PARLOR CITY PARADISE

Michael Sova

Kaylee,
Thanks for sending in
such a great photo.
Enjoy the Book!

5/2016

Dedication:

This one is for Mom. Thanks, for everything.

-1-

Skid Row stormed down the sidewalk, clenching his fists and not even glancing back as he unleashed a world class string of vulgarities at Arthur, McDonald's, bad luck, frogs, losers, liars, and the disgusting, rancid, puke-filled bowl of rotten cherries that had somehow become his life. Why couldn't he ever catch a damn break? Why couldn't, just for a change, just for shits and giggles, one damn thing go his way? He was twenty-four years old and, other than his rented room at the Y and a very few personal possessions, didn't have a thing to show for it. He'd never hurt anyone. He'd never done anything horribly wrong. So why, every time he thought things might be shifting in his favor, did they invariably turn into a steaming lump of dog crap?

The day had started out fine. He'd made it in on time, more or less, and Arthur had him working the counter, which sucked but was still a lot better than slaving over a hot grill. When the short lunch rush subsided, the place was as dead as road kill. That suited him fine. He could milk away the final hour of his shift and head home. Maybe even detour through the park to find Marco and score a little weed. He didn't have much cash but thought he could spare a few bucks for such a worthy cause.

Skid Row glanced over his shoulder. As usual, Arthur was in back, hunched over his desk and elbows deep in what had to be his fourth Quarter Pounder of the day. No wonder he was built like Mayor McCheese. Skid Row's stomach gave a heave and he averted his gaze. He began organizing ketchup and mustard packets, trying to appear busy so Arthur wouldn't make him mop the floor, or worse, clean the nasty, stinking bathrooms. You could scrub those things with bleach from top to bottom and they'd still smell like month-old horse piss. What the hell did people do in there anyway? Then again, based on the look of their regular clientele, mostly soiled, unkempt and grossly overweight, the true dregs of society, Skid Row figured the less he knew about their personal habits the better. He was wondering why that particular

McDonald's was such a magnet for losers when he first noticed the totally weird-looking dude making his way through the parking lot.

Skid Row moved a few steps to his right so he could see past the 2-for-1 Big Mac poster in the window. The guy had beady eyes, an oddly large mouth, small, knobby ears that stuck out from the sides of his shaved head, and a face that, at least from a distance, appeared wider than it was tall. In short, he looked like a frog, in beat up work boots and shabby, oversized gray coveralls that were torn at the knees.

"Keep moving, Pal," Skid Row muttered, knowing already it was wishful thinking. Not for the first time, he told himself he should find a job in a better part of town. So he hadn't graduated high school. Big deal. It wasn't like he was a total idiot. He had to be qualified to do something more than sweep floors, sling burgers and wait on weird-ass frog dudes. How had his life ended up so thoroughly in the shitter?

Deep down, Skid Row knew that simply moving to a better part of town wouldn't solve his problems. Dip a turd in chocolate. It may look and smell a little better but it was still gonna taste like a turd. The entire Binghamton area was an armpit, a haven for poverty, drugs, crime, high unemployment and low morale. Anyone with any sense had already packed up and left, so what was he still doing there? If he ever wanted to make something of himself, if he really wanted to find his way in the world, the first step was to get the hell out. That's all there was to it. Find a better job in a better town. There were plenty of nicer parts of New York. Or, Skid Row imagined, he could head straight down the east coast. Even working at McDonald's wouldn't be so bad if he was in Tampa, Daytona, or Fort Lauderdale. Bikini babes would be a big step up from frog dudes and ugly-ass losers. Of course, he had to get through the rest of the day before he could make any life-altering changes. So, he pasted a smile on his face and prepared to deliver the standard line. *Welcome to McDonald's. May I take your order please?*

Right away, Skid Row knew something about the guy was seriously off. He entered the small foyer, then paused like he wasn't sure what to do next. *There are only two doors,* Skid Row thought. *Come in or go out. It shouldn't be a tough decision.* Evidently, though, it was. Through the clear glass, he looked on as the newcomer slowly turned and studied the door he'd just come through. He started to reach for the handle as if he'd had a change of heart. No such luck. He turned again and, after another brief hesitation, pushed his way inside.

The first word that came to Skid Row's mind was "shifty." The guy's strange, buggy eyes kept flitting this way and that. Did he think someone was after him? Who the hell would want him? Or, Skid Row thought with a slight twinge of alarm, maybe he'd come in just to case the joint. He didn't think he'd ever heard of anyone knocking over a McDonald's but there was a first time for everything. It certainly wouldn't be hard to imagine a loser like this suddenly pulling a gun from beneath his dirty coveralls. Skid Row took half a step back and prepared to dive for cover. No gun was forthcoming and he slowly relaxed.

"You hiring?" the guy asked, speaking in a strange sort of whisper and never making eye contact as he approached the counter, walking, almost tiptoeing, like he was afraid the floor might give way under him at any moment.

Skid Row didn't respond right away, mainly because he had the distinct impression the guy hadn't really come in there looking for work. He definitely wasn't dressed for success. Along with his dingy, ill-fitting coveralls, his hands looked like they hadn't seen a bar of soap in days. Something dark and greasy stained his palms, and there was so much gunk underneath his nails he might have been wearing black nail polish. Skid Row was also still marveling at how much the dude really did look like a frog. It was creepy. His skin wasn't green, thank God, and he didn't have any visible warts or bumps; but it wouldn't have been a surprise to see a long, thin tongue come snapping out of that big mouth. *Do you want an order of flies with that?* Skid Row had to cover his mouth to hide a smile.

"You want to work here?" he asked, once he'd composed himself.

"Sure, Man. That would be great. You got an application? I can start right away."

Fat chance, freak. Skid Row knew they weren't hiring. Even fulltime employees recently had their hours cut because business had been so lousy. No point sharing that bit of information. "It's all online," he explained. "Just visit the website and enter the store number. You can fill out an application there and I'm sure someone will be in touch." No one would but that wasn't Skid Row's problem.

He figured that would be the end of it, but instead of walking away, the guy continued to stand there, his befuddled expression making him look like the world's stupidest statue. What was his deal?

"Is there something else I can do for you?" Skid Row asked, already knowing he wasn't going to like the answer. And that's when things really went to hell.

"Yeah," the guy said, blinking, clearing his throat and blinking some more. "I, uh... I was in here a while ago...."

He proceeded to stumble through a totally bogus story about the purchase of a supposedly burnt cheeseburger. Skid Row would have bet his entire measly paycheck that, not only had the frog man not been in there earlier that day, he'd never been in there period. Some faces you just didn't forget. He was trying to scam some free food and that's all there was to it. The problem was Skid Row couldn't come right out and say that. He couldn't just call the dude a liar. He thought of Arthur's oft-repeated mantra that the customer was always right. That, as far as Skid Row could tell, was the only piece of business acumen Arthur had acquired during his failed semester and a half at community college. Day shift manager was as high as the grease ball was likely to climb up the corporate ladder. That didn't alter the fact that he was still the boss. And, of late, Skid Row had had some "issues" with his customer interactions. One more slip up and there was a good chance he'd be out on his ass. Did that mean he had to put up with being lied to? He was still working on that one and his "customer" appeared to be getting a tad impatient. He glanced at the door and started rhythmically shifting his weight from one foot to the other, almost like he was doing some sort of amphibian fucking cheeseburger dance. It might have been entertaining if it wasn't so weird.

"So what are you going to do?" he asked. "You sold me bad food. I'd like a new burger or a refund."

Skid Row hesitated. Why did he even have to bother with this? A double cheeseburger was like a buck. If this Kermit-looking dude was that hungry, why didn't he just buy one? The truth was, if there were any burgers ready, Skid Row would have happily handed one over just to be done with the whole thing. It was no skin off his butt one way or the other. But, there were no sandwiches in the warming tray and nothing whatsoever on the grill. Everything had been tossed after sitting around too long. Vera was currently on her break and Randy was in back, either washing dishes or jerking off in the big walk-in fridge. Skid Row wasn't even supposed to be in the grill area. That meant that if any food were to be cooked, Arthur would have to get off his fat ass and do it. He wouldn't appreciate the interruption and Skid Row didn't want to do anything that would necessitate any extra conversation with his boss.

"Here's the thing," he finally said, spreading his arms wide and hoping to give the impression that he really did want to help. "I don't remember seeing you in here before." Is it possible you visited another McDonald's instead?" There wasn't another burger joint within a mile in any direction. Skid Row knew it and he figured his customer knew it too.

That would explain his red face and buggy eyes suddenly bugging even more.

"I'm a paying customer," he croaked, his voice going up half an octave. "Why are you giving me a hard time?"

How about because you're trying to rip us off? Skid Row thought and had to bite his tongue. "Please understand," he said, pointedly looking down at the guy's filthy but otherwise empty hands. "You don't seem to have the defective product." He liked the way that sounded. "Without that, I have no way of knowing that you really made a purchase."

There. It was smooth and subtle but he'd clearly called the guy's bluff and thought for sure that would be the end of the conversation. He was wrong.

"You're calling me a liar?" the frog man asked, his voice going up even more.

Hey, if the flipper fits.... "I'm not calling you anything, sir," Skid Row replied, trying to keep his own voice calm but beginning to lose the battle. "I just need to see some proof of purchase. Do you have the receipt?"

"Who keeps receipts from McDonald's?" he asked and then slammed his hand on the counter.

The only other person in the restaurant was Delmont. He was at his normal corner table and appeared to be talking to his biscuit as he used a plastic knife to carefully slice it in half. He looked up, gave them both a wide grin and then went back to his task.

"I'm sorry," Skid Row said, doing a mental eye roll, turning back to his customer and crossing his arms in a gesture of finality. "Without some proof of purchase, there's really nothing I can do for you."

"Oh yeah?" The frog dude started bouncing on his toes and a bubble of spit formed at the corner of his mouth. "Well what about this? What if I was in here before but you were too stoned to remember? Did you ever think of that?"

Up to that point, Skid Row thought he'd done an admirable job keeping their conversation on as calm and professional a level as possible. He'd kept his temper under control and hadn't said anything he thought Arthur would disapprove of, but that last comment crossed the line. So maybe his hair was a little too long to be considered stylish. Maybe he liked to toke-up once in a while. Maybe he enjoyed sitting in the dark listening to *Tripping Icarus* or *Sleep*. That didn't make him a stoner. Customer service or not, he wasn't about to just stand there and take a bunch of verbal abuse from some Alligator World escapee.

"I explained the situation in perfectly reasonable terms," Skid Row said, raising his voice and leaning halfway across the counter but keeping his company approved smile solidly in place. "If you still don't get it, you must be even stupider than you are ugly, and that's really saying something. If you have some sort of problem with me, you're more than welcome to take it up with my manager. He's eating a big cheeseburger right now so you may have to wait a few minutes. I hate the thought of wasting so much of your valuable time so here's what I suggest instead. Do us both a favor and hop back to your lily-pad or wherever the hell it is you came from. Thanks and have a nice day... Kermit."

For several moments, nothing happened. The shake machine hummed. The ice maker rattled. Temperature controlled air hissed through overhead vents. Then, with no warning whatsoever, Skid Row learned something he wouldn't have expected. His odd looking customer's resemblance to a frog extended beyond his physical appearance and somewhat squatty stature. The little fucker could jump. One moment, he was just standing there—blinking, gaping and generally looking like a moron. A split second later, he'd launched himself into the air and over the counter where he landed on Skid Row like a ton of unwashed bricks. Skid Row fought to keep his balance but his worn sneaker slipped on the tile floor. He flung out an arm for support but it was already too late. He was going down. His head smacked against the cup dispenser and a metal cabinet before hitting the floor. He saw stars and it took a moment for him to grasp what had just happened. He'd been crushed by the world's largest and ugliest frog.

-2-

Ricky Fixx sat in his high-backed leatherette desk chair, picking at bits of foam through a tear in the seat cushion and staring impatiently out the window. He couldn't actually see anything through the glass because the single pane had a large spider web of cracks in one corner and was coated with a decade's worth of grime. That suited him fine. There wasn't anything to see out there anyway, unless you counted the rusting chain link fence that separated his lot from the long-abandoned auto salvage yard next door. A nice clean window likewise would have provided more natural illumination than his cramped office really deserved. He was well aware of the warped walls, uneven floor, threadbare puke-green carpet, and dangerously sagging ceiling. The last thing he wanted was a good look at any of it.

He'd positioned an old brass floor lamp in one corner, its single forty watt bulb barely providing enough illumination to work by. Ricky didn't mind that either. Proper lighting would have given his clients a better view of the squalid surroundings and that wouldn't have been good for business. He also imagined that the long shadows cast by the lamp must make him appear more formidable and threatening. In his line of work, perception was everything.

Ricky straightened when he heard the crunch of tires on gravel. "About damn time," he said under his breath, and quickly pulled out his top desk drawer to check his reflection in a small mirror. He tried a few scowls, settled on one, slid the drawer closed, turned back to the window and waited. He'd practiced this routine and had it down to a science. It was all about the timing. He heard the thunk of a car door and seven seconds later, the sharp creak of the first wooden step. The man's tread was slow, heavy and, as he crossed the small front porch, Ricky could feel the entire trailer lean in that direction. He held his breath until he heard the slight rattle of the doorknob. That was the trigger. With his arms folded over his chest and his head tilted just so, he used a toe to push off from the wall. He swung slowly around and came to rest in perfect alignment with the doorway as his visitor entered the room.

"Sorry I'm late," Carl said, staring at Ricky but then immediately dropping his eyes. "I had a busy morning." He turned and tossed a beat-up brown briefcase onto a dorm size couch. He then looked up, sniffed and shook his head. “Are we gonna be getting out of here anytime soon? You said-- ”

"What do you got for me?" Ricky asked, both cutting him off and ignoring his question.

Carl frowned. “How ‘bout you answer me first?”

Ricky blew out a breath and flicked one finger toward the empty chair on the other side of his desk. "Have a seat," he said when Carl didn't move. When Carl still didn't move, Ricky grudgingly got to his feet. There were important business matters to discuss and he wanted to face the big man eye to eye, a feat made possible thanks only to the custom built eight-inch-high platform on which his desk stood.

Ricky needed special shoes to top out at five foot six. Carl was a solid foot taller and at least a hundred and fifty pounds heavier. Where Ricky had the slight build and sallow skin of someone who'd been frail since birth, Carl was a mountain, barrel-chested and burly. He had thick lips, sunken eyes, the type of beard any lumberjack would be proud of, and a mop of curly black hair which, as far as Ricky could tell, covered most of his body. Even his knuckles were hairy. His size and rather bestial visage made for a terrifying combination. That was the main reason, really the only reason he’d been given the job.

In Ricky’s expert opinion, Carl was a bungler. He was slow, clumsy, no good with firearms and not especially bright. Those things hardly mattered because he usually got what he wanted with a simple glower, which happened to be his normal expression. On those occasions where violence became necessary, he often exceeded expectations. On one hand, that created some problems. On the other, it sent a clear message that Carl was not to be messed with. And by extension, Ricky wasn’t either.

He wasn’t in the mood for Carl’s bullshit or his lousy attitude but Ricky knew he’d have to at least humor the man or they’d never get anywhere. “First off," he began, clasping his hands behind his back and pacing as far as his ten-by-ten platform would allow. “There is no ‘we.’ You work for me and I'll toss you out on your over-sized ass if you don't show me the proper level of respect. You got that?"

Carl winced and Ricky knew he’d gotten his attention. To his surprise, though, Carl wasn’t quite ready to back down.

"If you want *respect*," Carl said, stooping slightly to avoid hitting his head on an especially low section of ceiling, "maybe you shouldn't run your business from this upholstered bathroom stall of an office."

"We've been through this," Ricky said, again settling into his chair. After a few moments of silence, Carl sat as well, his own chair groaning under the weight.

"I know this place is a dump," Ricky said, picking up a pen and twirling it slowly in his fingers. "It's temporary. It's also necessary. Cops leave us alone because they don't know we're here. But as long as our customers can still find us, we'd be foolish to relocate. Besides, we're rent free."

Carl made a noise somewhere between a laugh and a grunt. "Rent free? That's because it's a cesspool. This entire road spent a week under water. Haven't you noticed that no one else lives or works around here? There's no telling what kind of mold and fungus is growing in these walls. We're breathing all that shit in. Doesn't that bother you?"

It did, but Ricky preferred not to think about it. The trailer had been scheduled for demolition following the 2011 flood that left much of Broome County and surrounding areas submerged. Ricky had had his trouble with local law enforcement and needed a new place to set up shop, preferably somewhere under the radar. It cost him five grand for the demolition crew hired by the City of Binghamton to overlook the single-wide on the banks of the Susquehanna River. Getting electrical service proved a bit more challenging until he got the right amount of money into the right hands. It wasn't exactly Trump Tower, but in his business, inconspicuous was the key.

Ricky didn't want anyone looking too closely at him, and with most of his clients being junkies, cons and losers, the situation seemed to work well for everyone involved. That didn't alter the fact that the place really was a shithole and undeniably unsafe. Ricky no longer noticed the foul stench that permeated the furniture, walls, carpet and everything else. He was, however, aware that the air he breathed was none too clean. He was averaging about one respiratory infection per month and started every morning by hacking wads of brownish gunk into his bathroom sink. It was even worse than when he'd been a two-pack-a-day smoker, a habit he'd given up on his thirtieth birthday after a sobering conversation with his doctor. He hadn't had a smoke in nearly eight and a half years.

Although he still drank too much coffee and booze and purchased most of his meals from a drive-thru window, overall, Ricky felt better about himself, or had prior to moving into the old trailer. He knew he needed to relocate, for his own health if nothing else, and he figured he'd have the necessary capital after one more big score, which was the main reason for the meeting with Carl.

Of course, if he were being completely honest, a business practice he tried to avoid, he knew they could move at any time. He was cheap so was naturally reluctant to leave a place with virtually no overhead. Mostly, though, he didn't want his partner to know how well they were really doing. Ricky also hadn't decided if, when the time came, he really wanted to take Carl with him. Shouldn't a change of scenery mean a change of partner as well? That could present complications but certainly nothing he couldn't handle as long as he planned accordingly. He'd already taken steps in that direction.

"So what's the story?" Ricky asked, rubbing his palms together and glancing pointedly at the briefcase Carl had brought in with him. "Is that thing full of sunshine?"

Carl's demeanor suddenly changed, confrontational morphing into something smaller and more submissive. He glanced to one side and then the other, his gaze finally settling on the small red notebook he always kept with him. His expression gave nothing away, but Ricky had been around the man long enough to recognize the signs. Something had gone wrong. He bit back a curse and waited for the bad news.

"I saw the Sweeny brothers," Carl began, studying his notebook as if it contained all the secrets of the universe. "I told them about the price increase. They didn't like it but they agreed."

"No choice," Ricky said. "They want my product; that's what it costs."

John and Jake Sweeny owned an electronics boutique called The Buzz, which was really just a front for pirated software and video games. Ricky had a connection with a cousin in New York City. He paid twenty percent of retail for knockoffs of all the hottest new stuff. He then tacked on a fifteen percent surcharge of his own before selling it all to the Sweenys. Prices fluctuated based on how much the same items were selling for on eBay. Ricky added his fifteen percent regardless and told Jon and Jake, or had Carl tell them, they could take it or leave it. They always took it because Ricky was the only game in town.

"So what else you got?"

Carl continued to study his notebook and Ricky wondered what, if anything, he had written there. It wasn't like they had hundreds of clients to keep track of. In fact, there was only one person Carl was supposed to go see. Was he so stupid he had to write it down so he didn't forget? Ricky knew he wasn't, which made Carl's fixation on the notebook more than a little troubling. He recognized a stall tactic when he saw one.

"I went to see Kristi," Carl said, still not looking up.

"That's great. Did she pay you off or suck you off."

Kristi was one of three aging hookers who looked to Carl and Ricky for protection. Ricky highly doubted the skanks needed it. The down-and-outs that paid for their services rarely posed much of a threat. Still, if it made them feel better to have a hulk like Carl looking out for them, Ricky had no qualms about taking their money. Besides, even if they weren't the most attractive creatures he'd ever seen, he wasn't above letting them show their gratitude once in a while.

"I got seventy bucks from her and another fifty from Debb. Never saw Trudi."

"Uh-huh." Ricky said, even more convinced the conversation was headed nowhere good. He didn't give a shit about this nickel and dime stuff. There was a grand total of one thing he did care about and Carl seemed determined to talk about anything and everything else.

"Let's see," he said, thick fingers fumbling as he flipped to a new page. "I stopped by T.J.'s place."

Ricky glanced at his watch and judged that his pulse was racing at about twice the speed of the second hand.

T.J. Tyson was a smalltime bookie with a big time lifestyle. He ate in the nicest restaurants, drove a late model BMW, wore fancy Italian suits and only bought and drank top shelf liquor. He also sometimes had to borrow money from Ricky when he didn't have enough left in the till to pay off his winners. In the past, he'd owed upwards of a hundred thousand dollars. Currently, however, his ledger was nearly clean. Collecting from him was not on the list of high priorities.

"I talked to the wife," Carl said, awkwardly crossing and re-crossing his legs. "She said T.J. is in Atlantic City for the week. I'll touch base with him when he gets back."

"And did you shake any school kids down for their lunch money?"

Carl offered a weak smile and hunched a little lower in his seat. He appeared to be attempting to retract his head into his own neck hole like a turtle disappearing inside its shell.

Ricky knew what was coming next. He'd known all along. He watched Carl squirm and might have been amused had the circumstances been different. Beads of sweat had formed along the big man's brow and he used the back of a hairy arm to wipe them away.

"I do have some bad news," Carl finally admitted, pushing against the back of the chair and trying to get as far away from Ricky as possible.

"You don't say." Ricky steepled his fingers, leaned back in his chair and braced himself for whatever was coming.

Carl swallowed and nodded.

"Then tell me!" Ricky demanded, a sudden edge in his voice. "And you better not leave anything out."

"Well," Carl wiped his forehead again. "I went to see him just like you said. I told him he was behind on his payments and he had to make good or things were going to get ugly."

"And?" Ricky picked up a paperclip and started twisting it in his hands.

Carl watched for several seconds and then continued. "I told him I really didn't want that to happen. I said we had an agreement and he wasn't living up to his end of the deal."

"Did you remind him that we haven't seen a penny from him in three weeks?"

"Yes."

"And what did he say to that?" Ricky asked, twisting the paperclip until the thin metal snapped.

"He said he didn't have the money. He said he had other obligations and that we needed to give him more time."

"We've already done that. I assume you explained that to him?"

Carl nodded and licked his lips.

"And what happened after that?"

"Um… Nothing."

Ricky leaned forward and placed his elbows on the desk. "Pardon my ignorance but what exactly do you mean by that?"

Carl squirmed and then met Ricky's eyes for the first time. "I told him he had to pay. I told him we'd given him all the time we were going to. He said he understood and then he… sort of ran away."

"He… what?"

"Ran away," Carl repeated reluctantly. "I took off after him but…" he shrugged. "He's a lot faster than me."

"And you did nothing to stop him?"

"What could I do?"

How about your fucking job? "So what you're telling me," Ricky said, closing his eyes and pinching the bridge of his nose, "is that your briefcase there is empty and his current whereabouts are unknown. Is that about right?"

There was no need for Carl to respond. His sullen features told Ricky everything he needed to know. It was only the latest in a long line of screw-ups.

Ricky knew they could find their target again. It wouldn't be difficult, but that wasn't the point. He'd given Carl a very simple task and the idiot had been unable to deliver. That meant he'd have to wait even longer for his money. That was irritating, but what bothered Ricky even more is that Carl had made him look incompetent and unprofessional. He didn't like that one bit. He glared across the desk and then stood and took a step toward the window. Then, without warning, he spun around, grabbed a snow globe paper weight and hurled it at the wall. It struck a framed picture of former Jets quarterback Mark Sanchez and his infamous butt fumble. The glass shattered and the picture crashed to the floor.

-3-

"UN-FUCKING-BELIEVABLE," Skid Row snarled, kicking a plastic cup into the road and trying to put as much distance between himself and the McDonald's as possible. He hadn't even bothered changing out of his dorky blue uniform before exiting the premises. He had, however, spared a few seconds to tell his former boss exactly what he thought of him and his shit bag of a restaurant. As satisfying as that might have been, it did nothing to improve his current situation.

"What now?" Skid Row asked the broken windows and peeling paint of the vacant, dilapidated warehouse on his right. He pulled off his visor and scaled it towards a rusting metal trash can. "Just what the hell am I supposed to do now?"

"I'm really sorry."

Skid Row immediately stopped and spun around. He hadn't realized the frog-looking weirdo had not only followed him out of the restaurant but trailed him halfway down the block.

"What did you say?" Skid Row asked, not really caring one way or the other.

The guy couldn't even meet his eyes. "I said I'm sorry," he mumbled, fidgeting and staring at his feet. "I shouldn't have lost my temper like that."

"Yeah?" Skid Row put his hands on his hips. "Well a lot of good that does me. Has it occurred to you that, instead of apologizing for acting like a maniac, you shouldn't have told that bullshit story to begin with? None of this ever would have happened. What do you say to that?"

Without waiting for a response, he turned and again started walking, a little quicker than before. He didn't want excuses, apologies or explanations. He didn't want anything except to be left alone so he could figure out what to do. He had a bit of money stashed away, and his room was already paid through the end of the week. His last paycheck should get him through the end of the month. After that? Skid Row didn't even want to think about it but he knew he wouldn't be able to put it off for long. He'd have to either find a new job or come up with some other plan. Part of that plan had to include a new place to live. The YMCA is fine if all you want is affordable shelter, but the total lack of privacy, freedom, and any of the things that would normally be considered comforts of home get old in a hurry. He wanted his own place with his own furniture. Maybe he'd even get a dog. He'd always wanted one and his parents had always said no. Once he was out on his own, mostly living on the street and struggling just to make it from one day to the next, getting a pet, any pet, simply hadn't been possible. No reason that couldn't change.

Skid Row paused to let a garbage truck rumble past. He looked at the man clinging to the back. Clad in a bright yellow jump suit, he appeared to be near retirement age yet was still spending his days sucking in the delightful aromas of rotting food, dirty diapers and diesel fuel. So Skid Row was out of a job. Things could be worse. He was young, healthy, and still had ample time for a fresh start. He just needed to figure out where. His mother always said things happen for a reason. That was her excuse for getting knocked up by a bouncer in a night club but maybe there was some truth to it just the same. Maybe getting fired was the best thing that ever happened to him. It would put him on the right path. He crossed against the lights, contemplating various dog names and trying to decide between Lars, Elvis and Luther, when he was interrupted by the sounds of footsteps and heavy breathing. He didn't have to look to know who it was.

"What?" Skid Row asked, slowing and reluctantly turning around. After their last brief exchange, he'd assumed the dude had gone off to wherever frog people go. They had nothing to talk about; yet, here he was again.

"You're right," he panted, staring like he was expecting some sort of response.

"What the fuck are you talking about?" Skid Row asked, crossing his arms over his chest.

"You said I shouldn't have told that story," he said, clutching the fistful of McDonald's coupons Arthur had evidently given him. "I'm just saying you're right. I'm sorry."

Skid Row felt like taking a swing at the guy but he'd never been much of a fighter. Besides, if the dude's jumping ability was any indication, a physical confrontation would not be in his best interest. He had to content himself by spitting on the ground. "I just lost my job, dude! Is your stupid apology supposed to make me feel better?"

The guy shrugged but said nothing.

"I didn't think so," Skid Row said, spinning and again starting to walk away. "You said your piece. Everyone's all happy now. I've got things to do and I'm sure you do too. Thanks and have a nice day. See you around." *When hell freezes over.*

"Wait. Where are you going?" the guy asked, taking a few tentative steps forward.

"What do you care?" Skid Row asked, stopping and turning once more.

"I guess I don't. I mean, it doesn't matter; but is it all right if I tag along?"

Huh? Skid Row dug his hands into his pockets and leaned against a bent road sign for Chenango Street. "What's your deal?" he asked, thinking his day was getting weirder by the minute. "You don't even know me. I don't want to know you so why don't you leave me alone?"

"Okay," he said after a pause. "I can do that. It's just..."

"It's just what?" Skid Row asked when it seemed clear the guy wasn't going to say anything more.

"I..." He swallowed and looked away. "I got fired today too. I have no money and no place to go. It's a good thing I don't have a gun because I'd probably use it."

Holy shit, Skid Row thought. *Dude's a total basket case.* "You serious?" he asked, alarmed but also suddenly feeling a little better about his own situation.

"No," the guy said, shaking his head slightly as if he wasn't quite sure. "I don't think so anyway. Things just haven't been going my way lately."

"I heard that." Then after a beat, "I was headed for the park. Come if you want."

They walked along in silence for a few minutes, Skid Row leading the way and his new companion following so closely they kept bumping shoulders. Skid Row wanted to tell him to back off but, after the previous episode, was afraid of doing anything that might set him off.

"Do you know Marco?" he finally asked, really just to have something to say.

"Who's that?"

"Our neighborhood Good Humor man."

"You mean ice cream? I told you I don't have any money."

Skid Row almost smiled. "What Marco sells is way better than a hot fudge sundae. Ever smoke any weed?"

"Not much," the guy said. "I've been on the move for a while."

That seemed like a strange response but Skid Row decided not to comment. "So what's your name?" he asked instead.

"Call me Bullfrog."

At first, Skid row thought it was a joke. He started to laugh but stopped himself when he noticed the dude's sour expression.

"I know," he said with a shrug. "It's a horrible nickname; but if fits, right?" He gestured at his own face and Skid Row couldn't help but feel a little sorry for him. "So what about you?"

"Everyone calls me Skid Row." He made the announcement with pride even though he knew that wasn't much of a nickname either.

"How'd you get a name like that?"

"Long story," he said dismissively, already planning on ditching this Bullfrog character long before he had a chance to tell it. The guy said he didn't smoke. Skid Row figured he could get him high in about five minutes and then ditching him would be as simple as walking away.

"Let me ask you something," he said as they crossed the street against traffic. "Why the hell did you go nuts back there? That was insane the way you jumped across that counter."

"I've had a bad day," Bullfrog replied, his tone suggesting he'd prefer to change the subject.

Skid Row didn't give a damn what he preferred. "You gotta do better than that, dude. We all have bad days. You could have freakin' killed me."

"I said I was sorry. I don't want to talk about it anymore."

"Then blow," Skid Row said. "We got nothing' to say to each other and I don't want you hanging around anyway."

With that, he picked up his pace, hoping the whacko would finally take the hint and disappear. No such luck. As he made his way down the street, Skid Row could tell from the sound that Bullfrog had once again fallen in step behind him. He wanted to spin around and shout at the guy to fuck off. Instead, he tried to ignore him. He didn't understand what the dude was up to but decided it wasn't worth worrying about. He had more important things on his mind, starting with finding a new job. There were gas stations and convenience stores all over the place. They all had NOW HIRING signs in their windows. Those signs may as well say WORK HERE AND GET SHOT. The Hess station closest to the McDonald's had been robbed three times in the past month. Skid Row wasn't about to risk his life to protect a rack of Twinkies and pork rinds. Another fast food job might be his only choice, unless he went back to school. His parole officer was always telling him he should at least get his GED. It never seemed that important but now he wasn't so sure.

"You called me Kermit," Bullfrog said, so quietly Skid Row thought he might be talking to himself. He didn't respond and after a moment Bullfrog said it again. "You called me Kermit!"

"So what?" Skid Row said, not liking the knack Bullfrog seemed to have for restarting conversations that had long since ended. Hell, he'd ended that one himself by saying he didn't want to talk about it anymore.

"You told me your name is Bullfrog. I called you Kermit. What's the difference?"

"I just don't like it."

Skid Row snorted. "Too bad, dude. I don't like it when someone calls me a stoner and then attacks me for no good reason. I guess that makes us even."

"I overreacted. I've already apologized for that."

"Your apology doesn't get my job back."

Bullfrog evidently had nothing to say to that.

"So let me ask you something," Skid Row said, thinking he'd probably be better off just keeping his mouth shut. "If Kermit sends you off the deep end, why the hell did you pick a name like Bullfrog?"

"I didn't."

"Come again?"

"I didn't pick it," Bullfrog replied. "My parents did."

"Must not have liked you very much."

"It wasn't that," Bullfrog said. "When I was a baby, I never really learned to crawl. I sort of hopped instead. My parents started calling me Bullfrog. It kind of stuck."

"But now that you..."

"Now that I look like a frog too?"

"That's not what I was going to say," Skid Row said, even though it was exactly what he'd been thinking. He was also thinking that he didn't care for the new, overly personal direction of their conversation. "Now that you're older," he continued. "Why not ask your parents to call you something else? Or just go by your real name."

"My parents are dead," Bullfrog said flatly as he stared down at the sidewalk. "I still use Bullfrog because it reminds me of them."

This time, it was Skid Row with nothing to say. He didn't even glance in Bullfrog's direction as they made their way across the Bevier Street bridge towards the entrance to Otsiningo Park.

"I didn't mean to be such a downer," Bullfrog said.

Skid Row waved a hand. "Hey, it's been that kind of day. We'll find Marco and he'll make everything better."

"Are you sure he'll be there?"

"Tuesday afternoon and the sun is shining. He'll be there. And if you don't mind me asking," Skid Row said, "what's your real name?"

"You don't want to know."

"Come on. It can't be any worse than Bullfrog."

"Don't be so sure."

Well, now you've got to tell me." Skid Row said. "Fess up."

"Promise you won't laugh?"

"Dude, I got liquidated a little while ago. I ain't got nothin' to laugh about."

Bullfrog still seemed hesitant and Skid Row didn't try to force the issue. He was about to change the subject when Bullfrog finally spoke.

"It's Jeremiah," he said, keeping his head down so Skid Row couldn't see his face.

It took a moment for the words to really sink in. At first, Skid Row didn't understand what the big deal was. Jeremiah wasn't a bad name. He thought it may have even come from the bible. Okay, it wasn't all that common but.... And then it clicked. He stared at Bullfrog wide-eyed. "No fucking way!" he said, too stunned to even think about laughing.

"I know," Bullfrog said morosely. "Jeremiah was a bullfrog. You can go ahead and laugh. Everyone else does."

"No, man. It's cool. In fact, I kinda dig it," which proved to be a poor choice of words. It got him thinking about that Honey Smacks frog that said *dig 'em* all the time and, before long, he couldn't control himself. He burst out laughing. The more he thought about it the funnier it got. It didn't take long for Bullfrog to join in. They kept laughing and the few passers-by looked at them like they were both crazy.

"That's priceless," Skid Row said, once he was finally able to catch his breath. "Are you sure your parents liked you? I mean, that's a pretty rotten thing to do to a kid."

"They didn't know."

"Come on."

"I'm serious," Bullfrog said. "They'd never heard the song."

"Everyone's heard that song."

"Mom was a biologist. Dad was an accountant. They didn't spend much time listening to the radio. They never understood why people thought my nickname was so funny or why it bothered me so much. By the time they realized..." Bullfrog gave a palms up gesture. "The damage was already done."

"But you said your parents are... not around anymore. Start going by your regular name, or pick a different one. Who's gonna know?"

Bullfrog just shook his head. "I've been Bullfrog as long as I can remember. It's who I am. I can't change that now."

There was something almost tragic in the way he said it and Skid Row decided it was best to let the matter drop. "Well," he said as enthusiastically as he could, "I've got just the thing to lift your spirits."

They were on the main trail into the park. On their right, a flock of a dozen or so geese dotted the surface of a small pond. Ahead and to their left, they could hear yells and shrieks coming from the direction of the playground.

"We stay on this path," Skid Row said. "Third bench past the playground. That's where we'll find our man."

"He deals in a place like this?"Bullfrog asked as two roller-bladers whizzed past. "There are people everywhere."

"Yeah, so maybe you could keep your voice down? Marco knows what he's doing. We slip him the cash on our way by, pick up Maggie on our way back."

"Pick up who?"

"The weed, dude. Stick with me. I'll show you how it's done.

The thought of a smoke suddenly gave Skid Row a much better outlook on life. This Bullfrog character was weird but otherwise not so bad. He still planned on ditching him but it wouldn't hurt to get high together first.

"Do you come here a lot?" Bullfrog asked.

"No more than once a week. Marco's got his routine. Sometimes he's by the library, sometimes the laundromat. You got to know his schedule. Today is park day. We'll see him as soon as we round this bend up ahead. Don't stare. Don't even look at him. Walk by like you don't even notice he's there. I'll take care of everything."

As it turned out, there was nothing to take care of. For the first time since Skid Row's initial contact with him months earlier, Marco's bench was empty.

-4-

Ricky Fixx made an illegal left turn and pulled his silver Lexus into the only available parking spot. It was reserved for the handicapped but he paid no attention to the sign and bright blue paint.

"You know what you're doing, right?" he asked, killing the engine and turning in his seat so he could reach the nondescript gym bag that he tossed onto Carl's lap.

"Sure," Carl said, unclipping his safety belt and reaching for the door latch. "I just need to deliver this."

Ricky stopped him with a hand on his arm. "And what else?"

"We've already been through this," he said. "I need to tell him we'll be back to collect."

"Don't forget!" Ricky jabbed a finger in his face. "And be very specific. No more confusion. No more screw-ups. You'll meet him in the usual place in exactly twenty-four hours. Understood?"

"Yeah," Carl said. "No problem." He again reached for the door.

"He pays in full," Ricky said as Carl levered his bulk out of the seat. "We can't afford to give anyone any more extensions right now. Make sure he understands that."

Without another word, Carl picked up the bag, turned, and started to lumber away, but only after slamming the door a little harder than necessary.

Ricky pressed the button to lower the passenger side window. "Hey," he called. "Don't take too long. We've got other stops to make."

If Carl heard he gave no sign, just kept walking until, a few seconds later, he'd disappeared around the corner.

"Moron," Ricky muttered once the man was out of sight. He'd obviously ticked Carl off by being so blunt but that was too damn bad. He knew from painful experience that his super-size partner could find new and unlikely ways to mess up even the simplest jobs. Not three weeks earlier, he'd been told to send a message to another one of their delinquent clients. The guy owned a used car lot and his vehicles were often used for transporting any manner of illegal merchandise. He and Ricky had been working together for years. But, it turned out he was working for one of Ricky's biggest competitors too, sometimes playing one against the other in an ill-advised attempt to maximize his own profits. He needed to be reminded that such underhanded business practices would not be tolerated. Ricky assumed Carl understood the situation and would act accordingly. That usually meant roughing the guy up a bit--scaring him but doing no serious damage. Instead, Carl started what he'd described as a "small fire" in the office at the dealership, unfortunately failing to notice the large propane tanks at the rear of the building. The entire structure burned to the ground, as did several vehicles, a Dominick's sausage wagon, and the brand new bridal shop that had just opened next door. The blaze was still under investigation but, at least as far as Ricky knew, Carl was in the clear. Thank God the owner had been too cheap to install any security cameras.

On the plus side, Carl's size and demeanor made him naturally intimidating. One angry look and people were shitting their pants. It didn't always work out that way, and that was when things usually got interesting. He might try to break someone's arm and have them end up in a body cast, or start a fire in a trash can and burn down half a city block. Still, for all his flaws, he was well-suited to act as Ricky's right hand man; hell, his left hand man too. With Carl doing the brunt of the dirty work, Ricky was able to conveniently keep both of his own hands clean.

He figured it should take about fifteen minutes for Carl to deliver the bag and the message, and then make his way back to the car. Ricky spied a bakery across the road and considered going in for a donut and coffee. He hadn't eaten any breakfast. But, he was parked illegally and there were no empty parking spots in sight. The odds of a cop coming by in the next few minutes were slim. He still didn't think he should take the chance. Ricky checked his reflection in the visor mirror, adjusted his shades, straightened his tie, and looked around for babes. It was a disappointingly brief inspection. The only woman in sight was a block away and old enough to be his mother, maybe even his grandmother. She walked with a limp and appeared to be deep in conversation with the sweater-clad mangy brown flea bag tugging at the end of a leash. Ricky watched with disgust and then turned his attention to the car stereo. He hit the scan button, ignored Rihanna, Benny Mardones, Five Finger Death Punch and the B-52's, almost stopped on the Zac Brown Band and finally settled on the Doobie Brothers. Had Carl been with him, he would have chosen classical, not because he especially liked it or even because he knew Carl despised it, but because Ricky believed listening to highbrow music somehow enhanced his image. When he was alone, though, he normally went for rock and roll or the brand of modern country that sounds like rock. He checked his reflection again, angled the mirror slightly, then sat back and waited for his partner to return.

"Any problems?" Ricky asked, a string quartet reaching a crescendo as Carl opened the door and slid into the car.

"No," he said, turning the knob to lower the volume. "He accepted delivery and knows I'll be back tomorrow to collect."

"That's it?"

Carl stared at him. "Yeah," he said evenly. "What else did you expect?"

What Ricky expected, or at least had to consider, was the possibility that Carl misunderstood his instructions, delivered the wrong message, or found some other way to royally fuck things up. He kept his concerns to himself, turning the stereo volume back up and then cranking the engine.

"Where to next?" Carl asked, retrieving his notebook from a shirt pocket and making a quick notation.

Ricky studied him briefly and then put the car in gear. "We gotta see Geno."

"Ahhh," Carl groaned, slamming his head against the back of the seat. "I knew it. You brought in food from that dump three times this week. The stuff is garbage so I figured there had to be something else going on."

"I'm impressed," Ricky said and he meant it. It always surprised him when Carl proved he wasn't quite as dumb as he looked. "And you're right," Ricky went on. "That food isn't fit for a dog."

"So what have you two worked out?"

"Nothing so far," Ricky said, letting a Schwan's delivery truck roll past and then easing the Lexus into traffic. "His little pizzeria is a money-laundering hole. You know it. I know it. He damn sure knows it."

"What's he into?"

"Mostly gambling," Ricky said. "It didn't bother me much at first. It's a big pie. I didn't mind him taking a small piece."

"But his piece is getting bigger?"

"That seems to be the case. I've lost some business and I think he's the reason. It's going to keep getting worse if we don't do something about it now."

"I assume you've talked to him already?"

"Until I was blue in the face." Ricky mashed the button to turn off the radio because a female opera singer had started doing her impression of a sea lion being slowly poisoned.

"Thanks," Carl said. "I might have put my head through the dashboard if that had gone on any longer."

"You just don't appreciate culture."

"Culture, huh? Sounded more like a chipmunk being sodomized by a goat."

Ricky agreed but did his best to look offended and disapproving.

"So what's the plan with this guy?" Carl asked.

"Very simple. You're going to offer our services and convince him that he can't live without them."

"Think that will be enough?"

"It will if you use all your unique powers of persuasion."

"Are we going in together?"

Ricky had anticipated the question. "I don't think so," he said slowly, pretending to give the idea serious consideration. "I think I'll drop you off at the end of the block. There's a diner there with pretty good food. Get yourself some lunch. I recommend the chicken fried steak."

"And what are you gonna do?"

Ricky ran a hand over his chin. "I'll take one more crack at Geno. I'll get a slice of today's special, try to eat it without puking all over the counter, and give the sales pitch one more time. If he doesn't go for it, which I know he won't, I'll give you a call. You got your cell, right?"

Carl patted his back pocket and nodded.

"Good," Ricky said. "So we've got a plan. Any questions?"

The conversation with Geno went as Ricky expected. He walked into the quote-unquote *restaurant* and, as usual, there wasn't a customer in sight. There were no workers in sight either. He set a string of bells jangling when he pushed through the glass door but, other than disturbing a family of flies that had been busy investigating a puddle of something sticky on one of the empty booth tables, the noise elicited no response. He approached the counter, trying to avoid looking at the pizza carousel that was slowly rotating the same three slices of pizza that had probably been there since the last time Billy Joel had a hit record. Pizzerias were supposed to smell like garlic, sauce and cheese. Geno's smelled more like a boy's locker room with a delicate hint of fish hatchery. Ricky wrinkled his nose, thinking that, compared to this place, his moldy trailer was as fresh and clean as an April morning.

There was a handwritten sign on the counter instructing patrons to ring for service, but the closest thing Ricky saw to a bell was an empty metal napkin dispenser. "Hello," he called, wrapping his knuckles against the cracked laminate countertop. "Anybody home?"

"Ricky!" Geno said, emerging from somewhere in the back, wearing a dingy apron and a smile that could have almost passed for genuine. "You come ina for lunch?"

Geno was no more Italian than Barack Obama but he did his best to play the part.

"No," Ricky said, casting a suspicious glance at those spinning slices of salmonella. "I had a big breakfast."

"Ifa you say so. Then what can I do for you today?"

"I thought I'd try one more time to get you on board with us. I think you'd find it very beneficial. I have a lot of connections."

"I don't understand this," Geno said. "I keepa telling you. I'm just a small businessman. I sella the pizza. Why would that interest someone like you?"

"Geno," Ricky said. "My friend. We're not going to get anywhere if we're not honest with each other. You're an... entrepreneur, like myself. I think we can both be a lot better off if we decide to work together."

Geno shook his head sadly. "I don't know where you get these ideas. I sella the pizza. I can maybe give you job if you want to work here. That's best I can do."

"I have partners," Ricky explained. "They're going to be very upset when I tell them what you said. It could get unpleasant."

"I'm sorry," Geno said. "But no hard feelings, ay? You come in for free pie anytime."

Ricky walked out more confused than surprised. He certainly never expected Geno to willingly hand over a portion of the take from his various gambling endeavors. Prospective *partners* usually didn't see the light until they'd had a visit from Carl. Normally, though, they were a lot more up front about their illegal activities. Geno hadn't admitted a single thing. Ricky knew damn well what he was up to. It just would have made it much easier to proceed if they could have gotten past Geno's *I sella the pizza* bullshit. Well, they'd get past that soon enough.

Ricky unlocked the Lexus, slid into the driver's seat, and fished his cell phone out of his inside jacket pocket. It was his policy to never say or text anything that, if read or overheard, could be considered incriminating. He pulled up his contacts, found Carl and sent a totally innocuous three word text. "He's all yours."

-5-

Breathing hard, Andrew Cullen braked to a stop, slid off his sleek Eddie Merckx EMX-525 and removed his helmet and riding gloves. There wasn't a cloud visible in the predawn sky but he bypassed the curbside rack and wheeled his bike up the short flight of stairs, through the small, well-appointed lobby and into the elevator. Beautiful day or not, with a price tag north of four thousand dollars, he wasn't about to leave his prize possession out on the street.

Checking his gold TAG Heuer wrist watch, he pressed the button for the fourth floor and leaned back against dark wooden paneling. He had the elevator and probably the entire building to himself, unless there was a member of the cleaning crew still around. He knew that wasn't likely since they normally made their rounds in the late evening and were long gone by midnight. About the only time that changed was if they were doing something out of the ordinary like waxing floors or shampooing the carpets. Nothing like that appeared to have happened overnight, and Cullen was thankful because he didn't want to stop to talk to anyone right then. He was aware of the perception that he didn't want to socialize with blue collar workers. Really, though, he just wanted to complete his daily workout without interruption and his time was limited.

Steering the bicycle with one hand, Cullen dug for his keys with the other. He used one key to unlock the door for Cyber Force Technologies and a second unlocked his spacious corner office. He ignored the blinking light on his phone and the neatly stacked message slips Carrie had left in the center of his desk. He tossed his keys aside, propped his bike against the wall and dropped to the floor where he did a hundred push-ups, a hundred sit-ups and a hundred squat-thrusts. Dripping sweat, he headed for his private bathroom. Twenty minutes later, he was showered, shaved, and sitting behind his desk in a charcoal suit, cranberry shirt, and dark blue pin-striped tie.

"Coffee's made," he called when he heard Carrie enter the office.

"Good morning," she said, sticking her body halfway through the door and bringing a wave of chill air with her. Her cheeks were flushed and, not for the first time, Cullen fantasized about bending her over the end of his leather sofa. She wore a long skirt, high boots and a tight-fitting leather coat, all of which served to accentuate the best ass he'd ever seen. Her skirt was a deep purple, and he imagined running his hands over and then under the soft fabric.

"You look cold," he said, shifting in his chair, keenly aware that parts of his own body had gotten noticeably warmer.

"It can't be more than twenty degrees out there," Carrie said, rubbing her hands together and then hugging herself. She glanced at Cullen's bike. "I can't believe you rode this morning. What is it--ten miles?"

"More like twelve," he replied, making the conscious effort to look his office assistant in the eye rather than admiring the more interesting parts of her body. She had a pretty face: big brown eyes, small nose and a heart-shaped mouth, all framed by thick, shoulder-length, curly, dark brown hair. Her makeup and clothing were always impeccable, but it was her traffic-stopping body that had Cullen drooling into his desk drawer.

"What's on the agenda today?" he asked, wondering how she'd respond if he asked her to clear his schedule so they could spend the day playing Who's Your Daddy in the luxury suite at the Holiday Inn. Cullen had never made any attempt to act on his fantasy, not because she was half his age, not because of the boyfriend she talked about far too often, not even because he had a wife waiting for him at home, but because Carrie Flynn was the daughter of Leo Flynn, of Dwyer, Cartwright and Flynn, a large law firm most known for its constant litigation of sexual harassment and sexual discrimination cases. Carrie had never given any indication that she might go running to papa if he stepped out of line. She even flirted from time to time. Did that mean she was really interested or merely yanking his chain, so to speak? He didn't know and wasn't about to take the chance to find out.

Cullen hadn't yet hit the Big Five-O but he had the milestone solidly in his sights. Physically, he was in the best shape of his life. He knew he looked good too, the bit of gray at his temples serving only to make him appear more distinguished, more successful. Attracting women had never been a problem. He felt sure he could walk into practically any bar in town and walk out with the most gorgeous available female. Still, you always want the one you can't have, and Carrie had been driving him crazy on a daily basis from the moment he'd hired her eighteen months earlier. She always dressed professionally leaning towards the conservative but he would have bet a thousand bucks and given five to one odds that she wore a thong. Sadly, he'd never know.

"You have an eleven thirty lunch meeting with Leonard Price," she said.

Cullen looked at her blankly and it was a few seconds before he realized she was responding to his question. "Leonard Price?" he asked, trying to get his mind back on business and out of her hypothetical underwear.

"Southern Tier Staffing…."

"Right," Cullen said. "The temp service. And what's this meeting for?"

"Mr. Price would like to discuss payroll software. They've had some problems and he's looking to upgrade."

"Sure," he said. "We can do that. Anything else?"

"I'll have to double check but I think your afternoon is fairly open."

"Fine," he said. "Let's try to keep it that way. I may need to head out early."

"Sounds good. Is there anything I can do for you before I get to work?"

Cullen's eyes involuntarily flicked to the couch. "Not right now," he said. "I've still got messages to go through and some other things to follow up on. I will need your help later."

"Sure thing," she said, turning away and leaving him with a far too brief view of exquisite backside and the slightest hint of perfume in the air.

When she'd gone and Cullen could once again think straight, he turned his attention back to the stack of pink message slips. He had appreciated the diversion, but knew it was just that. He also knew that fantasizing, harmless as it may be, was not going to solve any of his problems. For the better part of an hour, he went through his messages one by one, responding to some and putting others aside for later consideration. When he was done, he had just one message slip left. It had been on top of the pile when he sat down and he'd immediately reallocated to the bottom. Now it was front and center again and could no longer be ignored.

He had known that particular message would be waiting for him. That was one of the reasons he'd ridden his bike on such a frigid morning. Cullen had hoped the combination of air and exercise would help clear his head. It hadn't. He closed his eyes but could still see the message slip and knew exactly what it foretold. He was, by his own estimation, completely fucked.

-6-

"I don't get it," Skid Row said, as he and Bullfrog retraced their steps out of the park, across the bridge and back down Chenango Street.

"Are you sure you had the right bench?"

"I've met the guy there like a hundred times. Course I'm sure."

"Well maybe he's sick or something. Or maybe he found a better spot."

"I don't know," Skid Row said, stepping on an empty Genny Cream Ale can and crushing it flat. "It don't matter anyway. I'm just pissed I walked all that way for nothing."

"Is there anywhere else you can buy your… stuff?"

"If necessary," Skid Row said. "But I'm happy to report I still got a couple Aces stashed at my place."

"A couple what?"

Skid Row gave him a sideways look. "You really don't get out much do you? Bombers, Straws, Fingers, Goof Butts…."

Bullfrog stared at him blankly.

"Marijuana cigarettes," Skid Row explained. "You've heard of those, right?"

"Sure," Bullfrog said. "I figured that's what you meant."

Skid Row doubted that but let it pass. They were walking past New York Pizzeria and the smell of garlic hit him full force. "You hungry?" he asked.

"More like starving," Bullfrog said. "I haven't eaten since last night."

"Why the hell not?"

"No money," Bullfrog said.

"You got a job don't you? Wait, you said you got fired too. What happened?"

"Let's grab something to eat and then I'll tell you."

"Listen," Skid Row said. "I guess I don't mind you tagging along but I can't afford to buy you a meal. My finances aren't exactly in great order either."

"Don't worry about that," Bullfrog said. "It's my treat." He pulled out the wad of coupons Arthur had given him.

"I can't go back in there," Skid Row said. "That fat fucker would probably have me arrested."

"I'll go in," Bullfrog said. "It's the least I could do."

Skid Row waited outside a gas station while Bullfrog crossed the lot and entered the McDonald's. Five minutes later, he was back with noticeably cleaner hands and a sack bulging with burgers, fries and apple pies.

"Arthur say anything to you?" Skid Row asked as he unwrapped a cheeseburger.

"Nah," Bullfrog said. "I think he was about to tell me I couldn't use all the coupons at once. Something made him reconsider."

"Probably thought you'd go all freaky-frog again. I wouldn't want to be on the receiving end of that shit."

"Having people think you're nuts does have its advantages. Maybe I should go crazy more often."

"As long as I'm not in the line of fire. So what happened with your job anyway? You attack somebody there too?"

"It wasn't like that," Bullfrog said, stuffing a handful of fries into his mouth. "I was working at the bus station."

Skid Row made a face. "Land of the losers."

"Well put."

"So what were you doing there, driving old ladies to Atlantic City?"

Bullfrog shook his head. "That would have been an improvement. I was a luggage handler, making minimum wage to be treated like crap."

"Join the club pal."

"I'm not kidding."

Skid Row wasn't either but he let that go. "What was so bad about it?"

"My boss was an asshole. Whenever something went wrong, he never bothered to find out what actually happened. He just blamed whoever was closest to him at the time."

"I take it something happened today."

"You could say that." Bullfrog finished his fries and started in on one of the pies. "Bus came in from Philly. One of the things I unloaded was this guitar case. It was all beat up. It looked like it had been tossed off a five-story building. The case was cracked. One of the hinges was broken, and I didn't have to open it to know the guitar inside was all sorts of messed up."

"And?"

"And it was worth over ten grand."

Skid Row whistled.

"Yeah. There's no telling where the damage occurred. It could have been Philly. It could have been somewhere further down the line. The owner said he'd come all the way from Minneapolis. The guitar probably fell off a cart or something. Whoever was responsible loaded it up without saying a word. I was there to unload so, as far as my boss was concerned, it was my fault."

"You serious?"

"As a heart attack. The jerk told me he was going to withhold the whole ten grand from my pay. I told him exactly what I thought of that plan and, well, you can figure out the rest."

"Man, that's bullshit. Doesn't the bus company have insurance for stuff like that?"

"Of course they do. Lot of good that does me. Today was supposed to be pay day. The boss kept my check for what he called a down payment. He'll never see another dime from me. I promise you that"

"He kept your money? That totally sucks. Even Arthur wouldn't pull something like that. You gonna try to fight it?"

"How? I can't afford a lawyer."

"Guess you got a point there."

"I didn't like the job anyway. The place was filthy and lugging suitcases around gets old in a hurry."

"So what are you gonna do?"

Bullfrog shrugged. "I'll either find another job or hit the road. I haven't decided which. Where are we headed anyway?"

Skid Row remembered Bullfrog's comment about being on the move. Now he was talking about hitting the road. Was the guy just a drifter? He didn't look the part. Then again, what exactly did a drifter look like? Maybe dirty hands and coveralls were the universal drifter uniform. Skid Row wanted to ask more about his personal situation but decided it was really none of his business.

"We're headed to my place," he said instead. "I got a room at the Y."

"That's right near the bus station. Is it an okay place to crash?"

"It's a bed," Skid Row said. "You're not going to get much more for seventy-four bucks a week."

"That's not bad. Maybe I'll check it out if I decide to stick around."

Skid Row looked at him. "You can have my room," he said. "I've been there long enough and I'll be relocating at the first opportunity." He had no idea how soon that opportunity would come.

They entered the building through a pair of large double doors. Skid Row turned left and headed for a staircase but was brought up short by a black man large enough to play linebacker for any pro football team.

"Don't go up there," he said, in a voice much higher and quieter than his size and physique would suggest.

"Hey, Tyrone," Skid Row said. "Kill anybody yet today?" He expected a smile but the big man only stared. "So what's up?" Skid Row asked. "Somethin' goin' on upstairs?"

It wouldn't be the first time. A few weeks before, the residential wing had been closed off for hours because some idiot made a bomb threat. The cops were called in and they searched the place from top to bottom. All they found was a shoebox-sized package wrapped in plain brown paper and smelling of seafood. It contained nothing more dangerous than a moldy tuna sandwich.

"By the way," Skid Row said, jerking his head at his new companion. "This is Bullfrog. He may want to talk to you about getting a room here. Got any vacancies?"

"We definitely have one," and something in his tone brought Skid Row up short. Tyrone always tried to look mean, with his bulging muscles, gold hoop earring, and the hand that never strayed far from the handle of the billy club that hung from a loop on his utility belt. It was mostly an act--except today, Skid Row was pretty sure he wasn't messing around.

"We need to talk," Tyrone said, turning and striding toward his office. He clearly expected Skid Row to follow.

"Sure, Man. Whatever you say." Then to Bullfrog, "Just hang here. I'll be right back." He hoped he sounded cool and casual because he felt about ready to shit his pants. Skid Row had known Tyrone for a while and could tell the dude was pissed. Why, he couldn't imagine. He'd never caused any trouble there, at least nothing to speak of.

"Sit down," Tyrone commanded, unlocking his door and tossing a large ring of keys onto his desk.

Skid Row looked around. He was surprised at the size and comfort of the office. Tyrone had a black leather chair, or at least one that looked like leather, and a real wooden desk. It was old but solid and obviously well-made. The walls looked freshly painted and the carpet, though industrial grade, somehow gave the space a bit of character and authority. Tyrone didn't have any windows. What he had instead were half a dozen television monitors, the first showing local news and the rest providing views of halls, stairwells and doorways. Skid Row had seen a few of the security cameras but he'd had no idea the place was that well wired. Could Tyrone flip a switch and look into private rooms? That was a sobering thought.

Skid Row still didn't know why he was there but he had more than a sneaking suspicion that it wasn't going to end well for him. He sat and tried to stay calm while he waited for Tyrone to tell him what it was all about. He didn't have to wait long.

"Anything you want to tell me?" Tyrone asked, but it came out as more of a demand than a question.

"No!" Skid Row said, shaking his head. "I mean, I didn't do anything. I don't know what this is about."

"Really." Tyrone stared at him in much the same way he might stare into a container of leftover Chinese takeout that had stayed in the fridge a few weeks too long.

Skid Row fidgeted but said nothing.

With a heavy sigh, Tyrone reached into a shirt pocket and withdrew a small plastic bag. He studied it for a few seconds, then flipped it casually onto his desk. "Ever see this before?" he asked, his tone suggesting he already knew the answer.

Skid Row recognized the little bag at once. It was, in fact, the very item he'd come to collect. "What if I say no?"

Tyrone sighed again and sat up straight in his chair. "Then I'd lose even more respect for you." He looked at Skid Row with more sadness than anything else. "Man, I thought you were smart enough not to keep that shit here." He poked the bag with disgust. "You realize you've left me no choice."

Skid Row didn't know what to say. He supposed he could still deny the marijuana was his. That would be a tough sell, especially since he knew right where it had been found, tucked into a small slit in his own mattress. Maybe he could claim he was holding it for someone else. Tyrone would have a hell of a time proving otherwise. They both knew the truth, though, and Skid Row realized there was nothing to be gained from trying to delay the inevitable.

"I'm really sorry," he said, unable to meet Tyrone's eyes. "It won't happen again. I swear."

"I'm quite sure that's true," Tyrone replied, bending down behind his desk and coming up with a plain cardboard box. He slid it across to Skid Row. I've taken the liberty of gathering your belongings. You're welcome to go through them to make sure everything is there."

"You're kicking me out?" Skid Row had known that was coming but it still somehow took him by surprise. "Dude, you can't do that. I mean, at least give me a second chance."

Tyrone folded unnaturally large arms across his chest. "You know the policy," he said. "This is a drug free environment; no exceptions and no second chances. I'm sorry. I really am."

Skid Row knew the YMCA was about as drug free as a college frat party. No point saying so. He'd gotten caught and that was the bottom line. "Where am I supposed to go?" he asked instead, trying and failing to keep the note of panic out of his voice.

"You'll have to figure that out for yourself," Tyrone said evenly. "You're no longer welcome here."

-7-

Ricky Fixx left the pizzeria and headed toward his car. He'd only gone about a half a block when his stomach started to growl. He glanced at his watch and saw that it was nearly noon, and that reminded him that he hadn't eaten anything all day. Ricky hadn't had any trouble refusing Geno's offer of lunch, but once he was out of range of all the *aromas*, his hunger returned with a vengeance. He looked longingly in the direction of the diner. That's where Carl was, no doubt savoring the very chicken fried steak Ricky had been kind enough to recommend. His mouth watered as he imagined that golden brown coating and the tender, juicy strip steak inside. Had Carl ordered the homemade fries or the garlic mashed potatoes? Both were delicious, and he'd surely finish things off with a selection from the large pastry case up front. Ricky usually went for the coconut cream pie, one of the house specialties, but they probably had a dozen other items to choose from. His stomach growled again as he thought about rum cakes, half moon cookies, and chocolate mousse. He was more than a little tempted to stroll in there, grab a seat across from Carl and place his order. Ricky knew that wouldn't do. He had plans and they depended on him being out of sight when Carl paid a visit to Geno. If they ate together, separating afterwards could prove difficult.

With a sigh, he took one more look at the diner and then walked the other way. He wasn't in a hurry. He knew Carl wasn't about to rush through a good meal. Ricky still didn't think he'd have enough time to find another restaurant, sit down for the sort of lunch he was in the mood for, and get back in position before Carl was finished. Irritated by nothing more than simple jealousy, he drove a couple blocks and swung into a Wendy's drive-thru where he ordered a burger and a baked potato. Then, still thinking about chocolate mousse, he added a Frosty once he got to the window. Ricky paid, parked in the shade of a large oak tree and ate his lunch in his car, trying hard not to think about what he was missing.

It was going on twelve-thirty when he tossed his food containers out the window and made the short drive back to Geno's. He didn't have to pass by the diner to know Carl was still there. Not wanting his Lexus right out in plain sight, Ricky turned the corner and found a parking spot at the far end of a lot adjacent to a small consignment shop. There was only one other vehicle in the lot. It was a white Corolla and clearly empty but Ricky still took a quick look around before popping his trunk and removing a leather camera bag containing a Cannon PowerShot SX 510 along with a telephoto lens he doubted he'd need. The camera's built-in 30x optical zoom should be more than sufficient to get the job done. Checking to make sure the mini tripod was in its customary spot in a side pocket, Ricky zipped the bag closed and slung the strap over his shoulder.

Once he was sure the coast was clear, he jogged across the road, slowing as he passed a small corner liquor store. When he got to the rear of the building, he let himself in through a broken metal gate. He squinted as his eyes adjusted to the sudden gloom. He was in a narrow alley, the back of the liquor store on one side and a dry cleaner on the other, the air heavy with smells of garbage and laundry chemicals. Ricky picked his way past overflowing dumpsters and stacks of cardboard boxes bearing names like Jack Daniels, Ketel One, Beefeater, and dozens of wines he'd never heard of and would have had a hard time even pronouncing.

Focused entirely on his destination, he nearly fell headlong over a pair of legs jutting out from beneath one of the larger piles of boxes. Someone, it appeared, had constructed a cardboard castle. Ricky saw worn black shoes, sickly pale skin, no socks, and the lower half of a pair of threadbare tweed pants. A mostly empty bottle of Mad Dog 20/20 was wedged between the man's knees. At least Ricky assumed it was a man. They were men's shoes, and he could hear what he guessed was masculine snoring coming from somewhere within the depths of the makeshift shelter.

With a look of disgust, he detoured around Rip Van Wino, and then started paying a lot more attention to his surroundings as he picked his way carefully to the far end of the alley. Ricky didn't notice any other slumberers, but suspected there could be an entire wino colony hidden beneath the piles of boxes. He doubted it mattered. Even if he was seen well enough to be identified, homeless people weren't the most credible witnesses. They also weren't likely to do anything to draw attention to themselves. Besides, he wasn't doing anything illegal. Well, he supposed he might have been guilty of trespassing. No one in the immediate vicinity was about to accuse him of that. What was that saying about the pot and the kettle?

With a last glance around, he grasped the bottom rung of an old steel ladder and hoisted himself up, once again wondering why the thing was there. The first time he scouted the location, he'd assumed it was a fire escape but that made no sense. The liquor store was only a one story building. From street level, it looked like there might have been a small attic or storage space above the actual store. That still didn't explain the ladder because there were no windows on the back side of the building and no interior roof access. He knew that because he'd been on the roof twice before. The only thing up there was a ventilation system of some sort. Unless it broke down a whole lot, why go to the trouble and expense to have a permanent ladder installed? Ricky's only other theory was that it had something to do with the building next door. That one had a second story which might have once been a private residence. He supposed the ladder could have been part of their fire exit plan. What the hell difference did it make now? The apartment, if that's what it was, showed every sign of being long vacant and the mysterious ladder was perfectly placed to serve his needs.

Keeping a tight grip on the strap of his camera bag, he clambered up the nineteen rungs, swung his legs over a low brick wall and dropped carefully onto the roof. He realized there was no real need for stealth. The roof's surface was coated in something industrial that felt like rubber underfoot. He figured he could run a jackhammer up there without too much fear of discovery. There was still no point taking chances. Ricky ducked low as he half walked, half tip-toed to the opposite side of the building. Peering over the edge, he had a full, unobstructed view of the entire street.

Directly across from Geno's dung heap of a restaurant, Ricky could now see right in through the front window. As he'd anticipated, the angle was a bit of a problem. The back half of the restaurant was completely out of sight. Ricky powered the camera up and adjusted the zoom. He could see the front door, a few of the booths, and maybe a third of the counter. He hoped that would be good enough. At least the overcast sky meant there'd be no issues with glare. He snapped a couple shots of nothing in particular and studied the results in the small display window.

"It'll do," he muttered, and then screwed the tripod into the bottom of the camera, picked out what he thought would be the best spot to shoot from, popped a peppermint candy into his mouth and sat back to wait.

Carl exited the diner at exactly twelve forty-one, or so said the Cannon's date and time stamp which provided a permanent record of the event. Ricky lined up his shot, adjusted the zoom and got a charming picture of Carl belching and scratching his ass. He plodded off down the street and, two and a half minutes later, was standing outside Geno's . A car backfired a block away and Carl turned to look. The timing couldn't have been better. Ricky snapped a shot that showed Carl's face almost head on, the sign for Geno's clearly visible in the background.

"Perfect," he said, as he snapped a second shot of Carl reaching for the door handle, and a third where he was actually entering the restaurant. Then, nothing happened; at least nothing Ricky could see.

Carl was in there, and presumably, Geno was too. They seemed to be having some sort of a disagreement. Ricky heard a muffled thump and imagined Carl slamming a hand, or maybe Geno's head, down on the countertop. That was followed by raised voices, or was it just one voice? He strained but couldn't make out who was speaking or what was being said. And to his great dismay, everything was happening just out of range of his camera lens. He'd occasionally catch a glimpse of Carl's arm, his elbow, or the back of his head. Geno remained completely hidden somewhere towards the back of the restaurant.

"Shit!" Ricky swore, shifting his weight from one knee to the other and starting to think the whole thing had been a waste of time. The liquor store was fairly low but not low enough, and the knee-high brick wall that rimmed the edge of the roof made it even worse. The angle was too sharp, and no matter how he maneuvered, Ricky couldn't see far enough into the restaurant to tell what was happening, let alone get any decent pictures. He was about to give up--had the camera halfway back in the bag--when inspiration struck.

Ricky grinned, wondering why in the world he hadn't thought of it sooner. The Cannon's small display window not only flipped open but could rotate over a hundred and eighty degrees. That meant he didn't have to be looking through the viewfinder to see what the lens was seeing. He adjusted the display so it was facing straight up. Then, jamming a toe under a metal pipe for support, he leaned over the wall as far as he dared, holding the camera with both arms extended. He knew he was running the risk of being spotted. If anyone saw a man dangling from a rooftop, camera in hand, they'd be sure to call the police. Ricky wasn't overly concerned, though. There hadn't been much traffic on the street, pedestrian or otherwise, and it was his experience that people almost never looked up. He still couldn't help feeling somewhat exposed and vulnerable. There was nothing to be done about that.

He shifted slightly, trying to ignore the way his belt buckle had started digging into the soft flesh of his stomach. He also worried that he might be ruining a perfectly good pair of suit pants. He couldn't do anything about that either. His eyes fixed on the digital display, Ricky began panning slowly back and forth until he again found Geno's front window. Bent double and looking down at the camera, he found it surprisingly difficult to zero in on his target. He kept moving the camera too much, and then he'd overcompensate by going too far back the other way. It was several uncomfortable seconds before he was finally able to again zoom in on Carl.

Still far from perfect, the angle was better now. He could see more of his partner, more of the counter, and part of what must have been Geno's dirty apron. Ricky squinted and wriggled forward a few more inches. Stretching out as far as he could, he took a picture that showed the bottom half of Geno's face, and then nearly toppled off the roof when he saw Carl lunge across the counter, grab Geno by the crotch and launch him into space.

"Holy fuck!"

Ricky flinched, slid, and came dangerously close to plummeting to the pavement fifteen feet below. He would have dropped his camera right then had he not had the foresight to twist the strap once around his wrist. He gritted his teeth, balancing precariously over the wall, with one hand gripping the Cannon and the other jammed painfully against the side of the building and supporting what felt like about ninety percent of his body weight. The rough brick bit into his left palm. He imagined it tearing the skin and starting to bleed. His hand would then get slippery, begin to slide and he'd be a goner. A fall from that height wouldn't kill him, probably. It would still hurt like hell, maybe break a bone or two and damn sure attract attention.

Ricky heard a crash he could only assume came from Geno's. It was sort of hard to tell hanging upside-down with all the blood rushing to his head. He wondered what was going on but recognized that, right then, he had more important things to worry about. He'd lost his small toe hold and his legs flailed wildly as he tried to inch his way backwards. He made no progress at first. Then, pushing with his free hand and wriggling his pelvis painfully into the brick, he gradually got his body moving in the right direction. It took a lot longer than he would have liked but he finally made it back to safety. He collapsed onto the roof: flushed, out of breath, and ticked at himself for doing something so stupid.

Ricky wasted no time counting his blessings because, right then, he heard another shout followed by another crash. He scrambled to his feet and, hands still shaking badly, snapped hurried pictures of his thumb, the rooftop, and the rear end of a Volkswagen before finally getting himself under control.

"Settle down," he murmured as Carl once again appeared in the frame. But where was Geno? Ricky zoomed out and panned slowly this way and that. The little grease ball had vanished. He'd survived the nut grab. Ricky knew that because of all the noise that followed. So where was he now? A moment later, Ricky had his answer. Carl bent down then straightened, grasping Geno by the scruff of the neck. The little prick mouthed something that looked a whole lot like "NOOOOOOO!" right before he was slammed face first into the front window. Ricky laughed out loud. That one might be worth framing. He had Carl. He had Geno. He had glass splintering in every direction. He was also fairly sure he had a new client.

-8-

Bullfrog tossed another log on their small camp fire and slid his blanket a little closer. Skid Row watched him in silence, still not sure how, in less than twelve hours time, he'd lost his housing and his job, and was now taking shelter under a bridge. The nighttime chill had begun seeping into his bones but that seemed to be the least of his problems. He looked on as his new companion poked at the coals with what might have once been a pair of old hedge clippers. They were so bent and discolored from age and weather that it was impossible to say for sure. Bullfrog had obviously used the tool many times before. He maneuvered bits of wood and, when the fire was crackling away to his satisfaction, eased two cans of baked beans closer to the flames. Skid Row didn't especially like beans but he had to admit the food smelled good. The last thing they'd eaten was the grub from McDonald's and a lot had happened since then.

Skid Row remembered sitting in Tyrone's office and being asked, actually told, to vacate the premises. Next thing he knew, he was out on the sidewalk, all his worldly possessions in a pathetically small box tucked underneath one arm. He had a couple pairs of jeans, a few T-shirts, a hoodie sweatshirt, socks and underwear, and a New York Giants ball cap someone had left in the bathroom at the McDonald's a month before. He didn't really like football or the Giants but it was a good hat so he kept it. In addition to his clothes, the box held a pair of shades, basic toiletries, a few CD's with nothing to play them on, and a tattered three by five picture of his mom. That was all he had to show for his life. Pathetic. Thank God Tyrone had given him back his bag of weed. It was small consolation but Skid Row had a feeling he'd need it.

He slid a hand into his pants pocket and once again fingered the other item Tyrone had given him. The man had never given him anything before, had never shown any real affection, for him or anyone else, so what on earth had prompted him to fork over twenty bucks? Being head of security at the Binghamton YMCA couldn't pay a hell of a lot. Tyrone had a wife, at least a couple kids, and a twenty-year-old Chevy that spent more time at the garage than on the street. He obviously couldn't afford to replace it or even fix it right. Yet, he'd given Skid Row some cash. Why?

He remembered the look of Tyrone's old brown wallet, torn at one corner and faded to almost white along the crease. Was that twenty dollar bill the only money he had? It was possible, perhaps even likely, and he'd handed it over to an undeserving stoner loser with no prospects. It made Skid Row feel incredibly grateful, and humble, and awful. He barely knew the man yet somehow felt like he'd let him down. Skid Row shook his head, wondering what he'd manage to screw up next.

Hours before, he'd been fantasizing about how nice it would be to get out of his cramped, cruddy, and totally impersonal room and into a real apartment. Staring sullenly at the cardboard box at his feet, he now had a much clearer understanding of how ridiculous, how totally asinine the idea had been. What the hell would he do in an apartment? He didn't have any furniture. He didn't have any lamps. He didn't have any towels, blankets, cookware, silverware, or dishes. He literally didn't have a pot to piss in. What he did have was a growing sense of dread. For all its faults, the Y had put a reasonably priced roof over his head and given him a sense of security that, until a little while ago, he'd completely taken for granted. He'd assumed he would stay there until he was ready to leave and never considered what might happen if the decision were taken out of his hands. Now that it had been he felt completely unprepared.

Skid Row took quick stock of his situation. Thanks in part to Tyrone, he figured he had enough cash in his pocket to pay for a night in a cheap motel. He also had one more check coming. With the hours he'd worked, it would be around eighty bucks and he'd have to wait nearly a week to get it. What was he supposed to do until then, especially if he spent his entire life savings on a bed for the night? He had lived on the street before and knew he could survive the ordeal again if necessary. He just wished he didn't have to. Those had been the loneliest, most depressing, most humbling days of his life and he thought he'd left them far behind.

He remembered, nearly ten years before, throwing some clothes in a back pack, telling William to fuck off one final time, slamming the front door and never looking back. He'd never regretted the decision, well, almost never; but it's hard not to second guess when you're cold, hungry and completely destitute. In his darkest hours, Skid Row swore to himself that, somehow, someday, he would prove his father wrong. He'd thought he was finally starting to live up to that promise. But now he was all the way back at square one. Had the son of a bitch been right all along? Skid Row couldn't accept that but at the moment was having a hard time denying William's assertion that he was and would always be a fuck up.

"So what happened?" Bullfrog asked, stretching short legs out in front of him and leaning back on his elbows. "You get in trouble or something?"

He obviously knew Skid Row had been kicked out of the Y. He'd seen the evidence. Skid Row just hadn't shared any of the details of his brief interaction with Tyrone. In fact, when he left the office, he hadn't said a single word, brushing past Bullfrog and trying to rub the sting from his eyes as he elbowed his way through a group of young men who'd just come in. A few of them called out greetings but Skid Row didn't respond or acknowledge them in any way. He'd simply pushed through the doors and moved off down the street, evidently not caring whether or not Bullfrog chose to follow. Bullfrog did follow, and caught up with him about the time Skid Row reached the end of the block. They continued along in silence, and at one point Bullfrog ended up leading the way. He said he had a place they could go, and Skid Row never questioned it

"A dude set me up," he said now, moving a few inches closer to the fire. "That had to be it." He started to explain but stopped and shook his head. What difference did it make? He had his theory. Whether it was true or not, he was still out.

"They got me with the goods," he said with resignation. "Simple as that."

"That sucks," Bullfrog observed. "What do you think you'll do now?"

"Fuck if I know. I guess I'll take advantage of your hospitality and these beautiful surroundings."

In the dark, he didn't think the place looked half bad. Bullfrog had set up his small camp in a clearing about ten yards from the water's edge, in an area of sandy soil dotted with random patches of scrub grass. The Susquehanna River sprawled in front of them, motionless and tranquil, at least compared to the steady drone of traffic from above. They were at the base of an old bridge he surely could have identified if he were looking at it from street level. From down here, it was just a bridge, loud and dirty. In the daylight, he suspected he'd have a glorious view of crumbling supports, graffiti, and the empty beer cans, broken bottles, and other trash that were undoubtedly strewn all over the ground. *Home sweet home*, he thought sourly. The place was a dump, but at least it was his dump, or theirs anyway, and far preferable to bedding down on a park bench. Besides, with the bridge right there, at least they'd be able to keep dry if it rained.

"Stay as long as you want," Bullfrog said, seemingly reading Skid Row's mind. "And thanks for the food." He indicated the small pile of bread, peanut butter and canned goods.

"No sweat," Skid row said. As much as he might have enjoyed a nice, soft motel bed right about then, he knew that would have been a serious waste of money. Instead, he'd gone into a thrift shop where he'd purchased a second hand sleeping bag and a winter coat. It wasn't yet the middle of October but he knew he'd need warm clothing soon enough. Better to get it while he still had the dough. Then he and Bullfrog had stopped by a Weis grocery store and bought enough stuff to at least last a few days. Bullfrog wasn't lying when he said he didn't have any money. Skid Row picked up the tab for the whole thing. It wasn't much and he really didn't mind. He just knew he wouldn't be able to support both of them for long.

"How long you been camped out here?" he asked.

"Couple weeks I guess."

"Mind if I ask why? I mean, you said before that you've been on the road for a while. What's up with that?"

Bullfrog sat up and began busying himself with the fire. Their cans of beans had started to bubble and he carefully eased them off to one side. He dug into a canvas bag and came out with two spoons. Then, still not looking at Skid Row, he disappeared into the darkness and came back a few moments later with an armload of wood. He tossed a few chunks into the flames and glanced around like he was looking for something else to do.

"Listen," Skid Row said. "It's none of my business. If you don't want to tell me--"

"It's not that," Bullfrog said, dropping heavily onto his blanket. "It's just tough to talk about."

"So don't."

Skid Row was curious, though. Bullfrog was a little odd but he seemed bright enough. He was also young, close to Skid Row's own age, and looked perfectly healthy. What was he doing living under a bridge in a crap hole like Binghamton? True, Skid Row was now living under the same bridge in the very same crap hole. He saw his own situation as extremely temporary. Bullfrog, on the other hand, looked like he'd been living off the land for a while. Why? He was dying to know but wasn't going to force the issue. If the dude didn't want to talk, that was his own business.

"My parents were killed," he finally said, handing one can of beans to Skid Row and taking the other for himself. "Careful," he added. "They're pretty hot."

"What happened?" Skid Row asked.

Bullfrog dipped a spoon into his beans but didn't take a bite. "Car accident," he said evenly. "Couple years ago. Snow storm. Bad roads. Their car went over an embankment. I don't know a lot of the details but I guess it was pretty nasty."

"Man, I'm sorry," Skid Row said. "And you've been on your own ever since?"

Bullfrog nodded.

Skid Row didn't know what else to say so he started to eat while at the same time studying Bullfrog out of the corner of one eye. His story was tragic but also incomplete. He had said his dad was an accountant. And his mom? Skid Row couldn't remember but it had sounded like they were both professionals, white collar for sure. That usually meant well off. They must have had a will or at least some assets. So how, so soon after their death, did their kid end up penniless and on the street?

"You got any brothers or sisters?" Skid Row asked.

"No," Bullfrog said with a hitch in his voice. "I don't have anybody. Not anymore."

"And your folks didn't leave you anything?" Skid Row knew his question wasn't appropriate but he wanted to know.

Bullfrog hung his head and set his untouched dinner aside. "Actually," he said, "they left me a nice house, a new Toyota Camry and a decent amount of money."

"So what happened?" Skid Row asked, concentrating on his beans and wondering how the guy could have blown the family fortune in such a short period of time.

"My mom had this step-brother," Bullfrog said. "They weren't real close but we saw him a few times a year. Seemed like a decent enough guy."

He stood and walked to the river's edge. Skid Row started to follow but something in Bullfrog's body language made him reconsider. For several moments, neither of them moved or said a word. The brief silence was broken when an eighteen-wheeler rumbled overhead. Without warning, Bullfrog grabbed a large stone and hurled it at the underside of the bridge. It clanged off something metal and, a second or two later, splashed into the water.

"FUCK!" Bullfrog shouted, his voice echoing hollowly and sending some critter of the night scurrying off into the weeds. "Fuck," he repeated, but much quieter.

"Dude, are you all right?" Skid Row had known Bullfrog less than twelve hours and had already witnessed two violent outbursts. He'd been on the receiving end of one of them and didn't relish the idea of being in that position again. His best bet might be to grab his new sleeping bag and few belongings and find some shelter elsewhere. He'd have to leave the food behind but that was no big deal. He could buy more tomorrow. He started to rise when Bullfrog turned to face him.

"I'm sorry about that," he said. "I try not to think about it. Sometimes, though," he gave a shrug. "It just comes out."

Skid Row sat back down but stayed on his guard. He wanted to be ready to move if Bullfrog flew off the handle again and went into attack mode. Then he had a thought. The best way to avoid another explosion was to do something to ease the tension. He had just the thing. He dug into his pocket and came out with two marijuana cigarettes which he lit in the campfire. "Here," he said, handing one over. "This should make you feel better."

"Thanks," Bullfrog said, studying the weed before taking a tentative puff. He immediately started hacking.

Skid Row laughed. "You are a rookie. Look. You do it like this." He demonstrated by inhaling deeply and holding his breath for several seconds before blowing slowly out again.

Bullfrog tried to copy, again started coughing but then began to get the hang of it.

"We're going to need more of this," Skid Row observed. "You're way high strung."

Bullfrog was too busy smoking to respond.

"So," Skid Row said after a while, "you want to finish your story?"

Bullfrog looked confused but then seemed to remember. "The guy's a f-fuck," he said, slurring his words a bit.

"What did he do?" Skid Row asked. He assumed, correctly as it turned out, that the fuck in question was the step-brother.

"He screwed me." Bullfrog made a sound that might have been a giggle. "And it didn't even feel good."

"What do you mean?" Skid Row asked, hoping Bullfrog could tell his story before getting too stoned to communicate.

"He... told... me... he'd... put... my...f-f-finances in order," Bullfrog said, speaking in a sluggish monotone and seemingly mesmerized by a dark stain he'd discovered on his left work boot. He poked at it with an extended finger and looked surprised when his finger didn't penetrate the hard leather. "What…did…I… know?" he asked his boot. "I…thought…he…was…going…to…help…me."

"I take it he didn't?"

Bullfrog started to shake his head but must have forgotten what he was doing halfway through. His gaze wandered from his boot to Skid Row's sneakers, and then up to Skid Row's face which he didn't seem to see at all. His eyes kept floating up until they fixed on something high above. Skid Row figured he was hallucinating but he took a look just the same and damned if there wasn't something up there--green flashing lights of a plane, a satellite or a fucking UFO. Whatever it was, it had captured all of Bullfrog's attention.

Beautiful, Skid Row thought, realizing their conversation was probably over. He still figured he'd give it one more try.

"So what did he do?" he asked, thinking it must have been pretty damn bad.

"Huh?' Bullfrog's head moved slightly in Skid Row's direction but he was still in some other hemisphere.

"Your… step uncle or whatever the hell he is. What did he do to you?"

Bullfrog didn't respond for a long time and Skid Row thought he'd completely drifted away. Truth be told, he was a little jealous. He'd hoped for a nice high but really wasn't feeling it at all, or maybe that was only because Bullfrog was in the fucking clouds somewhere.

"Papers," Bullfrog said, an odd smile on his face. "He gave me papers."

-9-

The phone on Andrew Cullen's desk buzzed. He started to reach for it automatically, but stopped with his hand hovering just inches above the receiver. Line four, his private line, was flashing which meant the call had not gone through Carrie. There were only a handful of people who had his private number. Only one person used it on a regular basis and he didn't want to talk to her right then. He wasn't really up for talking to anyone. He withdrew his hand but kept an eye on the light until it finally stopped flashing. Line one lit up for half a second and then went dark. Either Carrie had picked up that quickly or, more likely, Sara hung up as soon as the call rolled over, assuming it had really been her. That suspicion was confirmed not thirty seconds later when his iPhone gave a soft chirp. She always did that--tried one phone if she couldn't get him on the other. It didn't necessarily mean the call was important. She may have just wanted to see if he was free for lunch. He knew he should answer, and knew he wouldn't be able to bring himself to do it. He waited, and after a few beats, his phone chimed. She'd followed that second call with a text. He glanced at the display, and then put his head in his hands.

Cullen didn't waste time worrying about or even questioning the long series of missteps and poor decisions that had brought him to this point. What's done was done. Water under the bridge, whatever the hell that meant. It was just a shame that bridge wasn't high enough to jump off. He had considered suicide, briefly, and rejected the idea just as quickly. For one thing, he knew he'd never have the guts to pull the trigger, swallow the pills, or seal up the garage, crank the car engine, and sit in the driver's seat long enough for carbon monoxide fumes to do their deadly work. Even more troubling was the possibility that his death, untimely or otherwise, might actually make things worse. He'd be off the hook, but what about the mess he left behind? Sara and the girls might be made to suffer on his behalf. Cullen couldn't live with that, or, he noted bitterly, die with it either.

He glanced at the text message one more time, then went back to contemplating that same pink message slip he'd been staring at for the past hour. Carrie's neat, precise hand writing had recorded a name, phone number, and time the call was received--five twenty-seven the previous afternoon; and in the memo space, she'd written the single word *personal*. Had she had even the slightest inkling how true that was? Right then, there was nothing more personal in Cullen's entire life. He'd dug his hole and it was up to him to somehow find a way out.

He'd been stupid, and it wasn't the first time. Cullen was painfully aware that he hadn't been an especially good husband or father. He still loved his family, even if he didn't deserve them. His eyes moved to the silver framed eight-by-ten he kept on the corner of his large mahogany desk. In the background, the Poconos were spread out, snow covered and majestic under a leaden sky. And in the foreground, his wife, blonde and beautiful, her arms wrapped around Kristin and Kayla, both looking triumphant after skiing one of the black diamond slopes for the first time. Cullen wasn't in the picture but knew he should have been. At the time the photo was taken, he guessed he was no more than a hundred yards away. He was an excellent skier in his own right, and had been looking forward to seeing if he could still keep up with his daughters. Then, something else came up. He ate breakfast with his family, but then started complaining of a headache. With promises to catch up with them later, he headed back to their room where he spent the rest of the morning and a good part of the afternoon receiving *private* instruction from Lina, a voluptuous Swede he'd met in the resort bar the evening before. She had a world class set of slopes and, once they'd made eye contact, he knew he wouldn't rest until he'd given them a try. He'd felt like crap afterwards but knew he had no one to blame but himself.

In addition to a family vacation, he and Sara had been celebrating their twentieth anniversary. He'd given his wife a pair of stunning emerald earrings with matching bracelet, and then spent the day banging another woman. As sick and remorseful as he'd felt after the fact, Cullen knew that, if given the chance to do it all over again, he would.

Despite his daily workouts, his demanding exercise regiment, the marathons, biathlons and triathlons he'd competed in and, on occasion, even won, Cullen knew he was weak. He could bench press three hundred pounds without breaking a sweat but resisting even the slightest sexual temptation was often too much. The only exception was Carrie, and that was only because he feared serious legal repercussions if he made even the slightest misstep.

Disgusted with himself, he stood and walked to the large windows that took up all of one wall. Tears stung his eyes when he realized he might never have the opportunity to make up for all the damage he'd done, the hurt he'd caused. Sara had never said anything. She'd never even let on. He still suspected she knew, if not about Lina then about at least one of the others. There'd been several over the Years. Why had she stuck with him for so long? Maybe she clung to the hope that, in time, he'd settle down. Or maybe it was for the girls. Either way, he thought she'd come to regret her decision to stay by his side. So far, he'd only hurt her emotionally; but what would she think of him when she learned the rest? The fact that she would learn seemed, at this point, a foregone conclusion.

He ran a trembling hand through short brown hair. As much stress as he'd been under, waking up in a cold sweat at least once a night--that was on the increasingly rare nights he was able to sleep at all--he was surprised his hair hadn't fallen out altogether. He felt run down: old, tired and beaten. He knew he'd been drinking too much and his diet of late had consisted mostly of power bars and vitamins. At the rate he was going, it was something of a surprise he hadn't already dropped dead of an aneurism. If it were up to him, he supposed that wouldn't be a bad way to go.

He paced from one side of his office to the other, never completely taking his eyes off that message slip. The call time seemed telling. Five twenty-seven. Cullen normally left the office between five-thirty and six. Yesterday, however, he'd left a bit early so he could meet with a prospective client. He'd locked his office door around five-twenty, given some brief instructions to Carrie and then left the building. He doubted he'd even made it to his car when the call came in. Did that mean anything? Maybe. It could have been mere coincidence, or the caller might have been giving him until the end of the day to get in touch, something Cullen had promised he'd do. He'd been thinking about it, dreading it all afternoon. But since he had nothing but bad news to report, he finally decided it could wait until morning. The message might have been a subtle reminder that, no, it really couldn't wait, or to let him know someone was keeping tabs on him. Carrie didn't always record call times, so had she written the time randomly or was she requested to do so? He could pick up the phone and ask her, and then she might start asking him questions he really didn't want to answer.

Cullen had made a deal and now found himself unable to live up to his end of the bargain. That was the grim bottom line. Anyone with a shred of common sense would have instructed him not to make the deal in the first place. He hadn't sought anyone's advice, thinking he could handle the situation just fine on his own. He'd be made to pay for that mistake: literally, figuratively, or both. And given recent events, he knew the price he'd pay would end up being a lot higher than he'd planned.

Cullen stopped pacing, grabbed the pink square of paper, and then dropped it like he'd been burned. Then, as anger flared, he snatched it up again, wadded it into a tight ball and flung it across the room where it bounced off a Tiffany lampshade and fell silently to the floor. He stared at it in disgust, despising himself and his new, unfamiliar feelings of helplessness and desperation.

He looked at the phone and then quickly looked away. What if he didn't call? What, Cullen wondered, if he never called? At best, that might buy him some extra time. And at worst? He hated to even think about it. He'd already kicked the hornet's nest once. He hadn't meant to. It just sort of happened in the heat of the moment. They'd have to respond, and the next communication would undoubtedly be a lot more menacing than a message slip.

He thought he could try to help his cause by being proactive, but Cullen currently did not have the one thing he knew they wanted. That left him no choice but to stall, which meant the constant fear of retribution would hang over his head like a guillotine, the heavy blade descending a little further with every passing hour. He'd be afraid to cross the street, to start his car, to do…anything. And when he returned home, when he pulled into his drive, admired his large, more than comfortable house and greeted his family, he'd be reminded of how quickly everything he cherished could disappear.

Cullen turned back to the window and rested his forehead against the glass. He surveyed the flowing traffic, a group of college students boarding a Binghamton University bus, a woman pushing a stroller, two men walking briskly toward the courthouse, a young couple holding hands. To Cullen, they all looked like they didn't have a care in the world. Maybe they didn't. He remembered feeling like that. He had the world on a string and no concept of how quickly the string could break. He watched a moment longer, longing for the days his own daughters were still in strollers.

"Enjoy it while it lasts," he said, not even realizing he'd spoken the words aloud. Then, with a last glance at his phone, he grabbed his suit coat and headed for the door.

-10-

Skid Row woke early with his entire body shivering, his back aching and his head pounding like the Energizer Bunny on Red Bull. It took a while to remember where he was. He opened one eye and saw rocks, water, weeds, and tiny curls of smoke from the ashes of a camp fire.

What the hell? he thought, totally baffled by his unfamiliar surroundings. He tried to remember if he was scheduled to work that day, then things started falling into place. The sudden blast from an air horn brought him all the way back.

"Fucking trucks," he mumbled as he struggled to sit up, his sleeping bag slightly damp from an overnight frost that was only just starting to melt away.

He heard the scrape of metal on metal and looked to his right. Bullfrog was awake and feverishly digging into a can of what had to be nearly frozen baked beans. Skid Row felt his stomach tighten and had to turn away.

"How can you eat that shit?" he asked, thinking he would have given just about anything right then for a cup of hot coffee.

"It's not bad," Bullfrog said between mouthfuls. "Besides, I'm starving."

That made Skid Row smile when he remembered how quickly Bullfrog forgot about his dinner, and everything else, as he succumbed to the mystical powers of wacky weed. He'd spent what seemed like a solid hour staring off into space, and then got into an in-depth conversation with the campfire. He asked where it came from, where it went when it died, and what all the different colors meant. It seemed to be a one-sided exchange, but that failed to dampen Bullfrog's enthusiasm. Skid Row amused himself by poking the fire every time Bullfrog asked a new question. Each poke sent a fresh shower of sparks high into the air. That was all the response Bullfrog needed. He'd stare in wonder as if he was witnessing a miracle. He kept saying things like *amazing, unbelievable,* and *no way.* Skid Row found the whole thing pretty funny but, after a few failed attempts to start a real conversation, he gave up and went to bed.

"Ready to hit the pavement?" Bullfrog asked, smacking his frog lips and using the edge of his spoon to scrape the last of the bean goop out of the can.

"What are you talking about?" Skid Row asked as his stomach gave another heave.

"Gotta find jobs," Bullfrog said. "Our supplies won't last forever."

That was true enough. Skid Row again considered ditching his new friend. Since he was the only one with any money at all, anything they needed would be his responsibility. If he were on his own, he'd be able to reduce his necessities by half. On the other hand, although Skid Row had spent time sleeping on sidewalks and dumpster diving for his meals, that was all long ago and he'd really forgotten what it was like. Being homeless required a very specific skill set. You had to know how to find the soup kitchens, where to take care of your personal hygiene, and where you could crash once it got too cold to sleep outdoors. Bullfrog presumably knew the ropes already. Skid Row decided that, at the very least, he should hang with him for a day or two, until he knew his own way around. And if he got a job quickly, he could concentrate on finding a more permanent place to live. Then he had a sobering thought.

"How the hell are we supposed to find jobs?"

"What do you mean?" Bullfrog asked, looking confused. "We grab a paper and check the want ads, or just look for places with signs in the windows. They're all over the place."

"Right," Skid Row said. "So let's say you want to apply at the donut shot right up the road. What are you going to do?"

Bullfrog stared at him. "I'm going to go in and ask for an application."

"Yeah, and it's going to ask for a name, address and phone number. Don't you see a problem there? We don't even have cell phones. How is anyone supposed to hire us if they can't fucking reach us?"

“Oh,” Bullfrog said, smiling. "That's no problem. I always make up an address and put in a number for a pay phone."

"And then you just hang out by that phone all day?"

"No. You just tell them you can only be reached at certain times. Tell them you have another job and you don't have an answering machine. There are ways to work it out."

Skid Row was still doubtful but there didn't seem to be any point in voicing further objections. Bullfrog had obviously done this before and Skid Row really had no choice but to follow his lead. Maybe one of them would get lucky. Even working overnight in a gas station was better than nothing. He'd have heat, food and a bathroom. And if someone put a bullet in his head, he wouldn't need those things anymore anyway.

"So finish your story," Skid Row said, rolling his sleeping bag into a tight bundle.

"What story?"

"Last night," Skid Row prompted. "You were telling me about your mom's step-brother or whatever. You got a little distracted and never finished."

"How much did I tell you?" Bullfrog asked, his expression somewhat guarded.

"You said he was going to help you with your finances, and something about papers. Nothing you said after that made any sense. Dude, you were all sorts of fucked up." Skid Row grinned but that faded as soon as he saw the look on Bullfrog's face.

"What he did," Bullfrog said, turning to busy himself with his own bedding, "was take me for everything I had."

"Seriously?"

"Do I look like I'm joking?" He made a wide gesture that encompassed their dismal little campground. "He had these documents drawn up. He told me they would *protect my interests.* He told me I had to guard myself against people who might try to take advantage of my situation. I was so messed up by my parents' deaths I didn't question it. I didn't even read the stuff he gave me. I just signed my name about a hundred times. When I was done I had nothing because he'd taken it all.

"Shit." Skid Row said. "That's cold."

"As a snowman's nut sack."

"And there wasn't anything you could do?"

Bullfrog shook his head. "The guy's a dirt bag; I mean a lawyer. They're pretty much the same thing. He had the whole thing all worked out. I never stood a chance."

"Damn," Skid Row said. "That totally sucks. So what did you do... afterwards?"

"Pretty much crashed and burned. Everything happened toward the end of my junior year at Southern Maine."

"That a college?"

Bullfrog nodded. "I was studying music theory."

"No shit?" Skid Row didn't really know what that meant but he thought it sounded impressive.

"Yeah," Bullfrog said. "My parents thought I was wasting my time but they supported me."

"What did you want to do?"

He was silent for several beats, staring at nothing and clearly remembering another place and time. "It doesn't matter," he finally said. "I'm somebody else now."

Skid Row didn't know what to say to that. He tried to imagine what he would do if he'd suddenly gone from having everything to having nothing. Since he'd never had a nice house, a stable home life, or any formal education beyond the tenth grade, he couldn't even begin to put himself in those shoes. He was used to having nothing, though, and no matter how you got to that point it sure did blow.

"You never finished school?"

Bullfrog answered with a look.

"So why not go back? I mean, I know you don't have the money right now but there must be student loans and stuff."

"I told you," Bullfrog said. "That's not who I am anymore. I couldn't return to that school anyway."

"How come?"

He sighed. "There was an…incident. It was after all the mess with my parents but before the end of the semester. My plan was to finish up and then take some time to get my head straight."

"That makes sense."

"I thought so too, but I guess I was under more pressure than I realized. I got into a fight in the dining hall. A guy said something to me and I just…lost it. I broke his nose and loosened a couple teeth. It would have been even worse if people hadn't been there to break it up."

"Damn," Skid Row said. "So you've always been a bad ass."

"No!" Bullfrog shook his head. "I'd never hit anyone before. Anger management wasn't a problem. It came out of nowhere and," he shrugged, "kind of freaked me out. I was afraid something like that might happen again."

"And that's why you bailed?"

"Pretty much. They would have expelled me anyway. I decided it was time to take a little break from society."

"So you gonna spend the rest of your life drifting around then? That's no way to live."

"As opposed to flipping burgers and getting high? I don't think you were exactly on top of the world either."

That stung but Skid Row knew Bullfrog was right. "Sorry," he said after a while. "That wasn't cool. I guess I ain't exactly the poster boy for fine living."

"It's all right," Bullfrog said. He turned and studied the river. "I don't know who I am right now. I'll probably keep moving around until I figure it out."

Something in his tone told Skid Row it was time to shift the conversation in a different direction. "So how'd you end up here?" he asked. "We're a long way from Maine."

Bullfrog stood. "I don't mind telling you my life story but we can't spend our whole day hanging out here. We got things to do." He walked to the river's edge with his empty bean can, filled it, and returned to dump the water on what was left of their fire. It hissed and sputtered, and sent a cloud of thick gray smoke into the air.

"That should do it," he said. "We'll need to gather more wood when we get back here tonight."

"What about our stuff?" Skid Row asked, wondering how it would look if he showed up for a job interview carrying a sleeping bag and a box of clothes.

"There's a spot over there," Bullfrog said, pointing at one of the bridge supports. "We can hide everything and it will be safe enough."

And if not, Skid Row thought, who really cared? It wasn't like either of them was loaded down with valuables.

"I'll be ready to go in a second." Bullfrog pulled a couple garments out of a worn canvas bag and unselfconsciously changed out of his torn coveralls and into a pair of dark green cargo pants and a black t-shirt. He then returned to the water's edge where he washed his hands and face and quickly brushed his teeth.

Skid Row left his jeans on but pulled on a fresh shirt and the Giants ball cap. "Where do we go first?" he asked.

"Library," Bullfrog said. "We need a newspaper."

-11-

For the second day in a row, Ricky's shit for brains associate had shown up at the office with a briefcase full of excuses. Trying to keep his mounting anger under control, he closed his eyes, leaned back in his desk chair and ran his hands through his hair. He didn't know what he should do. Part of him longed to reach across the desk and grab Carl by his fat neck. He knew that wouldn't solve anything and, although he'd never admit it to a soul, his partner scared the hell out of him. He'd never go after Carl with anything short of an elephant gun. With fingers itching to do something, he began roughly massaging his temples, hoping that might make the throbbing pain in his head subside. It didn't. The hissing and wheezing of the ancient window air conditioner sounded like a freight train hurdling straight through the middle of his skull. How had he ever ended up paired with a moron whose only real talent seemed to be a knack for making every bad situation inestimably worse? It just wasn't fair.

Ricky straightened, opened his eyes, and was almost disappointed to see Carl still sitting there. "Go ahead," he said wearily. "Tell me."

Carl sighed and placed a ham-sized hand on his knee. "It wasn't my fault," he began.

Ricky stopped him with a raised hand. "I'm not blaming you," he said, even though he was. "I just need to know what transpired."

"You need to know…what?"

"What the fuck happened!" Ricky snapped, his anger and impatience getting the better of him.

"Oh," Carl said. "Nothin'. I mean, I went to see him just like you said."

"Where?"

"Same as always. That construction lot over by the baseball stadium."

"And?" Ricky coaxed, already knowing this was going to be like pulling teeth.

"What do you think? He didn't have the cash and asked if we could give him one more day."

"What the fuck is this? I'm not running a community service here."

"I know," Carl said, "and I stressed that to him. I also told him he had to give me the money or return the product. Those were his only two choices."

Ricky didn't want the product back but he already knew that was long gone. "Okay," he said. "So what happened then?"

Ricky watched as Carl suddenly became fascinated with the cuffs of his black denim work shirt. He played with the buttons, then undid them and began methodically rolling up his sleeves. This task required all his attention as he concentrated on making each fold perfectly straight and smooth. His body language was unmistakable. Ricky had seen it a hundred times before. They'd reached the part of the story Carl didn't want to tell.

"I'm waiting," Ricky prompted, picking up a pen and tapping it against his chin.

In response, Carl inspected his newly rolled sleeves to make sure each was completely wrinkle free. He then opened his mouth, closed it again, and finally reached for his little red notebook.

Ricky almost stopped him, but decided he'd rather let the man squirm. Carl's brow furrowed as he opened the book and fumbled from one page to another. To Ricky, he looked like that goof-off student trying to convince his parents that he really was studying. It was tempting to let him sit there and suffer, and he might have had they not had work to do. Ricky reached across, plucked the notebook from two fat fingers and sailed it across the room. Carl watched it go, and kept watching until Ricky redirected his attention by wrapping his pen sharply on the edge of the desk.

"Hey!" he said. "Remember me? You were telling me a story. I think we were almost at the part where you royally fucked up. Why don't you take it from there? Tell me what happened and then maybe come up with at least one good reason I shouldn't can your giant ass right now."

Carl gaped, obviously at a loss without his precious notebook. He rubbed his face, crossed his arms, uncrossed them, then stuck a couple fingers in the left shirt pocket where the notebook was usually kept. He sat that way for a moment, his mouth hanging half open, and Ricky couldn't decide if he looked more like a seriously ugly fish or a total retard.

"He bolted," Carl finally said, seemingly surprised by his own admission. "And I'll tell you, the little punk could move."

"Isn't that what you said the last time you were sitting here? Two different people and you let them do the same fucking thing? How does that happen? What the hell's gotten into you?"

Ricky was annoyed but also somewhat relieved. He had contacts all over the city. If the kid went into hiding, it wouldn't take more than a few calls to track him down and flush him out. And unlike Carl's other blunder, this one wouldn't have to be handled as delicately. He automatically reached for his cell phone but stopped halfway there.

"No," Carl said, his tone suggesting that the bad news had not yet been delivered. "I wasn't gonna let him get away—not after last time. He took off but then tried to jump this barbed wire fence. He always wears those stupid baggy jeans and they got caught on the wire. He was just dangling there with his ass hanging out. It was actually kinda funny. He looked like a--"

"What did you do?" Ricky asked, cold and quiet.

Carl spread his hands. "I grabbed him. I was going to bring him back here so we could have a private chat."

"And?" Ricky asked, a sinking feeling in his stomach.

"He resisted," Carl said. "He took a swing at me. I eat steaks bigger than him and the dude thinks he's gonna take me on. I had to teach him some manners."

"You hit him," Ricky clarified.

"That's what you pay me for, right?"

That wasn't exactly the point of his employment but Ricky chose to take the high road on that one. "Did he retaliate?"

Carl looked confused but then his face cleared. "No, man. He didn't have any fight left."

"So you just hit him once?"

"That's right," Carl said, a little pride creeping into his voice. "That's usually all it takes."

Even that was often too much but Ricky bit his tongue on that one as well. They could discuss it once the immediate issue was resolved. His headache had become more concentrated, a tiny flaming ball somewhere behind his left eye. He opened his desk drawer and began digging for the Advil.

"So how bad is he hurt?"

Carl paused. "I don't exactly know."

"Just what in hell does that mean?"

Carl began pulling at his fingers and Ricky wondered if he was counting to make sure they were all there. "He went down," he explained, "and didn't get up right away."

"Did you try to help him?"

Carl shook his big head. "I couldn't. There were people nearby. I thought it was best to take off before someone called the cops."

Ricky looked up, hoping and praying he'd misheard. "Are you telling me you assaulted a man in broad daylight in front of witnesses?"

"He owes us money," Carl stammered, "and he tried to run. What was I supposed to do?"

Ricky slammed his desk drawer and thought he heard something inside crack. "I don't fucking believe this!"

Carl shrank back in his chair. "I don't think he was hurt bad. Really. I'll find him and collect. I can make this right."

"Oh yeah? He said he didn't have the money, correct?" Ricky didn't wait for an answer. "So how's he supposed to get it if he's in the damn hospital?"

"Then I'll pay you," Carl said. "I promise. I will."

"Oh, that's rich. And you're not by the way. Do you even know how much he owes, total?"

Carl reached for his pocket and stopped when he remembered the notebook wasn't there. "About three grand?" he guessed.

"It's more like five. Under the current circumstances, how much of that do you suppose we'll ever see?"

"I can pay it," Carl insisted. "I'll think of something."

"No offense but I didn't hire you for your brains. The less thinking you do the better off we'll both be. Now get out of here. I'm sick of looking at you."

"Where am I supposed to go?'

"What the fuck do I care? I just want you out of my sight!"

Carl hung his head, then got slowly to his feet and shuffled out of the room, but not before stooping to retrieve his notebook. He gave Ricky a look: part guilt, part hurt, maybe a trace of anger, and then he was gone.

"Fuck him," Ricky grumbled, pulling on his desk drawer and discovering it would no longer open. He grasped the handle in both hands, braced his feet and gave a mighty tug. Wood splintered, then he had the drawer in his lap with most of the contents scattered on the floor. "Fuck him," he said again. He found the Advil and swallowed three pills dry.

Ricky sat for a moment, marveling at the path of destruction Carl always seemed to leave in his wake. They'd stopped in to see Geno that morning, just to make sure he was fully onboard with their new business arrangement. He'd hidden in back, refusing to come out of his office until Carl had retreated to the car. After that, he agreed to everything Ricky proposed, the only stipulation being that Carl never enter his restaurant again. Geno had wasted no time replacing his broken front window but the black eyes and broken nose he'd suffered would be visible for a while. He also walked with great care. Ricky assumed that must have something to do with the crotch grab. He had to give Carl credit for one thing. He'd damn sure gotten results. Even better, Ricky was now in possession of several highly incriminating high resolution photos. In the end, they might prove to be far more valuable than anything Geno's small business brought in.

Ricky stood, found a glass which he rinsed out in the cracked and rusting bathroom sink, then returned to his desk, the glass in one hand and a half-empty bottle of Jim Beam in the other. He poured two fingers and sipped at the drink while he fired up his state of the art laptop, a gift from T.J. Tyson the last time the bookie had been unable to pay his bill. Ricky needed to take a good long look at the company finances, something he couldn't easily do with Carl constantly hanging over his shoulder. With his troublesome partner temporarily out of his hair, he had to decide if he really wanted or needed him back.

Their arrangement was simple enough. They split the profits fifty-fifty, at least so far as Carl knew. But since Ricky handled the books, found most of their business, had all the contacts and was undeniably the one in charge, he thought it only fitting that, on occasion, he take a slightly or perhaps significantly larger cut. He felt entirely justified, and doubted Carl would argue much even if he knew.

Ricky still never found himself obligated to bring the subject up. He was the real brains of the operation. He should be properly compensated and shouldn't have to answer to anyone, especially an oaf like Carl. Truth be told, Carl was the biggest reason Ricky found it necessary to have some extra cash set aside. There was no telling when it might be needed to cover legal fees or silence someone who'd heard or seen too much. Carl was good at getting his message across--not so good at covering his tracks. Ricky always had to be there, money in hand and prepared to smooth things over. So, it was for Carl's own benefit that he'd been skimming off the top for years. Now, however, Ricky was questioning if Carl had gotten to be more trouble than he was worth. This latest slip-up was one more nail in the coffin.

A full ninety minutes later, Ricky was still staring at the computer screen. He'd filled and drained his glass a couple more times but was no closer to coming up with anything like a resolution. He thought he had enough in the coffers to go it on his own, even if outstanding debts were never collected and he had to set up shop elsewhere so Carl couldn't find him. He also had his little insurance policy which all but guaranteed Carl wouldn't make too much of a stink. That was all good. The one problem was that Ricky didn't have a suitable replacement. He didn't need Carl, but before they went their separate ways, he would need someone to take over that role. He'd have to get the word out, quietly, and see what developed.

Ricky yawned, stretched and decided it was time to knock off for a while, maybe step out for a bite and some fresh air. He was about to shut the computer down but thought he should catch up on the news first. He typed pressconnects.com into his browser. Seconds later, he was staring at the homepage for the Binghamton Press and Sun Bulletin. At first, he didn't fully grasp what he was looking at. And then he did.

"Get down here," Ricky snarled as soon as Carl answered the phone. "Right fucking now!"

-12-

“So why Skid Row?" Bull frog asked.

"Huh?"

They were walking along some old railroad tracks and Skid Row was so absorbed in his thoughts he'd completely lost track of his surroundings. He had, in truth, forgotten he wasn't alone.

"Skid Row," Bullfrog prompted. "That's got to be a nickname, right? So how'd you get it?"

"It ain’t worth talking about."

"Come on," Bullfrog said, stooping and picking up what looked like a section of old fence post. He started using it as a walking stick. "I told you how I got my nickname. I even told you my real name is Jeremiah. Now it’s your turn.”

"Finish your story first."

"What?" Bullfrog asked. "I already told you."

"You told me that dude ripped you off," Skid Row said. "What happened after that? After you left school and everything?'

That's what he'd been thinking about since he and Bullfrog hid their meager possessions and vacated their riverside campsite. The guy had talked about a house and a car. It sucked that he’d lost all that. But to Skid Row, it still didn’t explain how he'd ended up working in a bus station in a crappy town many hours from where he'd started out. It didn't explain how he'd hit the skids so completely. Okay, so he hadn't graduated, but even the semesters he’d completed had to qualify him to do something more than the lowest levels of manual labor.

Skid Row didn't have a damn thing going for him but he'd done well enough professionally to at least put a roof over his head, even if it was a room at the Y. Bullfrog had been living under a damn bridge and seemed fairly comfortable in that setting. It made no sense.

Bullfrog used his new walking stick to bat at some twigs and rocks. Then he swung the hunk of wood like a baseball bat and sent it spinning far off into the weeds. "It’s like I told you before. I fell apart. I had a mental breakdown or something. I'd say I lost faith but religion has never meant a whole lot to me. That bastard left me with nothing. I could deal with that. What I couldn't deal with was the feeling of…emptiness, betrayal even. It seemed like everything I believed in was gone. And after that fight,” Bullfrog said, keeping his eyes on the ground, “it was like I didn’t even know myself anymore.”

Skid Row studied him. “You said yesterday if you had a gun you’d use it. You ever--?”

“Nah,” Bullfrog said. “Not seriously. My folks did a lot for me. It wouldn’t be right to pay them back with a gutless move like that.”

"So what did you do?"

"This is going to sound weird but I just started walking. I headed north at first. Ever heard of Acadia?"

"No," Skid Row said, thinking it sounded like the name of a commune.

"It's a big national park. My parents took me there when I was a kid. I loved it. Anyway, I had this screwed up idea I could go up there and just sort of disappear. I wouldn’t have to be around anyone. I could live off the land or whatever.” Bullfrog shrugged. “I’m sure that sounds dumb but it worked for a while"

"And then what?"

"Winter," Bullfrog said. "You ever been to Maine?"

Skid Row shook his head.

"It gets cold. I hadn't really considered that when I came up with my brilliant plan. I toughed it out as long as I could and totally froze my butt off."

"What’d you do then?”

Bullfrog laughed. "I headed south again. But, I knew I wouldn't get far that time of year. I picked up some odd jobs--made enough to pay for a room in this old woman's house. Once it was warm enough, I hit the road again."

"Where were you going?"

"Don't know," Bullfrog said. "Stupid, right?"

Skid Row wasn't so sure. "And Binghamton?" he asked. "This couldn't have been a planned destination. How'd you end up here?"

"Oh, just lucky I guess. I still don't have anything you might call a plan for the future. I'm just getting by day to day. That's okay for now. I finally feel like I'm starting to get my head right. The time on the road has done me a lot of good. You might not think so looking at me but it’s true."

"I'll take your word for it."

Bullfrog ignored that. "In terms of Binghamton," he said. "I've been working my way gradually southward. I haven't been in a big hurry. I just want to get far enough that, if I had to spend the winter outdoors, I could do it without it killing me."

"So?"

"So I was hitching along Route 88. This was a month or so ago. I got caught in this monstrous rainstorm, just torrential. So I'm standing there getting soaked and this old dude pulls up in one of those little U-Haul trucks. He tells me he can take me as far as Binghamton if I'll help him unload once we got there. I'd never heard of Binghamton. I didn't know where it was and I really didn't care. I just wanted to get out of the rain. Unloading the truck seemed like a small price to pay. I was sure wrong about that."

"Why? What happened."

"What happened is that the guy was a geologist."

"What's that?"

"Geology is one of the physical sciences," Bullfrog explained. "Basically, it's the study of the earth."

"Yeah? So what's wrong with that?"

"Nothing, except the guy was seriously into rocks and he was transporting his personal collection."

"The whole truck was filled with rocks?"

"All the way to the top. I carried two hundred and twenty-seven fully packed boxes. Each one had to go down to his basement."

"Holy shit!" Skid Row said.

"My back hurt for a week. But it got me prepared for the lousy job at the bus station. Compared to thousands of pounds of rocks and minerals, lugging some suitcases around was a piece of cake."

Skid Row couldn't imagine why anyone would willingly live the kind of life Bullfrog had chosen for himself. He'd only been homeless for a night and the thought of staying that way long term scared him to death. He didn't say anything but Bullfrog must have sensed what he was thinking.

"I know it's weird," he said, as the two of them waited for a line of traffic to pass by on Court Street so they could make their way across to the library. "I have a feeling I won't be doing this too much longer."

"How long you gonna hang around here?"

Bullfrog gazed up at the steeple on top of St. Mary's church. "That's a good question. I'd planned on being gone already. I was going to cash my last paycheck and hit the road, probably be somewhere in Pennsylvania by now."

"Why stay?"

Bullfrog shrugged. "I don't like to start hitching when I'm totally broke because you never know how long it will be before you get a ride."

"So you're gonna be here until you get a job and work long enough to get paid?"

"I guess. It may not take that long. Some places will pay under the table. If I can find something like that, I may only need to stick around another day or two."

Skid Row held the door for an old man with a cane and they entered the library.

"Do we need a card or something?' The last library he'd been in was in his junior high school and he certainly hadn't spent much time there.

"Not to read the paper," Bullfrog said. "You only need a card if you want to check something out or use a computer. Follow me."

He led Skid Row to the periodicals section and pulled out a chair at a long wooden table.

"Here," he said. "I'll be right back."

Skid Row sat, but not before catching a disapproving look from a silver haired woman at the help desk. She appeared to be in her late 60's. Thick framed glasses hung from a chain around her neck and her hair was pulled back from her face and secured with some sort of black clip the size of a softball. It looked to Skid Row like a torture device. The woman didn't say anything but her sour expression made it clear she didn't welcome the intrusion. Either that or she just didn't like the look of the two new visitors.

"Here we go," Bullfrog said, dropping a copy of that day's *Press & Sun Bulletin* in the center of the table and sitting down. "Let's see who's hiring."

There were plenty of options but most required a degree or were in retail. Everyone was adding extra staff in preparation for the holiday season. Skid Row somehow couldn't see spending his days perched behind a counter hocking perfume and lingerie. He didn't have the wardrobe or the temperament. "Where are the man jobs?" he asked, shoving the paper aside.

"Don't worry about it," Bullfrog said. "There are plenty of jobs that aren't listed in the paper."

"So let's go find one," Skid Row started to rise. "I don't feel like we should be here anyway."

"Relax." Bullfrog placed a hand on his arm. "This is a public building and we have every right to stay as long as we want."

"Tell that to the bitch over there." Skid Row said a little too loudly, causing her to raise her head and give him the hairy eyeball.

"Relax," Bullfrog said again. "We haven't done anything wrong. What can she do?'

"I don't know," Skid Row mumbled. "I just don't feel like I belong."

"We'll be on our way soon enough, but not before you answer my question."

Skid Row was confused. "What question?"

"The one I asked before. You never answered . So why Skid Row?"

"Do we have to talk about it here?" There was a story there but Skid Row didn't really want to tell it. It was none of the dude's business. On the other hand, Bullfrog had been pretty open and honest, at least as far as Skid Row knew. The least he could do was respond in kind. He tipped back in his chair and crossed his legs in front of him. "My father gave me the name," he said, his eyes moving from Bullfrog's face, to the newspaper, to the tall shelves of books and magazines.

"Kinda mean, wasn't it?"

"Yeah, well he was a mean guy."

"What did your mom say about it?"

"Nothing. She...sort of split."

Bullfrog didn't say anything and Skid Row blew out a long breath.

"My real name is Sebastian," he said. "That was my mom's idea. She was pretty wild. She loved hard rock and heavy metal, and once she really got into a band, she'd follow them all over the place. She once hitched all the way to Columbus, Ohio to see Motley Crüe. She had a thing for the drummer."

"I've heard of him," Bullfrog said. "Wasn't that the guy that spun around in the metal cage?"

Skid Row nodded. "Mom was into all those old bands: Twisted Sister, Scorpions, Great White, Judas Priest, and her absolute favorite was this band called Skid Row."

"Never heard of 'em."

"I'm not surprised. I don't think they were all that big but my mom went nuts over them. Saw them in concert twenty-three times. One of the shows was at some club in Delaware. She tried to get backstage and this asshole working security told her he'd give her a pass if...well, you know."

Bullfrog nodded but said nothing.

"She lived up to her end of the bargain," Skid Row said, picking at the edge of the table with a fingernail. "He didn't. Instead of getting to meet her idols she got herself knocked up. He did the decent thing, if that's what you want to call it, and they got married. When I was born, Mom named me Sebastian after Skid Row's lead singer. I think Mom did that part as tribute and part to stick it to my dad. After all, he sure stuck it to her."

"So they called you Skid Row because of that band? That's kind of cool."

"It wasn't exactly like that. Mom figured out pretty quick she couldn't be a groupie and a mother at the same time. She hung around for a while--did her best I guess. Then, when I was in second grade, Metallica came to town. When their bus left, she was on it. She didn't say goodbye or nothin'. I didn't take it too well. I was already having trouble in school. I started acting out, getting in fights, shit like that. Me and William, that's my dad, never got along great and it just kept getting worse. I blamed him for Mom leaving. I think he blamed me for the same thing, and everything else. It didn't make for a happy upbringing."

"I'm sorry," Bullfrog said, looking like he really meant it.

"When I was in fifth grade," Skid Row went on, "I got expelled for getting into trouble three times in the same day. I was caught smoking in the bathroom, letting air out of the principal's tires and trying to steal an electric pencil sharpener."

"What were you going to do with that?"

Skid Row shrugged. "Who the fuck knows?" He looked around to see if anyone had heard. Mrs. Tightbritches obvious
ly had and gave him a look sharp enough to cut glass. Skid Row was tempted to flip her off but instead lowered his voice. "It was just something to do," he said. "I've been told I was seeking attention. If that was the case, my master plan really backfired. William didn't want anything to do with me after that. He told me I'd never amount to anything. I was Skid Row from that day forward."

"That stinks."

"What stinks," Skid Row said, "is that he was right. He wasn't the world's greatest dad or anything but at least he tried, working two jobs so he could provide for me. That was a heck of a lot more than my mom was willing to do. I repaid him by acting like an ass."

"Did you ever tell him you're sorry?" Bullfrog asked.

Skid Row shook his head. "I never told him anything. We sort of coexisted for a while. I left home when I was fifteen and, as far as I know, he never bothered looking for me. Why would he?"

"So where is he now?"

Skid Row looked away and shrugged. "We haven't spoken in almost ten years."

"And how do you feel about that?'

"I don't know," Skid Row said, abruptly pushing his chair back from the table. "It don't matter."

He could have said more; could have told Bullfrog how much, at least at first, he'd enjoyed his new-found freedom. He'd enjoyed not having anyone yelling at him, checking up on him and constantly putting him down. Those feelings changed over time, and he might have also said that, if given the opportunity, he'd sort of like to apologize to his dad for making things so tough. He just didn't know if he'd be able to talk around the lump that had suddenly formed in his throat. Besides, he'd talked too much already.

"Let's blow," he said, getting to his feet. "We got things to do."

"Sure," Bullfrog said, a strange look on his face. "Just let me put this back." He picked up the paper and started to turn away.

"Holy shit!" Skid Row said, snatching it from his hands and suddenly so distracted he didn't see the library attendant come halfway out of her seat. He and Bullfrog had been so focused on the want ads, they hadn't even glanced at the front page. Until now. Skid Row stared in disbelief.

"What?" Bullfrog asked, reading the bold faced headline.

BINGHAMTON MAN SLAIN.

"That's why he wasn't at the park yesterday," Skid Row said. "Marco is dead!"

-13-

When Carl finally showed up, a full forty-five minutes after he was ordered to get his ass back to the office, Ricky Fixx was still staring at his laptop and seething. He kept telling himself it had to be a mistake, knew it wasn't, and wondered how in hell he'd bail the moron out this time.

"What's up?" Carl asked, coming into the room and smelling faintly of soy sauce. He dropped into a chair.

Ricky noticed a smear of something dark and greasy on Carl's left hand. He'd obviously been into the Chinese food, one of his many weaknesses. The asshole probably spent his afternoon parked in front of the television, watching soap operas and stuffing his face with spare ribs, egg rolls and who knew what else? Meanwhile, Ricky had been busting his butt trying to save their business. Did the guy even care?

"So how's it going?" he asked, studying his partner, *for the time being anyway,* and searching for remorse, deceit, or some sort of indication that he knew just how badly he'd fucked up. Ricky saw nothing, and that somehow pissed him off even more.

"Oh, fine," Carl said, picking something out of his teeth and then wiping his hand on his pants. "I was actually about to take a nap when you called. I had a busy day." He smiled, and seemed to have completely forgotten about the argument they'd had just hours before.

Ricky didn't know if he should slap him or feel sorry for him. It boggled the imagination but he was beginning to think Carl really was as dumb as he looked.

"Was there anything," Ricky began, sitting back and steepling his fingers under his chin, "that you...perhaps...neglected to tell me?"

"About what?" Carl asked, blinking but not looking nervous or even concerned.

Shit. Was it possible he really didn't know? Ricky glanced at the monitor and then back at Carl. "You had a job and it didn't go according to plan."

Carl's face clouded and then cleared. "Yeah." He looked suddenly sheepish. "I am sorry about that. I'll find him and make it right, just like I said."

"And you don't anticipate any problems?"

“No way,” Carl said, cracking his knuckles. "He got the best of me once. It's not going to happen again."

"I'm sure."

Carl's brow creased but he must have decided he'd been complimented because his smile returned. "You know you can count on me. We'll have that money in the bank by lunchtime tomorrow. You'll see."

Ricky's eyes again flitted to the computer screen. "And I can trust you, right? You'd never lie to me?"

Carl looked around as if he was hoping someone else might field that one. He finally stopped, looked at Ricky and shook his head.

"So let me ask you again. Think very carefully. Was there anything at all you didn't tell me?"

Carl started to shake his head again but then seemed to think better of it. "Like what?" he asked. "It went down just like I said."

Ricky stood and walked around to perch on the corner of his desk. He was directly in front of Carl, so close he could smell his breath, and the big man had to draw his legs in to avoid being kicked. "If you'd be so kind," Ricky said, spreading his arms expansively, "tell me again just how it *went down*."

Carl obviously sensed he was about to step in it. He swallowed, cleared his throat and swallowed again, all the while shrinking down in his seat as much as his large frame would allow and trying not to meet Ricky's eyes. "I told you before, I…" but he trailed off without saying anything more.

"What you told me," Ricky said, "was that Marco tried to run. You grabbed him when he got stuck on the fence. He swung at you. You hit him, once, and that was the end of the altercation. You didn't hang around because there were people in the vicinity. Is that about right?"

"Yeah," Carl said, nodding vigorously. "That's exactly what happened."

"And there isn't anything you'd care to add?"

"I don't know what you mean."

But Ricky was suspecting he was starting to get an idea. "Well," he said, crossing his arms. "Let's start with this. Were there any weapons involved?"

"I didn't bring a weapon," Carl insisted, his expression exhibiting surprise and something a little more telling.

"I don't care what you brought.' Ricky said, thinking Carl knew damn well where this was headed. "Did you use a weapon or not?"

Carl stared but said nothing.

Ricky tried counting to ten but only made it as far as two. "ANSWER ME!" he shouted, flinging out an arm, striking his whiskey glass and sending it flying. It bounced off Carl's shoulder, hit the floor and rolled halfway across the room.

Carl started to rise as if he wanted to go after it.

"Leave it!" Ricky demanded.

He froze, half in his chair and half out, one arm awkwardly extended. He looked pathetic, and Ricky might have pitied him had the circumstances been different.

"Sit," he said, gesturing with his chin.

Carl did, but kept a firm hold on the arms of the chair, almost as if he were prepared to leap up again at any moment.

"You didn't take a weapon with you," Ricky said. "I know that because I told you not to and you generally don't need one to do your job. What I'm asking, though—follow me closely here--is if any sort of weapons was used at any point."

Carl looked toward the door and Ricky half hoped he'd dash through it and never come back. That would solve all sorts of problems and he knew full well he'd never be that lucky. He watched as Carl bent over and began methodically untying and retying his shoes. Ricky gritted his teeth but said nothing because he knew it would only lead to another explosion. Thinking it might be better to give the man some space, he returned to his own chair, sat and leaned back, feet propped on the desk and fingers laced behind his head. He wanted to give the impression that, if necessary, he was ready to wait all night.

Carl looked at him and finally spoke up. "Not at first," he said.

"Meaning?" Ricky lowered his feet but kept his hands in place, in part to maintain his casual demeanor but mostly to keep himself from ripping Carl's lips off.

"Well," he began, "I think Marco was pretty scared when I pulled him off that fence. I know he wanted to run but I had him cornered. There weren't nowhere for him to go."

"So?"

"So he picked up this stick off the ground and swung it at me."

"And then?"

"I took it away from him."

"Was that all?"

"Well, I guess I might have hit him with it. "But he pissed me off," he added quickly. "What was I supposed to do?"

"You *might* have hit him with it," Ricky repeated, his fingers beginning to twitch. It would have felt so good to smack that clueless expression right off the jerk's face.

"Okay," Carl said, "I did hit him, but only once--just like I said before. I didn't hurt him bad. I would have stayed to talk to him but...."

"But there were people around," Ricky finished.

"Yes!" Carl shrugged like he really didn't understand what the big deal was.

Ricky wondered what, if anything, he did understand.

"It's no problem," Carl assured him. "He knows he owes us money. Once I find him, I'll make sure he understands he's on borrowed time."

Ricky couldn't take it anymore. He jackknifed forward and slammed both hands on the desk. "He's not on borrowed time you dumb son of a bitch! You are!"

Carl's mouth fell open like he'd suddenly lost control of his jaw muscles. He seemed to have lost the power of speech too. His lower lip quivered but the only sound that came out was a ghostly moan.

While Ricky had his full attention, he used a finger to spin the laptop so Carl had a good look at the screen and the full color image taking up most of the top half.

"You didn't hit him with a stick," Ricky hissed. "You skewered him with a fucking axe handle!" He scrolled down so Carl could read the headline. BINGHAMTON MAN SLAIN. "He's dead you dumb shit. You fucking killed him!"

"I didn't," Carl stammered. "I only hit him once. I swear!"

"That may be," Ricky said, taking one more look at the monitor and then pushing the laptop aside. "But as usual, you went overboard. He bled out before paramedics even got to the scene. Is there some reason you didn't think to mention that earlier?"

"I didn't know," Carl insisted, shaking his head and holding his hands out in front of him as if trying to ward off an attacker.

"And you somehow didn't notice all that blood either?"

"Maybe a little," Carl mumbled. "It didn't look bad. I'm sorry."

"Sorry?" Ricky echoed. "Is that what you're going to tell the jury when they're deciding whether or not to fry your ass?"

All the color drained from Carl's face and it looked like he might either pass out or burst into tears. Ricky didn't want to see either one.

"Steady," he said. "We might still be able to manage this. "Where did you ditch the murder weapon?"

"I didn't murder anyone," Carl whined. ""I--"

"Call it what you want," Ricky said. "The dude is dead and the cops want to know who did it. Do you still have that ax handle?"

Carl shook his head almost imperceptibly.

"So you ditched it somewhere?"

Another headshake.

Ricky stared at him, his stomach sinking. "Let me get this straight," he said. "You're telling me you left the weapon at the scene?"

Carl's entire body started to shake and Ricky had his answer.

-14-

"This is unbelievable," Skid Row said," staring at the newspaper while running thin fingers through his hair.

After his last outburst and another dose of stink eye from the old biddy in the library, he and Bullfrog decided it was time to move on. They took the paper with them and she didn't object, probably figuring it was a small price to pay to finally be rid of them. They left the building, crossed the street and sat down on the large stone steps of St. Mary's Catholic Church.

"You all right?" Bullfrog asked.

Skid Row looked up and was surprised to see genuine sympathy on his face. He almost had to laugh. "Oh, yeah," he said, his eyes again dropping to the front page. "It's not like we were buds or anything. I barely knew him other than to make purchases once in a while. It's just weird that he's...dead. You know what I'm sayin'?"

Bullfrog nodded as he read over Skid Row's shoulder. "Says here witnesses reported seeing him argue with a large white male. Does that sound like anyone you know?"

"It sounds like half the dudes in Broome County. Hell, it sounds like Arthur. He's white and definitely large. Have the cops set up an information hotline? Maybe I'll phone in a tip."

Skid Row smiled to himself, enjoying the thought of making the fat fuck sweat it out in an interrogation room or in the back seat of a cop car.

"Actually," Bullfrog said, pointing, "there's a phone number right here. The police are requesting information. It doesn't sound like they've got a whole lot to go on. There was a physical confrontation of some sort."

"Yeah?" Skid Row said. "Well I'd say my man lost in a big way."

According to the article, Marco, whose full name was Jonathan Marcus Ryan, was twenty-six years old and had three prior arrests and one conviction for possession with intent to sell. He'd spent ninety days in jail and was still on probation. Police seemed to think the altercation was a drug deal gone wrong. If he had any illegal substances on his person, that information had not been shared with the media. He was killed by a single blow from what police later identified as a wooden axe handle.

"What the fuck is *internal hem-orr-haging*?" Skid Row asked.

"Bleeding," Bullfrog said. "Probably ruptured his spleen or something."

"Whatever you say."

Bullfrog studied the mug shot style photo. "You sure that's him?"

Skid Row leaned back and folded his hands behind his head. "No doubt," he said. "I never knew his full name but I'd recognize that ugly face anywhere."

"Well, I'm sorry."

"Nothing to be sorry about. The world lost another drug dealer. We're probably all better off."

"But where will you...?"

"Buy my weed?" Skid Row shrugged. "Not a high priority at the moment, and not exactly in the budget anyway. Maybe it's a good time to quit."

Part of him wanted to believe that. Another part badly craved a blunt right then. Skid Row knew Marco's death didn't really impact him but the news still put him on edge. Getting fired, becoming suddenly homeless and now this. He felt as if the sand kept shifting under his feet and might give way altogether at any moment. Maybe somebody was trying to tell him it really was time to clean up his act. He'd been on his own for almost a decade, working one crap job after another and never really getting anywhere. For a while, the hand-to-mouth lifestyle suited him fine. He didn't have a wife or a family--no one in the world to answer to--so what was the point of busting his ass? He was doing okay. Skid Row also had the nagging suspicion that his dad had been right all along and he'd never amount to anything no matter what he did. Lately, though, he'd begun wondering if that was his true belief or merely an excuse to stagnate. He'd considered going back to school, considered finding a job that at least had some chance for advancement. He'd even briefly considered joining the military. What had he actually done? Nothing. He hadn't even managed to save enough money to buy an outfit suitable to wear to a real job interview. It was pathetic. How could he ever hope to get anywhere if he lacked the gumption to pull his own head out of his ass?

Skid Row wondered if that had been Marco's problem too. He certainly hadn't set out to become a smalltime drug dealer in one of the most depressed counties in the state. Maybe he'd had big plans for tomorrow. He wasn't the picket fence type, but Skid Row supposed Marco might have dreamed of one day becoming a wealthy businessman. Except now he was dead. The thought of following a similar path made him shiver. Then, it gave him an idea. He sat up straight and stared off down the road.

"What?" Bullfrog asked, turning quickly to see what he was looking at.

Skid Row held up a finger. He didn't just have an idea. He had a brainstorm--a fucking revelation. And if he played his cards right, it could be the answer to all his problems. He stood and brushed off the seat of his pants. "Come on!" he said, bounding down the steps and heading towards downtown. "There's someone we need to see"

"Who?" Bullfrog asked, leaping to his feet and hurrying to catch up. "Where are we going?"

"For now, back to the Y."

"What for?" Bullfrog asked, almost jogging in order to match Skid Row's fast pace and long strides. "Do you think they'll let you back in?"

"No chance," he said over his shoulder.

"Then what are we doing?"

"Shut up," Skid Row said distractedly. "I'm trying to think."

Marco was history. That sucked but what could you do? What Skid Row hoped to do was step into his shoes, at least on a very temporary basis. He had a brand new business opportunity staring him right in the face. It was all about supply and demand. He'd lost his supplier, which meant plenty of other people were in the same boat. They were wondering right now where they were going to get their crack, or their smack, or their meth, or whatever it was they were doing. Skid Row only smoked a little weed now and then but he knew plenty of people into much heavier stuff. They all needed their fix. Skid Row needed a job, and Marco's untimely demise created an opening, one that could potentially be very lucrative.

Someone was going to have to take Marco's spot at the park, the laundromat, and all the other places he hung out and served his clientele. If Skid Row didn't step up to the plate, somebody else would. And for once he had the proper wardrobe and enough experience in the field to feel qualified. He didn't know Marco's whole routine but he didn't think it would be tough to figure out. All he had to do was ask around. It was perfect. And if Bullfrog wanted to get in on the action, they'd be able to work two locations at once and, at least in theory, double their profit. Skid Row didn't know how much Marco had been making but assumed he'd been doing pretty well. He was always sporting a new gold chain and two hundred dollar Nikes that looked like they'd just come out of the box. Skid Row had no interest in bling. He did, however, have plans for the future and thought this could be his golden ticket.

Of course, there was one minor detail yet to be worked out. To the best of his knowledge, Marco was in sales, not manufacturing. He wasn't growing pot in his back yard or cooking up batches of meth in his kitchen, although plenty of people did. With his large selection of recreational drugs, he had to be getting his product from somewhere. He had to have a source, and that was the person Skid Row needed to find.

"I don't know," Bullfrog said, once he'd heard the plan. "Drugs are serious stuff. Maybe we shouldn't mess with it."

"We're not doing the drugs," Skid Row explained. "We're just selling them."

"That's even worse! Do you even know anything about it?"

"What's to know?"

"What's to know?" Bullfrog echoed. He glanced around like he was afraid someone was following them and listening in on every word. "Do I need to remind you that your Marco friend was *just selling drugs* until he was killed with an axe handle? Doesn't that concern you?"

"So he got careless," Skid Row said, brushing hair out of his eyes and beginning to walk even faster. "He was also working alone. We'd be together. Strength in numbers."

Bullfrog gave him a look. "What are you, a hundred and forty pounds? And I'm not exactly Captain America. Do you really think we're going to intimidate anyone? And what about all the gang activity in Binghamton? It's in the paper all the time. You really want to mess with that?"

Skid Row waved a hand as if it wasn't even worth discussing. "Listen," he said. "It doesn't matter because we wouldn't be doing it long enough to get into any trouble."

"How do you mean?"

Skid Row turned to face him. "You really think I want to push dope the rest of my life?" He didn't wait for a response but added, "I'm not that stupid. We make a few quick sales, get a pile of cash and get out."

"It still sounds dangerous." Bullfrog gnawed a thumbnail. "Do you really think it could work?"

"Well why not? Someone's got to take over his territory. Why shouldn't it be us?"

"How many reasons do you want?"

"Hey, you don't have to do it. I'm just not crazy about sleeping outside and eating my dinner out of a can."

Bullfrog was quiet and Skid Row figured he was considering the possibilities. They could find part-time jobs, earn minimum wage and continue to scrape by. Or, they could begin a career in sales and get some serious coin in a hurry.

"Do you even know who to talk to?" Bullfrog asked, and Skid Row could tell he was coming around.

"Not yet, but I will."

"Yeah? How?"

"I told you. We're going back to the Y."

“To see Tyrone?”

Skid Row shook his head. “No, man. That dude's as straight as the road to hell. He wouldn't have the info we're after. We need to find Zatts."

"What the hell is a Zatts?"

"Unless I miss my guess, he's the reason I'm out on the street."

"He had you kicked out?"

"Probably," Skid Row said. "He came looking for weed a couple nights ago. I didn't have much left so I turned him down. He was pissed and I think he got back at me by telling Tyrone where I kept my stash."

"You gonna call him on it?"

"What for?" Skid Row asked. "What's done is done. Besides, if I piss him off again, he won't be willing to help us."

"He sounds like a jerk," Bullfrog said. "Why would you want his help anyway?"

Skid Row smiled. "Zatts is definitely a jerk. He also knows every low-life, scum-bag, good-for-nothing, drug-selling, drug-using piece of garbage in the entire Binghamton area."

"He knew Marco?"

"He knows fucking everybody, at least everybody at the bottom end of the food chain."

"So he can tell you who Marco's supplier was?"

"I hope so."

"But why would he?" Bullfrog asked. "If he's the one that got you kicked out, why turn around and do you a favor now?"

"He wouldn't," Skid Row said, slowing as their destination came into view. "Not if he knew why I was asking. We'll need to be smart about it. We need to be quick too. I'm sure I'm not the only one to have this idea. That's why I want to make sure we're at the front of the line."

"Okay," Bullfrog said, "but wouldn't this Zatts guy just go to the supplier on his own? I mean, if he knows him, he could probably just step right in."

"Ain't happenin'," Skid Row replied. "For one thing, Zatts couldn't be trusted with an empty coffee cup, let alone a pile of cash or drugs. It's also a good bet he doesn't know Marco's no longer with us. He's not one to read the newspaper."

"He still could have heard," Bullfrog said.

Skid Row realized he had to at least consider that possibility. Zatts wasn't the sharpest knife in the drawer but he was connected and it wouldn't do to underestimate him. If he suspected what Skid Row was up to, he'd clam up tighter than a frozen nun. It was certainly possible the information could be acquired elsewhere but that would take a lot more time than Skid Row thought he had. The key, he decided, was to get what he wanted without tipping his hand.

"So how do you want to play this?" Bullfrog asked.

"Not sure," Skid Row said, not liking the idea that his entire plan hinged on the cooperation, willing or otherwise, of one burned-out loser. He took a deep breath and tried to steady his nerves. "First thing is to find him, preferably without running into Tyrone."

"Why? What would he do?"

"Probably nothing. It's not like I'm not allowed to be on the property. I just don't want to have to answer a lot of questions."

That was really only part of it. As Skid Row's hand strayed to his front pocket, he realized he didn't want to see Tyrone because of the feelings of guilt and remorse that would surely follow.

As it turned out, he had nothing to worry about. When they got within about thirty feet of the building, the front door flew open and a tall, thin black man strode out. He wore orange camouflage pants, a black tank top and high top black sneakers. Both arms were covered with tattoos, and he sported a gold hoop earring in his left ear and a faux diamond stud in his upper lip. He stretched and surveyed his surroundings as if he were in charge of the whole block. When he spied Skid Row, he broke into a broad grin.

"Sebastian, my man," he said, brushing long dreadlocks away from his face. “Good to see you again. You keepin' it real?"

"Real enough."

"Where you crashin' these days?"

"I'm around." Skid Row couldn't miss the subtle taunt but decided to let it pass. "This is my friend Bullfrog.”

Zatts approached, then cocked his head to one side and made a show of studying him from top to bottom. "Bullfrog, huh? I guess that's about right. It's a pleasure," he said, extending a hand but sliding it casually into a pocket when Bullfrog reached to shake.

"Forget about it," Skid Row muttered out of the corner of his mouth. "It's what he does."

"So what brings you around, Sebastian?" Zatts asked. "I thought old Tyrone asked you to vacate the premises."

"Oh yeah? Who told you that?"

"You know," Zatts said. "People talk."

"They sure do. Sometimes too much." Skid Row stared at him pointedly but he didn't seem to notice.

"So," Zatts said, "you slummin' or what?"

"I got a place," Skid Row lied. Then, before Zatts could ask any other questions, he added, "I was planning on relocating anyway. Definitely time to move on"

"Good deal," Zatts said, looking disappointed.

"So what's been happening around here? You seen Marco lately?"

"Same old," Zatts said. "You lookin' to make a score?"

"Funds are a little low right now, but I thought I could introduce him to Bullfrog here. We stopped by the park yesterday but he wasn't there. Thought you might know where I could find him."

Skid Row had decided his best approach was to play dumb, and Bullfrog thankfully seemed to know enough to keep his mouth shut.

Zatts inspected the python tat that curled elaborately around his left forearm. "I don't think you're going to see Marco again for a while. Somebody offed him."

"Shit!" Skid row said, giving his best surprised face. "You serious?"

"Heard about it this morning. Killed him with a shovel or some shit."

"Man," Bullfrog said. "That sucks."

Zatts looked at him but said nothing.

"So what happened?" Skid Row asked.

Zatts shrugged but Skid Row could tell he was enjoying being the deliverer of such grim news. "Pissed somebody off I guess. Wouldn't be the first time."

"What do you mean by that? Did you ever have problems with him?"

"Let's just say he wasn't very accommodating."

Skid Row could tell Zatts wanted to say more so he waited.

"It's bullshit," Zatts said. "Say some crack whore wants a score but she doesn't have any dough. What does she do?" He didn't wait for a response. "She spreads her legs and gets what she wants. What am I supposed to do, lube up and bend over? No fucking way."

Skid Row and Bullfrog exchanged a look. The conversation had gone in a very different direction than the one Skid Row had intended and he tried to get it back on track. "So you weren't buying from Marco?" he asked.

"Sometimes," Zatts said, "if I had the cash."

"And if you didn't?"

"I went to Twig. He and I could always reach some sort of...agreement."

Skid Row didn't think he wanted to know what that meant. He knew Zatts was adept at swiping car stereos. Maybe that was how he paid his debts.

"So what if I didn't want to go to Twig?" Skid Row asked. "What else could I do?"

"You don't like Twig?" Zatts looked stunned, like Skid Row had said he didn't like Santa Claus, sex or pizza.

"I caught him messing around with my sister," Skid Row said. He didn't have a sister, nor did he have the slightest idea who this Twig character was. He just didn't think it would be wise to involve any more people in his scheme than necessary. There was also no way in hell he'd start a business relationship with any friend of Zatts'.

"You got a sister?" Zatts asked. "You never said."

"She moved away last year." Skid Row wanted to get off that subject as quickly as possible. "Listen," he said, deciding it was time for a more direct approach. "You got any idea where Marco got his stuff?"

Zatts crossed his arms in front of his chest. "Now why would you want to know that? He don't sell direct to the public."

So Zatts did know. Skid Row had to bite back a smile. He was close. He could feel Bullfrog's gaze on him but his own eyes didn't stray from Zatts' face.

"I don't want to buy from him," Skid Row said easily, "but if Marco's gone, I'll need someone to go to. Maybe he can hook me up."

"I can hook you up," Zatts said, spreading his arms like a proud salesman about to show off his wares. "Tell me what you want. I'll have it in your hands in less than twenty-four hours. I can get anything and that's a promise."

Skid Row knew a promise from Zatts was worth about as much as the *signed document* Lucy gave Charlie Brown right before she whipped the football away and he fell on his ass. And even if Zatts was true to his word, he'd undoubtedly take a sizable service fee off the top. The guy was probably scheming already.

"The thing is," Skid Row said, choosing his words carefully and keeping his tone as friendly as he could, "I'm way over on the other side of town now. Bullfrog is too. Getting here ain't exactly convenient, ya know? We need somebody closer"

"Sure," Zatts said. "That's cool," but he didn't sound like he meant it.

"So you got a name?" Skid Row asked, hitching thumbs in his pockets and trying to look unconcerned while his heart pounded in his chest.

Zatts studied him, and then he spent some time looking up and down the street. "Ricky Fixx," he finally said. "That's your man. But you didn't hear it from me."

-15-

Andrew Cullen picked up his vodka and tonic, his third of the afternoon, but put it down again without taking a sip. The dealer, a tall Asian man with a ponytail and eyebrow piercings, eyed him expectantly. Cullen again glanced at his cards but nothing had changed. He was staring at a seven of hearts and eight of clubs. The dealer was showing a king of diamonds.

"Shit," he mouthed, and fingered his dwindling pile of chips. He'd been there two hours and lost far more hands than he'd won. Nothing was working for him and every choice he made seemed to be the wrong one. He knew he shouldn't take a hit but bad luck streaks had a way of clouding one's judgment. Cullen was living proof of that.

"Tough luck there, Champ."

He looked to his right and immediately looked away again, not wanting to encourage further conversation. There were two other players at the table. The first, the one who'd just spoken, was a middle-aged man with a scrawny beard, tobacco-stained teeth, and one of the worst toupees Cullen had ever seen. He'd been running his mouth nonstop, commenting on nearly every card that hit the table, and he didn't know the first thing about playing blackjack.

The man, who asked to be called Jimmy, wore store brand jeans, a Molly Hatchet t-shirt, a hideous denim vest with a poorly airbrushed American flag on the back, and he had a ring of keys clipped to his over-sized belt. Cullen would have pegged him as a scrap metal collector or perhaps the guy responsible for refilling the toilet paper dispensers in rest stop bathrooms. What was someone like that doing at a fifty dollar table? Where'd he get fifty bucks to begin with? Rule of thumb: if a single chip is worth more than your entire wardrobe, you're probably in the wrong place. There was one problem with that theory. He had about two thousand dollars stacked up in front of him and played the game like he didn't much care if he won or lost. The worst part was, despite utter ineptitude and what appeared to be total indifference, he kept winning. It was driving Cullen nuts because he couldn't catch a break no matter what he did.

With a sinking feeling, he motioned for another card. It turned out to be the queen of spades, bringing his total to twenty-five--another loser.

"Dern, " Jimmy said. "You've got all the luck of a blind man at a titty bar."

Cullen agreed but chose not to respond, instead trying to gauge the reaction of the other player at the table, an attractive but serious looking blonde in a cocktail-length black dress, emerald and gold bracelet with matching earrings and necklace, and, Cullen noted, no wedding ring. He guessed her age at thirty-five but wouldn't have been shocked to learn she was a decade older. Her skin, well-tanned for the time of year, was tight and smooth and might have been the beneficiary of some professional attention. She definitely worked out. Cullen thought she looked like a runner or maybe a yoga instructor. He bet she could teach him a thing or two about flexibility.

Although he couldn't discern any of the usual telltale signs of age, something in the way she carried herself suggested she had more miles on her than she was letting on. She looked expensive, even smelled expensive, and he was dying to know her story. If things went well, he'd get the opportunity to uncover a lot more than that. He knew it would take some doing. He'd made a few attempts at small talk. Her monosyllabic answers to even the most casual questions sent a clear message. She wasn't buying what he was selling, and had no interest in becoming friends, lovers, or anything in between.

Cullen suspected her vibe of indifference was deliberate, the chilly veneer intended to keep Jimmy at arm's length, and why not? The guy was repulsive. But if she struck up a conversation with one man, the other might assume she was fair game and subject her to his crude version of charm. Cullen tried to catch her eye to let her know he understood. If she noticed, she gave no indication, all her attention focused on her cards.

When she first sat down, the stool making her dress ride up enticingly high on her legs, Cullen was hoping to show her some of the finer points of blackjack. She obviously didn't need the help. Occasionally consulting the small strategy card on the table in front of her, she played with style and confidence and the handful of chips she'd started with grew steadily larger. That was far more than Cullen could say for himself. He was having a hard time remembering the last time he'd won two hands in a row.

"Let's do it again, Sport," Jimmy said, pushing three fifty dollar chips into the betting circle. "Daddy needs a new pair of shoes."

Cullen was thinking what *Daddy* really needed was a toothbrush and some manners but he kept that to himself.

"Hey, Sweetie." the idiot called, waving his empty Budweiser bottle at a passing waitress. "I can't concentrate when I'm thirsty."

Concentrate, Cullen scoffed as the waitress hurried away. What the hell did Jimmy know about that? The hand before, he'd taken a hit on sixteen, been dealt a four and won. And before that, he'd held on fourteen, but won again when the dealer busted. That had nothing to do with concentration. It was plain, dumb luck, “dumb” being the operative word.

As if to prove the point, Jimmy was dealt a pair of tens and immediately decided to split them. Cullen nearly fell out of his chair. The object of blackjack, as he assumed Jimmy knew, was to get as close to twenty-one as possible without going over. Play with even a modicum of common sense and no game in the casino gives better odds of winning. The only reason to split a pair was to improve those odds. Split aces and eights every time. You never split tens because you had an almost sure winner already--bird in the hand and all that.

Jimmy either didn't know or didn't care. If there was a poker god, he'd be rewarded for his stupidity with a two and a three. Cullen wasn't a bit surprised when he was instead dealt a nine and a jack. Both turned out to be winners. Cullen stayed at seventeen and lost once again. It simply wasn't his day.

Flipping a chip to the dealer, he drained his glass, scooped his remaining chips into a coat pocket and stood to leave.

"Stick around, Champ," Jimmy said, flashing his pearly yellows. "This table's hotter than a bitch in heat."

Cullen gave him a look, and briefly considered saying something chivalrous about watching the language in front of the lady. He again tried to catch her eye but she was oblivious to the whole thing. Too bad. He would have happily stood up for her if there was a chance she'd return the favor by going down on him. That, evidently, wasn't in the cards.

Her loss, Cullen thought, running a hand over his silk tie as he walked away. He'd come to the casino for two reasons: to solve his problems with a big score, or forget about them for a while with a score of a different and more physically stimulating variety. He hadn't yet found a willing participant but the afternoon was young and the place was crawling with women.

He stopped a waitress and ordered another drink and then left the casino, going just far enough so he could no longer hear the myriad beeps, bleeps and bells of all the slot and video poker machines. He leaned against the wall, pulled out his iPhone and told Siri to call his office.

"It's Andrew," he said once Carrie picked up.

"Oh, hi."

He heard the click of computer keys and pictured her staring at the screen and biting her lower lip. He shook his head to clear the image. "So what's happening?" Cullen asked in his most businesslike voice.

"Hold on a sec."

More clicking.

"Okay. So I was able to reschedule your meeting with Leonard Price. It's now tomorrow afternoon at three"

"That should work."

"I hope so. He didn't sound happy about the change."

"Not much I could do about that," Cullen said. "What did you tell him?"

"Just what you said when you called before. You had an emergency meeting and it was unavoidable."

"And you apologized for me?"

"Of course." Concern had crept into her voice. "Is everything all right?"

Cullen muted the phone as a tipsy woman moved past, giggling and clutching her husband's arm for support.

"Sure," he said. "Everything's fine, but I'll probably be here a while longer. I'm in some pretty heavy negotiations and things have gotten a little complicated. I can't really say more right now. I'll fill you in in the morning."

He spent a few seconds contemplating how nice it would be to *fill her in* and then moved onto other business. "So what else you got?"

"It's been quiet," Carrie said. "We have some clients with contracts that will soon be up for renewal. I've started reaching out to them so we can schedule those meetings."

"Thank you. I've been meaning to get to that."

"Also," Carrie continued. "A Mrs. Banyard called from First Niagara. She needs to speak to you at your earliest convenience."

"Great!" Cullen replied. "I've been looking at a piece of land for development. I'm sure that's what it's about." But what he was thinking was that things were going to hell even faster than expected. The shit hadn't exactly hit the fan yet, but it was close enough to impact that the blades were really starting to spread the smell around.

Janet Banyard was the manager of First Niagara Bank and possessed nearly as much charm as an impacted wisdom tooth. If things had been escalated all the way to her desk, and it appeared they had, he was going to have to come up with something and pretty darn fast.

"That it?" Cullen asked, extremely thankful his beautiful office assistant couldn't see him right then. His heart was pounding and beads of sweat had formed across his forehead and on the back of his neck.

"Just one other thing," she said. "You had a call from a gentleman yesterday. He left a number but no name. He said it was personal and you'd know."

"Right. Old college buddy of mine."

"Well, he called again this morning right after you left, and once more about a half hour ago. I've got his number here someplace"

He could hear her sifting through papers. "Don't bother," he said. "I know it. Was there any message?"

"Just that he's looking forward to talking to you. He said he may even come for a visit. He thought you guys could go for a bike ride."

"That would be great," Cullen said, sinking onto a padded bench before his knees had the chance to completely give out under him. "Well, I'd better get back into this meeting. Call me if anything important comes up."

Carrie started to say something but he pressed the button to end the call. Then he leaned forward, put his head in his hands and fought the urge to throw up. "It's over," he said, pulling at his hair until his eyes started to water. "It's all over."

Earlier that morning, he bolted from his office, not remembering until he was out on the street that he'd ridden his bicycle to work. He wasn't about to go back in to get it. Carrie would ask what he was doing, and right then, he really didn't know. All he did know was that he had to do something. The comfortable life he'd built for himself and his family had started coming apart at the seams. His business wasn't far behind and it wouldn't be long before it all came down on top of him, unless....

Cullen had always been a gambler. He started playing cards as a teen. It kept money in his pocket and, when it came to strip poker, was a major source of entertainment. Those were the only games he ever cheated at. Hell, he would have done just about anything to get Pamela Swinson out of those tight jeans. If that meant an ace or two up his sleeve, it was all for a good cause. Usually, though, he played for money and the more the better. He'd nearly flunked out of SUNY Buffalo for all the time he spent at the casino, but then realized a lot of his Long Island classmates had more money than brains. He started hosting poker games in his dorm room nearly every Friday and Saturday night, supplying the beer and pizza and usually pocketing a few hundred dollars. He was a skilled player and enjoyed more than his share of good luck. The cards just seemed to fall his way.

Once out of school, putting in thirty-seven and a half hours a week and earning minimum wage offering online computer support, Cullen still relied on poker playing as his major source of income. He bet on some horse races and sporting events as well but mostly stuck to cards. His Midas touch continued, and in 1995, he purchased his tech firm with the proceeds from a high stakes hand of five card draw. He was dealt crap and immediately decided to bluff. He bet over a thousand dollars holding nothing but a nine and a queen, not even of the same suit. He accepted three new cards, and put his poker face to the test when he picked up a king, a ten and a jack. Suddenly holding a king-high straight, he changed his strategy, betting more conservatively so he could increase the pot without scaring off the other players. He wanted them to think his hand wasn't that great. His ploy worked because everyone stayed in the game and he made them pay, literally.

Cullen didn't host or even attend many poker games anymore. When he did, he generally played for nickels and dimes. As far as his wife knew, those infrequent card games were the only gambling he ever did. He'd made that promise to Sara on their honeymoon after he'd abandoned her in their beachside bungalow. He'd gone out for ice, ducked into a casino to play a quick hand of blackjack, and been gone over six hours. She'd dined alone, drunk alone, and still had plenty of time to get pissed. He'd spent every penny of his winnings and then some on a stunning tanzanite necklace but she didn't crack a smile until he swore it would never happen again. Even with the promise, he'd spent the next two nights on the pull-out sofa in their suite.

Cullen kept his promise, at least in the sense that he never again left her sitting alone in a hotel room. He stayed out of casinos altogether if there was even the remotest chance she might find out where he'd been. But, as much as he tried, he found he couldn't completely resist the temptation. That meant a few more business trips than might have been strictly necessary. He could spend time gambling and no one was the wiser.

At first, he felt bad about violating a trust, but spending time in casinos often led to other activities that, as a married man, he really shouldn't be engaging in. He learned how to keep that part of his life entirely separate. He'd crossed the line occasionally, like with that Swedish snow bunny, but those incidents were few and far between.

Okay, so he'd missed some dinners, a few of the girls' sporting events, some school activities and a family wedding. He always made it up to everyone and always left the casino with more money than he went in with. Well, almost always. But lately, his life-long lucky streak had been letting him down.

In the past six months, Cullen had lost something north of half a million dollars. He wasn't sure exactly how far north. He'd been borrowing money from his money market account, his checking account, and various corporate accounts. Over time, he'd sort of lost track of how much he'd taken from where. It really hadn't seemed like a big deal. He'd hit a rough patch for sure but knew his luck would turn around eventually. It had to. He'd started moving money to cover his tracks, and was spending more and more time in the casino so he could win back what he'd lost; at least that was the plan. Instead, he'd ended up spending money he really didn't have and gambled himself to the brink of total financial ruin. He could have lost his house, his business, everything.

Seeing no other choice, he talked to some gambling buddies, got a few names, and arranged the type of loan you can't get from a bank. The interest was astronomical, and the failure-to-pay penalties were even worse. Cullen wasn't concerned. Empty coffers aside, his business was thriving. He figured that, with fifty thousand dollars in cash, he could pay off his more pressing debts, right the ship and begin to put his life back together. He'd need to make some adjustments, tighten his belt a bit, but he'd be earning enough to stay afloat and, more important, pay off the money-grubbing bastard who'd bailed him out. All told, he calculated it would take about five years to get completely out from under. He knew it would be tough, but it beat the hell out of bankruptcy.

Of course, there was another way. He'd never shied away from taking risks and five years was such a long time. What if the economy tanked? Could he really count on a consistent revenue stream for the next sixty months? It made sense to do what he could to expedite that timetable. If, for example, he had a hundred grand instead of fifty, he could speed things up by fifty percent or more. He'd built his company on a gamble. Couldn't he save it on one as well? Things had been going so bad for so long, he was bound to catch a break. So, instead of going to the bank and depositing the money in his numerous depleted accounts, he'd headed back to the casino where he pissed it all away in a matter of hours. Those phone messages were reminders. His first payment was due, and Cullen had no idea where he was going to get the money.

That morning, after dashing out of his office, he'd found himself on the street with no transportation and no idea what to do next. After a few moments' deliberation, he hailed a cab, and was dropped off in front of his house twenty minutes later. Twenty minutes after that, he was behind the wheel of his black Jag, one of Sara's credit cards tucked into a shirt pocket. She thankfully hadn't been home. And with any luck, he'd have the Visa safely back in her top dresser drawer before she ever had a chance to miss it. All he needed was a nest egg--just enough to get him started. He could do the rest. Once again, though, as Jimmy had so eloquently stated, he had all the luck of a blind man at a titty bar. In no time flat, he'd turned a few thousand dollars into a few hundred, and seemed to dig a deeper hole with every card that landed in front of him.

Cullen was responsible for every one of his dumb ass actions. He knew that. He accepted it. But, until his conversation with Carrie, until she'd given him the message of an impending visit and the possibility of a *bike ride*, none of it had seemed real. When he was withdrawing money from one account after another, when he was converting that money into chips and then watching them disappear before his very eyes, even when he was meeting with a loan shark, shaking hands and accepting the battered briefcase full of tens, twenties and fifties, he felt like he was in a dream or maybe watching himself on film. It was him, but it wasn't him so nothing really bad could happen. He knew now he'd been fooling himself all along. He was, in every way, shape or form, screwed. It was that bike ride comment that brought it all home.

He'd never told his new benefactor he sometimes biked to work, hadn't told him he even owned a bike. The guy obviously knew, which meant he'd been keeping a close eye on Cullen even when Cullen wasn't aware of it. It wasn't much of a stretch to imagine him keeping an eye on his wife and daughters too. The message was a threat, and Cullen was so scared the sweat on his back had spread all the way down to the crack of his ass.

"Are you all right, sir?"

He looked up. The waitress was there with his drink.

"Sure," he said. He straightened and ran a hand across his forehead. It came away damp and he figured he must look almost as bad as he felt. "Just a little upset stomach. I'll be fine in a minute"

She took half a step back. "Maybe you should go home."

Home. Cullen wondered how much longer he'd have one of those. "I'm fine," he insisted. "What do I owe you for the drink?"

"It's six fifty-but I can take it back if you don't want it."

He flipped a ten onto her tray. "Keep the change."

She stood and watched as he drained the glass in a single gulp and then headed back into the casino.

-16-

Bullfrog said exactly what Skid Row had been thinking from the moment they walked away from Zatts and the Y.

"That was easy."

"Just like fucking Staples," Skid Row muttered.

"What?"

"Forget it," he said, chewing on his lower lip and trying to make some sense out of what had just happened. It had been easy--too easy--and that made the whole thing feel wrong. Zatts was definitely no genius. He'd once asked Skid Row how they got the mashed potatoes inside of French fries. Okay, he'd been a little stoned at the time but it was a stupid question just the same. Still, he had to have enough working brain cells to realize what Skid Row was up to. The story about why he wanted to find Marco's supplier was totally lame. Anyone with the intelligence of a bread crust should have seen right through it. Zatts hadn't, or hadn't seemed to anyway. He hadn't asked any questions or, and this is what Skid Row found the most troubling, asked for anything in return. Almost without hesitation, he'd given them a name and at least a general location. Why? It was highly un-Zatts-like to be helpful, cooperative, or anything other than a total dick. Skid Row couldn't help but wonder what he was playing at. Maybe he really didn't care or was just too lazy to get involved. There was one other possibility Skid Row couldn't afford to overlook. Zatts knew the score full well and was trying to set him up.

"But how could he know?" Bullfrog asked, as he and Skid Row boarded a B.C. Transit bus and began the slow, rumbling ride across town. "It's not like you really told him anything."

"I know," Skid Row said, dropping into a seat near the front and trying not to make eye contact with any of the other passengers. "It just bugs me."

"So let's come up with a new plan," Bullfrog said. "I don't like this one anyway."

He'd made no secret of that and Skid Row couldn't really blame him. He kept thinking about Marco's picture under that bold headline. He definitely didn't want to end up like that. Was the potential reward worth all the risk? But really, what were the alternatives?

"So what do you propose?" Skid Row asked.

"Simple. We do what anyone else would and find regular jobs. That would be a lot safer."

Safer, sure, but where had that gotten him so far? Skid Row turned and stared out the window. They passed a dollar store, an adult book store, a pawn shop, a rundown garage, a Taco Bell, and a boarded up building with a hand painted signs stating FOR SALE OR LEASE. "Tell me," he said to his reflection, "which of those fine establishments do you want to work at?"

"There are other places."

"You're right," Skid Row said. "So let me ask you. How much were you making at the bus station?"

"Eight twenty-five an hour. Why?"

"We call that minimum wage. And how many hours were you getting per week?"

"I hadn't been there long but usually about twenty."

Skid Row didn't have to do the math because he'd seen similar figures enough times on his own paychecks. "Around one sixty a week," he said, "and that's before taxes. Once you pay Sam and his flunkies, you're lucky if you've got a hundred bucks left."

"Sam?'

"Fucking government, dude. They're like the world's biggest condom. They say they'll protect you when all they're really doing is screwing you over. And you know what that hundred bucks will buy ya? A sleeping bag under a fucking bridge!" Skid Row punched the seat back in front of him and got a dirty look from the oversized driver in his oversized rearview mirror. It seemed like he was getting a lot of dirty looks lately but he really didn't care. "Screw you," he said, only half under his breath.

The bus driver glared but said nothing.

"What's your problem?" Bullfrog asked.

Skid Row made a face like he couldn't believe anyone could be that dense. "It's hopeless," he said, gesturing vaguely out the window.

"What is?"

"Just look," he said. "Do you really want to work at any of those places? Do you want another job with part-time hours, shit pay and no benefits?"

"It's not that bad"

"Said the guy who just went crazy over a cheese burger. I've been out of work one day and I'm already digging through pocket lint to come up with bus fare."

That wasn't quite true. He'd sifted quickly through his bills and discovered that, largely thanks to Tyrone, he still had around thirty dollars. That was a relief, but not so much of one that he didn't still think twice before handing over the four bucks so he and Bullfrog could board the bus. He couldn't remember the last time he'd ridden a bus anywhere and saw immediately that he hadn't been missing anything. The passengers looked miserable. The driver looked miserable. The whole place was hot as balls and smelled like the purple powder the old school janitor used to throw on the floor when somebody ralphed. Skid Row was tempted to turn away right then, but his feet ached already and getting all the way to Conklin Ave. on foot would have taken hours. He felt sure they didn't have that much time.

"It's a damn sauna in here," Skid Row said, using the sleeve of his sweatshirt to mop his forehead. The bottom few inches of each window were covered with a thick layer of condensation yet the vent at his feet continued to blast hot air. He shifted in his seat to try to get out of the line of fire. When that didn't work, Skid row peeled off his sweatshirt, wadded it into a ball and dropped it on top of the vent.

"Thanks," Bullfrog said. "I was about ready to pop."

Skid Row studied his companion and wondered what they would do if his plan didn't work out. Of course, they didn't have to remain a team. Best intentions and all that, he couldn't avoid the simple fact that his money would last longer if he didn't have to share. He felt a flash of resentment, again reminded that if it hadn't been for Bullfrog he'd still have a job and a steady source of income. And now the dude was freeloading--catching free bus rides, eating Skid Row's food and otherwise sapping his ridiculously limited resources. It was high time to put a stop to that shit. He opened his mouth to speak but didn't get a chance.

"Thanks for the bus fare," Bullfrog said. "Thanks for everything. I owe you and I promise I'll pay you back when I can."

"Don't worry about it," Skid Row said, suddenly feeling like a jerk. He'd been having his internal debate over thirty lousy dollars. Whether he shared it or not wasn't going to make a hell of a lot of difference one way or the other.

"I've never been to this part of town before," Bullfrog said, leaning forward so he could get a better view out the window. The bus slowed and made a left turn across from the large Frito-Lay plant. "Where are we going?"

"You know about as much as I do," Skid Row said, inhaling deeply and savoring the distinctive aromas of hot oil and potato chip production. "We need to find an old trailer. It's supposed to be somewhere along the river but Zatts didn't know the exact location. Either that," Skid Row reflected, "or he knew but wasn't telling."

"Would he do that?"

"You met him," Skid Row said. "What do you think? He might have sent us out here for nothing. He'd think that was pretty funny. This trailer might be clear on the other side of the county or may not exist at all."

"Then why are we bothering?"

Skid Row shrugged and reached for his sweatshirt. "This is our only shot. Besides, Zatts told us enough to make me think there was at least some truth to his story."

"Such as?"

"That bit about it being flooded out and condemned," Skid Row said. "That didn't sound like something he'd just make up."

"So you think we'll be able to find it?"

"I didn't say that," Skid Row admitted. "He mentioned a rusty mailbox. They could be a dime a dozen out here. A few years ago, this whole county was flooded. A lot of those buildings we passed had water all the way up to their roofs."

"I think I remember hearing about it," Bullfrog said.

"It was bad news, dude. This entire area was washed out and Conklin was hit really hard. Most of the town runs right along the river. I don't know if it's the Chenango or the Susquehanna but it's right fucking there." He pointed to indicate just how close.

"So you're saying we could see a lot of rusty mailboxes?"

"Be shocked if we don't."

"He also said there's an upside-down number six on the post."

"And that's our quest my friend. I hope you feel like walking because we may have to cover some ground."

"Should we split up?"

Skid Row considered. "No, man. We got no way to connect if one of us found something." He brushed hair out of his face and started to pull his sweatshirt back on. "There's one area I know is really flood prone. We'll start there. If we strike out we can try something else. That work for you?"

"Sure," Bullfrog said, not sounding eager.

Skid Row wasn't real jazzed about their prospects either. Odds were good they'd spend the rest of their day chasing shadows. He tried not to think about that, or the money he'd have to spend later to get them back to their side of town.

Before long, they were dropped at the corner of Bedford Street where they stood on the side of the road, stretching their limbs, taking big gulps of refreshingly cool air and at a total loss as to what to do next.

"So where to?" Bullfrog finally asked.

Skid Row didn't immediately answer because his brilliant idea suddenly seemed not only hopeless but stupid. Even if he and Bullfrog were somehow lucky enough to stumble onto this mystery trailer, what were they supposed to do then? You didn't just ring a doorbell and tell whoever answered that you wanted to sell drugs. How would they even know if they had the right trailer or the right person?

Zatts hadn't provided any kind of physical description. He'd just given them a name--Ricky Fixx, which, Skid Row thought now, sounded made up. He'd never considered what sort of name a major drug dealer might have but Ricky didn't seem to fit the bill. But, they were here now and the bus was already a quarter mile away. Nothing to do but proceed and see what happened. They'd probably head home later with tired feet, less money, and nothing else to show for their efforts.

Skid Row looked up and down the road, trying to make up his mind. He didn't see any big billboards advertising the best prices on meth or weed. What he saw instead were businesses, houses, and nothing whatsoever that provided any real clue as to which direction they should go. There'd be no help from Bullfrog. He was staring expectantly and not about to make the first move. *Okay,* Skid Row thought. *This was my hair-brained idea. I should be the one at the controls.*

"This way," he finally said, turning to head in the direction the bus had come from. "About a half mile back, we passed some new construction and a few lots that looked like they'd been cleared. That might have been from flood damage. We'll take a look. Keep your eyes peeled. That damn trailer could be anywhere."

"I wish we had more food," Bullfrog said, after they'd walked the half mile, plus another half mile, plus at least a mile after that.

Skid Row didn't comment. He was hungry too, but he did his best to ignore his growling belly as well as the nagging suspicion they were going the wrong way. He wanted to turn around, thought they probably should, but couldn't help thinking their destination might be just ahead. So, they scuffed along, Bullfrog in his worn boots and Skid Row in his tattered sneakers, neither saying much but their body language suggesting they both knew they'd messed up.

"Tell you what," Skid Row eventually said, but then froze.

Bullfrog had been staring at his feet, hadn't seen Skid Row stop short and nearly walked right up his backside. "What the heck?" he said, flailing his arms and stumbling as he tried to avoid a collision.

Skid Row barely noticed. He'd been about to say that they'd go as far as an old warehouse-looking place a couple hundred yards ahead and turn around. No sooner had he reached that decision and started to put it into words when, out of the corner of his eye, he spied a rusted mailbox mounted to a pole leaning so far to one side that the mailbox itself couldn't have been more than a couple feet off the ground. Screwed to the pole, Skid Row saw a small silver square of metal or plastic displaying a stenciled number six in black. And it was upside-down.

"Son of a bitch," he said, slow and quiet.

"What?" Bullfrog asked. "Are we going back now? It's about time. I think that Zatts guy was full of --"

“Look,” Skid Row said, pointing.

"What?" Bullfrog asked again. “I don’t--”

But Skid Row saw his expression change as he took in the mailbox, the pole, the number six, and then the old trailer, nearly invisible behind a row of overgrown shrubs.

"That's it!" Bullfrog said. "We found it.”

I found it, Skid Row thought, and that brought him up short. From the time they'd boarded the bus, hell, from the time they left Zatts standing outside the Y, he realized he'd never really expected to make it this far. That perhaps explained but definitely did not excuse the fact that he'd spent exactly no time coming up with a plan of action.

"Are we going in?" Bullfrog asked, striding forward with far less trepidation than he'd shown when approaching the counter at McDonald's the day before.

"Hold on!" Skid Row hissed, grasping his arm hard enough to spin him around.

"What the heck?" Bullfrog asked, pulling away. "This is the place, right? So let's go," and he started to move forward again.

Skid Row didn't know what to do. The guy obviously didn't get it, but he should at least have enough sense to realize you didn't march up to a drug dealer's place of business like you were selling fucking Girl Scout cookies.

"Just wait a second," he said, keeping his voice low so they wouldn't be overheard, not that that was likely over the hideous sounds emanating from a seriously dented and rusting window-mounted air conditioner. It leaked a steady stream of grayish water, and whined and moaned like it was breathing its last. A second window was completely boarded over and a third was so crusted with dirt and grime it was impossible to make out anything that might lie beyond.

Skid Row thought he saw a flicker of movement but that could have been a reflection or, more likely, his own imagination. He still thought it was a good bet there was someone indoors. A dark blue F-150 took up most of the small parking area and an aging silver Lexus sedan was tucked nearly out of sight around the far corner of the building.

His first instinct was to turn and run and, had Bullfrog gotten any closer to the door, Skid Row might have done just that. Thankfully, the guy had been smart enough to stop in his tracks and was evidently now waiting for further instructions.

Something wasn't adding up. Skid Row kept thinking about Marco's gold chains, nice clothes and new threads, and trying to somehow reconcile that with the shithole trailer right in front of him. If this Ricky Fixx guy was some sort of major player, as Zatts had suggested, why was he driving a ten-year-old car, assuming the Lexus was his, and living or at least working in a structure that didn't look suitable for livestock?

Even on a bright sunny day, the place seemed dark and foreboding. A sagging wooden deck stretched from the scarred metal door to one end, and Skid Row assumed there'd been an awning there at one time. The single bent and corroded support rod was all that remained. The trailer itself, an indeterminate color somewhere between brown and green, appeared to be on the verge of collapse. It looked like it was tipping in several directions at once, held up by stacked cinder blocks at one end, metal jacks at the other, and what might have been construction vehicle tires in the middle. It didn't seem possible that anyone would willingly set foot inside. Someone had, however. He knew that because the groan of floor boards could suddenly be heard even over the racket of the laboring AC unit.

"Come on," Bullfrog said, taking another step closer. "We can't just stand here all day."

"Dude, slow down," Skid Row said. We can't just… "

But that was as far as he got. With a crash, the trailer door flew open and slammed against the wall. A huge man filled the door frame, his large squarish head atop shoulders as big as nightmares.

Skid Row wanted to run but his legs had turned to stone.

"Get in here!" the behemoth said, his menacing tone and intense stare leaving no room for debate. "Ricky wants to see you."

-17-

Ricky Fixx had a decision to make. Carl was his partner and, Ricky had to admit, his closest friend. He'd also become a liability. Like it or not, he realized it might be time to start forming his exit strategy. He'd protect Carl as best he could. But there was no point sticking his neck out for a lost cause and he thought there was an excellent chance the man was going down. Ricky wasn't about to go down with him. He inspected his gloomy surroundings, alternately drumming his fingers on the desktop and sipping at a Styrofoam cup of gas station coffee. It was too hot to have any flavor, which he figured was probably a blessing.

What, Ricky wondered, if everything went south and he had to run? He'd thought about it before but never really believed he'd have to take such drastic measures. How far should he go? Could he try to stay local, or would it be safer to pull up all the stakes and start fresh somewhere entirely new?

Ricky hated the thought of leaving. His family had been in the area since the late nineteenth century. Back then, Binghamton was the second largest cigar manufacturer in the United States and earned the nickname "The Parlor City" because of all the large, stately homes. Distant relatives had once owned one of those homes, or so he'd been told. That was at least five generations ago. The home was gone, and the meager family fortune had disappeared long before so many Binghamton-based businesses had either moved or shut down. The city had been in a serious recession for more than two decades and recovery was slow at best.

Ricky's father had been one of thousands of IBMers and had gotten out just ahead of the massive layoffs. He'd taken a hefty severance package with him and evidently hadn't wanted to share. Without a word to anyone, he packed a suitcase, left a note and a check barely large enough to cover the rent and power bill and that was it. Ricky never heard from him again. If his mother did, she never let on. She definitely never received anything like child support. She made ends meet waiting tables at the Skylark Diner, and changing sheets and scrubbing toilets at the Binghamton Motor Lodge. She never complained, not even when she started to age well ahead of her years and chronic back pain forced her to quit one job and then the other. She was mostly bedridden before she turned sixty and died of a stroke not long after.

Ricky blamed his father, although he knew he was just as guilty. What had he ever done to ease her burden? He was earning his keep at the age of fifteen, and blowing every cent he made on girls, cigarettes and clothes, usually in that order. And in his free time, he started running in the wrong circles and getting into trouble. He supposed his mother got a few more gray hairs each time the police knocked on her door in the middle of the night. She'd tried to talk to him, tried to set him on the right path, but working two fulltime jobs, how much energy could she really devote to looking over his shoulder? He'd thanked her for her efforts by abandoning the family name of Frederick, going with Fixx because he thought it was better for his image. He switched from Richard to Ricky for the same reason. He couldn't switch back now, which meant his only lasting connection to his mother was the struggling city where they were both born and raised.

Ricky knew he had no real reason to feel nostalgic. He was a criminal. If he suddenly folded up his tent and left, he wouldn't be missed or even remembered. For better or worse though, the old Parlor City was still his home. That, however, wasn't the main reason he chose to stick around. A shitty economy meant opportunity for a guy like him and he wanted to continue to take advantage of it. Whether or not he'd be able to do that depended entirely on what happened with Carl.

Ricky doubted his partner really posed much of a threat to him. He knew enough about the business to make things difficult for sure. That was only assuming the police could make him talk. Carl had a record and had even spent a little time behind bars. As a result, he hated cops more than classical music and Geno's pizza put together. He was also tough. He wouldn't say a word...intentionally. He could be tricked and that was a concern. Good thing Ricky still had his little insurance policy. He planned on making damn sure Carl knew about it and fully understood the need to keep quiet. If he played his cards right, maybe it would work out after all, even if *working out* meant throwing Carl to the wolves.

Ricky's eyes moved to the far corner of the room. The floor there was as warped and discolored as everywhere else. However, directly beneath the rickety floor lamp, one board moved a little easier than the rest. Some pressure in the right spot and the whole thing would pop free. Beneath it, Ricky had stowed a small lock box. It contained some papers, about two thousand dollars in emergency cash, and most important, half a dozen thumb drives. Ricky never left anything incriminating on his laptop. It was too risky. He even cleared his browsing history at the end of every day. Two of the thumb drives held his important files, all encrypted. The others were full of Carl's greatest hits: hundreds of photos and dozens of audio and video recordings. If turned over to the proper authorities, he'd never again see the light of day. And with a fresh murder charge potentially hanging over his head, he was already on dangerously thin ice. Ricky felt bad but what could he do? Sometimes, all you could do was look out for number one. He knew that if it came to it he could be in the wind in as little time as it took to collect his few personal items and toss them in the back of the Lexus. Ricky was wondering if there was any real reason to wait when he heard the familiar rumble of Carl's truck followed by the crunch of tires on gravel.

"Damn," he said, automatically checking his watch. He hadn't expected Carl back so soon, and wouldn't have been too surprised if he didn't come back at all.

"You look like hell," Ricky observed, before Carl had even made it through the door.

Based on his initial reaction, it had become clear to Ricky that Carl really had not realized what he'd done to Marco or how serious the situation was. Once the truth sunk in, it hit the man hard. He'd wandered out of the office in an obvious daze, unwilling or unable to say where he was going. And now, Ricky couldn't miss his pale skin, trembling hands, hollow eyes, and hair and beard that somehow looked even more wild and unruly than usual.

"Here," Ricky said, sliding the coffee across the desk. "You need this more than I do."

"Thanks," Carl grunted, collapsing into a chair and accepting the cup with all the enthusiasm a death row inmate might devote to his final meal.

"So where've you been?"

Carl glanced around as if not entirely sure how he'd gotten there. "Just driving," he said. "I was thinking about turning myself in."

Ricky shuddered, knowing how easily he could be implicated. He came around the desk and gave Carl's shoulder an awkward pat. "Let's not do anything too drastic. We'll talk this through and figure something out. Really."

It was a weak promise and Carl seemed to sense it. He hung his head and wiped a hand across his eyes. A couple fingers came away damp.

"Well," Ricky said, unsettled and not really knowing what to do. "Let's get busy then."

Carl didn't speak or even look up, so Ricky continued.

"According to the latest reports, police are talking to witnesses. That could mean one of two things. First, you really were seen. Or second, the cops are just blowing smoke."

"Hmpf," Carl said. "They can blow me."

Ricky half smiled, relieved his partner was showing signs of life. "Interesting idea." He went back around his desk and sat down. "But not terribly productive. I want you to think about what happened yesterday."

"That's all I've been doing. I still can't believe he's...."

"I know," Ricky said. "Try to forget about that for now. Just picture the scene: where you were, where he was, and concentrate mostly on your surroundings. Do you think you were seen well enough to be identified?"

Carl thought about it. "I don't know," he said. "It happened fast and no one was real close. I doubt anybody could have seen much."

"That's good," Ricky said. "But if just one person tells the cops he saw a big hairy dude hanging around, how long before we've got the fuzz on our doorstep?"

"They don't know where to find us."

"They don't know because we haven't given them any real reason to look. Gangs control most of the drug trade, and no one gives a crap about boot leg video games, a little gambling and the rest. We're small potatoes and I've made a point of keeping a low profile. That's a lot tougher when you're talking about a murder rap."

"Don't say that," Carl said, shaking his head and putting his hands over his ears. "I didn't mean to hurt him. I didn't mean to do anything. I just wanted to stop him"

"You damn sure did that."

Carl recoiled as if he'd been slapped.

I'm sorry," Ricky said. "But the only way we're going to get past this is to deal with it head on. Are you still with me?"

Carl nodded weakly.

"Okay," Ricky said. "So the first step is to find out what the cops really know."

"How?"

Ricky held up his cell phone. "Simple. I'll give Ronnie a call."

Carl almost smiled.

Ronnie Tripp had been a member of the Binghamton Police Department for more than thirty years. He started as a beat cop, moved up to detective, and then his career was derailed when he was caught tampering with evidence in a major drug case. Several kilos of high grade cocaine disappeared, and a closer look at Tripp's activities revealed that was only the tip of the iceberg. He'd spent years shaking down local drug dealers, agreeing to let them off in exchange for a small, powdery contribution. Ricky knew all that because he and Tripp had had some business dealings. The Binghamton P.D. was only recently recovering from a major corruption scandal and the acting chief didn't think they could survive the firestorm of another. As a result, Tripp was allowed to keep his job if he would likewise agree to keep his mouth shut. He'd been behind a desk ever since. He'd gone through all the required substance abuse counseling classes but never entirely got over his taste for Big C.

"You think he'd be willing to help?" Carl asked, a glint of hope in his downcast eyes.

Ricky gave a wry laugh. "You kidding? I know his weakness. Besides, they don't call me Ricky Fixx for nothin'. One cellophane baggie and he'll spill his guts."

"What if he doesn't know?"

"He pushes paper all day," Ricky explained. "Ronnie can find out anything if he puts his mind to it."

"What are you gonna ask him then?"

"Easy. To identify our witnesses."

Carl looked confused. "But what good will that do?"

"Use that big head," Ricky said. "Let's say one of those witnesses got a real good look at you. They not only noticed what you were wearing but can give a detailed physical description right down to the scar on that ugly mug of yours."

Carl self consciously moved his hand to his left cheek. "I'd be screwed," he said, slumping over in his chair.

"True enough," Ricky said, a sly smile creeping across his face, "unless we could somehow convince that witness to change his story."

Carl brightened immediately. "I can be very convincing."

"I know you can. And if one witness has some sort of... well, let's call it an unpleasant experience...."

"The rest will clam right up."

"Now you're getting' it," Ricky said. "You see? This might not be as bad as we thought."

"So call him right now," Carl said, excited.

Ricky set his phone on the desk. "I will call but we've got a more serious problem and I don't know what we're gonna do about it."

"What?"

"That axe handle," Ricky said. "You left physical evidence behind and it places you at the scene. That ain't good."

"Could Ronnie get it back?" Carl asked, his suddenly ashen expression suggesting he already knew the answer.

"No chance in hell. And your finger prints are probably all they need anyway."

"Then I may as well go ahead and turn myself in." Carl looked around and then started to hyperventilate.

"There's no need to panic," Ricky said, thinking that, if he were in Carl's size fourteens, he'd be half way to North Dakota by now. "What you want to do is lay low for a while. You got somewhere you can go?"

"Can I stay with you?"

Ricky's blood pressure immediately jumped twenty points. "You could," he said, scratching his chin. "But if the cops moved in, they'd take both of us together. Once inside, I wouldn't be able to do anything to help you."

"So I'll stay here."

The last thing Ricky wanted was Carl sitting on top of all his important files if things got hot and he needed to skip town in a hurry. "It's an option," he said. "I just don't know how safe it would be."

"Then where can I go?"

"For now, just stay off the street. Park your truck someplace random and public, a grocery store maybe. Then stay out of sight."

"But where will I sleep?"

Carl again started with his finger counting routine, pulling on one finger after another. He was obviously scared and Ricky couldn't blame him.

"Crash at the train yard tonight. You'll be safe enough there."

His eyes got big. "I can't do that."

"Sure you can. I've done it plenty of times," Ricky lied. "Just find an empty box car and hop in. Even if a watchman finds you, which he won't, the worst they'd do is make you leave."

"I don't know," Carl said, still looking worried.

"Don't sweat it. It's not like you'll have to sleep on trains the rest of your life." Although, Ricky thought, that would still beat the hell out of a jail cell. "I'll talk to Ronnie, figure out which way the wind is blowing, and by this time tomorrow we'll have a much better idea of where we stand."

"But if they've already got my prints," Carl said, pulling a pair of black leather gloves out of his back pocket and beginning to knead them like a stress ball, "it's just a matter of time."

Ricky stared at him. "Hold on," he said, nodding at the gloves. "Any chance you had those with you yesterday?"

"Sure. It was cold out."

"At the construction lot, when you had your little run-in, you had those gloves on?"

"Yeah."

"The whole time? You're sure?"

"Yeah. Why?"

"Go home," Ricky said. "Get some rest. I'll talk to Ronnie but I don't think you have anything to worry about."

"But..." and then it clicked. "Hey, you're right." He broke into a huge grin.

"Don't get carried away," Ricky said. "I'm still pissed at you. You cost us a lot of money and I want to know how you're going to make good."

Carl started to speak and then they heard a loud yelp from outside.

"What the fuck was that?" Ricky asked and they both moved toward the door.

-18-

Skid Row blinked several times and tried to will his eyes to adjust to the sudden dimness. He was still in a state of shock after being charged by a man who looked even larger than the trailer from which he'd just emerged. Before Skid row knew what was happening, he and Bullfrog had been grabbed, then half dragged, half carried inside, the giant's strong grip on their arms making it impossible to resist. He pushed them through the door and dumped them unceremoniously onto a small couch with torn fabric and its springs so sprung they may as well have been sitting on the floor.

"What's the deal?" Skid Row asked, his voice cracking. He tried to sound defiant but was so scared he thought he might piss his pants. His mammoth escort was still looming over him, so he directed his question at the only other person in sight. He was smaller, further away, and his suit and tie suggested he was the one in charge. Besides, he looked a whole lot less threatening.

"You were on our property," the man said easily, stepping up onto a low platform and walking around to sit behind a desk. Once he did, his entire upper body disappeared in the shadow cast by the only light in the room. "This is a place of business," he went on, "and you two were trespassing."

"What kind of business?" Bullfrog asked and Skid Row immediately elbowed him in the ribs.

"We didn't mean to trespass," he explained, squinting in a vain attempt to read the guy's expression. "We were looking for someone and we sort of got lost. It was an accident."

"And who were you looking for? I know a lot of people. Perhaps I can be of assistance."

"No, it's cool," Skid Row said quickly. "He isn't around here. I think we must have been given some bad information. We'll be going now." He started to rise but was halted by a big, hairy arm as rigid as a crowbar.

"Boss asked you a question," he said, his voice deep and threatening. "I suggest you answer."

Skid Row tried to shake free but it was like trying to shrug off an avalanche. He gave up and sank back into his seat. "Like I said, we got bad--"

"We're looking for Ricky Fixx," Bullfrog cut in. "Do you know him?"

Shit! Skid Row couldn't believe his ears. Couldn't believe Bullfrog's stupidity. Didn't he understand what was going on? Skid Row shot him a nasty look but the guy just sat there, a bump on a damn log, face to face with a couple obvious thugs yet not seeming to realize the danger they were in.

The room had fallen silent, all except for the rattling, wheezing air conditioner unit. Skid Row was grateful for the noise because it covered up the pounding of his heart. He knew he and Bullfrog were in trouble and there wasn't one single thing they could do about it.

The two men exchanged a glance, the meaning of which Skid Row could only guess at. Then, the big one stepped forward, hands on hips as wide across as a picnic table. Skid Row was ready to begin begging for his life right then. He prayed the bearded giant wouldn't be given the command to kill because he looked both willing and able. And if, he thought, by some miracle they actually made it out of there alive, he vowed to kill Bullfrog or at least kick the living hell out of him.

"What do you know about Ricky Fixx?" the smaller man said after what felt like several minutes.

"Nothin',"' Skid Row replied, jumping in before Bullfrog had a chance. He brushed hair out of his eyes and concentrated on keeping his voice steady. "We were just told he might be somewhere around here. That's all."

"But why do you want him?"

Skid Row knew that question was coming and had no idea how to answer. He had the feeling the person they sought was sitting just a few feet away, and Zatts, incredibly, had not steered them wrong after all. Skid Row, on the other hand, had fucked up in epic proportion. He hadn't planned ahead or anticipated an immediate confrontation, and it somehow hadn't once occurred to him that a drug dealer might keep a big hunk of muscle nearby. He was petrified of saying the wrong thing now so he said nothing. And this time, Bullfrog had enough sense to keep his mouth shut too.

Ricky studied his visitors and tried to determine what they were up to. They were a strange pair, both looking like derelicts. The first was scrawny to the point of malnourishment and couldn't seem to sit still. His hands kept wandering to his hair or his face, and his fingernails were bitten to the quick. The other one, shorter and stockier but just as unkempt, bore a disturbing resemblance to a frog. He had frog ears, frog eyes, and his unusually wide head looked like it had mistakenly been put on sideways. It also didn't help that the guy was bald as a baby's ass. He sat hunched over with his knees spread wide apart and Ricky had no trouble picturing him springing up, maybe to go after one of the flies bouncing determinedly against the window. He bit back a smile even though he was pretty sure no one could see his face.

This is interesting," he said, glancing at his computer and tapping a few keys. The only thing he was looking at was a desktop image of a bikini clad brunette with bongos the size of bass drums. She was smoking hot but he frowned at the screen, trying to give the impression that he had access to the world's deepest, darkest secrets and wasn't liking what he was seeing. Ricky always preferred to negotiate from a position of authority and, in his experience, a little fear went a long way.

"There seems to be a difference of opinion as to what you two are actually doing here. One of you," he looked at Skid Row, "claims you were lost and ended up on my property *by accident.* Let me just say that no one ever finds me by accident. But you," he shifted his gaze to Bullfrog, "say you were looking for this Ricky Fixx person. You've got two different stories so what am I supposed to believe?"

No one said anything and Ricky turned back to his computer screen. He frowned again and pulled at his lower lip. "What do you think, Carl?"

"Buncha bullshit," he grumbled. "Want me to take care of it? I can make 'em disappear in the river just like the last pair."

Ricky almost laughed. There'd been no *last pair*, but Carl understood the situation and knew what Ricky was after. The new comers were certainly fooled. The scrawny one tried again to leap to his feet while the frog-looking one sat there, his mouth opening and closing but no sounds were coming out.

Ricky sat back and clasped his hands in front of his chest. “The river,” he said, staring up at the ceiling as if considering the possibility. "Do we have any cinderblocks left?"

"A whole pallet."

"Oh, we won't need that many." He started rubbing his hands together. “What about chains?”

"These two are pretty small," Carl replied matter of factly. "We got enough."

"Just a fucking minute!" the scrawny one exclaimed, squirming under Carl's firm grip. "You can't do that. We weren't doin' nothin'."

Ricky ignored him. "Garbage truck been through yet? We could toss them in that big dumpster. That might be safer, unless we want to just stash them somewhere until after dark."

The scrawny one went pale and looked ready to puke. The other guy was borderline catatonic. He blinked occasionally, but otherwise barely moved. Ricky supposed he'd pushed things far enough. The losers no longer seemed capable of speech and definitely didn't pose any kind of a threat. It was time to break the ice and see what this was all about.

"It so happens that I am Ricky Fixx." He sat up and placed both hands flat on the desk. "Now that you found me, just what in hell do you want?"

There was another long pause, and then the scarecrow finally spoke up. "My name is Skid Row, and this is Bullfrog. We're looking for work."

Ricky stared at them, at Carl, then back at them again. "Looking…for work?" he repeated. "Does this look like an employment agency?"

He wasn't sure what he'd been expecting but it definitely wasn't that. If anything, he thought the two might be looking to score some drugs. They looked the part, but that still wouldn't explain how they'd ended up on his doorstep. He never dealt with his customers first hand, and that meant someone had been running his mouth. Ricky would have to deal with that, but first things first.

Skid Row cursed himself for how badly he'd botched the whole thing. In his defense, he'd been caught completely off guard, and not just by the way that big Carl dude had rushed out at them. That was scary for sure, but he could handle it. His real problem was Ricky Fixx. The guy didn't come close to fitting the mental image Skid Row had created. He'd pictured someone a lot less weasely. His suit was obviously cheap and just sort of hung on his thin frame. His shirt had tattered cuffs and didn't really match the suit or tie. He also had the type of high-pitched, whiny voice that made you want to punch him right in the mouth. It would have felt good, at least until Carl ripped both his arms off and shoved them straight up his ass.

To Skid Row, the setting was all wrong too. Zatts had told him to look for an old trailer. He still hadn't imagined he'd end up in a place that looked like hell and smelled like moldy socks. His nose twitched from the stench, and the place looked worse than it smelled. The walls were crooked. The carpet was so dirty the original color was no longer identifiable. Half the ceiling tiles were missing and the whole thing looked ready to cave in.

He thought again about Marco and wondered why his employer worked in such squalor and looked like a small-time mafia wannabe. None of it seemed to gel. And what about Carl? Was he there just to give Ricky credibility? If so, it worked. The monster had finally taken a seat in front of the desk. It gave them some space. Skid Row no longer felt like he was in immediate danger but he was still having a hard time getting his breathing under control.

There was, he realized, one possibility he hadn't previously considered. It went back to Zatts being a total shit head. True, he'd told them how to find Ricky Fixx, but nothing Skid Row had seen indicated that Fixx was anything more than what he appeared, which was just this side of worthless. In other words, he wasn't much different than Zatts. Maybe the two were buddies and would get together later for a good laugh at his and Bullfrog's expense. Fixx tried to come off like a bad ass, and Skid Row had to admit it was a good act. Without Carl, though, he'd have nothing. So why wasn't Carl the one in charge? Skid Row hoped to figure it out. In doing so, maybe he'd learn there was more to Ricky Fixx than met the eye.

Of course, the first thing he needed to do was try to level the playing field a bit. He and Bullfrog had come off looking like a couple of jerks, not knowing where they were going or what they were doing. Then there was all the talk of chains and cinderblocks. It was all crap, empty threats meant to intimidate. Skid Row just hadn't understood that until he'd had time to think. Even if Ricky and that Carl character were criminals, and they almost certainly were, they weren't likely to off someone just for wandering onto their property. No one was that crazy. And, no criminal worth a damn would risk a stunt like that for no good reason. Feeling safe enough for the moment, Skid Row decided he'd try to get some answers.

"We know you ran into some trouble recently," he said, sitting up as much as the sagging couch would allow. "We think we can help you out."

"You're gonna help me?" Ricky asked. "That's rich." He winked at Carl. "That's the funniest thing I've heard all week. You two comedians or something? You gonna come in here every day to make me laugh? How much will I have to pay for that service?"

"We can help you," Skid Row insisted. "We just need to know you really are the person we were told to look for."

"You want ID? I've got some right here." He reached below the desk. "It says my name is Louisville Slugger."

Carl started to stand but Ricky waved him down.

"I don't know what you guys are after, but I suggest you spill it before this gets ugly."

For emphasis, he placed a baseball bat on the desk in front of him. The paint was flaked and it was dented in several places and had clearly seen plenty of action. Somehow, Skid Row doubted any of the dents had been caused by a baseball. Skull cracking seemed a lot more likely.

"We came about Marco," he said, glancing at Bullfrog who was staring fixedly at the floor, his Adam's apple bobbing up and down. It appeared he'd finally realized they were in serious shit. Skid Row knew that too, and decided their best bet was to put their cards on the table and see what happened.

Ricky was taken aback. The cops hadn't fingered Carl yet so how had these two deadbeats zeroed in on him so fast? That had to be what this was about. They knew Marco was dead, somehow knew Carl had killed him, and now they were going to demand money for their silence. Or, maybe they wanted to trade information for drugs. Either way, it wasn't happening. He could meet their demand now but, sooner or later, they'd come back for more. He'd have to make sure their silence was permanent, and there was really only one way to guarantee that. They wouldn't end up in the river or the dumpster but they'd damn sure disappear.

He was about to give Carl orders to that effect when a couple things occurred to him. First, it really wasn't conceivable that these two knew a thing. Even if they had been at that construction lot and witnessed the crime first hand, how would they have tailed Carl all the way back here? He had a pickup truck and they were apparently on foot. And, if for the sake of argument they already knew or had been told where to find him, it made no sense that they'd shown up alone, unarmed and obviously confused. The sight of Carl had not only surprised them but scared them too. That told Ricky they hadn't been prepared for any sort of confrontation. They also didn't look like they had the guts to try to shake anyone down. There had to be something else going on.

"This... Marco person," Ricky said slowly. "What do you know about him?"

"He's dead," Skid Row replied. "We saw it in the paper."

Carl stiffened and the floor creaked. Ricky looked his way and tried to relay the message that there was nothing to worry about.

"I think I saw that story too," he said. "But what does it have to do with me?"

Skid Row blinked. "He worked for you, right? That's what we were told."

"Ricky smiled like that was the most ridiculous thing he'd ever heard. "The newspaper indicated that that was some sort of drug deal gone wrong." He spread his hands. "Do I look like the type who would associate with druggies and hoods?"

The answer was yes and everyone in the room knew it. Skid Row didn't want to force the issue but, at that point, he didn't have much to lose. "It's what we were told," he said again.

"And who told you?" Ricky asked, his expression hardening noticeably.

"Guy named Zatts," Skid Row answered without hesitation. He hoped Ricky knew him and would dispatch his bulldog to knock Zatts down a peg or two. The jerk had it coming, and Skid Row had a vision of Carl plucking out those dreadlocks one by one.

"Zatts," Ricky said, stroking his chin. "Can't say the name is familiar."

Skid Row didn't know if he should believe that or not. Although Ricky hadn't exactly denied knowing Marco, that was certainly what he'd tried to imply. They'd have to get past that or their conversation had no hope of going any further. Skid Row already had his toes in the water so he supposed he may as well jump all the way in.

"You're gonna need someone to take over Marco's territory." He nodded at Bullfrog. "We can do that for you."

Bullfrog stirred but still hadn't found his voice.

"Let's say, just for the moment, "Ricky said, holding up a hand, "that I did know Marco. What do you think was the nature of our business?'

Skid Row hesitated but only for a second. "He sold for you, right? Now he's dead. You need someone to take his spot."

"And by *sold*, I suppose you are referring to drugs?"

Skid Row nodded. "I bought weed from him once in a while. Not often," he added quickly. He didn't want Ricky thinking he was a stoner. "And I never touched the heavier stuff. Marco always offered so I know he had it."

"And you think he got it from me?"

Skid Row nodded again. He was so nervous he could feel his balls sweat but he'd said his piece and it was up to Ricky to take the next step.

"I must say," Ricky said, standing. "You've certainly taken me by surprise. I'm not sure I can help you but I'd like to have a brief word with my associate. Would you two gentlemen mind stepping outside?"

"So what do you think?" Bullfrog asked? standing on the trailer's warped front porch and straining to hear through the door. For the past several minutes, they'd heard some murmuring and the occasional creak of floorboards but that was about it.

"I wish I knew what was going on in there," Skid Row said, digging hands into his jeans pockets and shaking hair out of his eyes. "I don't trust those guys."

"I don't either, but what difference does that make? We're just gonna rip 'em off, right?"

"Shh," Skid Row hissed, looking around uneasily. "You want them to hear us?"

"Relax. If we can't hear them, they can't hear us either."

"I still wish you'd keep your voice down." Skid Row scowled. "And you're awful brave all of a sudden. What were you thinking in there? 'We're looking for Ricky Fixx.' You could have gotten us both killed."

"Hey. At least I got things moving. You didn't know what to do."

"Well I'm sorry," Skid Row said. "That big dude freaked me out."

"He is big," Bullfrog acknowledged, glancing at the door. "Mean looking too. I wouldn't want to mess with him."

Skid Row looked off down the road. He was trying to decide if he should put his thoughts into words.

Bullfrog saved him the trouble. "So maybe we should just split."

Skid Row turned to stare at him. "It is starting to feel like coming here wasn't such a hot idea." He paused and gnawed a fingernail.

"So let's go." Bullfrog said. "We could head towards the river and be out of sight in like ten seconds. I doubt they'd waste much time looking for us."

"You got a point," Skid Row said. "And they're probably gonna tell us to shove off anyway."

"Then let's do it on our terms."

They'd barely gone a step when the door swung open and Carl waved them back inside.

-19-

Andrew Cullen shifted into a lower gear as he began the long climb up Airport Road. He had just over three miles to go and most of it was uphill. He gritted his teeth against the burning in his upper thighs as he pushed himself harder. Despite the pain, which never went away no matter how many miles he logged, he actually looked forward to this part of the ride because it never failed to fill him with feelings of accomplishment.

When he'd first started cycling nearly five years earlier, he couldn't do the hill at all. He'd try, but had to stop before he'd covered the first half mile. Sometimes he'd walk the rest of the way, wheeling the bicycle alongside. Other times he'd call Sara. She'd drive down with the SUV to bring him and his bike home. He kept working at it, getting a little further each time, and eventually he made it the whole way. He'd never admit it to anyone, but he was prouder at that moment than he had been on his wedding day or even when he held his firstborn just minutes after she'd come into the world.

There was no way Cullen would have called Sara tonight, whether he'd made it up the hill or not. He had phoned her late that afternoon, and given her a bullshit story about an important business dinner. He told her he should be home by nine; but it was just past eleven when he flashed past the marker indicating his turn would come in one more mile. He was trying to come up with a believable explanation for being so late when he heard a car approaching from the rear.

Cullen flinched involuntarily and considered pulling off the road. He had an open field to his left and, on his right, a low guardrail and then the ground dropped away sharply. He couldn't remember what was down there, maybe a line of trees or a dry riverbed. It was too dark to see all the way to the bottom and steep enough to make any exit that way potentially suicidal. He was effectively trapped.

Cullen fingered the switch for his handlebar-mounted headlight, hesitated, and then flipped it on. He hadn't bothered with the light before, in part because the moon provided plenty of illumination, but also because he hadn't wanted to draw unnecessary attention to himself. He knew he was being paranoid. He also knew there was a chance, perhaps a good chance, someone really was out to get him.

He kept going back to his last conversation with Carrie and the message from his so-called *college buddy.* That bit about going for a bike ride together--that was meant as a threat, or at least a warning. The guy was watching, as he'd said he would be, and had learned at least part of Cullen's routine. That was scary shit. He always trained alone, running through the woods, cycling late at night or early in the morning, and keeping that same schedule when it came to swimming laps in the pool at the Y. He'd never thought about it before but he'd been making an easy target of himself, and he'd ridden home tonight feeling like there were eyes on him every inch of the way.

Now, on a quiet road without another house or building within a quarter mile in any direction, Cullen realized he was a sitting duck. Someone could drive up, put a few bullets in him, toss him over the embankment and it might be days before his body was discovered. His rational mind told him that wouldn't happen. He knew the vehicle bearing down on him was most likely somebody on the way to the airport or headed home after a long day's work. But his thudding heart and over-stimulated imagination were telling him a very different story. Staring straight ahead, he hunched low and pumped his legs as fast as he could, all the while feeling like he had crosshairs on the back of his head. He was wearing his helmet, but was fairly sure a few ounces of plastic and foam would be no match for a high velocity projectile.

The engine got louder as the vehicle closed in on him. Cullen wanted to look so he'd at least know what was coming but his arms were shaking so badly it was all he could do to grip the handle bars and keep his front wheel pointed in the right direction. Why hadn't he at least called the guy back, argued his case and begged for more time? It was too late for any of that now, and he wouldn't even get to apologize to Sara. He thought about his lovely girls, and wondered what they'd think of their father once they learned the truth about him.

"I'm sorry," Cullen said, the small, jittery beam from his own headlight suddenly lost in the vehicle's high beams.

He moved as far to the right as he could, his right knee nearly brushing the guardrail. For a second, he considered veering across the road, dumping his bike in the weeds and taking off across the field. With any luck, he could make it as far as the distant tree line.

With any luck, he thought bitterly, knowing his had long since run out. The car, or truck, or fucking steamroller would probably run him down before he even made it across the center line.

"I'm sorry," he said again, ducking even lower and bracing himself for whatever was about to happen. He hoped it would be quick and painless.

Moments later, Cullen choked out a laugh when the car, an old Mazda compact, finally chugged past, pulling all the way into the left lane to give him plenty of room. In the glow from the dashboard lights, he could see that the driver was female and couldn't have been any more than eighteen. She barely glanced in his direction, instead singing and bopping her head to a pop song he couldn't quite make out over the engine noise. The car disappeared and Cullen was once again alone. His legs immediately turned to rubber and he had to get off the bike and walk the rest of the way to his house. He was sweating profusely and couldn't get his muscles to stop twitching even after stowing his bike in the garage, doing five minutes of stretching exercises, then retrieving a Sam Adams OctoberFest from his beer fridge and downing it in three long pulls.

The house was quiet and dark, which Cullen was thankful for. He'd been afraid he'd find Sara waiting up for him. She'd ask a bunch of questions he'd have no good answers for. That would lead to a fight, which would in turn lead to a pillow, a blanket and a lumpy sofa. The fact that she'd gone to bed indicated she was already pissed. Even so, at least he'd now have until morning to come up with a plausible excuse for his lateness. He could also spend some serious time taking stock of his situation and, God willing, coming up with a solution. He felt sure there had to be a way out. He just needed to find it.

He grabbed a second Sam Adams, let himself into the house, careful his ring of keys didn't knock against the metal kitchen door, and then tiptoed down the hall to his office. He paused in the doorway, listening for anything out of the ordinary. Hearing nothing, he entered and turned on a floor lamp but only after closing and locking the door behind him. Cullen again paused, trying to shake the lingering feeling he was being watched. He lowered the blinds, did a lap around the room and finally settled himself behind his pool table -sized desk. He set his beer bottle on the blotter and powered up his laptop, rocking in his chair until the Windows logo appeared.

His office was his sanctuary and had always been his favorite room in the house: dark wood, oriental rugs, leather wingback chairs, a bookshelf full of first edition classics, mostly unread, a crystal chess set, and the obligatory globe. The desk itself was an antique that had once belonged to a French duke. Cullen had paid almost five grand in transportation costs alone. He thought the globe was an antique too but couldn't remember where it came from. He certainly hadn't picked it out. His primary contributions to the decorating motif were limited to the sixty inch wall-mounted plasma television and his fully stocked wet bar. Looking in that direction, he considered a cocktail but, wanting to keep a clear head, decided it was best to stick with beer.

Once his computer's startup process was complete, Cullen opened Google Chrome, navigated to the First Niagara website and logged in, entering an email address, a password, and answering a series of security questions. He jumped through the requisite hoops, and then was able to view his various accounts. On the plus side, he hadn't borrowed enough money from Sara that she was likely to notice, even on the off chance she checked. He also hadn't ended up using her credit card, perhaps the only bit of good judgment he'd shown all week. The rest of his finances were, in short, a disaster.

As much as he would prefer to avoid it, Cullen knew he'd have to call Mrs. Banyard first thing in the morning. He could already picture that rotten potato face and hear her rusty car door of a voice as she painstakingly explained the obvious mess he was in. She might have the personality of a constipated rhino, but he'd still have to play her game because she possessed the power and maybe even the inclination to strip him of his home, his business, and all his material belongings.

At that moment, he was having a hard time caring because, regardless of what transpired at the bank, Janet Banyard wasn't likely to break his arms, take a baseball bat to his kneecaps or go after his family. He of course still had to deal with her but that was something he thought he could manage. A little fast talk, some money back in the till and perhaps a nice fruit basket and she'd be off his back, at least temporarily. That was all well and good except for one small detail. He wasn't immediately sure where he'd find the necessary capital since his latest foray to the casino hadn't exactly gone as planned.

After leaving the blackjack table where he'd met Jimmy the jerk off and the hottie in the cocktail dress, Cullen placed a few bets at the roulette table, won back at least a little of the money he'd lost, then spent an hour playing craps, a game he usually avoided. A black man in a wheel chair, an army coat and with a glass eye and missing right leg had been rolling the bones with a seriously hot hand. Cullen wanted to ask the guy if he'd suffered his injuries in combat, wanted to thank him for his service but wasn't about to mess with the man's mojo. He kept betting, rolling and winning and Cullen was only too happy to ride his military coattails. He got back to the break-even point, maybe even a few bucks ahead, and then the man abruptly stopped playing. Without a word to anyone, he scooped his chips into his lap, spun his chair around and wheeled away.

By that point, Cullen thought his own lucky streak had returned. He considered heading back to the blackjack table to show Jimmy how it was done, and probably would have had he not struck up an enticing *friendship* with the redheaded waitress who'd been bringing his drinks. She had smallish boobs, big thighs, and an annoying habit of finishing every sentence with a giggle. Cullen still wanted her because he'd never met a single redhead who didn't know how to fuck. Mandy, or maybe it was Candy or Brandy, proved to be something of a letdown in that department. He still had a good time with her especially when she let him play rear admiral, something Sara never allowed. He hadn't even had to spring for a room because she lived five minutes from the casino. They'd taken their own cars to her tiny apartment, which made Cullen's departure forty-five minutes later that much easier. He was afraid she'd beg him to stay but she seemed done with him almost as soon as he was done with her. So much the better.

He drove home feeling dirty, dishonest, and unfaithful. He knew that would all pass. And sex, even illicit sex, had always helped clear his head. Sure, he was doing something he shouldn't be doing but wasn't that preferable to gambling away even more of the family fortune? Cullen thought so and rationalized that if she knew, Sara would agree. It was true that his infidelities started long before his current financial troubles but that was ancient history. His job as a husband and a father was to do everything in his power to make things right. If that meant a quick tumble with a total bimbo what was the harm? At least it got him out of the casino. He'd had his fun, driven back to the office, left his car and retrieved his bike, but not before showering and changing clothes. He knew he'd have to shower again once he got home. Even on a cool night, he couldn't bike upwards of twelve miles, much of it uphill, without working up a serious sweat. Maybe his exertions would have masked any lingering smells of women and sex but it wasn't worth taking the chance.

Cullen picked up his beer, took a sip and held the bottle against his forehead, enjoying the sudden chill on his skin. He sat that way for several moments, then set the bottle aside and grabbed a Post-It and pen. He jotted down Janet Banyard's name and underlined it twice, not because she represented the biggest threat, far from it, but because that problem seemed to have the most immediacy and, in theory, should be the easiest to resolve. If he didn't get the bitch off his back, she might feel the need to call Sara, tell her what was going on and then all hell would break loose. He definitely wasn't ready for that.

Cullen was thinking in the short term because he thought that might be all he had. He stared at the name he'd written, underlined it a third time, then plucked a calculator out of his top desk drawer. He poked some keys, chewed a fingernail, then poked a few more, eventually sitting back and studying the digital display. If his calculations were correct, he figured he'd need around ten grand to get wolf number one away from the door. That sounded manageable enough, or would have if not for the bigger and badder wolf already breathing down his neck. Cullen knew that wolf had ears to hear and eyes to see. How sharp those teeth were remained to be seen. He wanted his money, and if Cullen was unable to deliver it, might come looking for a lot more than a pound of flesh. A second name was jotted down. Cullen looked at it briefly then slumped forward in his chair, not stopping until his head thumped against the desk.

-20-

"This bites," Bullfrog said for perhaps the tenth time.

"At least we're dry," Skid Row observed, picking up a flat stone and scaling it toward the river. He wanted to see how many times he could make it skip but the angle was wrong and his stone sliced into the water and disappeared with barely a ripple.

Bullfrog watched for a moment and then spat on the ground. "Who cares about dry?" he said. "I'd rather have something to smoke or something to eat."

"So eat me," Skid Row turned and grabbed his crotch. "Be the best meal you've had in days."

"Be the smallest anyway," Bullfrog muttered, staring at the rain pelting into the Susquehanna. The deluge was soundless, at least compared to the constant drone of traffic from above.

"That's not what your mom said.

"Yeah, and your mom's so dirty she has to wipe her feet before she goes outside." Bullfrog spat again, then looked up as an eighteen wheeler rumbled past. Ancient bridge supports rattled and bits of dirt and debris cascaded down. "You know what?" he said. "If that thing collapsed right now, if the whole bridge crumbled apart and landed in my lap, if, all of a sudden, I got buried under a pile of concrete, steel and whatever, that would probably be the best thing that's happened to me all year."

"That's pathetic."

"But it's true."

"What the hell's gotten into you?" Skid Row asked, walking in a circle and being sure to give Bullfrog plenty of room. "You've been acting like this ever since we left Ricky's place."

"Ricky's place. You make it sound like you two are buds. He's slime and that Carl guy is flat- out nuts. Did you see the way he was looking at us? Bullfrog shivered. "He wanted an excuse to tear us apart and didn't like it that his little boss man wouldn't let him do it."

Bullfrog picked up the top half of a broken Budweiser bottle, examined the jagged edges, then gripped the bottle by the neck and began digging a trough in the dirt.

Skid Row watched in silence and then turned to stare at the leaden sky. If anything, the intensity of the rain had increased. The clouds were low, dark and heavy, and there was no indication of the situation improving anytime soon. It would be dark before long, so at least he wouldn't have to look at their depressing little area he now called home. He tried to keep a positive outlook but, in the end, had to agree with Bullfrog's most recent status update. This did bite. They'd been camped out, hiding out was more like it, under the bridge for the past several hours. They'd devoured their small stash of food and a pile of smoldering ashes was all that remained of their camp fire. No big loss there because they'd about run out of firewood too. There was plenty in easy walking distance but it wasn't worth getting drenched. And thankfully, the night was warm enough that they didn't need a fire for heat.

"We got our stake," Skid Row said, eyeing the black duffle Ricky had given them. "Two grand could get us a long way."

Bullfrog made a noise somewhere between a grunt and a cough. He didn't look up from his task, using both hands for leverage as he gouged methodically at the soil.

Skid Row watched, his expression a combination of curiosity and concern. "If you don't mind me asking, what in hell are you doing?"

"Digging, why?" Bullfrog used the sleeve of his jean jacket to push a pile of newly excavated dirt out of his way.

Skid Row lowered himself onto the ground. "If I know what the goal is here, maybe I can give you a hand. You gonna try to get all the way to China? I could go for some Lo Mein."

Bullfrog made his grunting sound again.

Skid Row studied his progress for a while and then laid back on the hard ground, using the duffle as a makeshift pillow. He thought about retrieving his sleeping bag but decided it wasn't worth the effort. It felt good just to be off his feet for a while. Ricky had had Carl drive them back to town. That was nice and it saved them the bus fare. But, Skid Row didn't need Carl or Ricky knowing where they were living. He'd asked to be dropped off in front of a rundown apartment building over a mile away. He and Bullfrog had walked from there and the rain started to fall just as they neared their bridge.

All things considered, Skid Row thought the day could have gone a lot worse. Despite everything, his hair-brained plan had somehow worked. Ricky actually gave them a bag stuffed full of weed, crack, meth, and heroine, and told them exactly how much to charge for each item. He then explained when and where they needed to be on any given day, and instructed them to steer well clear of any gang-controlled areas or, as Ricky put it, "You'll end up fucking worm food just like

Marco." Twice a week, they'd meet and exchange money for drugs, and that would continue as long as all parties were satisfied.

There was one minor detail Skid Row had not counted on. Ricky had made it painfully clear that, at least in the early going, he and Bullfrog would be watched, by Ricky, by Carl, or perhaps by both. If Skid Row believed that claim, and he absolutely did, it would be damn near impossible to make a quick score and take off with the money. That left him with two choices. He could risk it, make a couple grand and leave town as quickly as possible. Or, he and Bullfrog could peddle drugs for as long as it took to gain Ricky's trust. That was by far the safer option but neither plan had much appeal. Unfortunately, it was too late to turn back. He couldn't very well return the drugs and say thanks anyway. Ricky had made that clear too. Now that Skid Row and Bullfrog knew something about his business they were, for better or worse, connected to him. He wouldn't let them simply walk away.

"We can still make this work," he said, talking as much to himself as to Bullfrog.

The only response he got was the sound of more digging. It increased in intensity, then the bottle cracked and Bullfrog swore. When Skid Row looked over, he was sucking on a finger.

"Is it bad, he asked, seeing a small dribble of blood.

"I'll live," Bullfrog said, "but who knows how much longer?" He tossed what was left of his bottle into the river. "Selling drugs. Wouldn't my parents be proud?"

"You don't have to do it," Skid Row said, propping himself on an elbow. "I'll tell Ricky you took off. As long as I'm still around, he wouldn't have any reason to look for you. Stick with your plan and get another dead end job somewhere."

"At least dead end jobs are safe," Bullfrog said.

"And why would you want that? A few minutes ago, you were wishing that whole bridge would come down on top of you."

Bullfrog looked up but said nothing.

Skid Row watched him for a while and then lay back down. He couldn't help feeling bad. The whole thing had, after all, been his idea. But, he never thought they'd be in danger because he never really believed they'd make it to this point. He hadn't thought Zatts would help them, hadn't thought they'd ever find Ricky or his trailer, hadn't really believed either existed. Even when Ricky disappeared into one of the trailer's back rooms, coming back a couple minutes later with the duffle, none of it had seemed real. Yet, there they were, literally sitting or at least lying on a couple thousand dollars. Bullfrog wasn't happy about it. *Well,* Skid Row thought, *too fucking bad.* It may have been his idea but it was Bullfrog's damn fault. He'd cost Skid Row his job, tailed him down the road afterwards and refused to leave him the hell alone. No one had forced him to do any of that. He still had the option to walk away. If he didn't do it, that was his problem and there wasn't any reason for Skid Row to feel responsible.

He closed his eyes and wondered what he should do. He actually considered digging into the bag for a free sample. They could both use a few tokes of relaxation. In the end, he didn't dare. Skid Row didn't know what that big goon might do if their very first transaction came up a few dollars short but it definitely wasn't worth finding out. Their best bet was to follow instructions, make a few sales and then see where things stood. There was one thing they had going for them. Normal jobs would have meant waiting a couple weeks for their first paychecks. This new endeavor would pay much quicker dividends.

Skid Row wondered where he should go when he finally had some real money in his pocket. He didn't especially dislike Binghamton. It just didn't seem to have much to offer. Maybe that was his own fault. He was dissatisfied but had to admit that he'd never made any real effort to better himself. And now? Could selling junk to crack heads and tweakers really be considered a step in the right direction? He tried to convince himself that it was--tried to rationalize that, at least for the short term, his plan made sense. He likewise did his best to ignore the nagging feeling that he'd made a terrible mistake.

Skid Row was dimly aware of Bullfrog moving around. There were footsteps followed by the sound of splintering wood. Either the rain had stopped and Bullfrog was attempting to revive their fire, or he just felt like breaking stuff. He didn't bother to look. His mind wandered. Before long, he started thinking about his father. It seemed like that had been happening more often lately. That was probably because his life was crap so his relationship with William naturally came to mind. At least the guy had never been abusive, not physically anyway. But, he sure knew how to throw an insult. Was it really any wonder? His wife left him and he'd been stuck with a punk kid. Skid Row's response was to lash out, directing every bit of his anger at his dad. In short, he'd done everything he could to make a bad situation worse. That didn't mean William was totally innocent. He hadn't had many good things to say even when Skid Row's mom was still in the picture. That may have been part of the reason she left. It was hard to say because Skid Row only had his father's side of that story. At least William had tried to make it work. Skid Row had to give him credit for that. He wondered where his dad was and what he was doing right then. He was still wondering that when he drifted off to sleep.

Skid Row woke to the sound of snoring. He opened an eye and saw Bullfrog, a few feet away and curled up in a tight ball. His mouth hung open and he was drooling.

"Lovely," Skid Row mumbled." He rolled onto his back and reached for his pillow, remembered he didn't have one and reached for the duffle bag. It wasn't there. He rolled onto his stomach and then got to his hands and knees. Everything looked completely normal. He saw his sleeping bag along with his small box of personal items. He saw Bullfrog's few belongings along with a pile of wood he'd evidently collected the night before. He saw Bullfrog's rusted campfire tool and the remnants of their last meal, and that was it. The black duffle bag was gone.

-21-

"Congratulations," Ricky said as soon as Carl opened the door and slid onto the passenger seat of the Lexus.

"What for?"

"Not fucking up for once."

Carl eyed him, dropped the duffle onto the floor and then shook his head, water droplets from his hair and beard spraying in every direction.

"Hey!" Ricky exclaimed, shrinking away. "You're soaking wet. You want to ruin my leather?" He opened a center console, grabbed a handful of napkins and began dabbing at the seat and dashboard.

"It's raining," Carl said; "or hadn't you noticed?"

"I noticed. I've been sitting here for the past two hours."

"That must have been rough on you with your nice comfy seat, your music and," he sniffed, "is that a hazelnut latte? I'm so sorry I kept you waiting."

Ricky ignored the snotty tone, concentrating instead on mopping up water. When he was done, he lowered his window and dumped the wad of sodden napkins onto the sidewalk. "Any problems?" he finally asked.

"Nope."

"They didn't see you?"

Carl frowned but didn't reply.

"Then what in hell took so long?"

"I stopped at a whore house along the way. I guess time just got away from me."

Ricky gave him a look.

"I had to wait for them to fall asleep. What do you think? You spent the last two hours sitting here. I spent the last two under a damn bush. I'm soaked to the skin and I may have rolled in poison ivy." He examined some pinkish splotches on his left wrist.

"Good thing you got all that hair. It probably protected you."

"I appreciate your sympathy." Carl turned to stare out at the rain. "You know, I would have bet money those two didn't really live in the apartments where I dropped them off but I wouldn't have thought they were homeless either. That's gotta be tough."

"You feeling sorry for them then? You want to take the bag back?"

Carl smiled thinly. "I was surprised you gave it to them in the first place." He poked the duffle with the toe of his boot. "You'd think they'd be more careful. You told them we'd be watching, but from the time I dropped them off, they didn't look around one time. It was like they were in their own little world. I was able to ditch my truck and still follow them without any trouble."

"So they're idiots," Ricky said. "What's your point?"

Carl poked at the bag again. "You gave them two grand worth of junk. I just returned it to you. That helps clear my ledger, right?"

"You kidding?"" Ricky said with a laugh, starting the Lexus, putting it in gear and pulling a fast U-turn, nearly flattening a NO U-TURN sign in the process.

Carl immediately reached for his seatbelt.

"We ain't even close to square. For one thing," Ricky said, "all you did was retrieve my property. It's not worth any more now than it was a few hours ago. And for another," he smirked, "the contents of that bag aren't worth anywhere near two thousand dollars."

Carl stared at him. "But you said--"

"I lied," Ricky cut in. "I lied to a couple of losers. I told them what was in the bag and how much it was worth. It's not my problem they were stupid enough to believe me without even checking. And before you get all judgmental, I'd like to remind you that you weren't exactly truthful when you threatened to dump them in the river."

"That was different."

"How so?" Ricky asked, swerving around a beat up Buick with Domino's Delivery on the side.

Carl clutched the hand hold above the door. "You made a deal."

"Yeah? Well I just changed the terms. You got a problem with that?"

"But why?"

Ricky sighed. He didn't understand why Carl seemed so bothered. It wasn't like shady business dealings were anything new to them. "I don't need to explain myself to you but I'll do it anyway. That scrawny kid..."

"Skid Row," Carl offered.

"Whatever. He came right out and told me he only smoked weed. I could tell he wasn't a serious tweaker and didn't know much about hard drugs. And that other guy..."

"Bullfrog."

"He didn't seem to know much about anything. I don't think he even wanted to be there."

"What makes you say that?"

"It doesn't matter. The point is, I knew they were in way over their heads and I saw a way we could capitalize on that."

"How?" Carl asked, looking interested but still unhappy.

"Simple. They now think they owe us two large. They're already scared shitless so they'll be highly motivated to pay us back."

"But that's what I don't get. They looked like bums. Where are they supposed to come up with that kinda money?"

"Not my problem," Ricky said. "They'll have to figure it out."

Carl sat, gazing out the passenger side window, his jaw working silently. Ricky studied his reflection in the windshield and could tell Carl was struggling to put it all together. He obviously had something to say and seemed to be debating whether or not he should say it.

"What is it?"Ricky asked, sailing through a yellow light just as it changed to red, and then wheeling into the Binghamton Plaza parking lot. The Lexus lurched violently as he bumped over a series of water-filled potholes. "Shit!" he swore, struggling to hang onto the steering wheel. He hadn't been wearing his seatbelt and nearly slammed his head against the roof of the car.

"You could try slowing down," Carl suggested.

"Are you saying that was my fault? Someone should fill those things in. Better yet, bring in a bulldozer and level the whole place."

Carl didn't reply, and Ricky headed to the far end of the lot where they'd met earlier in the evening. He passed the K-mart, a card shop and a couple empty storefronts, and then pulled into a parking spot right next to Carl's truck.

"So what's your problem?" he asked, killing the engine and turning in his seat. "I can tell this is bugging you. Why?"

"I don't know," Carl said. He glanced at the duffle bag and then went back to staring out the window. "It seems like you're messin' with those guys for no reason. It doesn't seem... I don't know... fair I guess."

Fair? Ricky was baffled. Since when had that mattered? He'd never known Carl to have anything resembling scruples and it was really throwing him off.

"Why would you even care?" he asked. "Those guys don't mean anything to you. Besides, I'm doing you a favor."

"Me?" Carl tapped his own chest and shook his head like he really wanted no part of it.

"You bet your ass," Ricky said. "You owe me because you screwed things up so badly with Marco. He's got an outstanding bill I'm pretty damn sure won't be paid. And that ain't your only mistake lately either. You can't afford to pay me back. I've worked it out so someone else is on the hook. Am I a genius or what?"

Carl looked down and began fingering his little red notebook.

"I don't get this," Ricky said. "You should be thanking me. You should be ready to suck me off, but you're sitting there acting like I've done something horrible."

"Yeah," Carl said. "I just--"

"You just what? You created the problem. I came up with a solution. End of story."

"But those two guys," Carl gestured as if they might be standing right outside the car. "They offered to take Marco's place. They wanted to work for you."

"Right," Ricky said. "And what do you suppose would have happened if I'd let them do it?"

Carl blinked. "They would have earned back the money and then some."

"No!" Ricky said, banging a fist on the steering wheel. "That's the part you don't understand."

"But someone's got to take over for Marco, right? You had two guys willing to do it and, well, you sort of screwed them."

"And I was doing them a favor too."

Carl opened his mouth but closed it again without saying a word.

"Let me ask you something," Ricky said, growing irritated. He didn't appreciate the way Carl was questioning his actions, but had to control his temper because he knew this wouldn't work if Carl wasn't fully onboard. "What," he asked, "do you think would happen if no one did take Marco's place?"

Carl thought for a moment. "I guess gangs would probably move in after a while."

"Hey, bright boy. Except it's a good bet they've started moving in already. I think we lost that territory as soon as you turned Marco into a piñata."

"You sure?"

"No, but it's not worth taking the chance."

Carl looked at him.

"Marco came from one of those gangs," Ricky explained. "He had connections. He had... street cred. We can't replace that. It's really the only reason they left him alone. It definitely wasn't out of respect for you or me. Now that he's gone," Ricky shrugged. "I'm pretty sure they'll take advantage of the situation."

"And you think..."

"If we sent those two out there," Ricky said, "they would have been eaten alive in no time. Marco didn't have a lot of territory but he had his steady customers. His death will end up costing us a lot more than the money he owed."

Carl considered. "But maybe we could have used them for a while, just until we found somebody better."

Ricky shook his head. "They wouldn't have lasted an hour. They'd have been scared off, ripped off, or killed, and probably all three. We have to face facts. We've lost that particular revenue stream."

Carl looked like he wanted to object but Ricky didn't give him the chance.

"You gotta trust me on this one," he said. "It wasn't worth the risk." He watched as an old man, swaddled in a bright yellow trench coat, materialized from somewhere behind the K-Mart. He had a pronounced limp and appeared to be in the middle of a heated discussion with the shopping cart he pushed in front of him. It was overflowing with cans, bottles, clothing, and what looked like an empty bird cage. Maybe he was talking to the bird that was supposed to be in there. Ricky muttered something about lunatics and drunks and refocused on Carl.

"I know we had our problems with Marco when it came to paying on time. He still came through in the end and, bottom line, we could trust him. You know what I'm sayin'? We kept all the issues in-house. No matter what happened, he'd never use our names in connection with anything.

Now think about how those two losers looked the first time they saw you. They were scared to death and all you'd done was opened the door. How long would it take them to give us up if they were questioned by the cops or some bad-ass gang leader? We don't need that kind of hassle. Thanks to you and your axe handle, we may already have some of Binghamton's finest looking at us more closely than I would like."

"Okay, then why deal with Skid Row and Bullfrog at all? You obviously don't trust them."

"Of course not."

"Then why do it? You could have just sent them on their way. Hell, if you hadn't identified yourself, they would have left on their own. They didn't know what you looked like."

"True," Ricky said; "but they'd gotten my name from somewhere. I don't like that."

"They mentioned somebody named Zatts."

"Right," Ricky said, rubbing at the stubble on his chin. "We may need to... follow up on that if you catch my drift. I don't know who's talking about me but it needs to stop."

"I can take care of that," Carl said, starting to reach for the door handle.

"Not yet," Ricky said. "You should probably try to keep your head down for now. Besides, you've got a more important assignment."

"Skid Row and Bullfrog?" Carl asked, as if he didn't like the taste the two names left in his mouth.

"That's right."

"So what do you want me to do?"

"Not sure yet. By swiping that bag," Ricky jabbed a thumb towards the floor, "we've put them in a tough spot. They'll have to react. We need to figure out how to take advantage of that. And no thanks to you, we've had a lot more money going out than coming in. I expect you will remedy that very soon. In the mean time, seems we have ourselves a couple new puppets. If we pull their strings the right way, they can make up for everything we lost and then some."

"Meaning?"

Ricky smiled dangerously. "You get to do what you do best. The way I see it, they'll be on the move as soon as they realize the bag is gone."

"How do you know that?"

"Easy," Ricky said, spreading his hands. "They got no choice. They sit still and we know exactly where to find them. My guess is they'll be trying very hard to stay out of sight. They might even try to skip town. Of course, their resources will be limited. Do you think you can find them and keep track of their whereabouts?"

"In my sleep."

"Fine," Ricky said. "Then that's what I want you to do."

"Discretely, right?"

Ricky started to nod but then reconsidered. "Actually," he said, a new plan beginning to form, "I only want it to look like you're trying to stay out of sight."

"Then you want..." Carl started and then stopped.

"I want you to...occasionally...make your presence known. Don't get close to them. Don't speak to them. Don't lay a hand on them. Just make sure they see you once in a while. We told them they'd be watched. They need to think we're looking over their shoulders no matter where they go."

"Then what?" Carl asked, sounding like he might be starting to warm to the idea.

"I'll make contact when the time is right. By then, I think they'll be willing to do just about anything I ask."

-22-

"I knew it!" Bullfrog muttered, only half out loud.

Skid Row wanted to respond but knew there wasn't a hell of a lot he could say. He caught Bullfrog's nervous glance over his shoulder. "There's nobody back there," he said, resisting the urge to do the same thing.

"Yeah? You so sure about that? "They followed us back to the bridge yesterday."

"We don't know that."

"Well it's a damn good guess. Besides, they told us they'd be watching. What makes you think they're not doing that right now?"

They hurried along, skirting a line of trees that ran parallel to some old train tracks. Rain from the night before had given way to blue sky and sunshine. That didn't make their current outlook any brighter.

Skid Row shook hair out of his eyes. "You really need to calm down."

"I'll be happy to if you can come up with one good reason why I should." He looked backwards again and nearly tripped over his bedroll.

"Nobody's following us." Skid Row insisted. "How could they? There's nowhere to hide."

He hoped that was true, and tried inspecting their surroundings without making it look like that's what he was doing. The trees were sparse and mostly bare. Even the few evergreens were too small to conceal an adult body, especially one the size of Carl's. The closest building was well off in the distance, with not much in between but rocks, weeds and shrubs. Skid Row still looked twice at every shadow, and nearly jumped out of his shoes when a large crow cawed indignantly and took flight.

Bullfrog snickered. "I guess you're not so tough after all."

"It just surprised me."

"Scared you is more like it. And you should be scared too--not of birds but of raving maniacs."

"We don't even know it was them."

Bullfrog gave him a sideways glance. "It was them."

"You keep saying that but there's no proof."

"What kind of proof do you want? Wait a minute," Bullfrog added, slapping his forehead as if he'd just had a revelation. "I almost forgot. How about the missing bag? Is that good enough for you, or were you gonna try to tell me someone else took it?"

"It's possible," Skid Row said, thinking that sounded lame even to him. He still wasn't ready to give in to Bullfrog's fear and paranoia. "Other people use that camp," he argued. "They were walking through all the time. It's not private property. Someone could have wandered in while we were asleep, seen the bag and took off with it."

"And you really think that's what happened?"

Skid Row didn't, so he tried a different tack. "Are you sure you didn't move it?"

Bullfrog looked at him with scorn. "I told you six times already. It was right between us when I went to sleep. I didn't move it. I didn't touch it. Do you want me to take a stinking polygraph?"

"No," Skid Row said. "I'm just trying to figure out what happened."

"I told you what happened," Bullfrog snarled, a line of spittle forming at the corner of his mouth. "Your buddies screwed us."

"But that doesn't make sense. And they're not my buddies."

Bullfrog stopped and looked at him. "I don't see why this is so tough for you to get your head around. They gave us the bag. They're the only ones who knew we had it. Now the bag is gone. What does that tell you?"

"I know what you're saying. It still doesn't add up. Why would they give it to us only to swipe it again a little while later? What's the point?"

"What's the point?" Bullfrog's mouth fell open. "Did you really just ask that? We now owe them two thousand bucks!"

"But, dude, just look at us." Skid Row spread his arms wide as he took in Bullfrog's threadbare work pants, well-worn boots and dingy flannel shirt. His own wardrobe was no better. "We got nothing,'" he said. "It's not like we're strolling around in gold chains and leather. We have no possible means of paying them back so what would they gain from double crossing us?"

He thought he must have scored a point with that one because Bullfrog didn't respond. They continued along in silence for several minutes, each carrying his own pitifully small supply of personal belongings. Skid Row shifted his cardboard box from one arm to the other. It had gotten heavy and he thought about just dumping the whole thing right there by the train tracks. With the exception of his sleeping bag and clothes, it was pretty much all junk anyway.

"We can't just carry our stuff around forever," he observed, really just to have something to say.

"We can't go back to the bridge either," Bullfrog pointed out. "We gotta find a new place."

"You got anything in mind?"

"Sort of," Bullfrog said. "The river is over... that way," he gestured with his head. "I say we keep moving in that direction."

"Great. We can build a raft and float the fuck away."

"Not a bad idea," Bullfrog mumbled.

"Seriously?"

"We were talking about getting out of here. This might be the perfect time."

Skid Row knew Bullfrog was joking, about the raft anyway, but that wasn't their only option. He stared off down the tracks. He'd never been on a train and wondered what it would be like: rattling along, looking out at the changing landscape, leaving his worries far behind as towns slipped past one after another. Of course, with no means for buying a ticket, he'd be doing all his sightseeing from the hard floor of a freight car. He might end up sharing his glorious tour of the countryside with farm animals, industrial fertilizer or barrels of toxic waste. That was assuming he could sneak into one of those cars in the first place. It always looked easy enough in the movies, but life, he'd long since come to realize, was no movie.

"No moolah, dude," Skid Row said. "That's what got us into this mess."

"It doesn't cost anything to walk."

It didn't cost anything to hop a train either but transportation wasn't their only problem. "What about food?" Skid Row asked. "That's never free."

"So we'll figure it out. I made it all the way here from Maine. A lot of it was on foot. What do we have to lose?"

Skid Row remembered what Bullfrog had said about his travels. He had come a long way for sure, but worked a lot of jobs and never moved on until he had some cash in his pockets. Those pockets were empty now, but it really wasn't worth arguing about. He blew out a breath, eyeing his cardboard box and thinking about what it represented. The sad truth was, he couldn't come up with one good answer to Bullfrog's question. He had--they had--nothing to lose because neither one of them had anything. It still didn't feel right to just run. He'd been in Binghamton a long time. It was familiar, and with familiarity came a certain level of comfort, misguided or otherwise. He didn't think he was ready to turn his back on that.

"You can go," Skid Row said. "I don't want to, not 'til I know there's a need."

"You should know that already."

"All I know is that the bag is gone. I don't know who took it or why."

Bullfrog started to speak but Skid Row didn't give him the chance.

"I know," he said. "You think it was Ricky and Carl. Maybe you're right. That doesn't mean we're in any danger."

Bullfrog's eyes got wide. "How can you say that?"

"Easy." None of it made any sense but there was one thing Skid Row thought he knew for sure. "If they wanted us dead we'd be dead already. They could have done it at their trailer or back at the bridge, or anywhere in between. They didn't, which means it was never part of their plan."

"But--"

"But nothin', man. If they took the bag, we don't have anything to worry about until we know what they're up to."

"So what if they didn't do it?" Bullfrog asked.

"Then they don't even know it's gone. We're in the clear until it's time to pay them back."

"I don't like it," Bullfrog said.

"Shit, dude. I don't like it either. I'm just not going to run until I know who or what I'm running from."

"Then what do you want to do?"

Skid Row didn't have much of an answer for that one. He examined their surroundings. He saw train tracks, rocks, weeds, trees and more trees. "Like you said, we need a new camp, somewhere we're not gonna be found. I want a few days, just so I can try to figure out what's what."

"And then?"

Skid Row shrugged. "I guess that depends on what I find out. You can take off now. I'll give you half the money I've got left." He only made the offer because he knew or at least thought he knew it wouldn't be accepted.

"A few days?" Bullfrog echoed.

"Sure," Skid Row said. "Just so we can see."

"I guess that would be all right."

"We'll just need a place to hole up for a while."

"Fine," Bullfrog said. "I'll find us a new camp and you figure out what in hell is going on."

-23-

Andrew Cullen sprinted down the sidewalk, sweat streaming as he pushed himself to run even faster. His calf muscles screamed and his breath burned in his chest but he didn't let up. He'd set his alarm for five but was up and out of the house long before it went off. He biked the long way to work, going a good five miles out of his way. He still made it to the office before sunrise. He deposited his bike, then returned to the street to begin his run. He had about forty-five minutes so planned out a course that he figured was between six and seven miles. It was mostly flat which allowed him to maintain a hard, steady pace. He needed to be back in time to get cleaned up and still make it to First Niagara Bank when they opened for business.

Physical pain notwithstanding, Cullen felt a little better about himself because he finally had some semblance of a workable plan. He'd start by getting his bank accounts in slightly better order, and that began with a three thousand dollar withdrawal from the wall safe in his office at home. He would have taken more if he could, but the safe was now empty with the exception of some documents and a few pieces of Sara's pricier jewelry. He'd considered taking some of that too. She had more than she needed, including an exquisite diamond bracelet that was worth at least eight grand.

In one of his more desperate moments, he'd actually thought about staging a burglary. His antique globe alone would probably fetch enough to get Janet Banyard off his back and everything was well-insured. He'd just have to mess up his office, break a few things, throw books and papers around, and take a crow bar to the door of the safe. What he liked about the idea was that it would allow him to double dip, making claims for items that hadn't really been stolen. He could then sell those items on the side.

There were, of course, drawbacks. First, he'd be screwed if he got caught hawking his own shit. Next, insurance claims took time, a commodity he was currently running short on. And finally, and this was the big one, he could not subject himself or his family to a police investigation. His financial situation might come to light, and if the cops found a loose thread, he knew they'd tug. That would lead to all sorts of uncomfortable questions, and the whole mess would be right out in the open. Cullen couldn't take the chance on a risky stunt like that because, with the amount of stress he'd been under, he knew he wasn't thinking clearly enough to pull it off. He'd do or say something stupid and that would be the end of it.

He told himself such drastic measures weren't yet necessary anyway. He had the three large, and that should prevent Mrs. Banyard from spitting in his face. He also anticipated having a lot more money to give her by the end of the day. It was just as well he'd left his Jag at work the night before. It would make it that much easier to sell.

The car was conveniently due for service. Cullen decided he'd tell Sara the mechanic discovered some engine problem and a repair would cost more than it was worth. He hated the idea of unloading his beautiful Jag but knew that was the quickest way to get some cash in his pocket. How far could he downgrade without raising suspicion? He thought about the rattletrap Mazda that had scared him so badly on Airport Road the night before. What would the fam say if he cruised into the driveway behind the wheel of a rust bucket like that?

Even if Cullen's new plan worked out, he knew he had a far heavier weight still hanging over his head. In addition to the ten grand or so he needed to deposit ASAP, he still had to come up with twice that amount, and that was only to cover the slightly overdue interest on his loan. Two weeks down the road, he'd owe that much again. Just where in the hell was he supposed to come up with it? Maybe he could renegotiate. And maybe, Cullen thought bitterly, he was totally insane for agreeing to such horrible terms in the first place. The interest payments would continue unless he could somehow pay down on the principal. He probably wasn't going to score a hundred large on a lottery scratch off or in a box of Cracker Jacks so he needed to be more proactive.

The Jag was the first of many personal belongings he thought he could liquidate. Unfortunately, with employees, wives and other family members looking on, he would have to proceed with caution. He couldn't, for example, replace his ornate desk with something made of glass and tubular metal that he'd ordered from Ikea, anymore than he could sell off the privately commissioned marble statue in the office lobby in favor of a potted fern. People wouldn't just wonder what was going on. They'd think he'd completely lost his mind.

Cullen started a mental list of things he thought he could safely part with. It included a couple high end rifles he hadn't used in years, a minor real estate holding, some sports memorabilia, including a baseball signed by most of the key players on the 1969 Mets World Series team, and some other odds and ends. He wasn't sure how much the stuff would bring but had no doubt it wouldn't be near enough.

As he jogged past the Veterans Memorial Arena, ignoring the burning cramp that had begun working its way steadily up his right side, Cullen had the glimmer of an idea, and it soon morphed into something larger and more promising. It was, he decided, a stroke of pure genius. There'd be some risk. He knew that; but if handled properly, it could be the answer to his prayers.

The previous fall, he'd raced in the Tri-Cities Triathlon, an Olympic length competition consisting of a 1.5 kilometer open water swim, a 25K bike race and a 10K run. Despite not training as hard as he might have, Cullen still finished with an overall time that placed him twelfth for his age and gender class. He won some small prizes, all provided by various corporate sponsors. It was only later that he learned the race had a number of private benefactors as well. One of the biggest was a former Binghamton resident named Jonathan Ruben.

Ruben, Cullen now knew, had made a fortune in pharmaceuticals before shifting his focus to natural health options. A triathlon competitor himself, he became one of the nation's largest advocates for proper diet and exercise. He died at the age of ninety-two, just weeks after running a half marathon.

Ruben had donated millions of dollars to fitness centers, local parks, youth sports and physical fitness education. He'd been instrumental in starting the Tri-Cities Triathlon, participated in the event for nearly three decades, and typically offered a thousand dollars to anyone who finished ahead of him. Most years, he didn't pay out a dime. Upon his death, however, event organizers learned he had set up a trust. It was worth fifty-thousand dollars a year, and would only be paid out as long as certain criteria were met. First, other sponsors had to match him dollar for dollar. The first year that didn't happen, the trust money would disappear forever. Second, one hundred percent of the money collected had to be paid to the various winners. And third, exactly half had to go to the overall winner for men age forty-four to forty-nine. It was no big mystery why Ruben chose that particular age group to favor. He was forty-seven when he sold off all his pharmaceutical interests and started down a new, healthier path. Cullen didn't give a shit what the guy's motivations were. To him, it meant a shot at fifty grand.

In addition to the possibility of a nice windfall, preparing for the triathlon presented a few other benefits. A rigorous exercise schedule would keep him out of the casinos and away from all the related temptations. He'd be out of the house a good sixteen hours a day too. He and Sara were in a bit of a rough patch, even if she wasn't fully aware of it yet, and Cullen supposed keeping his distance was the safest way to avoid a major blow up. And most important, training for three events at once, he'd have to alter his schedule and that would make him less predictable and a lot harder to track down. That's what he was hoping anyway. He still didn't know if anyone was really looking for him, but if not, they surely would be soon enough. Why make it easy on them?

The triathlon was just under three weeks away. That was both good and bad. He'd have to bust his ass to get ready in time. It would suck but he thought he could do it. On the plus side, assuming he won, he'd only have to wait nineteen more days to collect his prize. How he would survive that long was still anyone's guess. He'd sell off what he could, collect as much cash as possible, appease Mrs. Banyard, *the ugly old bitch,* give his money-grubbing grease ball loan shark enough of a deposit to hopefully buy some time, and then do everything in his power to stay under the radar.

As Cullen approached the front door of the bank, his business-suited reflection looking far more confident than he felt, two aspects of his plan still troubled him. Who was he kidding? The entire thing was one giant disaster waiting to happen. There were, however, two specific details which could potentially set off the whole powder keg.

First, although staying under the radar sounded like the most sensible course of action, Cullen knew it would be far easier said than done. He had a home and a job. He could vary his hours to a degree. He could log-on to the network remotely and work from anywhere. He could even arrange a business trip. There were clients he could see--enough to keep him on the road for several days. That was a far cry from the nearly three weeks he needed. Eventually, he'd have to go to the office and he'd have to go home. If someone was patient enough, determined enough, he could stake out either location and simply wait for Cullen to walk into the trap.

It was, Cullen supposed, at least conceivable the little weasel didn't know where he lived. The odds of that were probably about the same as the odds of Janet Banyard winning a beauty pageant or a congeniality award. Cullen wasn't about to take the chance anyway--not with Sara and the girls just sitting there, unaware of the danger and totally defenseless.

And second, and this was the thought that had his balls shriveling a little more with every step, he couldn't completely disappear even if he wanted to. Sure. With the three grand he already had, Cullen knew he could return to his Jag, drive the few miles to the airport and purchase a ticket to Canada or Mexico or somewhere. Or, he could go straight past the airport, keep driving and filling the gas tank until his supply of cash was gone. He'd be safe, at least for a while, but he'd be walking away from his family, his business, and all possible sources of revenue. Sara would have to sell the house to pay off debts she didn't even know existed. She'd also report him missing, and he doubted it would take long for police to follow whatever trail he left. He'd end up broke, humiliated and probably divorced too. That wouldn't do. Cullen had to at least begin to make things right, and that meant a face to face meeting with the person, people actually, he'd been trying so hard to avoid. It couldn't be avoided anymore.

"Good morning," Mrs. Banyard said, opening her office door and gesturing for him to come in and sit down. "It's nice to see you."

The banker's tone and cold expression suggested she meant nothing of the kind. Cullen was too distracted to be offended. She held his fate in her hands but about all he could think about right then was Ricky Fixx and his scary-ass partner.

-24-

"Where in God's name are we going?" Skid Row asked as he picked his way through a tangle of wild berry bushes. The branches were bare of everything but prickers and he swore as they raked at his clothes and skin.

"Stop complaining," Bullfrog called over a shoulder. "We're almost through and you'll be thanking me in a few minutes."

"I bet," Skid Row groused. He slapped at a mosquito and it left a wet, sticky smear along the side of his neck. "If this is a joke, notice I ain't laughin', dude."

"You want a new camp, don't you?"

"That doesn't mean I want to go all…" he tried to come up with someone bad ass and outdoorsy but that Crocodile Hunter freak was the best he could come up with. "I just don't want to walk all the way back to Maine."

"I figured we'd try Canada instead," Bullfrog answered, deadpan.

"Real fucking funny."

"Just trying to brighten your day. You see? Here we go." Bullfrog picked up his pace as brambles gave way to a thick bed of pine needles.

Skid Row looked around in amazement. The Binghamton he knew had completely vanished. He felt like he'd somehow stepped onto another planet. Huge trees surrounded him on all sides, their branches swaying in the breeze and creating ever-changing patterns of sunlight and shadow. Gone were the car horns, blaring rap music and shrieking sirens. Instead, he heard buzzing insects and the soft call of what he thought was a mourning dove. Of course, for all he knew about birds, it could have as easily been an ostrich. He just knew he liked the sound. He also knew he wasn't about to share that information. Skid Row resented the fact that Bullfrog had somehow taken charge of their situation. He let him because he had no choice but it still pissed him off.

"You got a destination in mind or are we just gonna wander around until dark?"

"Is there somewhere else you need to be?"

"As a matter of fact, yes."

Bullfrog turned to look at him.

"Marco had a routine," Skid Row said. "At noon today, he's supposed to be near a payphone on the corner of Clinton Street. That's so he can sell to all the Binghamton High School students when they're out on their lunch breaks."

"You're gonna sell drugs to kids?" Bullfrog looked disgusted.

"I'm not selling to anyone," Skid Row said. "I got nothin' to sell. Remember?"

"Then why go?"

Skid Row gave a sly smile. "Because that's where Ricky and Carl will expect us to be, and that means that's where they'll be."

"Are you nuts? They'll catch you."

"Give me some credit," Skid Row said. "It's not like I'm gonna hang out right there by the phone and wait for them to show up. I'll find an out-of-the way place where I can watch and see what they're up to."

"What if they don't show?"

Skid Row shrugged. "Might still find out something. And if they are there, I bet I'll be able to tell whether or not they took the bag by how they act."

"Yeah? You a detective now?"

Skid Row frowned. "I just think it's worth a try."

"It's got to be about ten-thirty," Bullfrog said, looking up at the treetops. "Should we just head that way now?"

"We're not heading anywhere," Skid Row said, feeling like he was gaining the upper hand again. "We go together and there's a better chance we get spotted. We'll set up a camp now. And, since it looks like it's going to be in the middle of freakin' nowhere, we'll need some supplies. You buy food while I scope out the payphone. We'll meet up later and see where we're at. "

"But what if something happens?" Bullfrog asked.

Skid Row used a hand to brush hair away from his face. "Then take your bag of food and go. You didn't want any part of this anyway."

Bullfrog started to object when a sudden rapping brought them both up short. They stared at each other and then spun around.

As incredible as it seemed, Skid Row's first thought was that Ricky and Carl had followed them after all. He had just about gotten over his paranoia but now it was back with a vengeance. And if they had somehow been tailed into the woods, he knew they were done for because it proved there was nowhere at all they could hide. His sleeping bag was the closest thing he had to a weapon. Maybe he could stuff it over Carl's head and at least slow him down long enough to attempt a getaway. Except, Carl wasn't there. Ricky wasn't either. Their little forest was as quiet and as empty as it had been moments before.

"What the...?" but Skid Row's words were interrupted when the rapping started up again. His eyes immediately flew upward.

"Stupid woodpecker," Bullfrog spat, turning and continuing on his way.

Skid Row watched for a few seconds, wondering how an animal could spend his days repeatedly slamming his head into solid wood without getting dizzy or suffering splitting headaches. How in hell did the thing even stay balanced? He shook his head, turned and hurried to catch up.

"Almost there," Bullfrog said.

"How do you know?"

To Skid Row, it didn't look like their surroundings had changed. The ground started to slope down somewhat. Otherwise, everything seemed pretty much the same. He wondered if Bullfrog had any real idea where he was going and why they'd spent so much of the morning traipsing around in the woods.

Damn waste of time, he thought. Just because their bridge was no longer safe, at least according to Bullfrog, that didn't mean they had to go on a walking tour of greater Broome County. Okay, so they needed a camp. They could have found one closer to town. Skid Row was irritated: at Ricky and Carl for scaring them so bad, at Bullfrog for leading them who knew where, and at himself for getting them into trouble in the first place. But really, that was Bullfrog's fault too, because none of it would have happened if he hadn't acted like such a fucking whacko.

His eyes fell on a fat gray squirrel, busy trying to carry two large nuts up a tree. His destination appeared to be a small hole maybe eight feet off the ground. He got both nuts in his mouth, started to climb, then half of his cargo came tumbling to the ground. It happened twice, and each time, the squirrel went chasing after the runaway nut, as if he was afraid a rival squirrel would scurry in and snatch his prize. Skid Row wanted to help him. He also had the urge to rush over, kick the little rodent right in the acorns and tell him to wise up. He thought that was maybe what he needed to do too.

He'd only known Bullfrog a couple of days. In that time, his life, which hadn't been all that great to begin with, had been completely turned upside down. Bullfrog wasn't exactly speeding down the road to success either. Wouldn't they both be better off if they just parted ways?

Skid Row studied Bullfrog's departing back. He'd gotten well ahead, and looked totally fixated on something Skid Row couldn't make out from such a distance. He wondered what it was, but realized he didn't really care. He also realized that, by simply changing course, he could fade into the trees in a matter of seconds. Would Bullfrog even bother looking for him? Maybe, Skid Row thought, but not very long or hard.

Bullfrog was accustomed to living off the land and would do fine on his own. Skid Row felt far less prepared for whatever lay ahead, but also didn't like the idea of relying on anyone for help. He'd been flying solo for years and decided he wanted to keep it that way. He told himself it was all for the best, and took a couple hesitant steps to his left. His decision made, he was about to break into a run when he heard a startled yelp, and he turned just in time to see the top of Bullfrog's head disappear from view. That was followed by another shout and a hollow thump. He rushed forward to see what had happened.

"You all right?" Skid Row called.

"Yeah," Bullfrog said, his voice oddly muffled. "Just beautiful."

Skid Row approached a spot where the ground dropped off sharply. It had also gotten much rockier and many of the rocks were covered in some sort of greenish moss. He didn't need to step on one to know it was slippery, and Bullfrog had evidently found out the hard way.

"You sure?" Skid row asked, clinging to a sapling as he peered over the edge. When he spotted Bullfrog, he had to stifle a laugh.

His clothes and other things were scattered all around him, all except for his bedroll which was still tangled around his legs. Bullfrog had worked himself into a sitting position, his back against an old tree stump, and was busy spitting out leaves. "Watch that first step," he said. "It's a doozy."

"I see that." Skid Row began making his way downward, placing each foot carefully and grasping at weeds and rocks with one hand while holding his box with the other. "Let me help you."

"Little late for that," Bullfrog said. He got to his knees and finally to his feet. "Let's go." He turned and continued his trek downhill. "Not far now."

"What about your stuff?"

"Leave it," Bullfrog called. "We'll come back for it all once we find a better way in."

Skid Row shrugged and dropped his box. Even if they never came back, what the hell was the difference? "You ready to tell me where we're going?"

"You don't hear it yet?"

Skid Row stopped and cocked his head. He heard something, and he realized he'd been hearing it for a while. It hadn't really registered and he thought he must have automatically dismissed it as the drone of traffic. He realized now the sound was too steady and pitched a little too high. It sounded more like white noise, and then it clicked.

"How did you know?" he asked, looking all around but still seeing nothing.

Bullfrog's gaze was on his feet. "That first year after my parents died, I spent a lot of time wandering around the woods. I told you about that, right?"

"A little."

“It was hard living but I learned a lot."

"About what?"

Bullfrog was silent for a while. The muscles around his jaw tightened and he was obviously still dealing with a lot of pain. Skid Row was suddenly glad he hadn't abandoned his odd new companion. Bullfrog might be more self-sufficient. That didn't mean he'd be better off alone. He could see that now.

"I guess I just learned how to survive," Bullfrog said. "I know how to find water, shelter, whatever...."

"What about food?"

"It was easy enough at first--a lot tougher once the snow came. Hell of a lot of snow in Maine in the winter time."

"Couldn't you...trap animals and stuff?"

"Like a moose?" Bullfrog gave a humorless laugh. "I'm happy to say it never came to that. I caught fish, crabs, stuff like that. That's as far as it went."

"You're not gonna find much of that around here."

"I know. Like you said before, we'll bring supplies in. That will hopefully be enough to get us by."

Skid Row's right hand automatically went to his pocket. He had some money left but it wasn't enough to last long. Unfortunately, he had no idea how long it might take to dig themselves out of their current mess. When they left Ricky's trailer the day before, he’d truly believed their problems were behind them. He couldn't have been any more wrong.

Skid Row still wasn’t convinced Ricky and Carl were responsible for the missing bag. It wasn't that he trusted either one of them. They were obviously lowlifes and crooks, and in the business of taking advantage of people. But in the case of him and Bullfrog, what could they possibly have to gain? On the other hand, if they hadn't made off with the bag, who in hell had and what was their play? Skid Row again thought of Zatts. He was about as trustworthy as a social disease. It still didn't seem like he could be involved. The guy didn't possess the gumption or the smarts. So where did that leave them? Skid Row didn't have the foggiest idea.

-25-

"Tell me you found them," Ricky Fixx said, the remains of a steak and cheese sub spread out on the desk in front of him.

Carl eyed the food and then sank into a chair, the trailer floor creaking under his weight. "Sort of," he said and licked his lips.

"Don't give me *sort of.* I don't want to hear that. *Sort of* tells me you fucked up again."

"No," Carl said, shaking his head. "I think they must have split up. "I found Skid Row."

"That the skinny one?"

Carl nodded and licked his lips again.

"Tell me everything," Ricky ordered, shoving a French fry into his mouth. "And stop fucking drooling. Didn't you eat while you were out?"

"Yeah. That just looks good."

"Well it's mine so get over it." He sucked grease off his fingers as noisily as he could. "Now, what you got for me?"

Carl stared for a moment and then retrieved his notebook.

Ricky watched with growing impatience as he opened it and began thumbing through one page after another. He seemed to be taking a lot more time than was necessary and Ricky couldn't help wondering if he was doing it on purpose. He was about to scream at him to get the fuck on with it already when Carl finally spoke.

"O--kay," he said, holding the notebook in one hand while scratching an ear with the other. He then tilted his big head from side to side and Ricky heard something in his neck crack with the sound of a dry branch being snapped. Carl repeated the process and then began working his shoulders.

"You about finished?" Ricky asked, but Carl didn't seem to have heard, clearly caught up in his range of motion exercises.

Ricky watched and did a silent ten count. It was either that or grab Carl's big beard and feed it into the paper shredder. "You trying to piss me off?" he asked when he couldn't stand it anymore.

"No," Carl said. "Why?" He stared like he really had no idea.

"Forget it!" Ricky said, biting off the words. "Just tell me."

"I was about to."

Carl blinked and dropped his eyes to his notebook. He wasn't quite quick enough and Ricky would have sworn he saw the hint of a smile. Carl covered it by running a hand across his face.

That son of a bitch is playing me, Ricky thought, but then decided it must have been his imagination.

"I went to the phone booth on Clinton Street," Carl began.

Ricky hadn't been expecting that. "I didn't send you there."

"I know," Carl said, "but that was one of Marco's spots. I wanted to see if there was any sign gangs were moving into that territory. Maybe we haven't lost it yet"

"That's good thinking," Ricky replied, surprised he hadn't thought of that himself. It was probably because he'd been so busy trying to clean up Carl's latest mess. There'd be time to talk about that later. "So what's the story?"

"Hard to tell," Carl said. "The way high school kids dress these days, they all look like gang members to me."

"You didn't see anybody trying to sell?"

Carl shook his head. "Not that I could tell. I did see plenty of tweakers looking to buy. I--"

"That ain't my problem." Ricky cut him off. "But," he added, thinking aloud; "we should probably keep tabs on what's happening there. Marco's other spots too. What else you got?"

Carl paused and looked like he might have been doing a ten count of his own. "As I was about to say.... " He shot a glance at Ricky then quickly looked away. "I saw Skid Row there too."

"You what?" Ricky's eyes flew open. "What the fuck was he doing?"

"If I had to guess, I'd say he was looking for us."

"How do you know that?" Ricky asked, flabbergasted. "And how'd he know you'd be there?"

"No idea," Carl replied. "Maybe he's smarter than you thought."

"I doubt that. But back up and tell me the whole thing."

"All right," Carl said, stretching his legs out in front of him. To Ricky, they looked like a couple denim-clad tree trunks.

"You said there might have been witnesses to Marco's...accident."

"Yeah," Ricky said. "So what?"

"So, I don't know what the cops know or if they think there might be a connection to me. I'm sure they're still investigating."

"I'm sure they are."

"Yeah, well, they might go to the places he did his business. I don't know how likely that is but I thought it would be best if I stayed out of sight."

If you were that concerned, Ricky thought. *Why the hell did you go there at all?* He glanced toward the door, impatient because he was having a hard time following Carl's train of thought.

"Anyway," he went on, "I wasn't about to hang out right near the phone booth, especially since I was really just there to observe. Didn't want to scare people away, you know?"

"Sure," Ricky said.

"I stayed at least a block away all the time. See without being seen. I'm pretty good at that stuff."

Carl paused as if giving Ricky a chance to praise him on a job well done. Ricky ate a few more fries, drank from a Big Gulp cup and stared without saying a word. Carl finally continued.

"I just walked a big circle," he said, "stopping anywhere I had a good place to watch from. Man, some of those high school girls...."

"Don't even think it!" Ricky cut in, sitting up straight and giving Carl a glare. "You're in enough trouble already."

"I'm just sayin'...."

"Well don't. It makes me nervous."

They sat in silence for a while, Carl stewing and Ricky wondering when in hell he'd get to the point. He knew from long experience that trying to force the issue would only slow things further so he sat, grinding his teeth and waiting for his partner to get on with it.

"At first," Carl said, eyes downcast and speaking so softly Ricky had to strain to hear, "I didn't really see nothin'."

"I thought you said you saw Skid Row."

"Not right away. There were so many kids and I was trying to figure out if any of them looked, you know, out of place."

"Like they might have been there to sell?"

"Right," Carl said. "But I didn't see nothin' like that. It was sort of tough because I didn't want to get too close."

"That's good," Ricky said expansively, hoping their conversation might actually go somewhere if he threw Carl a bone. His ploy paid immediate dividends.

"I was about to leave," Carl said, "and that's when I saw him."

"By that phone booth?"

No." Carl shook his head. "Hiding behind a dumpster."

Ricky straightened. "You sure that's what he was doing? He looks like he hasn't had a good meal in a month. Maybe he was searching for food."

"Maybe," Carl said, tugging on his beard, "but that's not how it looked to me. I'll bet you a steak and cheese sub he was watching for someone and that someone was us."

-26-

Skid Row took a quick look behind him and then darted into the woods. He was about ninety percent sure he hadn't been seen but that wasn't good enough. He jogged a short ways until he spied a huge oak, its trunk wide enough to provide cover. He positioned himself behind the tree, ducked down and waited. Nothing happened, and the only thing he could hear was his own ragged breath. He swallowed and tried to get himself under control. He hadn't been followed. Of the few people in the immediate vicinity, no one had paid him the slightest attention. He knew that, but it somehow didn't make him feel any better.

Skid Row didn't know how long he stayed that way, hunched over, fingernails digging into tree bark as he peered cautiously around the trunk in the direction from which he'd just come. The sun hung low in the sky, casting strange, long shadows that seemed to move of their own accord. He knew it was a trick of the light and tried not to let his nerves get the best of him. Skid row still kept thinking he was seeing something out of the corner of his eye. When he turned, there was of course nothing there. Oddly, that made him even jumpier. And as the sun sank lower, shadows lengthened, darkened, and began pressing in from all sides.

It was the rapidly diminishing sunlight, along with his cramping knees, that finally got him moving. He straightened and took a moment to get his bearings. He had to find their new camp site and at first wasn't sure which way to go. Every tree looked just like every other, and further complicating things, Skid Row hadn't followed the same path he and Bullfrog used earlier that day. He was coming in from a completely different direction and it was totally throwing him off. After a few frustrating detours, circling around and getting hopelessly lost, he felt pretty sure he was finally on the right track.

Gotta give the little dude credit for one thing, he thought, walking along and chewing on a blade of grass. *He did find us a good camp.*

Much to Skid Row's surprise, Bullfrog had unerringly led them to a stream and, eventually, an honest-to-goodness waterfall. That was the weird sort of white noise he'd started hearing right about the time Bullfrog fell on his ass.

Skid Row still couldn't quite believe it. He'd lived in Binghamton for years and thought he'd seen it all. He'd definitely seen his share of bums and crack heads. He'd come to assume that was about all the city had to offer. He certainly hadn't known anything about lush forest, wildlife or fucking waterfalls. Still, Bullfrog had found one. It wasn't tall, no more than ten or twelve feet, but that was more than enough to serve their purposes.

He could hear that white noise again and knew he was getting close. And if he needed further assurance, Skid Row could smell the slightest hint of a camp fire. That got his mouth watering. He'd given Bullfrog all his money and, as a result, hadn't eaten anything all day. He hoped the fire meant dinner would soon be served. It didn't matter what was on the menu as long as it was warm and filling.

Skid Row wondered just how he'd go about telling Bullfrog what he'd learned that afternoon. He could, he supposed, simply keep it to himself. It wasn't like the new information really changed anything for them. Well, maybe it did a little, in the sense that it made their situation that much more tenuous. He figured it was only fair to let Bullfrog know. On the plus side, there was always the chance that once they discussed it all, it wouldn't seem quite as bad as he thought.

As he neared their small clearing, Skid Row saw Bullfrog sitting on a rock, an undeniably worried expression on his face. He kept looking nervously this way and that, but the bright light from the fire obviously prevented him from seeing very far into the gloom. That had to be the reason he hadn't noticed Skid Row's approach. The sound of the water must have dulled his senses too. Making no effort to be stealthy, Skid Row got to within thirty feet and Bullfrog still had no idea he was there.

He realized they would need to be aware of that. If they weren't on their guard, someone could easily sneak up on them. Skid Row considered putting that to the test. If he came up from the rear, he was sure he could stroll right up and tap Bullfrog on the shoulder. He grinned, thinking about how high he could make the frog jump. Then, he noticed the bag of groceries at Bullfrog's feet. A little further away were Skid Row's sleeping bag and cardboard box of mostly useless stuff. So Bullfrog had done what he said he'd do, buying food and collecting all their belongings. It wouldn't be nice to show his gratitude by scaring the living shit out of the dude.

"So what'd you buy?" he asked, stepping into the circle of firelight.

"Jesus!" Bullfrog said, snapping upright and putting a hand to his chest. "Where did you come from?"

Skid Row pointed with his head. "I found a new way in. I think it's a little shorter. Didn't mean to scare you."

"That's okay. What have you been up to?"

"Let's save that for later. Please tell me you got some grub in that sack. I'm starving."

"Fire out?" Skid Row asked.

"Yep," Bullfrog said, feeling his way along the wall until he was at Skid Row's side. "Ain't nobody gonna find us in here."

Skid Row was still amazed at Bullfrog's discovery. He sat on the ground, a rock wall at his back and a wall of water not two feet from his outstretched legs. He looked up but it was too dark to make out any real detail. The water, he knew from his earlier inspection, cascaded over a small ledge a dozen feet over their heads. The area immediately behind the falls was bone dry and almost completely hidden. It wasn't big, maybe eight foot long by six wide. That was plenty for their purposes. They just needed a place they could stay out of sight for however long it took.

"So what's the deal?" Bullfrog asked, sitting down heavily. "Did they take the bag or not?"

Skid Row didn't answer, focused on the water and the way the moonlight filtering through gave it an odd, other-worldly sort of glow.

"Well?" Bullfrog prompted after a good thirty seconds had gone by.

Skid Row blew out a breath. "I don't know. I made it to that phone booth in plenty of time and I found what I thought was a good spot to watch from."

"So what did you see?"

"Not much at first. Kids were hanging around and I think some of them were looking to score. I maybe saw a couple private transactions but no one that looked like a real player."

"What about Ricky and Carl?"

Skid Row ran both hands through his hair. "I…didn't see them either."

Bullfrog looked at him sharply. "Then why do I get the sense there's something you're not telling me?"

"Maybe because I don't want to tell you."

Bullfrog stared and then hung his head.

"Here's the thing," Skid Row said. "I hung around for like an hour. I was super careful too. I didn't get close enough for anyone to see me. I was next to this old dumpster and it smelled like holy hell."

"And?" Bullfrog asked, his tone wary.

"Like I told you before, I don't think they took that bag. I mean, they got no reason to, right?"

Bullfrog clearly didn't agree but he kept his mouth shut.

"So if they didn't swipe it," Skid Row continued, "they wouldn't know it was gone. They'd be out checking up on us and making sure we were selling their junk."

"And that didn't happen?"

"No."

"And you don't think it's because they knew darn well we had nothing to sell?"

"I don't know!" Skid Row said, "but this is where it gets really weird. I couldn't take the smell of that dumpster anymore and I finally had to get out of there. I stood up and turned around... and I would have sworn I saw that Carl dude walking in the opposite direction."

There was just enough light for Skid Row to see Bullfrog's mouth fall open.

"Did he see you?"

"Hell, I don't know. He must have I guess."

"But he didn't do anything?"

"No, and that's what's so fucked up about this. He just walked away."

"Then he didn't see you after all," Bullfrog said as if that settled the matter.

"But that doesn't make sense either." Skid Row got to his feet, saw that there was no room to pace and slid back down to the ground. "He should have been looking for us. He should have been right out in the open."

"I don't know if I follow."

"They said they'd be watching, right? Wouldn't they want us to see them doing it? Isn't that the whole point? Why stay back in the shadows?"

"But you weren't even where you were supposed to be. You weren't at the phone booth."

"That's what I'm saying!" Skid Row shouted, and then he pounded a fist against the rock. "We weren't there. He saw that we weren't there. So why did he still stay out of sight? It's almost like he was spying on me."

"Why?"

"I don't fucking know! And I'm sorry but I didn't run after him to ask."

"Then they took the bag after all," Bullfrog said quietly.

Skid Row sagged. "That doesn't explain it either. If they had it the whole time, why go near the phone booth at all? I went hoping to learn something but now I'm more confused than ever."

"So where is Marco supposed to be tomorrow? We could always try again."

"I don't think so," Skid Row mumbled, resting his head on his drawn up knees. "There's something I haven't told you."

"I don't like the sound of that."

"Go with the feeling," Skid Row said tiredly and then he sat up. He didn't want to tell Bullfrog the rest but knew he had no choice. They both needed to know what they were up against.

Bullfrog seemed to sense Skid Row's discomfort. Rather than pressing him for information, he sat and waited, occasionally flipping pebbles or bits of wood into the torrent of water where they immediately vanished. Skid row watched, wishing all their problems could be so easily washed away.

-27-

"Let me get this straight," Ricky Fixx said, still trying to comprehend what Carl had just told him. "You're saying you saw that Skid Row guy, and you think he was looking for us?"

"Well, he was looking for someone. There's no other reason to be hanging out by a stinky old dumpster."

Ricky had nothing to say to that. Hands crossed behind his back, he stalked from one end of the trailer to the other, trying to come up with a more reasonable explanation. The only conclusion he could draw was that Carl was wrong. It damn sure wouldn't be the first time for that.

"Just for the sake of argument," he said, staring at the sagging ceiling and speaking as much to himself as to Carl. "Let's say it's true and that he really was looking for us. What would he be hoping to gain?"

Carl shrugged and Ricky figured that was about all the response he was going to get. *Thanks for nothing.*

"And he didn't see you?" Ricky asked, returning to his desk and sitting down.

"Not until I wanted him to."

"Come again?"

Carl broke into a grin. "You said you wanted me to make sure those two knew we were watching them, but I thought it was more important to figure out what Skid Row was up to.

Ricky frowned at that because he didn't like the idea of Carl making decisions on his own or ignoring the instructions he was given. His logic did seem to make sense, though. Ricky wasn't about to admit that so he gestured for Carl to continue.

"I stayed behind him as long as I could," he said, "just sort of observing, you know? He had no clue I was there. I'm sure of that. But when I could tell he was getting ready to leave, I casually moved out onto the sidewalk."

"And you think he saw you there?" Ricky asked, already knowing the answer. Nothing Carl did was ever casual and he had no trouble being conspicuous when he wanted to.

"I'm pretty hard to miss," he said, sitting up, flexing and stretching the seams of his shirt to their limits.

"You got that right. So what happened next?"

Carl glanced at his notebook and then slipped it into a pocket. "I wanted to find out where he was going, see what he was up to."

"So you followed him?"

Carl paused. "That was the plan."

Ricky closed his eyes. He'd noticed the hesitation as well as the new, defensive note in Carl's voice. "I take it something went wrong."

"Well I couldn't just run after him. He was a block away and there were a lot of people around. How would that have looked? And I didn't want to totally spook him. I would have lost him for sure. I thought I knew which way he'd head and figured I could just circle around and come up from behind."

"But...."

Carl shook his head. "But he was nowhere in sight."

"You're telling me you lost him," Ricky said, leaning back, lacing his fingers behind his head and beginning to swivel back and forth.

"He must have just high-tailed it out of there. Guess I can't really blame him."

"No," Ricky said; "but I can sure as hell blame you. You had him and you let him get away."

"It's not my fault."

Ricky waved a hand, wishing he had a blow job for every time he'd heard that.

"Besides," Carl went on. "I was following your orders. You told me not to get too close. And if I hadn't gone over to Clinton Street, I wouldn't have seen him in the first place. Maybe you should thank me instead of always giving me a hard time."

And maybe you should follow my orders all the time and not just when it's convenient.

The conversation was going nowhere and Ricky decided it was time to back off. "What do you want to do now," he asked, thinking Carl might respond a little better if he thought he actually had some say in it.

He raised one eyebrow. "Not sure, but we know what we need to."

"How's that?" Ricky asked.

"Skid Row is still around, right? He showed up once, he'll show up again."

"What about the other guy?"

"Who? Bullfrog?" Carl looked unconcerned. "What about him? If they're no longer together, he's probably long gone. Ain't much we can do about that."

"Maybe they just split up for the day."

"Maybe. It don't matter anyway. Together or not, they're never going to be able to repay the money they think they owe."

"You let me worry about that," Ricky said. "Your job is to find those two, wherever they might be."

Carl crossed his huge arms. "If they haven't left town, I'll find them. You can bank on that"

Ricky looked at his partner and shivered, glad the man wasn't coming after him. Despite his various ineptitudes, he had always been dangerously effective. The two losers wouldn't stand a chance.

"And once you track them down," Ricky said, "you have my permission to tighten the screws."

"You want me to bring them in then?"

Ricky thought about that. "No," he said. "Not yet anyway. You can talk to them. Make sure they know they're on the hook."

"They'll say the bag was stolen."

"Fine. You make it clear that's not our problem. The money is owed and they have one week to pay."

"I don't get this," Carl said, staring with evident disapproval. "You may as well make it ten grand. They'll never come up with it. Why even bother with them?"

Ricky stood, walked to the window and tapped a finger against the dirty glass. "I'm surprised you haven't caught on yet." He turned to lean against the wall. "I know they can't pay. I want them to try and fail. I want them scared and desperate. I want them on their knees."

"But why?" Carl protested. "They're nobody."

"Don't you see?" Ricky said through a thin smile. "That's exactly the point. I can use them. If it doesn't work out, I'll throw them away. Or," he added with a leer, "you will."

"I don't want any part of that. They didn't do anything to us. Why put 'em through it?"

"Because," Ricky said, beginning to lose his temper. "I've been losing money right and left. I give you a job and you fuck it up. Those fuckups always end up costing me. You want to get out of this trailer, right? You want to move somewhere nicer? Somewhere more respectable? How do you suggest we do that if there's no money?"

Ricky didn't wait for a response and Carl didn't look ready to give one.

"You want to talk about Marco? You were sent out to collect. Instead, you fucking killed him. You know what that means? I'll tell you. We lose everything he owed PLUS everything he ever would have brought in. Do you know, do you have the slightest idea how much we're talking about? And that's only the latest. Do I need to remind you there's another huge debt you have yet to collect on? You want to talk about that?"

"Not really," Carl mumbled, his eyes everywhere but on Ricky. "Should I go look for him now? He might--"

"What I want," Ricky said, his voice raised, "is for you to stop questioning everything I do. I'm trying to run a business and it doesn't help when my employee isn't on the same page. And as it happens, you can forget about that other matter for now. I'm handling it personally. I may need you later on. In the meantime, Bullfrog and Skid Row, nice fucking names by the way, are your only responsibilities. Find them. Track them. Hound them. Scare the hell out of them. Is that understood?"

Carl's face clouded.

"What now?" Ricky asked, growing tired of all Carl's candy ass concerns.

"Just one thing. Will I have full…freedom of movement?"

"What are you talking about?" But Ricky thought he knew.

"Ronnie," Carl said, a quaver in his voice. "Did you talk to him?"

He was of course referring to Ronnie Tripp, their dirty cop friend. Ricky still wasn't happy with Carl's attitude and considered letting him dangle in the wind for a while. The guy had caused a lot of problems and deserved to suffer. Ricky considered telling him Ronnie wasn't in, that he'd retired, or that there were a dozen witnesses ready to pick him out of a lineup. In the end, he couldn't stand the prospect of making a grown man cry and Carl looked ready to do just that.

"I called him this afternoon," Ricky said, not being able to resist putting on his most serious face.

"So what'd he say?"

"Initially, nothing. He was aware of the investigation but hadn't seen any of the reports."

"Can he get them?"

"He already has. He called a while before you got back."

"Well what'd he say?" Carl asked for a second time. He'd move to the edge of his chair and Ricky was afraid the whole thing might give way under his bulk.

"There were a couple witnesses that could place you at the scene."

"I was identified?" Carl asked, inching so far forward his chair started to tip.

"You might have been," Ricky said, holding up a finger, "if the witnesses could agree on one damn thing."

Carl looked worried, then confused, and finally relieved. "You mean...."

"I mean they ain't got shit. One of the witnesses is half blind. The other is like eighty-five years old. They couldn't agree on your clothing, the type of vehicle you were driving, or whether or not you had any facial hair, although, how anyone could miss that forest you carry around with you is beyond me."

"I'm in the clear then?"

"What did I just say? Yeah, you're in the clear. Cops got nothin' so get out of here and go find me a couple of losers."

-28-

"You're saying what exactly?"

Skid Row stared at his hands, which he could barely make out in front of him. The moon was obscured by clouds and their tiny shelter behind the waterfall was now as dark as his mood. That suited him fine because he felt like he'd gotten them into this mess and didn't want to see Bullfrog's face when he told him the rest of the bad news.

"I ran into this guy," he said, his mouth feeling dry and pasty from his baloney sandwich dinner. "I don't really know him. I'd see him around, you know? His name is Jake or something like that. Anyway, he was one of Marco's customers. I think he was there today looking to make a score."

"So he didn't know what happened?"

"To Marco?' Skid Row shook his head. "Guess not; but this ain't about that anyway."

"Then what is it?"

"I'm getting to that," Skid Row said, marveling at how his voice just sort of disappeared once it reached the wall of water in front of them. There was no danger of their conversation being overheard, even if there was anyone around to hear it.

"So this dude was walking by right as I was coming out from behind the dumpster."

"You mean when you saw Carl?"

"Yeah," Skid Row said. "Jake saw him too. It was weird. We're both just standing there watching when out of nowhere he says, 'You don't want to mess with that one. He's seriously bad news.'"

"You ask him what he meant?"

"Damn straight. He told me about this friend of his. He gave a name but I don't remember it. The dude was into some bad stuff, drugs and whatever, and somehow ended up at odds with Ricky and Carl."

"He mentioned Ricky?" Bullfrog asked, sounding alarmed.

"Not by name but I can put two and two together."

"So what'd he say?"

"I don't know what exactly went down but Carl ended up coming after him."

Bullfrog swallowed hard. "What did he do?"

"It seems he has a reputation for hurting people really bad. He showed up with a gun and threatened to shoot the guy in the knee cap."

"Did he do it?"

"He tried but missed and hit him in the famerial artery instead."

"In the what?"

"Didn't you say your mom was a biologist or something? You should know this shit. The famerial artery is like the biggest nerve in your body. It's in your neck someplace. Dude fucking bled out."

Bullfrog made an odd squeaking noise. "I think you mean…never mind. You're telling me Carl goes around killing people on Ricky's orders."

"I don't know if it's exactly like that, but I think we'd be wise to steer clear of both of them"

"You don't have to tell me twice. I didn't want any part of it anyway."

"Yeah, well you're a genius and I'm an idiot. Happy now?"

"I didn't mean it like that. I--."

"Forget it," Skid Row said. "You were right and I was wrong. I think that's pretty clear by now."

"You had a good idea. It just didn't work out."

Skid Row knew Bullfrog was only trying to make him feel better. It was nice but didn't help in the slightest. He knew--they both knew--how badly he'd fucked up.

"So that Jake guy say anything else?" Bullfrog asked.

"He wanted to, Skid Row said, pulling at a loose thread on his jeans, "but I got the hell out of there. I don't know what Carl was up to but I wasn't about to be standing around with my thumb up my ass if he decided to come back."

"Good thinking. So where'd you go?"

Skid Row gave a short laugh. "Once I heard that story, all I wanted to do was get out of sight as quickly as possible. I jumped a fence and took off through this dude's backyard. I thought the Yard was empty but the guy was up on a ladder fixing his gutters or something. I know I scared the crap out of him. He let out this weird noise and dropped a bunch of shit on the ground. For a second, I thought he was going to fall. The way my luck's been lately, I'm surprised he didn't."

"Where'd you go after that?"

Skid Row shrugged in the darkness. "I just walked, he said, yanking at the thread until it came free. He began twisting it around a finger. "I mainly stuck to alleys, backyards and parking lots because I was afraid to be out on the street."

"I don't blame you," Bullfrog said. "So I guess it's settled then. We'll hit the road tomorrow."

"Wait a minute," Skid Row said, not at all surprised that Bullfrog was all ready to just pack up and leave. "I still want to know what's going on."

"Are you crazy?" Bullfrog asked, his voice going up an entire octave. "There's a killer after us. Do you really want to hang around long enough to ask why?"

"No, but I don't want to just run away either. Not 'til I know there's a reason."

"That sounds...."

"Stupid?"

"Actually, I was going to say dangerous. Isn't it obvious they're after us?"

"I don't know," Skid Row said, the end of his finger getting hot as he twisted the thread tighter, cutting off the circulation. "I don't know anything. But while I was wandering around, I had a lot of time to think."

"What about?"

"Everything. For starters, what the hell was Carl doing there? It could be a coincidence but I don't believe that any more than you do. "

"What then?"

"Beats the fuck out of me. None of it makes any sense."

Bullfrog was silent and Skid Row could tell he was trying to come up with something to say. "Are you sure Carl even saw you?" he finally asked.

"Yeah. I mean, he kind of had to, right?"

Skid Row replayed the scene in his mind as he'd done at least a dozen times already. He'd been kneeling by the dumpster, completely focused on the area right around the phone booth. He'd stayed that way until the stench of over-ripe garbage got to be too much. He stood, stretched and started to turn... and there was Carl, back turned but no more than fifty yards away. There was no doubt it was him. He hadn't walked past, and there were no side streets from which he might have just emerged. That meant he'd been somewhere behind him for who knew how long? That thought was totally creepy and Skid Row couldn't imagine what he was playing at.

"It's like he was tailing me," he said, only half out loud.

"What did you say?"

"I'm just thinking," Skid Row said. "Based on where he was, and where I was, there's no way he couldn't have seen me. It's like he was watching me the whole time."

"But why?"

"Damned if I know."

"Then what do you want to hang around for?" Bullfrog asked, sounding exasperated. "He wouldn't have been there if he wasn't looking for you."

"So let's say he was," Skid Row said. "I was right there in front of him. Why didn't he do anything about it?"

"Maybe he..." Bullfrog began but then fell silent.

"He didn't do anything," Skid Row said, "because he didn't want to. That's not what he was there for."

"But--."

"But nothing. If he was really after me, I wouldn't be sitting here right now."

"I get that," Bullfrog said. "At least I think so. But if he wasn't interested in you, what the hell was he doing?

"I got no idea, and believe me, I had plenty of time to think about it. That's all I was doing while I was walking around, trying to stay out of sight and checking every five seconds to make sure he wasn't around."

"He didn't... follow you back here."

Skid Row shook his head. "He didn't follow me anywhere. I know that much. I saw him that one time and that was it. And it's not like a dude that big can hide behind a telephone pole." That still didn't explain Carl's sudden appearance, but the fact that Skid Row hadn't been torn limb from limb was proof enough that Carl had other things on his mind and, at least for the time being, he and Bullfrog were safe.

"Then how long do you want to hang around here?" Bullfrog asked, unhappy but resigned.

Skid Row felt bad, but not so bad he was willing to leave his home for no good reason. Who was he kidding? In the past seventy-two hours, his *home* had gone from a room at the Y, to a patch of scrub grass under a bridge, to their current refuge behind a waterfall. The way things were going, he'd be bedding down in a sewer pipe before another seventy-two hours went by. He still wasn't ready to pull up his meager stakes and head for parts unknown without good cause.

"Just give me some time," he said. "I feel like there's something going on and I want to find out what."

"Okay. How?"

Skid Row yawned and rubbed his eyes. "Tomorrow is laundromat day. I want to see if Carl shows up again."

"You're nuts!"

"Maybe," Skid Row admitted. "But Marco is our only connection. I went to one of his spots and Carl was there. If the same thing happens again...."

"You'll what?"

Skid Row laughed. "I don't fucking know, but I'll make damn sure he doesn't see me."

"Oh, I will too," Bullfrog said, "because I'm going with you."

-29-

Ricky found Andrew Cullen's road without any trouble, driving past a couple times and craning his neck to see what he could see. It didn't amount to much. The road curved around to the left and, even though the trees had already lost most of their leaves, he couldn't make out much more than a few distant rooftops. He knew the Cullen residence was the last on the dead end road and, according to Google Earth, that was exactly 0.6 miles from his current location. The property was large and set well apart from any neighbors, prime residential real estate for sure, and it should be ridiculously easy to survey because the odds of being detected were so low. Ricky knew he'd have to walk a little ways, but that was nothing compared to what he planned to get out of this little venture.

He drove until he found a suitably wide shoulder, pulled over and parked, thankful there wasn't much traffic. He highly doubted it would matter one way or the other. Even if his car were spotted, there was no reason it would attract any attention. He was out in the country. If someone saw his empty car, they would probably assume the driver was off hunting, bird-watching or making like a bear and taking a shit in the woods. Ricky locked up, grabbed his camera bag and a bottle of water, and was on his way.

He knew immediately that he'd made a mistake. There were plenty of trees to provide cover, and no one around anyway. He still felt totally conspicuous and sort of stupid in his suit and tie, and the smooth soles of his black dress shoes were less than ideal for overland travel. He should have worn boots and, if not actual camouflage, something more appropriate than his imitation Armani. The ground was blessedly dry with no real steep hills. He still slipped and slid, and had a hard time making steady progress.

"What in fuck's sake am I doing here?" he wondered aloud, trudging along and hoping fervently that he was still headed the right way. He stopped and took a swig from his water bottle. Ricky had lost sight of the road and didn't have a clue how far he'd walked or how much further he still had to go. It had been just over a half mile by road, or so said Mr. Google, but his more circuitous route made that information irrelevant. Cullen's was the fourth and final property. Ricky thought he'd passed two so far, although it was certainly possible he'd missed one. He was trying to stay close enough to the road to keep his bearings, but not so close someone might glance out a window, see him and wonder what the hell he was up to.

He checked his watch, knowing it wouldn't tell him a thing. He didn't know what time it was when he started walking so what possible difference could it make knowing the time now? He guessed he'd been at it for about twenty minutes. It felt a lot longer so he really couldn't be sure. He might have covered half a mile or perhaps twice that. It was also possible he'd walked in a big fucking circle and would soon stumble out of the woods right next to his own car. Most people, without any landmarks to follow, would walk in a circle eventually. He'd seen a TV show about that not long ago. These morons were dumped in the middle of a field somewhere, blindfolded and told to walk in a straight line. None of them could do it for more than a short distance. They all started out fine, but invariably began to turn toward... their dominant side? Ricky couldn't remember now. That wasn't going to happen to him anyway. He wasn't blindfolded and he wasn't a moron. He could see a trace of chimney smoke a ways off to his left. That meant there was a house over there somewhere. He made a slight course change and began heading in that direction.

As he walked, pausing every so often to pull up his thin dress socks while trying to ignore the increasing soreness of his feet, Ricky asked himself why he hadn't given Carl this job. That guy loved this sort of shit and he most certainly did not. He also had plenty of better things to do with his time. Unfortunately, Carl did too. Per Ricky's very specific instructions, he was, hopefully at that very second, hot on the trail of two deadbeat losers.

Carl might screw up once or twice along the way. That was generally the case with him. In the end, though, he would find them. Of that, Ricky had little doubt. What might happen next was far less clear. Skid Row and Bullfrog were wildcards. That couldn't be denied. But, since Ricky had nothing invested in them, he knew that was a bet he really couldn't lose. He just wasn't sure what would happen when he started pulling their strings. There was, of course, only one way to find out.

Afternoon sun began filtering through the tree tops and Ricky had to admit the warmth felt nice on the back of his neck. He was still a little freaked out by the total absence of familiar city sounds and smells. It didn't seem natural. The constant crunch of dry leaves underfoot was starting to get on his nerves too. He tried to put it out of his mind and focus on the task at hand. Despite all the recent setbacks: Carl's fuckups, Marco, the unexpected hassle from one Andrew Cullen, and all the rest, Ricky believed things would come together eventually. He thought it was happening already. And, with any luck, he would soon have all the ammunition he needed to expedite proceedings in a big way. Cullen would know Ricky meant business.

After what felt like hours, he finally made it to the rear of the Cullen residence. He was prevented from going any further by an eight foot high cedar fence. He could only assume it was there more for esthetic purposes than anything else. A privacy fence didn't seem necessary, as secluded as the place was, and if it was there for security, the installers should be sued for incompetence.

Had Ricky wanted to, he could have scaled the fence in no time flat, even dressed as he was. He actually considered it, but not knowing what he might find on the other side, he thought a more cautious approach was prudent. That brought him to security flaw number two. There were readily climbable trees all over the place, some with branches that actually overhung the fence. Had Ricky lacked the basic athleticism required to get over the fence on his own, he could have climbed a tree, shimmied out on one of those nice thick branches and dropped right into Cullen's back yard. If he'd been looking for a dramatic entrance, that definitely would have been the way to go. Today, however, he needed subtlety and stealth.

On that front, Ricky saw at once that he had a problem. Although the trees gave him excellent access, they weren't worth a shit when it came to providing cover, not with all the leaves dead and on the ground. He'd be perched up there, looking as out of place as a well dressed businessman in a fucking tree. He walked from one end of the fence to the other, searching for a hole or a crack or anything at all he could see through. It was useless. The wood looked so fresh and new it might have been put in that very morning. Ricky knew he could have walked all the way around and approached the house from the front, but he would have felt terribly exposed and didn't want to take that chance unless he had no other choice.

He stood, hands on hips, trying to figure out what in hell he should do. The answer was right there in front of him: big, green and oozing sap from every pore. If his goal was to stay hidden, the huge ass pine tree was his best and, Ricky figured, his only option. He stared at it, hoping and even praying something else would occur to him. If he wasn't properly attired for a walk in the woods, he damn sure wasn't ready for O Tannenbaum. The fucker had to be sixty feet tall. He thought of that scene from *Christmas Vacation.* "Little full. Lotta sap." Yeah, no shit, Clark.

Ricky knew he didn't have much choice. He could do what had to be done or leave, go back to the trailer, hook up with Carl and tell him he needed to come out here to finish a job he'd been unable to accomplish on his own. Carl would just love that, and Ricky would never give him the satisfaction. He'd sooner use a tweezer to pluck out all his nose hairs one by one. If he wanted what he'd come there for, there was just one way to get it and it meant going up that tree. He sighed and began removing his suit coat.

Ricky dropped the coat on the ground, followed by his tie and the now empty water bottle. He cracked his knuckles and circled the base of the tree, searching for an easy way in. None was to be had. Branches were so numerous that, even from his vantage point of maybe six feet away, he could barely see all the way through to the trunk. It looked like it thinned out a little ways up but he'd have to get there first. Ricky cursed Cullen and decided the interest rate on his loan had just gone up.

Not for the first time, he wondered if he should have given Cullen the money at all.

Ricky was used to dealing with tweakers, small-time crooks and the people occupying the lowest rungs on the social ladder, the ones who would find his shit hole of an office perfectly acceptable. They made poor decisions, and their stupid mistakes and bad life choices paid his bills. But most of his clientele had nothing to begin with. They were good for nothing losers, and destined to crash and burn whether he was around or not. He saw no reason not to benefit from that.

Ricky's rationale was simple. If you're already on a path of self-destruction, what difference does it make if you choose to speed up the process by spending every cent you have on meth or heroine? He took their money, gave them their fix and did it with a clear conscience. With Cullen, it was different. He was in a higher financial class, a higher social class, and he had a whole hell of a lot more to lose. Ricky wasn't used to dealing with people like that and he found the whole thing unsettling, especially now that Cullen was becoming a problem.

Under normal circumstances, when Ricky felt it was time to deliver a message, he'd send Carl in to torch the guy's house, trash his office or just rough him up a bit. It was possible that at some point such tactics might still become necessary. Ricky wanted very much to avoid that if he could. Although he didn't think it was likely, he supposed Cullen might go to the cops. He obviously couldn't tell them he was in debt to a loan shark but he'd come up with a story and they'd take him at his word. He was white and rich and, when it came to the judicial system, that pretty much gave him the keys to the castle. Ricky, on the other hand, would never get the benefit of any doubt.

And even if Cullen tried to keep things *in house*, which was what Ricky anticipated, that still presented problems. He could not, for example, stroll into the fancy Cyber Force office, grab Cullen by his expensively tailored crotch and start tossing him around the same way Carl had with Geno. As tempting an idea as that was, it just wouldn't do. Cullen wasn't untouchable and Ricky would make sure he knew it. But, his social standing did buy him a certain amount of protection. To Ricky, that just meant he'd have to be subtle. He was okay with that. In his experience, the subtle threats were often the most effective.

Carl didn't do subtle, and that was why Ricky was currently twenty feet off the ground, a broken off pine branch crammed halfway up his asshole. His shirt was torn and he had a nasty scrape on his left cheek. Who knew pine bark was so abrasive? Fortunately, he'd managed not only to hang onto his camera but it appeared to still be in working order. That was a surprise given how many times he'd knocked it against a branch, the trunk or his own shin bone.

Ricky was quite a bit higher than he'd meant to go. All he really wanted was a good view over the Cullen's fence but getting it proved to be a lot tougher than he'd thought. He'd been a city kid his whole life but still climbed his share of trees. As far as he could remember, the biggest challenge was always finding enough hand and foot holds. But with Cullen's mammoth pine tree, there were so many things to hold onto he sometimes found it difficult to move anywhere. Every branch seemed to have a dozen more sprouting out of it and each of those was covered with tiny, sharp, twig-like things that jabbed him every time he shifted his body. Ricky couldn't count the number of times he'd smacked his head, and he had little bits of pine gunk in his hair, in his ears and down his pants. If nothing else, he supposed he'd smell outdoorsy fresh for the next week. He also didn't think he had to worry too much about falling, not the way he was pinned in. He ran a much greater risk of getting hopelessly stuck when it came time to climb down.

Eventually, the going did get a bit easier. Branches got thinner as Ricky rose and they were spaced further apart. For the first time since he'd started, he could actually look around and get some idea of where he was going. He was surprised when he realized he'd somehow managed to work his way around to the opposite side of the trunk. Now that he had some breathing room, that was simple enough to correct. He shimmied around and soon had what he'd come there for, a mostly unobstructed view of the Cullen homestead.

The place was practically a mansion, at least by Binghamton standards. The Yard, if that's what you could call it, was a good two to three acres and absolutely immaculate, the grass, even in mid-autumn, so green and lush it looked suitable for any pro golf course. Ricky noted a line of rose bushes, all trimmed back in preparation for winter, some multicolored chrysanthemums that had probably just been planted, a small pumpkin patch with one very large pumpkin, and a few apple trees, bare of both leaves and fruit. He also observed a large, kidney-shaped swimming pool, the winter safety cover already in place, a hot tub that looked like it was still open for business, a utility shed and a pool house.

The main house put all that to shame. It stood three stories and had large, wrap-around decks on every level. There were skylights and lots of glass and it was all very modern. Ricky couldn't even guess at the square footage but thought it had to be well north of ten thousand. He couldn't help being impressed. *So this is how the other half lives,* he thought, thinking too that it would be a real shame if he had to send it all up in smoke.

Ricky began snapping pictures, starting around the pool area and working his way gradually toward the house, not really focusing on anything in particular. He wanted Cullen to know he'd been there, and hoped for at least one shot that would really grab his attention. As if on cue, the backdoor opened and Mrs. Cullen emerged from the house.

"Good afternoon, Sara," Ricky murmured, zooming in for a close up. "You're looking fine today."

She was too, in low cut blue jeans and a snuggly fitting black knit top. Ricky knew her name was Sara and that she did volunteer work at a local center for under-privileged children. He also knew, thanks to Cullen's *portrait of a perfect family* bio he'd posted on the Cyber Force website, that there were two daughters, one in eighth grade and the other in tenth, and their names were Kristin and Kayla. He didn't know which was which and he really didn't give a crap. He did not plan on making them part of this equation. No matter what happened with Cullen, Ricky wasn't about to go after the wife and kids. He wouldn't even have Carl stoop to that level--not without damn good reason. He was banking on the fact that Cullen wouldn't know that. He'd get the little care package Ricky planned on leaving for him, naturally assume the worst, and if he had any balls at all, do whatever was necessary to protect his family. If he believed they were in real danger, dealing with him should get very easy, very fast.

Ricky was still stunned it had even gotten to this point. He snapped a couple pictures of Sara as she stood on tip-toe, pouring birdseed into a feeder. She was a beautiful woman by any standard and carried herself with obvious style and grace. Her daughters were equally attractive and the Cullen home was absolutely gorgeous. In addition to all of that, Cullen owned a business which, as far as Ricky had been able to determine, was doing quite well. That was a lot to be proud of. So with all that going for him, what was he doing messing around, wasting all his time in casinos, and pissing away so much of his fortune that he had to come to a guy like Ricky for help? Ricky had no doubts about his own place on the social ladder. He was a bottom feeder plain and simple. With Cullen, though, his position was suddenly elevated. He had real power. The feeling was both invigorating and, he had to admit, disconcerting.

He tried not to think about that as he put the lens cap back on the Cannon. Ricky was about to begin his descent when he heard the rumble of a large vehicle coming down the road. He looked off to his right and saw a brief flash of yellow. He knew it had to be the school bus. He decided he'd give it another minute or two, just to see what happened. Not long after, he got what he knew in his heart was the money shot. Right before they turned to go into the house, perfectly framed, Sara Cullen, arm in arm with Kristin and Kayla. That picture alone should be enough to bring Cullen to his knees.

-30-

Andrew Cullen exited Mrs. Banyard's uncomfortably warm office and pushed through the chrome and glass front doors of the First Niagara Bank, resisting the urge to turn and give her the finger, grab his crotch, or make any other inappropriate yet satisfying gestures. He'd handed over three thousand dollars in cash, and she'd eyed it over the tops of tiny wire-rimmed glasses complete with neck chain. She'd then stared at him with an expression suggesting he'd just taken a steaming dump right in the middle of her desk.

"What am I supposed to do with this?" he could still hear her asking, as if he'd offered her a soiled condom rather than a handful of currency.

"I'd like to get my accounts in order."

"This will hardly do it," she'd sniffed. "You're at least forty-thousand dollars in arrears."

Leave it to a fucking banker to use the word arrears. "I'm well aware of that," Cullen said, smiling and hoping it didn't look as sickeningly insincere as it felt. "I made some financial speculations and they didn't pan out as I'd hoped. My business is still strong and I'll get the money back in the till soon. This is only a start." He tapped the pile of bills. "I need to collect on some outstanding debts and I'll have more money for you by the close of business today." Collecting outstanding debts actually meant selling a bunch of stuff, his car included, but Mrs. Banyard didn't need to be privy to that information.

"I hope you're right," the woman droned. "I think I've been more than patient but I do have my limits."

You also have the personality of tree fungus."Oh, I know," Cullen said, "and I really do appreciate it. I overextended. I realize that and regret any inconvenience I may have caused you. It won't happen again."

"I'm quite sure it won't," she replied, scooping up his money and sliding it deftly into a desk drawer. "At least not here. Do we understand each other?"

She gave him a look suggesting she'd like nothing more than to spell it all out for him. Cullen wasn't about to give her the satisfaction.

"I think so," he said, crossing his ankles and trying to adopt a casual pose. "Like I said, this was nothing more than an unexpected and temporary setback. I can assure you it won't be repeated."

Mrs. Banyard removed her glasses which did nothing to improve her appearance. She had the complexion of wood putty and some of her liver spots were as large as dines. Cullen knew he wasn't being fair. It wasn't really that the woman was ugly. Her features were just so drawn and tight that she exuded disapproval with every word and gesture. She hadn't seemed much friendlier even when he'd been a customer in good standing. He doubted she'd put him in that category anymore. However, if things went according to plan, he'd get that ship pointed in the right direction soon.

"You have a position in the community. I understand that. But you need to understand that it only carries you so far. First Niagara has a reputation too, and protecting that is my top priority."

Come on, Cullen thought. *Are you really implying that I'm making you look bad by getting a little behind on deposits? If you're that concerned with appearances, stay away from your mirror.*

"I appreciate everything you've done for me," he said. "And once again, I do apologize for any inconvenience. We've always had a strong working relationship and I'd hate to do anything to jeopardize that."

She looked at him like she'd just swallowed a toad, which was pretty much how he felt after spewing such a line of bull.

"Thank you for your time this morning," he said, rising from his chair. "I'll be out of the office most of the day, calling on delinquent clients," he added for good measure. "I'll have more money for you by close of business. If you need to contact me before then, I can be reached through my assistant. I believe you have that number."

"Yes," she said pointedly. "I've used it several times recently."

Under the circumstances, Cullen thought the meeting had gone about as well as he realistically could have hoped. After all, she hadn't actually torn him a new asshole. He supposed he should be grateful for that. He'd bought himself some time, and that was the main thing he had been after. The key now was to use that time to his advantage.

He sat behind the wheel of his Jag, thinking about where he should go next. He considered making arrangements to meet with Ricky Fixx. He'd already put that off longer than he should have, and knew he'd have to get in touch soon and work out some sort of arrangement, ideally one that would keep him out of the hospital.

Cullen had a plan and thought it had real potential. He just wasn't sure how best to sell it. Bottom line, he needed an extension, possibly as long as a couple weeks, and that was something he knew Ricky wouldn't want to hear. He'd have to sweeten the pot and somehow convince him waiting would be worth his while. With that in mind, Cullen decided to delay their conversation a bit longer, when he'd hopefully have a better idea of what he could bring to the table. He dug out his phone, thought for a moment, and then dialed his office.

"It's Andrew," he said when Carrie picked up.

"Oh, hey. Are you on your way in then?" as bright and fresh as ever.

"No," he said, wishing he could unburden himself to her. He wanted to talk to someone and Carrie could be trusted; he thought so anyway. He just didn't trust himself to get through the whole thing without breaking down. Somehow, that would have been more embarrassing, more humiliating than everything else he'd done up to that point. Maybe he'd confide in her someday. But Cullen knew that if he actually made it through all this, he'd probably never tell a soul.

"I don't think I'll be there for a while," he said, adopting his business tone. "I have some things to tend to. Do you think you can clear my calendar?"

"Let me see what you've got."

He heard her typing and humming to herself.

"I don't see anything that can't be moved to tomorrow. Am I going to see you at all today?"

Do you miss me? Cullen pushed that thought aside. He was in enough trouble already. "It's hard to say. If anything, I'll be in and out."

"Sounds good," she said, with what he hoped or maybe prayed was a trace of suggestion. "Is there anything I can do for you while you're out?"

"As a matter of fact, yes. Contact Paul Powers. He's the news editor at the paper. If we don't have his number on file, you can find all the info at their website."

"Sure. What do you need?"

"Get in touch with him and maybe the news editors at a few of the radio and TV stations. I've decided to run the Southern Tier Triathlon this year. I want to get the word out. It would be good publicity for the company. In fact," Cullen had a sudden inspiration. "Let's really get some mileage out of this thing and try to turn it into a charity event."

"You want to donate all the proceeds?"

"No!" Cullen said, a bit more forcefully than he meant to. "A portion of the proceeds for sure." *Fat chance.* "But what I was really thinking was that we could try to line up some sponsors. Corporate or private, it doesn't matter."

He thought that if he had a bunch of people throwing money at the cause, it probably wouldn't be hard to skim a little off the top before making a very public donation to some worthwhile charity. There was always that center Sara spent so much time at. The holiday season wasn't far off. That might be a good angle for a PR piece. Make a contribution and help give under-privileged children a happy Thanksgiving. The press would eat that shit up.

Cullen thought of three immediate benefits to his new brainstorm. Make that four. For starters, if he actually won, he'd be able to give Ricky a lot more than he'd initially thought. And if he didn't win, at least he'd still have something to pay. That was assuming he could find sponsors but he really didn't think that would be a problem. The last two benefits were more personal and had to do with Sara. She would think he was a hero for doing so much to support her charity. In addition, his selflessness would surely help smooth things over if, God forbid, she ever uncovered the mess he'd put them in.

"I'll tell you what," he said, still working things through in his mind. "Don't make any calls just yet. This could be huge and I want to make sure we do it right. Let me give it some more thought and I'd like you to do the same. We don't have a lot of time so we will need to move quickly."

"I'm on it," she said, computer keys clicking once again. "I'll start putting together a press release and we can add details as necessary."

"Great. If I can swing it, I'll give you a call and we can meet for lunch to get everything ironed out."

Cullen spent the next two hours finalizing a deal to trade in his beautiful Jag on a new Toyota Avalon. The one he selected was black, like the Jaguar, and from the previous model year so he got a fantastic deal on the car. It was nice: leather interior and loaded with features. And, thanks to a cash-back incentive, he pocketed about two thousand dollars more than he'd expected. He could appease Mrs. Banyard, hopefully without the need to sell off any more of his possessions. He still felt like the AARP poster boy when he drove out of the lot. *An Avalon*? Cullen sighed. At least it wasn't a Buick or and Oldsmobile. He wasn't sure what Sara would say about it but that was the least of his worries right then.

He considered calling Carrie back but decided it was probably too late for a lunch meeting. She usually left the office around eleven thirty and it was already past noon. He supposed that was just as well. He'd need her help to get everything organized, but he couldn't let her in on every aspect of his plan, especially if some of his donors were going to be somewhat off the books.

Cullen pulled into Michelangelo's Restaurant, got a table for one and ordered grilled tuna and a side salad, even though the Greek chicken or lasagna would have tasted a lot better. If he was going to get in shape for this race, he needed to start eating better as well. He ordered ice water instead of vodka and tonic, and even waved the waitress off when she started his way with a basket of piping hot garlic knots.

To take his mind off what he was missing, he pulled out his phone and began scrolling through his contacts. He thought he should at least test the waters, and started with the owner of the dealership where he'd just purchased the Avalon. Not five minutes later, he had the promise of a thousand dollars. Two more calls netted similar results.

Cullen was encouraged, but also realized this wasn't going to be quite as easy as he'd hoped. In all three cases, the people he spoke to wanted to pay by check and make those checks payable to the charity involved. That shouldn't have come as a surprise; he just hadn't thought it through. They wanted the tax write-off and a record of the transaction. No one, he realized, was just going to hand him a fistful of cash.

He sat back and drummed his fingers on the edge of the table, trying to come up with a solution. Cullen did have one thing working in his favor. If he handled this properly, no one would know how much anyone else had donated. So, if he brought in a hundred grand, ten or even twenty percent might disappear without anyone being the wiser. That was assuming he could resolve the check issue. Otherwise, not a penny of those funds would be available to him. He didn't mind supporting such a good cause, but there had to be something in it for him. He wasn't going to bust his ass just to help a bunch of kids who were used to having nothing. He'd have a lot of money slipping through his fingers. There had to be a way to hold onto some of it.

Cullen raised a finger to get the waitress's attention. He needed to think and the ice water wasn't cutting it. He ordered a vodka and tonic, followed by a second ten minutes later.

Ricky had been watching for the Jag and nearly missed Cullen when, at about quarter past six, he pulled up in front of his office in an Avalon, parked and walked rather unsteadily into the building. Ricky shook his head. He'd observed Cullen enough over the past couple weeks to know he hit the bottle pretty good. He'd obviously been at it again. But what was up with the new ride? Was it supposed to be an evasion tactic? If so, the guy was a dolt. He'd parked in plain sight and made no attempt even to hide his face when he exited the car.

What are you up to now? Ricky wondered, thinking the Toyota might be a loaner or rental. *Why would he need one?* That was easy enough to guess. Based on the way Cullen was moving, it was no trouble imagining him wrapping that gorgeous Jaguar around a utility pole. That would be a tragedy, but it made no difference to Ricky one way or the other. He had his quarry in his sights now and that was all that mattered.

He removed a slim manila envelope from an inside pocket and held it between two fingers. He considered making the delivery right then. He couldn't see into the lobby but knew Cullen must still be there. The drunk bastard was probably having a hard time finding his way to the elevator. How simple it would be to stroll in, drop the envelope into his hands, smile and walk away. Ricky guessed his phone would start blowing up before he'd even made it back to his car. Cullen would be blubbering, begging for mercy and ready to make any deal Ricky proposed. On the other hand, in his current condition, there was no telling how he might react. It could get ugly. Ricky thought about it and finally decided to wait around a while to see what transpired.

Cullen's sudden appearance had definitely taken him by surprise. He'd been sitting and watching the building for the past couple hours, and all along, assuming the guy was inside at his desk--exactly where he was supposed to be. Ricky knew now that had been foolish. Cullen had gone off the rails a bit and really shouldn't be counted on to act rationally.

Thankfully, the plan he'd come up with was about as failsafe and easily adjusted as possible. He'd wait for his target to come out, and then tail him to whatever bar or restaurant he stopped at on the way home. Ricky had no doubt he'd stop somewhere. And while he was inside, ordering three or four for the road, Ricky would slip a little surprise underneath a wiper blade. He even considered jimmying Cullen's car door and leaving the envelope right there on the driver's seat. That would make an impression for sure, even if Cullen was shit-faced when he found it.

Through the windshield of the Lexus, Ricky had a full and unobstructed view of the Cyber Force front entrance. No one would come or go without his knowledge. He hoped he wouldn't have to wait around too much longer. It was nearly quarter to six and several employees had already left for the day. Not fifteen minutes earlier, the hot little secretary, or receptionist, or fuck bunny, or whatever she was had walked past so closely that, if he'd wanted to, he could have rolled down his window, reached out and stuck his finger right up her ass. While he looked on, admiring every move, she'd exited the building, walked half a block to a CVS drug store, spent just over eight minutes inside, came out carrying a single plastic shopping bag, crossed the street to a parking garage, and emerged three minutes and seventeen seconds later, behind the wheel of a late model dark blue Nissan. He was sad to see her go, and actually considered following her, if only to catch another glimpse of her world class figure. In the end, he knew he'd be chasing a dream, more like a fantasy, so he decided to stay put.

Ricky knew from a previous trip that Cyber Force did have a rear door. It opened into a narrow alley and was mostly used by garbage and delivery men. If Cullen wanted to give him the slip, he could do so out the back and Ricky wouldn't know until it was too late. The odds of that seemed slim, so he hadn't even considered calling Carl in for backup.

Regardless of when and where Cullen exited, it still didn't explain what he was doing there in the first place. He'd evidently been out for all or at least a good part of the day. Why show up after hours, in a strange vehicle and several sheets to the wind? Then again, nothing Cullen did seemed to make much sense. Among other things, Ricky couldn't figure out how he could drink like a fish on a regular basis and still work out so hard and so often. He couldn't imagine biking up some mountain somewhere, let alone doing it with a hangover.

"Enjoy it now," he muttered, thinking Cullen would have to find some other way to get his kicks once Carl got hold of him. Tough to ride a bike with broken knee caps. *Well,* Ricky thought, *there's always the Special Olympics.*

He sincerely doubted it would ever come to that. Cullen might be physically strong but was almost certainly a coward at heart. As soon as he saw what Ricky had for him: pictures of Sara, pictures of his kids, that perfect shot of all of them together, he'd collapse faster than a dollar store umbrella.

Ricky leaned forward in his seat, peering up at the fourth floor windows, all but one of which was dark. He guessed that had to be Cullen's office, and as if in confirmation, he saw a flicker of movement. Someone was in there for sure, but he knew that already.

"Come on," he said, eager to get the show on the road. It wasn't so much that Ricky was looking forward to a confrontation. He'd just been in the car too long and it was getting damned uncomfortable. What started as a mild ache in the vicinity of his tailbone had quickly spread and intensified and was now working its way steadily up his spine. He knew it was a direct result of the pine tree enema he'd undergone earlier in the day. It was all Cullen's fault, and Ricky vowed to make him pay.

Climbing down from that tree had been a whole lot easier than going up. The entire experience was still a nightmare and one Ricky didn't plan on repeating. By the time he'd finally extricated himself, his shirt was torn in a couple places and his pants were so sap-stained he knew they'd never come clean. He'd gotten home and tossed the whole mess right into the trash. He then had to deal with the challenge of cleaning himself. He started with soap and hot water, scrubbing his hands so long his skin turned pink and raw. About all he really accomplished was ruining one of his good bathroom washcloths. He rummaged under the kitchen sink until he found a spray bottle of bug and tar remover he'd bought for the car but never used. It took care of most of the goo and a soak in the tub did the rest. He still had to wash his hair three times before that felt normal again.

Even when Ricky was sap free, dressed in a new suit and back out on the road, he still thought he smelled pine tree every so often. He didn't know if it had soaked into his pores, permeated the car's interior, or was simply in his head or perhaps his nose hairs. Whichever the case, it was driving him nuts and had put him in a foul mood. The throbbing in his lower back didn't help. He toggled the button for lumbar support and cursed himself for not bringing along some Tylenol or, better yet, a flask. If nothing else, a quick snort would help pass the time and definitely improve his outlook on things.

Ricky was wondering about Carl and whether or not he'd managed to find Skid Row and Bullfrog when Cullen's office window suddenly went dark. "And away we go," he said, reaching for the ignition.

-31-

"So where is this place?" Bullfrog asked as he and Skid Row moved down the sidewalk.

"Little further."

"And what exactly are we gonna do when we get there?"

Skid Row sighed and rolled his eyes. He was trying to be patient but Bullfrog was really ticking him off. "How many more times you gonna ask that?"

"Well I just--"

"Listen," Skid Row said, hoping to avoid the same argument they'd had several times already. "I think it's weird that that Carl dude showed up yesterday. I don't know what he's up to but I wanna find out."

"Why do you think he's up to anything?"

"You tell me," Skid Row said. "You're the one who thinks he and Ricky swiped that gym bag."

"Yeah? So what?"

"So if they did, they'd know damn well we had nothin' to sell, right?" He didn't wait for an answer. "Then why would Carl show up at that phone booth, right where we were supposed to be and where Marco would have been?"

"You mean if he wasn't dead."

"Of course, dumb ass! I don't think he's showing up anywhere now. I just don't get why Carl was there. That can't just be a coincidence."

"But why do you care?"

Skid Row brushed at his hair and began nibbling a fingernail. "Because I feel like it has something to do with us. I just don't know what."

"You mean other than the drugs they gave us that are now gone?"

"Shit!" Skid Row said, glancing around. "You want to say that a little louder?" There were people nearby but thankfully none within earshot. "That's just it," he said, lowering his head so he was speaking directly into Bullfrog's ear. "It's easy to say they took that bag. My spider sense tells me something else happened."

Bullfrog gave him a sidelong look. "And why shouldn't we trust such a reliable source?"

"Hey, you don't have to," Skid Row said. "And you don't have to hang around either. I told you that before. You're anxious to get out of town so go. I ain't stopping you."

Bullfrog stared at the sidewalk but said nothing.

Skid Row looked at him, still unable to get a read on the guy. He'd obviously been on his own for a while. Why did he seem so reluctant to be on his own again? Stranger still, why had he seemingly hitched his wagon to him? There had to be better options. In truth, Skid Row welcomed the company but wasn't sure how he felt about being questioned all the time.

He slowed his pace as their destination came into view. It was a Duds and Suds Laundromat, halfway down the block and sandwiched in between an insurance office and nail salon.

"Here's what I'm thinking," Skid Row said. "If Carl or Ricky shows up here, we'll know for sure that something's going on. That will help us figure out what to do next. And we don't have to wait long. We'll maybe give it a half hour."

"Then what?"

"I don't know," Skid Row admitted. "We'll have to see."

He'd noticed that the location of the laundromat, right smack in the middle of the block, was going to make it tough to find a place to see without being seen. Their best bet was probably the donut shop across the road. It had big glass windows, and they could sit all the way in the back and still have a good view.

Skid Row immediately thought of two problems. They wouldn't be able to see a whole lot to either side. That was a drawback but still better than being out in the open. But also he was down to his last few bucks. They couldn't loiter in a donut shop without buying something, and a couple chocolate éclairs, though tasty, wouldn't be a wise investment. He thought they might be better off if they simply kept moving. They could go up and down the cross streets, keeping an eye on the laundromat whenever it was in sight. Or...

"There's something you don't seem to be considering," Bullfrog said, interrupting his train of thought.

"Yeah? And what's that my man?"

"You said you think someone else took the bag. I don't buy it but let's just say you're right."

"Okay. I'm right. Sure glad that's settled. I hope you feel better now that you got that off your chest."

"If they didn't take it," Bullfrog went on, not even glancing Skid Row's way. "Then they don't know it's gone or that we've got nothing to sell."

"Been down this road, dude. What's your point?"

"Just this. They told us they'd be watching and they'd probably start with the places they thought we'd be. By going to the phone booth yesterday, and coming here today, we could be walking right into a trap."

Skid Row considered that. "Not buyin' it," he finally said. "When I saw Carl yesterday I--"

"Sup boys?"

The voice was oddly familiar but, for whatever reason, Skid Row couldn't immediately place it. He stopped, spun around, and for a split second didn't understand what he was looking at. He then realized it was a shirt button; specifically, the button on the left breast pocket of a very large black denim shirt, and only about six inches from his nose. He had a hard time tearing his eyes away, not because the button was especially attractive, black with flecks of silver and dark gray, but because he'd already figured out who it belonged to.

"Howdy," Carl said. "Looking for me?"

"Nnn-no," Skid Row stammered, stepping back, shooting a glance at Bullfrog and seeing that his eyes were bugged out even more than usual. His lips were moving too but he wasn't making a sound. "We were just...walkin'."

"Walkin' and talkin' from what I heard." Carl said with the smile of a great white shark. "What I want to know is what you were talkin' about."

Skid Row looked to Bullfrog again, and in doing so, happened to catch his own reflection in a storefront window. "We were...just talking about football."

"Yeah?" Carl smiled even wider. "I love football. And I see you're a Giants fan."

"Totally," Skid Row replied, touching the bill of his cap and silently thanking whoever had left it in that McDonald's bathroom.

"That's my team too." Carl nodded as if this bit of common ground was deeply meaningful. He paused, looked off down the block and then suddenly snapped his fingers. "Carl Banks!" he announced. "You must have been talking about him."

"Huh?" Skid Row gaped, no clue what he meant.

"You said you were talking football and I heard you mention Carl. I figure it had to be Banks."

"Right," Skid Row said. "Carl Banks. He's the man."

"You see that play Sunday night?"

Skid Row hadn't seen any play from any game as long as he could remember. But now that he and Carl were buddy-buddy, he had no choice but to go along. "Fucking epic," he exclaimed. "I couldn't believe it."

Carl gave a short laugh. "I couldn't either, and you know why?"

"Um.... Why?"Skid Row asked, not liking the odd glint in Carl's eyes.

"Because Banks fucking retired twenty years ago!"

As quickly as his grin vanished, Carl's long, powerful arm shot out and he had Skid Row by the throat, practically lifting him off his feet. Bullfrog let out a yelp but the best Skid Row could manage was a small gurgle.

Carl looked around, seemed to realize where he was and dropped both hands to his sides. "Lucky for you we're in public or things could get ugly."

Thinking it had gotten plenty ugly already. Skid Row staggered and might have fallen had Bullfrog not been right there to catch him. He hoped someone would yell for the police. Unfortunately, there weren't many people close enough to see what just happened and those that were seemed intent on looking the other way.

Beautiful, he thought. *He can break me into little pieces and no one will step in to help.* Skid Row knew he was screwed. They were both screwed and once again it was his fault.

He raised a hand to his throat where he could still feel the warm imprint of Carl's fingers. His brief chokehold hadn't actually hurt, at least not that much, but was still scary as all hell. He couldn't believe such a big, clumsy-looking man could move that fast. Where had he even come from? Skid Row would have sworn Carl hadn't been behind them even thirty seconds earlier. It was like he'd materialized out of thin air. It wasn't fair. A dude that size should have to wear a fucking bell or something.

He coughed and wheezed and made a pretense of struggling to catch his breath. Skid Row was really just stalling while he tried to wrap his head around this latest turn of events. He'd only worked out two possible scenarios for the day's activities. In the first, he would see Ricky, or Carl, or both, and that would somehow give him a clue as to what was going on. In the second, he wouldn't see them, although he hadn't spun that one forward far enough to decide what that might mean. The sneak-attack-by-Carl scenario hadn't occurred to him at all. It was like that first meeting all over again, when Carl had surprised and confronted them outside that nasty trailer. There wasn't anything Skid Row could do then and he felt just as helpless now. He considered making a run for it, and that's when he noticed that one of Bullfrog's hands was balled into a tight fist.

No way, he thought. *He ain't gonna swing at Carl. Be like punching a UPS truck.* Of course, Skid Row had seen firsthand what happened when Bullfrog was pushed too far and common sense was not part of the program.

No matter what the little nut job might be working himself up to Skid Row knew fighting wasn't the answer. Even together they'd have no chance against Carl. They couldn't run either. With his tremendous size and speed, it was doubtful they'd make it five steps. Besides, running would indicate they were guilty of something, which they damn sure weren't. He wanted Carl to know that, but preferably not at the cost of getting his skull crushed.

Thankfully, he hadn't made any more threatening moves...yet. He was just standing there, almost like he was waiting for them to do something stupid. Or, Skid Row thought, *is he waiting for instructions?* Was Carl acting alone or was Ricky someplace close by? He knew he should at least consider that possibility. If given the choice, who would he rather deal with? Carl definitely presented more of a physical threat. Ricky was just... slimier, and that was an entirely different kind of scary. Skid Row wished he could walk away from the whole thing. He wished he'd listened to Bullfrog while he had the chance. He hadn't, and the only way out now might be to talk their way out. He racked his brains to come up with something, anything he could say. It would have to be damn good because he'd already been caught in one lie.

"Why'd you take the bag?" Bullfrog asked, speaking up for the first time.

S*hit!* Skid Row thought. *He's suicidal.* So it appeared they would be taking the direct approach. Bullfrog looked Carl square in the eye, or at least as square as their height difference would allow.

For Carl's part, he stared back calmly and raised one Twinkie-sized eyebrow. "And which bag would that be," he asked, yawning as he plucked a small red notebook out of a pocket.

"Like you don't know?" Bullfrog drew himself up to his full height. Even to Skid Row, the sight was less than impressive. "You gave us that bag and then you stole it!"

"We gave you a bag," Carl said, licking the end of a pencil and making a quick notation before putting the notebook away. "Are you telling me it's gone?"

He looked at each of them in turn. There was nothing menacing in his words, his tone, or even his posture. Skid Row still wanted to melt into the sidewalk. Bullfrog was having a very different reaction. He squinted at Carl and his face turned red.

"You know it is!" he said, glaring and bouncing on the balls of his feet. "You took it and we want it back!"

Skid Row placed a hand on his arm to try to settle him down but Bullfrog shook him off.

"You know it's true," he said, pulling away and continuing to stare daggers at Carl. "I've been telling you all along. Let's see if he's man enough to admit it."

Carl reeled back like he'd been slapped, and Skid Row suddenly had a new hope for escape. He could flee while Carl was busy pounding Bullfrog into a bloody pulp. The dude had to have a death wish. Either that or he was flat-out crazy. Skid Row felt sure he'd be flat out on the sidewalk if he kept running his mouth.

Bullfrog seemed unaware of the danger, or maybe he just didn't care anymore. Chest heaving and muscles taut, he showed no signs of backing down. "Let's hear it!" he demanded, jabbing a finger into Carl's stomach. "Did you take the bag or not?"

Carl stared down at him and his finger as if he wasn't sure what to do. Skid Row guessed it had been a long time since anyone talked to him like that. Bullfrog continued to press his advantage, moving forward each time Carl gave an inch of ground. Skid Row wanted to cheer him on but was afraid to put himself in the middle of what he felt sure was about to happen.

To his amazement, Carl did not reach out and squash Bullfrog with a single blow from one of those huge hands. He had both hands out in front of him in what could only be described as a defensive position. Big-eyed, he looked to Skid Row as if asking him to call off his dog. Bullfrog was still right there in his face, and they stayed that way for a few nervous seconds. Then Skid Row sensed something starting to shift. It was in the body language. Carl stood up a little straighter while Bullfrog seemed to shrink. He hadn't yet lowered his finger but Skid Row could see it beginning to tremble. Before long, his entire arm was shaking. He still didn't retreat and Skid Row wondered if he'd be able to even if he tried. Realization of his situation might have frozen him in his tracks.

The sudden backfire from a city bus broke whatever spell was left. Skid Row flinched, Bullfrog jumped and Carl's lips curled in a sneer. He put his two hands together and gave Bullfrog one mighty shove. He went completely airborne, sailing over the sidewalk and landing on his ass in the road.

"Hey," Skid Row cried, but the deadly expression on Carl's face convinced him it would be unwise to say anything more. Instead, he moved to where Bullfrog was still splayed out on the ground, reminding Skid Row of the old Frogger video game. "Come on," he said, helping him to his feet. "You okay?"

Bullfrog nodded and began brushing himself off. He had an ugly scrape on one elbow but otherwise didn't look any the worse for wear. They both had bigger problems anyway as Carl was now looming over them.

"You listen to me," he growled, one hand clamped on Bullfrog's shoulder and the other gripping Skid Row by the hood of his sweatshirt. "Ricky gave you some product which you agreed to sell. If I understand the situation correctly, you're telling me the product is gone."

He leaned in so close Skid Row could feel the heat of his breath.

"Here's what you need to understand," he continued, smiling with all the warmth of dry ice. "I really don't give a shit. Maybe you're trying to scam us or maybe that stuff really is missing. Either way, it's your problem. You know what I'm saying? You owe Ricky money and he'll be expecting me to collect. I found you yesterday. I found you today. You can bet your scrawny white asses I'll find you again tomorrow. You won't even see me coming. And don't make the mistake of thinking it's just me and Ricky you have to worry about. We have eyes everywhere. I'll hound you until you pay back every cent you owe. Is that quite clear?"

Without waiting for a response, he turned and walked away.

-32-

Andrew Cullen knew he should head straight home, and probably would have had he not spotted an empty parking space no more than ten steps from the front door of Uncle Tony's pub. He debated, tapping knuckles on the steering wheel as he tried to make up his mind. In the end, he couldn't resist stopping in for one quick drink. He promised himself it would only be one, and he thought he could actually stick to that this time. He really was anxious to get home, see Sara and tell her about his decision to enter the triathlon. He knew she'd be supportive if not especially enthusiastic. That was because she'd be focusing on the extra time he'd have to put into his training. He understood. She was already upset he hadn't been spending much time at home lately, but Cullen couldn't help smiling to himself, knowing how quickly she'd change her tune once she found out he'd be doing it for charity--her charity. Past sins would be forgiven even faster than he could drop trow so they could celebrate in style.

It was after six so Cullen didn't have to worry about feeding the parking meter. He got out of the Avalon, whistling tunelessly as he studied his new key fob until he located the button to lock the doors. He went inside and was pleased to see the bar was mostly empty. The Binghamton Senators had a home game that night, against Rochester he thought, and Cullen knew a lot of the normal clientele would be there. He had always liked sports well enough but had never really been able to get into hockey. There wasn't enough scoring and he could never quite make sense of the rules, especially when it came to icing, off-sides, two-line passes and stuff like that. It was way too confusing. He much preferred football and college hoops.

"Good evening, Mr. Cullen. I haven't seen you in a while. I hope you're well."

"Hey, Gus. I'm doing great. Thanks for asking."

The old man had been serving drinks at Tony's for as long as Cullen could remember. He always wore black pants, a perfectly pressed white shirt and a black bow tie. He had to be in his mid 70's by now. His hair had thinned to a few grayish wisps and he'd begun to stoop but he still carried himself in a manner that commanded respect. Something about him had always reminded Cullen of Lloyd, the bar tender in that creepy-ass movie *The Shining*. Maybe it was the tie or that Gus always addressed his customers, even the regulars, with more formality than was necessary.

"Will you be having your usual?"

"Please. Gray Goose with tonic and...."

"A lime twist. Of course, sir." He mixed the drink, placed a cocktail napkin in front of Cullen and set the glass on top. "Will you be running a tab this evening?" Gus asked, using a towel to polish a bar top that already sparkled under the lights.

"Not this time." Cullen said, taking a small sip and smacking his lips with appreciation. "You make the best vodka and tonic in town but I have to limit myself to one."

"Do you have dinner reservation somewhere?" Gus inquired. He'd served Cullen enough times to know a single drink was not his norm.

"Nope. Just got some things I need to take care of."

Cullen wanted to tell Gus what those things were but he knew that would lead to a second drink and probably a third. Even if he didn't have somewhere else to go, he had to cut back on the booze or he'd never be able to get himself in shape. He'd overindulged at lunch and definitely couldn't afford to do it again so soon.

"I understand," Gus said, looking genuinely disappointed Cullen wouldn't be staying. The guy was nothing if not sincere. "That will be four twenty-five."

"You got it." He patted his breast pocket and then both his back pockets. His wallet wasn't there. He had a momentary panic but then had a vague recollection of having trouble manipulating his pockets after his mostly liquid lunch. He was sure he had his wallet when he left the restaurant and thought he remembered sliding it into the center console of the new car. Or had he put it in the glove compartment? He wasn't sure.

"Back in a second," Cullen said, taking another quick sip of his drink. "I left my wallet in the car." He prayed it really was there and that he hadn't actually dropped the thing in a parking lot somewhere and not realized it.

He left the pub, digging in his pocket for his keys but he froze as soon as he reached the sidewalk. To his amazement, a man in a dark suit was trying to open the passenger door of the Avalon. Finding it locked, he then began messing around with the windshield wipers.

"Hey," Cullen said. He only had a view of the man's back but something about him struck a nerve. He knew he'd seen him somewhere before.

At the sound of Cullen's voice, the man stopped and turned around. He did it slowly, and nothing in his body language suggested he was scared or even nervous. He had no reason to be.

Ricky Fixx smiled thinly, then leaned a hip against the car hood, crossed his arms over his chest and cocked his head. "Well, well. Andrew Cullen," he said, his tone giving away nothing. "As I live and breathe."

Cullen was completely at a loss. Of all the people he didn't want to see right then.... He had meant to call Ricky, probably would have later that night but only after all aspects of his plan had been carefully thought out. To his tremendous relief, he believed he had solved the problem about how to get his hands on a portion of donor contributions. He needed to do a little more research but that was definitely a step in the right direction. It didn't mean all systems were go. There were details, a lot of details he still needed to consider. Cullen wasn't ready to have that conversation, if for no other reason than he might end up saying too much and making promises, *more promises*, he wouldn't be able to keep.

Logistical problems aside, Ricky's sudden appearance had caught him totally off guard. Where had he come from? Had he followed him there? Did that even matter? All that really did matter was what would happen next. Cullen was bigger, stronger and faster. He was absolutely sure of that. If he ran, there was no way Ricky would catch him. If it came to it, Cullen also guessed he could take him in a fight. He didn't relish the idea of testing that theory. Ricky looked completely at ease, studying his fingernails and then rubbing at a spot on his tie, and his casual demeanor put Cullen on edge. His muscles tensed, not sure what he'd do yet but wanting to be ready.

Ricky must have sensed what he was thinking. "Time for us to chat," he said, cocking his head to the other side. "And before you do anything stupid," he plucked a cell phone from an inside pocket. "I've got my man on speed dial and I can have him here in about thirty seconds flat."

Ricky doubted Cullen would believe that. But under the circumstances, it wasn't likely the guy would be willing to take the chance.

"What were you doing there?" Cullen asked, nodding at his car and then glancing back at Tony's front door. He could see Gus through the window, busy washing glasses and thankfully paying him no attention.

"Is this yours?" Ricky asked, turning around and making a show of admiring the Avalon. "Bit of a downgrade," he observed, trailing his fingers along the hood. "Last I knew you were driving that pretty little Jag. I know you still had it this morning."

Cullen tried to keep the surprise off his face but knew from Ricky's reptile-like smile that he'd failed. The intent of that last comment was plain. Someone was keeping tabs on him, as Cullen already knew. More to the point, although he might be the one with the big house, the nicer car and the social standing, Ricky, cheap suit, ten dollar haircut and all, was undeniably in charge.

Cullen stared at him for a moment and then looked away. "Sold it," he said, almost like he was confessing to a crime.

"Now that is a shame. That was one sweet ride. Course," Ricky said, stroking his chin as if he'd just had a wonderful idea. "If you were driving a Jaguar then and you're putting around in a Toyota now, I'm thinking you must have a bundle of money for me. I sure hope so because you owe me a bundle and your payment is past due."

"I know," Cullen said. "I'm sorry."

"Sorry don't feed the bulldog."

"I know," Cullen repeated. He glanced up and down the street and then lowered his head in hopes that would make him somewhat less recognizable to anyone who might be looking his way. He really didn't want to be seen talking to this guy.

"What are you so worried about?" Ricky asked. "You afraid people will know you and me are buds? Are you ashamed of me?"

"It's not that," Cullen said, even though it was. And really, he was mostly ashamed of himself for getting in bed with the worm in the first place. What had he been thinking?

"Well what is it then? I tried calling you… oh, I don't know, maybe a dozen times. Had some nice talks with that secretary of yours. Fine piece of ass. You tap that keg yet?"

Cullen looked at him but said nothing.

"Well, I'm sure you've tried. She somehow got the idea we went to college together."

"I got your messages."

"That's good," Ricky said. "Would have been even better if you'd returned my calls. We're both businessmen. We had a business deal and you weren't holding up your end of it. What was I supposed to do?" He held out his hands like he couldn't possibly be more reasonable if he'd tried.

Cullen didn't know what to say. Ricky, after all, was right. He had not held up his end and Cullen was probably lucky he'd made it this far without suffering bodily injury or worse. He'd seen the goon Ricky hung out with. The guy looked like he ate nails for breakfast. He didn't want to think about what he might be capable of if angered. Ricky would probably be only too happy to tell him, but Cullen didn't want to conduct this little tete-a-tete in the middle of a very public sidewalk.

"I'm gonna need more time," he said, keeping his voice low. "I'm really sorry. And I'm sorry I haven't been in touch. You have every right to be upset."

"You're full of apologies," Ricky said, every trace of his smile gone. "That supposed to make me feel good? And for the record, I have every right to rip your balls off. The only question is whether or not I should do it right now."

"I'm going to pay you."

"Yeah? So show me the money."

"I don't have it right now, but I can get it. Soon."

Cullen took another nervous look around. No one, so far as he could tell, was paying them the slightest attention. Most of the people he saw were hurrying in the direction of the arena where the hockey game would soon be underway. He still felt uncomfortable. It wasn't that Ricky looked like a criminal, at least not exactly. His suit was a little too shiny and his hair was the type that looked greasy even when it wasn't. He also looked at Cullen in an unusually disconcerting way that made him want to go take a shower.

"Can we, uh, talk about this inside? I'll buy you a drink." He didn't want to bring Ricky into Uncle Tony's but didn't see where he had much choice.

"You can't afford to pay what you owe and now you're buying drinks? Maybe that's part of the problem."

"Please," Cullen said. He tried to give his voice the proper level of urgency without making it sound like he was begging. "This is important and I promise I'll make it worth your while."

"You promise," Ricky said, frowning. "A Hell of a lot of good that's done me so far." He made a show of studying his watch. "I'll give you five minutes. If I don't like what I'm hearing, I call my man and he comes down here to make sure you understand the seriousness of this situation. I have to warn you. He tends to be a little...well let's just say heavy-handed."

"That won't be necessary," Cullen said, swallowing against the rising bile in his throat.

"You better hope not."

Cullen turned to reach for the door, and as he did he saw Ricky pluck something from beneath the Avalon's wiper blade. He hadn't seen it before because of the way Ricky had been standing.

"What's that?"

"Oh, this? Ricky asked, holding a small envelope between two fingers. "I was leaving you a present. I didn't know I'd get the chance to deliver it in person. This should be fun."

Cullen blinked and took a step back.

"What's the problem?" Ricky asked. He held the envelope out and, when Cullen didn't take it, stepped forward and tucked it into the inside pocket of his sport coat. "There," he said," adjusting Cullen's lapels. "Safe and sound."

Cullen still didn't say anything so Ricky reached past him grabbed the handle of Uncle Tony's front door and opened it wide. "Allow me, he said, motioning Cullen inside.

"I... uh... hold on a second," Cullen said, feeling suddenly very weak in the knees. He pulled out his keys, nearly dropped them, and then found the button to unlock the doors.

"Going somewhere?" Ricky asked, making no move to stop him.

Cullen wondered if there was any chance of making a fast getaway. He considered, but knew how foolish and ultimately pointless it would be to even try and Ricky plainly knew it too.

"I just need to get something," Cullen said, opening the passenger door and, while Ricky looked on silently, fumbling around in the center console until he came out with his wallet. He pocketed it quickly, and kept both his hands in his pockets so Ricky couldn't see how badly they were shaking.

-33-

"Where the hell did he come from?" Skid Row asked, still shaking from the after-effects of fear and anger.

"Does it matter?" With a scowl, Bullfrog spat into his hand and rubbed his elbow which had swollen and continued to ooze blood.

"Shit, yeah. He said he can find us whenever he wants." Skid Row looked around like he expected Carl to pop up again any second. "How do we know he isn't watching us right now?"

He and Bullfrog had spent the past couple hours working their way indirectly toward their new camp, occasionally taking random turns or doubling back a block or two. They hadn't seen Carl, Ricky, or anyone else that seemed to be taking particular interest in their movements. Skid Row still felt like there were eyes on them every step of the way.

They passed a row of low-rent apartments, the angle of the late afternoon sun casting all the street-facing windows in shadow. To Skid Row, each pane of darkened glass looked like a perfect spot from which to spy on him. He imagined an endless string of informants, cell phones pressed to their ears as they reported on his progress. Such thoughts were stupid and irrational. He knew that but still couldn't get them out of his head. He even caught himself regularly inspecting rooftops, for what he wasn't entirely sure.

"You believe him?" Bullfrog asked, repeatedly bending and straightening his arm and wincing each time he did.

"Huh?" Skid Row was so busy trying to determine if there was something or someone hunched over behind the Salvation Army drop box on the other side of the street, he'd lost track of their conversation.

"He said he could find us anytime," Bullfrog replied. "Do you believe him?"

"Well, yeah. I mean...don't you?"

"Not even a little bit."

"How can you say that?" Skid Row asked, staring at him. "He found me, or us, the last two days. What makes you think he can't do it again?"

Bullfrog stopped next to a brown metal bench and sat down. Skid Row hesitated, not liking the idea pausing right there in the open and making such easy targets of themselves. He would have preferred to keep moving, but his feet really were killing him. It felt like he'd been doing nothing but walking for the past three days. Bullfrog was probably used to it. He'd walked all the way from Maine. Skid Row wasn't in the habit of getting that much exercise and his body was letting him know. He took one nervous look up and down the street and then perched on the edge of the seat.

"Listen," Bullfrog said, placing his hands on his knees and hunching forward in a rather frog-like pose. "You've got to admit you made yourself pretty easy to find."

"What?" Skid Row asked, his voice rising indignantly. "I was careful."

"I'd say predictable."

Skid Row wanted to protest but Bullfrog silenced him with a raised hand.

"I'm not blaming you," he said. "All I'm saying is, had that bag not been stolen, we would have gone to those same two places to sell."

"Yeah but--"

"We were right where they told us to be. It's no wonder that's where they went to find us."

"But if they're the ones that swiped the bag--"

"There's no IF about it; not anymore. Please tell me you see that by now."

"Okay," Skid Row said. "But it's not like I was standing around waiting for him. I was behind a fucking dumpster and he found me anyway."

"So maybe he got lucky," Bullfrog offered. "I don't know, but he definitely didn't have as much help as he wants us to believe."

"How do you know?"

"Think about the first time we saw those two," Bullfrog said. "Think about that rusted mailbox and Carl's beat up truck and that disgusting trailer they call an office. I've bedded down in some bad places but I've never seen anything like that. There was mold on the ceiling."

"So it was gross. Big deal."

"You're missing the point." Bullfrog leaned back and studied him. "From what we've seen, do you really think Ricky and Carl are at the top of some major crime network? Does that make sense to you?"

"Shit, dude. I don't know." Skid Row jerked his head to shake the hair out of his eyes. "I guess not. It still freaks me out."

"It freaks me out too. Those guys are bad news and Carl just told us we owe a bunch of money we don't have."

"I heard that," Skid Row said. "So why didn't you kick his ass when you had the chance?"

He and Bullfrog looked at each other and started to laugh.

"You're a piece of work," Skid Row said. "You really surprised me getting in Carl's face like that."

Bullfrog shrugged. "You know what? I surprised me too. I don't know what I was thinking."

"You weren't. I could see that much. He pissed you off and you reacted, just like you did at McDonald's."

"And just like I did in the dining hall at school." Bullfrog stared at his boots. "It happens sometimes. I don't know why. I just sort of lose control."

"Yeah, well you might want to work on that or it's gonna get you killed one of these days. You can't be throwing down with dudes three times your size."

Bullfrog concentrated on nursing his elbow, alternately rubbing and then holding it gingerly.

"That real sore?" Skid Row asked.

He immediately dropped his hand. "Nothing's broken. I'll live."

"Good thing he didn't kick your head in. He could have, you know?"

"There was never any danger of that."

"Right," Skid Row said, starting to laugh, but stopping again when he saw that Bullfrog was serious. "You don't really think you could have beat him in a fight."

"You kidding?" Bullfrog asked. "I wouldn't last ten seconds."

"Then--"

"He said we owe them money, right? They're not gonna get it if we're in the morgue."

Fair point, Skid Row thought, realizing that, even though Bullfrog sometimes acted bat shit crazy, he had a good head on his shoulders. Too bad he hadn't picked up on that sooner. They'd probably both be better off.

"So you're saying we've got a little insurance policy."

"You could call it that."

"Fine. Then let's blow this popsicle stand." He took one look up and down the street and then stood. "You ready?"

Bullfrog got to his feet. "And miles to go before I sleep."

"Huh?"

"Nothing," he said. "Let's get out of here."

Skid Row started off in the opposite direction of their camp.

"Where are you going?" Bullfrog asked.

"I'm just making sure…."

But Bullfrog had stopped and crossed his arms over his chest. "Didn't you listen to anything I just said?"

"Well, yeah. I just wanted to be sure."

"I'd think you would be by now. We've hardly taken a step all day without you looking around to see if anyone noticed. Carl isn't following us. No one is. Put your paranoia away and let's go. It's getting dark"

Skid Row wanted to argue but he knew he couldn't. Bullfrog's reasoning made perfect sense and although he had been looking, he hadn't seen anything remotely suspicious since their run-in with Carl. He'd left them standing on the sidewalk, driven past in his pickup a couple minutes later and that had been it.

"Okay," Skid Row said, and he made a conscious effort not even to glance behind him when they turned in the direction of their camp.

Carl was halfway through his second Whopper with cheese when his iPhone vibrated. He set the burger aside, wiped his hands on his pants and dug the phone out of his back pocket. Smiling, he read the single text message. His targets, one of them anyway, was on the move. Unconcerned, he took his time finishing the sandwich and large order of fries. He drained his Coke, belched loudly, and then picked up his phone again and activated the new app. It told him Skid Row was currently six blocks away and headed southwest at about four miles per hour. Carl didn't know or care if Bullfrog was with him. He had one of them and that was really all he needed. He thought briefly about doing a drive by, imagining the look of shock on their faces if he suddenly pulled up right next to them. It was tempting, but he decided it would be better not to tip his hand so soon. He cranked the engine, checked his mirrors, pulled a quick U-turn and headed toward the office.

-34-

Ricky studied Cullen across the table top. They shared a booth at Uncle Tony's, tucked into a corner and about as far away from the bar as possible. That was fine with him. He didn't appreciate the way the old guy behind the bar kept staring at him. Cullen called him Gus. That fit. An old fart name for an old fart. Ricky wanted to stand up and tell him to mind his own fucking business. He resisted, not because Cullen was obviously trying to keep their conversation private but because Ricky was quite a ways from his normal stomping ground. Keeping a low profile made sense, so he sipped his Jim Beam and didn't so much as sneer the next time the geezer caught his eye.

"You're on the clock," Ricky said, tapping the face of his watch for effect. "But before you tell me why you dragged me into this dump, I suggest you open that envelope. I think you'll find the contents very interesting."

In truth, Ricky thought the place looked pretty nice and whatever they had going in the kitchen smelled fabulous. He wasn't about to say that. He wasn't going to say or do anything that might help put Cullen at ease. Normally, he wouldn't have even agreed to meet on Cullen's turf. Ricky wanted as much leverage as he could get. That's why he'd planned on simply leaving the envelope. Cullen would find it, look inside, probably shit his pants, and then he'd call Ricky and Ricky could call the shots from that point forward. It hadn't worked out that way, but Ricky still felt like he had the upper hand. If Cullen didn't agree, he would as soon as he got up enough nerve to look at that first picture.

"What is this?" Cullen asked, holding the envelope as if he thought it might be filled with anthrax.

Ricky just shrugged, swirling the ice in his glass and doing his best to look indifferent.

The envelope was plain white and unmarked. Cullen stared at it for awhile, placed it on the table in front of him and slowly turned it over. It wasn't sealed and the flap hung open. That seemed to take him by surprise and, Ricky thought, gave him some courage.

We'll see how long that lasts.

He counted to seven. That was how long it took for Cullen to pull out the pictures, look at the one on the top of the pile, grasp what he was seeing, and then for most of the color to drain from his face.

"That's my favorite," Ricky said, sipping his drink and using the bottom of the glass to point at the picture. It was the shot of Sara

Cullen, arms around her two daughters as they walked into the house. "Beautiful family," he observed. "You should be proud."

"What have you done?" Cullen asked, his voice cracking and nearly disappearing by the time he got the words out.

"Who said I've done anything?"

"But that's... my wife." Cullen seemed unable to pull his eyes away from the photo.

"Very observant. And I believe that's Kristin and Kayla she's with. Lovely girls."

"If you..." But Cullen fell silent, unable to say anything more.

He sat and stared while Ricky looked on, biting back a smile. He was getting an even better reaction than he'd hoped. He hadn't even started tightening the screws yet and Cullen already appeared on the edge of collapse. His face was about as white and stiff as his starched dress shirt and he seemed to have a hard time catching his breath. That was good. Part of Ricky's reluctance to deliver the pictures in person was the possibility that Cullen would react violently. No danger of that now. It didn't look like he could find the strength to stand up, let alone mount an attack. That should make their negotiations a breeze. All he'd have to do was--.

"Mr. Cullen? Is everything all right, sir?"

Shit! Ricky looked over in time to see the nosey-ass bar tender approaching their table.

"We're just fine," he said quickly, sweeping the stack of photos aside. "I'm afraid I was the bearer of some bad news. My friend here is taking it hard."

"I'm very sorry. Is there anything I can do?"

You can get the hell out of here. "I don't think so," Ricky said. "He'll be okay in a minute. Actually... Gus is it? I suppose we could use another round. "

"Of course, sir. I'll be back in a moment." He gave Cullen a curious look and then turned back toward the bar.

"You know what?" Ricky said, pushing back from the table. "I'll come up and get them. I think Andrew could use a little space."

That was true enough but he really just wanted to keep Gus at a distance. The more he hung around the more likely it was Cullen would do or say something stupid.

"Be right back pal," Ricky said, placing a hand on Cullen's shoulder and squeezing hard enough to make his point. To Gus it would look like a friendly gesture of support, but Ricky wanted to make sure Cullen got the message that he'd better not try anything. No way to know if that message had been received. Cullen had barely moved a muscle and was still staring at the tabletop as if the pictures were still in front of him.

"Is he going to be all right?" Gus asked, pouring vodka and then tonic into a glass.

"Oh sure," Ricky said, trying to come up with a story that was suitably horrific but also impersonal enough that Gus would lose interest in their conversation. He finally decided to spin a familiar yarn out a little further.

"Andrew and I went to college together," he explained. "I found out today that our old business professor passed away. It was totally unexpected and he and Andrew were always quite close. I hated to be the one to tell him but it's probably best that it come from a friend."

"I understand. Those things can be so painful. Please tell Mr. Cullen I'm terribly sorry."

"Thanks," Ricky said, shaking his head sadly. "I'll do that. What do I owe you for the drinks?'

"This round is on the house."

Ricky returned to the table, thinking the old fart might not be so bad after all. And, he noted with satisfaction, Gus was no longer looking in their direction, focused more on the television and the new Wheel of Fortune puzzle.

"Pardon the interruption," Ricky said, setting the drinks down and settling into his chair. "Would you like to see the rest of these? I've got some good shots."

"I...." Cullen picked up his glass and took a large swig. "I don't think that's necessary."

Ricky agreed. His implied threat had clearly hit the mark. However, Cullen claimed not to have the means to pay off his loan and Ricky wasn't sure where his conviction would be after another hour or another day had gone by.

"I'll tell you what," he said, reaching over and tucking the envelope into Cullen's inside coat pocket. "I'm gonna put those there for safe keeping. Next time I try to contact you, I suggest you look at them before you decide to blow me off. Capiche?"

Cullen nodded and licked his lips. "Where'd you get 'em.?"

"What difference does that make?""

"I... I just want to know."

"You want to know," Ricky repeated. "It seems to me that you're not in much of a position to make demands."

"Please!" Cullen said, his eyes frantic.

"Fine," Ricky said. "If it's that important to you, I took them myself. You should be able to figure out where I was when I did it." He leaned in close. "I could have walked right into your house. I could have put bullets in their brains. I could have done…" he sat back and shrugged, "anything, really."

"You wouldn't."

Ricky's face hardened. "Just because I didn't doesn't mean I won't. You owe me a substantial sum of money. You will clear that ledger or be made to regret it. I am a reasonable man but I've had enough of your games."

Cullen blanched, which Ricky wouldn't have thought possible given his already ghost-like pallor.

"I…." He cleared his throat. "I really was gonna call you."

"Yeah. You said that before. And if I had sat at home waiting for my phone to ring, what would you have said other than to tell me that you're a no-good deadbeat?"

"I am going to pay," Cullen said, gripping the edge of the table as if to steady himself. He looked around the pub until finally meeting Ricky's eyes. "I just need a little more time."

"I might be able to give you an extension, as long as you understand that time is money."

Cullen nodded slowly.

"And how much additional time would you need?"

"Just two weeks."

"Two weeks," Ricky echoed. "The original loan was for two weeks. That's come and gone. And then you dicked me around for a few days more. Why do I feel like you're blowing smoke up my ass again?"

"I'll make it worth your while. I swear!"

Ricky paused and pursed his lips. "Now how are you going to do that?" He looked at Cullen with scorn. "And how can I believe you anyway? So far, you haven't even paid back the interest from the original loan." He spread his hands. "What am I supposed to do here?"

Ricky didn't expect Cullen to have much to say to that. What could he say really? If the new Avalon was any indication, he was already selling off personal belongings to pay his debts. What other assets did he have? There was the house of course but, for all Ricky knew, that might be mortgaged to the hilt. It probably was, which meant Cullen was stalling for time because that was the only commodity he had left. He might be asking for two extra weeks so he could scrape together a few thousand dollars. It was just as likely he'd try to pull a disappearing act. Ricky wasn't going to allow that to happen.

He contemplated his next move and tried to figure out just how far he was willing to go. It wouldn't bother him in the slightest to put Cullen in traction or, more to the point, tell Carl to do it. Would that really do any good? In the end, the only thing Ricky really wanted was his money. Was Cullen more likely to pay up with or without some freshly broken bones? He wasn't sure and that was pissing him off. He couldn't understand what motivated a guy like Cullen, who had everything in the world going for him, to fuck his life up so royally. He wished he'd left him to his own self-destructive devices. Too late for that now. And if Cullen didn't make good, Ricky would be solely responsible for a screw-up far larger and more costly than anything Carl ever did.

He picked up his glass, mainly because his other impulse was to smack Cullen around some just for putting him in this position. Ricky knew he couldn't do anything right then, not even if the bar was completely empty. *But maybe....*

His left hand drifted toward the pocket where he kept his cell phone. He could always reach out to Carl and have him waiting outside in all his hairy and muscular glory. Normally, Ricky didn't like to be around when Carl did his dirty work. Just this once, though, he thought he could make an exception. He remembered that damn pine tree and all the trouble he'd had getting those pictures. He'd spent half the day traipsing around in the woods and in doing so he'd ruined a perfectly good suit and all because Cullen had been such a pain in his ass. Yeah, he could make an exception for sure and he'd take tremendous pleasure in watching the guy get stomped. He started to smile, and that's when Cullen finally spoke up.

"I'll pay you double."

Ricky froze, Carl and the phone already forgotten. He studied Cullen's face. He was plainly still shaken but his color was returning and he'd regained some composure. Could he be bluffing? He owned his own company and had probably been involved in some big money negotiations. He also spent way more than his share of time at the blackjack table. He'd had plenty of opportunity to master his poker face and that made Ricky nervous.

"You'd better not be fucking with me."

"Double," Cullen insisted, his gaze unwavering.

"You're talking about a hundred thousand dollars," he said, thinking he'd gladly give his left nut for that kind of money.

"Conan the Barbarian!"

What the heck? Ricky looked toward the bar. There were big-screen televisions everywhere. Most showed college basketball. Some tennis tournament was on too. Gus was oblivious to everything but Pat Sajak and the overweight jerk in the hideous pink Hawaiian shirt. He was struggling to solve the current Wheel of Fortune puzzle. Everything was there but the N's but he still couldn't get it.

"Conan the Barbarian," Gus said again, shaking his head in disgust.

Ricky turned his attention back to Cullen. "I'm listening," he said. "This had better be good."

-35-

Skid Row woke to the sound of water pounding against the rocks. It took a few confused seconds for him to remember where he was and how he'd gotten there. He blinked, wondered what time it was and then realized it made no difference. It wasn't like he had anywhere to be.

The night before, at the end of a day during which he felt like he'd walked a hundred miles, not to mention having the living hell scared out of him by Carl, Skid Row had been so completely drained that he collapsed minutes after he and Bullfrog stumbled back into their camp. Without even bothering to eat, he lay down, closed his eyes and was gone, the noise of the waterfall barely even registering. But now, the ceaseless torrent was like a dull blade right through the middle of his eyeball. He groaned and rolled over, smacking his head in the process.

"F-u-c-k me," he said, his throat so dry his voice was hardly audible. That's when Skid Row first noticed the cold. It hadn't seemed that bad when he'd gone to bed, but the temperature must have dropped a good twenty degrees overnight. He could see his breath, and his fingers and toes felt numb.

Shivering, he burrowed deeper into his sleeping bag. He smelled smoke, which meant Bullfrog was already up, but Skid Row wasn't quite ready to join him. If he'd had a pillow, he would have used it to cover his head. Instead, he reached up to brush hair out of his face and immediately discovered why he was so damn cold. All of his hair was frozen, stuck to his head like hard-shell ice cream topping. *Note to self*, he thought, blinking up at the layer of mist that always hung in the air. *Gotta sleep with my head under the covers from now on.*

"Any chance you got coffee out there?" Skid Row called, rolling over and sitting up.

"Oh, sure. Fresh croissants too. Come get 'em while they're hot."

Skid Row dressed, pulling on jeans, t-shirt, sweatshirt and coat as fast as he could. If he had hat and gloves, he would have put those on too.

"Morning," Bullfrog said, once he had emerged. "Sorry but the croissants are all gone."

"Yeah, that figures." Skid Row looked around. Bullfrog had a nice fire going and was practically sitting on top of it. "How long you been up?"

"A while. Too cold to sleep."

“No shit.” Skid Row blew on his hands, rubbed them together and then stuffed them in his armpits.

“There’s breakfast if you want it.”

“Anything good?” Skid Row realized he was starving.

"A fried baloney sandwich is the best I can offer."

He made a face. "That would be my second choice. My first choice would be anything else."

“Stop complaining,” Bullfrog said. “It’s not that bad and it’s hot. You want one or not?”

“Guess I ain’t got much choice.” He moved over to stand near the fire. "We’ll need to hit a grocery store today. Can’t live on baloney sandwiches forever."

“That’s true,” Bullfrog said, holding the package up. “This is the last of it.” He looked at Skid Row but then looked away.

"It’s cool," Skid Row said. “I got a little money left. I'll also get a paycheck in a couple days. We’ll be all right.”

Bullfrog poked at the fire but didn’t respond.

"Something wrong?"

"Since you asked, yeah, there kind of is. I don't like being a freeloader. I want to pull my weight."

"You are," Skid Row said.

"Really? How? You paid for the bus tickets. You bought our food. You bought everything. All I did was get you fired."

"Big deal," Skid Row said. “It was a sucky job anyway." He was trying to lighten the mood but could see Bullfrog wasn't going for it. "Listen," he went on. "You do plenty. You found this camp. We’d be totally screwed without that"

“Aren’t we pretty screwed anyway?”

“Well, sure,” Skid Row acknowledged, “but now we’re screwed with a nice view and our own waterfall. That’s the American dream, dude.”

"Great. I found us a place to crash. That hardly compares to you paying my way."

"Okay," Skid Row said, sitting down next to him. "So maybe you did get me fired. Maybe I've been picking up the tab. I'm also the reason we owe a bunch of money and we've been forced to hide out. Without your help, there's no telling where I'd be right now but I'm pretty damn sure it wouldn't be good."

Bullfrog eyed him carefully. "You serious?"

"Yeah, man." Skid Row mostly said that for Bullfrog's benefit but he realized it was true. For all their problems, he thought they made a pretty good team. He also thought they'd probably need each other if they were ever going to get out of this mess.

"That paycheck," Bullfrog said, looking at least somewhat reassured. "How much is it gonna be?"

"I actually have two coming. I put in around thirty hours last week. That check will be pretty good. My last one won't. That's 'cause my pay period was cut short when this crazy dude went all super hero on me."

"So what do you think we should do today?" Bullfrog asked.

"I was hoping you'd know. None of my ideas have worked out that great."

"You mentioned supplies."

"Yeah. And then we might want to think about getting out of here."

"You mean leave? I didn't think you wanted to do that."

"I don't," Skid Row said, picking at a knot he'd somehow put in his shoelace. "But it's got to be better than whatever the bearded wonder's going to do if he finds us again."

"It's not like he's going to shoot us or anything. I mean, he's got to give us time to come up with the money, right?"

"Possibly," Skid Row said, "but why leave it up to him? We can disappear like a couple of smoke rings. He'll never know what happened to us and he and that Ricky dude can find someone else to fuck with."

Bullfrog picked up a charred piece of wood and began jabbing it at the campfire. "I definitely don't mind leaving. I wanted to be a ways south before cold weather sets in anyway."

"May be a tad late for that. Pretty fucking nippy this morning." He ran a hand through his hair. It had thawed, thankfully, but Skid Row also noticed how heavy and flat it felt. That reminded him of how long it had been since he'd had a proper shower. He'd definitely need to do something about that."

"That's just it," Bullfrog said, interrupting his thoughts. "I'm not sure it's wise to hit the road when we've got no money and it's already getting so cold at night. I've done that before and it ain't fun."

"Then what do you suggest?"

"We lay low until you get your next check. That way we'd have something in reserve if we needed to get a blanket, a hot meal or whatever. We could even buy bus tickets. Or you could anyway."

"I'm not gonna just leave you."

"You could. I mean, I wouldn't blame you. You don't owe me anything."

"I'm not gonna do that," Skid Row insisted, feeling guilty about the number of times he'd considered that very thing. He wondered if Bullfrog had any idea. "Where do you think we should go?" he asked, deciding it was best to change the subject altogether.

Bullfrog shrugged and poked at the fire some more. "It doesn't matter to me. It would be nice to settle somewhere for a while. Get a real job. I'm getting tired of moving around all the time."

"I thought you needed to... find yourself or whatever."

"I've been doing that and I don't think I like what I'm finding. Maybe it's time to start over."

Skid Row wasn't sure what to make of that. He got quickly to his feet, sensing their conversation had been on the verge of getting totally weird. He had enough to worry about without Bullfrog spilling his guts all over the place.

"I need to get cleaned up," he said, retrieving his box of belongings and digging for his soap and shampoo. "Give me a few minutes and then we'll head into town."

-36-

"Talk to me," Ricky said, practically bouncing in his chair as he studied Carl across the desktop. He had news but hadn't yet decided how much he really wanted to share. All of a sudden, Carl's pursuit of the two drifter types was of little consequence. Ricky might have told him to drop the whole thing if not for the deal with Marco and how badly Carl had fucked that up. He couldn't simply let that go. On the other hand, what difference did a couple grand make one way or the other? He'd hit a grand slam with one Andrew Cullen and was now having a hard time staying mad at his partner or controlling his own enthusiasm. Ricky knew things could still go sour. Hell, they probably would, and that's what he kept telling himself so he could work his facial features into a proper mask of disapproval.

"Were you able to find them?" he asked, biting the inside of his lip to keep his frown in place.

"Course," Carl said, "I told you it wouldn't be a problem."

"And what happened?"

He pulled out his precious notebook and began slapping it against his thigh. "They think we took the bag."

"Is that a fact?" Ricky asked, unconcerned.

"Oh yeah. The little frog-looking one came right out and said it. He was all sorts of pissed too. I thought he was gonna come after me."

“You can't be serious."

"He was ready," Carl said. “That one’s got guts. Wouldn’ta thought it.”

"And what’d you do?"

"What do you think? I knocked him on his ass. He went down faster than a crack whore"

Ricky stiffened, his good mood disappearing instantly. "You didn't kill him. Tell me you didn’t fucking kill him."

Carl shook his head. "I pushed him one time."

"That supposed to make me feel better? You said that same thing about Marco and he ended up getting his picture in the paper."

"It was nothing like that."

"You sure?"

Carl scowled.

"Don’t lie to me," Ricky said. "I don't want to find out he's in traction or on life support or anything."

"He's fine," Carl spat, his face darkening. "I shoved him once. He landed on his ass and got right back up again. End of story."

Ricky wanted to believe him but wasn't sure if he could. He thought about all the Years they'd been in business together. How many times before had Carl taken things too far? He rarely admitted it until there was no other choice. Was this yet another one of those situations? How was he to know? Ricky tried to read him, staring into flat brown eyes that gave away nothing.

"Okay," he finally said, wanting to move things along. "I'm only asking because we've been down that road before. No need to get testy."

"No need to piss me off either. You told me to find them and I did. I could do without the cross examination."

Well too fucking bad, Ricky thought, because he knew Carl's lengthy resume of monumental blunders warranted serious micromanagement. He wanted to point that out, but decided not to push it any further right then.

"The little guy wanted to take you on, huh?" he asked, hoping his question would help lighten the mood.

"He was tempted," Carl said, still looking annoyed. "Gotta give him credit for that."

"And what about the other one?"

"I don't think he's got the balls to run out of a burning building."

That was Ricky's impression too, but in his experience you could never be sure. That's why he tried to always be prepared and why, even though he'd promised Cullen he'd give him some space, he planned on monitoring him as closely as he could.

"So you found them," Ricky said, propping his feet on the edge of the desk. "That's good work. Tell me everything."

Carl went through it all, starting with his hunch that the laundromat would be a good place to look for them.

"I wouldn't have gone there," Ricky said, impressed in spite of himself. "I guess that's why you're so much better at tracking people down. You can think like the scum bags."

"Gee, thanks," Carl said, giving Ricky a look.

"So what did you tell them when they said we took the bag?"

"I didn't tell them shit, except that they owe us two thousand bucks."

"And how'd they take that?"

"Don't know," Carl said with a shrug. "I really took them by surprise and they were both pretty rattled. I'm not sure our conversation had really sunk in yet."

"Okay. Rattled means scared, and that means they'll do whatever they have to to get the money. So what will you do next?"

Carl stared at him blankly. "What do you mean?"

"I mean when will you meet them again? When did you tell them they have to pay?"

"I..." Carl began, but it was clear he had nothing more to say.

Ricky stared at him, bolting upright in his chair. "Are you for real?" he asked. "How long have you been doing this shit? Do I really have to spell out every fucking thing?" He ran a hand across his forehead and down the side of his face, struggling and failing to keep his anger in check. "You're telling me you just let them walk away? What were you thinking? Wait. I know. You weren't thinking at all--as usual!"

Something flashed in Carl's eyes but then was gone. He stared at his huge feet and seemed to shrink into himself.

Ricky watched him and wondered what was going on inside that big ugly head. Carl hadn't liked the idea of strong-arming Skid Row and Bullfrog. He'd made that clear enough. So was it possible he was intentionally giving them every chance in the world to escape? *No,* Ricky decided. Carl never planned that far ahead; probably wasn't even capable of it. Besides, he had found Skid Row once and then found both of them the following day. If he wanted to help them disappear, he wouldn't have gone to the trouble. Why then, after successfully tracking them down, had he let them waltz away--TWICE? It was infuriating. Was it Ricky's own fault for not giving specific enough instructions? *NO!* he decided. It was Carl's fault for being such a tool.

Ricky stood and began pacing back and forth behind his desk. He told himself the money didn't matter. He had a much larger score in the works. This wasn't about money, though. Not really. It was about Carl's inability to do what was expected of him. If he couldn't get the job done, why should Ricky continue to give him a salary and put up with all the headaches? He thought about Cullen's promise of a hundred large. That little windfall would go a lot further if he didn't have to split it with his bumbling partner.

He looked down and his eyes automatically found the floorboard under which he had enough incriminating evidence to cause Carl some real trouble. Could he actually use it? Ricky thought about that. If push came to shove, if it was a question of one of them going down, he knew he'd throw Carl into the fire without a second thought. But, could he go that far just to get the moron out of his hair? A week ago Ricky probably would have said no. But now? He pushed the thought aside, knowing it would return soon enough.

He placed his palms on the desktop and leaned forward. "Do you have any idea where they went?" he asked quietly. "Do you have even the slightest inkling where they might be right now?"

Carl looked at him, opened his mouth, closed it again and then shrugged.

"That's what I thought. And based on what's happened the past couple days, what do you suppose are the chances they'll go anywhere near any of the places Marco used to do business?"

"I don't know," Carl said, smacking his notebook against his leg once again.

"Well I do. The chances are ZERO because the only person stupid enough to do something like that is you!"

Ricky leaned forward even further but then drew back when he saw Carl's free hand tighten around the arm of his chair. *Careful,* he thought, realizing he was pushing it a bit far.

"So what do you figure?" Ricky asked, softening his tone as he dropped back into his chair.

Carl said nothing. He just sat, smacking his notebook and staring at a spot high up on the opposite wall.

He was obviously pissed. Ricky saw that and decided to give him a few minutes to stew. He powered up his laptop and played a quick game of solitaire, glancing over after every few cards. Any other time, he would have been perfectly happy waiting Carl out indefinitely. Or, he'd just get up and leave and Carl could sit there until the unidentified blackish toxin dotting the ceiling tiles took over the trailer and, in the process, caused his nuts to shrivel up and fall off. Tonight, though, he had things to do and dealing with Carl's little temper tantrum wasn't one of them.

"I need those two," Ricky said. "So how you gonna do it?" His tone was conversational but his question was direct enough that it couldn't be ignored.

Carl shifted in his seat and thankfully stopped with the notebook smacking. He still didn't look at Ricky, instead focusing on his hairy knuckles. "I got my ways," he said. "You should know that by now."

"Oh, I do. I was just wondering how you'd go about it."

Carl knew his stuff, but Binghamton was a big city with no end of places to hide. That was assuming Skid Row and Bullfrog hadn't left the area altogether. That's what Ricky would have done if he were in their shoes. And if he'd been tasked to go out and find them, he wouldn't have the first clue where to look. He didn't understand why Carl didn't seem more concerned but sensed this was not the time to pester him about his techniques.

"I'll leave it up to you then," he said, thinking they'd probably seen the last of the two losers. "Track 'em down and make arrangements for them to pay. You got that?"

Carl snorted and that was the end of the conversation.

-37-

Cullen's alarm started buzzing at four forty-five. He was tempted to hit the snooze bar, even reached for it, but then sighed and turned it off. He looked toward the window but couldn't distinguish the first hint of daylight. No wonder. The sun wouldn't rise for another hour and a half. He'd be done with his run and in the swimming pool by then. He sighed again and turned his head the other way. Sara had her back to him and was pressed against the far side of the bed. He extended a hand to her but then drew back. If the previous evening was any indication, she might tolerate his touch but definitely wouldn't welcome it.

He went over the conversation again in his mind. It had started out rough and pretty much went downhill from there.

"You missed dinner again," she'd said as soon as he'd entered the house.

Cullen didn't think he was that late but wasn't about to debate the point. "I know," he said, trying to work a note of fatigue into his voice. "I'm really sorry. Today was nuts, non-stop. I took the Jag in for service. The mechanic told me there was some sort of compression problem with the engine. He didn't have the parts to fix it and said it might take a week to get them. It was also going to cost a bundle. I didn't want to deal with that."

He thought Sara would cut in with a question or at least show some concern but she hadn't even turned from the kitchen sink where she was busy scouring the bottom of a frying pan. He could see her reflection in the window. Her cheeks were flushed, either from the hot water, her mood or both. She had her long hair pulled back in a ponytail but one thick strand had come free and was partially covering one eye. What he was thinking was, *you're beautiful when you're angry,* but he had the distinct impression that saying as much might score him the business end of the frying pan against the side of his head.

"So anyway," he continued, "I traded it in. I've got a new Avalon. It's, um, it's nice. You want to come see it?"

"And you made this transaction at eight o'clock at night?" she asked, completely ignoring his question.

"Well, no. I was on my way home at six-thirty but then I ran into a client and he held me up for a while."

Sara finally spun to face him. "And how exactly did you 'run into' a client on your way home? Did he throw himself in front of your new car?"

Damn, woman. What crawled up your ass? "Uh, no," Cullen said, realizing he should have chosen his words more carefully. He tried to come up with a good lie but her drawn expression told him he was on thin enough ice already. "I stopped at Uncle Tony's," he admitted. "I wasn't going to but--"

"But you can't pass a bar without ordering at least one drink."

"That's not fair."

"Really?" Sara pointed a soapy sponge at him. "When's the last time you were home on time, Andrew? When's the last time you had dinner with your family?"

"I…" he began but then realized there really wasn't much he could say. The sad truth was that he didn't know the answer to either question. She obviously hadn't expected a response anyway because she'd already gone back to her dish washing.

"Can I help you with that?" he asked, feeling like he needed to do something.

"She stiffened but didn't look at him. "You could help by being around once in a while."

That stung but Cullen knew she was right. He hadn't been around, and that got him thinking about his daughters. "So where are the kids?" he asked, realizing how pathetic it was that he didn't already know. What kind of father was he?

"Kristin had a soccer game in Oneonta. They went to Brooks Barbecue afterwards. She'll be home around nine. Kayla's in her room studying for a science test. Maybe you should go say hello."

"Right," Cullen said. "I'll do that. I can help her study if she wants." He started to leave but then paused in the doorway.

"Was there something else?" Sara asked.

"Actually, yes. In terms of me not being around…. I guess I have good news and bad news. *Christ,* Cullen thought. *Could I have come up with a worse way to say that*?

She again turned to face him and everything from her tight lips to her narrowed eyes told him his timing totally sucked.

Cullen thought belatedly that he should have waited awhile, maybe earned some points by spending time with Kayla and helping her prepare for her exam. That would have also given Sara some time to cool down. Too late for that now so he decided to press on.

"I registered for the Southern Tier Triathlon," he said. "It's coming up in a couple weeks."

"How nice for you."

Ouch. "I'm doing it for charity," Cullen added. "It will be a big time commitment but I think it's worth it."

"Do what you want," she said. "I'll take care of the house and the girls. I'm used to that by now. Do you want me to reheat your dinner?"

Okay then. Cullen hadn't spent much time thinking about how she might react to his news but total indifference was something he definitely hadn't foreseen.

"Hey," he said, taking her hand as she started to move toward the fridge. She let him do it, but there was no warmth in her touch. He would have gotten the same response from a manikin. He gave a little squeeze. She didn't, and he let her hand drop after a few awkward seconds. He knew she was ticked, but also knew she'd come around once he had a chance to explain.

"I didn't tell you the best part," he said, searching her eyes. "I'm doing this for you…and your center."

"You're doing what for me?" saying it like he'd just offered to give her herpes.

"The Triathlon," Cullen explained. "I'm getting local businesses to sponsor me. It will be great PR for Cyber Force and the donations will help those kids."

"Why?" Sara asked, arms crossed.

"Because they mean so much to you. I thought--"

"No, Andrew. Why are you doing it? Why now? You've never paid any attention to my work. Why is it suddenly so important for you to help out?"

Work? She was a volunteer. It wasn't like she had a real job.

"I'm just trying to do something nice."

"How very noble. So what's in it for you? It's got to be something or you wouldn't do it."

Damn! He'd known he'd have to sell her on the training and time commitment but didn't expect her to question his motives when it came to the charitable donation. And she was so cold too. What in hell had happened? He had the panicked thought that she'd spoken to Janet Banyard, or worse, Ricky, but no. If that was the case, she would have come right out and said so. However, it was possible she'd learned about his *their* financial difficulties some other way. That would explain the hostility.

Cullen was about to come right out and ask what was wrong but, deep down, he thought he already knew. It wasn't just his daughters he'd lost track of. It had been far too long since he'd had any sort of meaningful conversation with his own wife. The last time he'd come home late, she hadn't even bothered waiting up for him. That should have told him she was near her boiling point, but instead of cluing in, he’d only been relieved he'd avoided a confrontation.

Cullen realized now they hadn't spoken since then. She hadn't even texted him, something she'd normally do a dozen times a day. He hadn't noticed because he'd been too absorbed in trying to clean up a mess he'd made and she, God willing, still knew nothing about. That was guaranteed to change soon unless he ran the triathlon, won it, and cleared enough money to cover his losses, pay off that slime ball Ricky and make a large enough donation to the underprivileged children's center that it would all look legitimate.

He leaned against the kitchen counter, a headache beginning to take hold. What could he say to make things right? What would happen if he sat her down and told her the whole sordid tale? As much as he might be tempted, he knew he could never do it. After all, the main reason his life was in the toilet was because he'd lost so much money at the casino, and that was after swearing to her he wouldn’t gamble anymore. There was no way he could tell his story without also telling how completely, repeatedly and catastrophically he'd broken that promise.

"I’ll make this up to you," he said. "I hope you can believe that."

She stared at him and then turned and left the room.

-38-

Carl sat in his pickup, staring out at the empty windows of what had once been a Hess service station. The pumps were still in place but it had been years since anyone used them to fill their gas tank. His tank was already full and he was prepared to drive around all day if necessary. He hoped he'd be going somewhere soon. He was bored and starting to get cold.

He cranked the engine, warmed his hands in front of the heater for a minute and then checked his phone. As expected, Skid Row and Bullfrog were two blocks to the south and moving in roughly the same direction they had been for the past half hour. Contrary to what he'd told Ricky, he knew his targets had set up a camp somewhere in the middle of a large wooded area. Had he wanted to, he could have flushed them out at any point over the past twelve hours. He hadn't done that, in part because it was easier to grab them on the street where there were fewer places to hide, but also because he didn't want Ricky to know he could track them so easily.

He thought about his boss, and their most recent meeting at the shithole trailer. What was it he'd said? *You're good at it because you can think like the scumbags?* It was something like that. And like so many of Ricky's compliments, it was so back-handed it practically left a red mark.

What exactly he would do about Ricky was something Carl hadn't yet figured out. He enjoyed his job, usually anyway. He had no qualms about being rough with people who had it coming. However, when it came to guys like Skid Row and Bullfrog, guys whose only crime was making the mistake of crossing paths with Ricky, Carl's conscience sometimes got in the way. He would have preferred to just let them go, but his nature prevented him from openly disobeying Ricky's orders. That might have been because, and Carl hated admitting this even to himself, Ricky sort of scared him. Lately though, Carl realized he'd been getting more defiant and he found that somewhat troubling too.

Skid Row and Bullfrog were headed away from him and Carl considered moving his truck to keep them close. He placed his hand on the gear shift, but instead of shifting into drive, he reached for the key and killed the engine. He had no immediate need to go anywhere. The two were walking at a snail's pace, and even if they got an a bus or hijacked an airplane, he'd still be able to find them, at least as long as Skid Row kept his sweatshirt on.

Carl's stomach growled, probably because it was just as bored as the rest of him. He picked up his bag of Doritos and saw that it was empty, but still tipped the bag up so he could dump the few remaining crumbs into his mouth. He chewed, looked around, then opened the glove box where he sometimes kept a stash of candy. He came up dry, finding only napkins, a straw, his vehicle registration, a used Band-Aid, and a pack of Juicy Fruit that had been there so long it had solidified. He put it back, sighed and again checked the display on his iPhone. Nothing had changed but the Retrievor app was still doing exactly what it was supposed to. The nice ganja icon he'd created for Skid Row continued to monitor his sluggish progress.

Carl was still amazed that a device so small and cheap could do so much. The program allowed him to set up a zone around the target. He could even customize the size and shape of that zone. He'd receive a text message, email or phone call whenever said target ventured beyond the designated area. Or, as he was doing now, he could receive what amounted to a series of pings that told him where his target, in this case Skid Row, was at any given time. He'd receive those status updates as frequently or infrequently as he wanted. He had total control. About the only thing Retrievor didn't tell him was whether or not Skid Row was traveling alone. He was curious and had gotten close enough once to make visual contact and verify that Frogman was still tagging along.

Carl sat back and smiled to himself, proud of his little secret. He'd been damn slick and he knew it. He'd managed to sneak up behind Skid Row and Bullfrog as they approached the laundromat. Then, when they were both so stunned they couldn't have found their own assholes with a flashlight and a map, he'd grabbed them by the shoulders, and while he had a hold of Skid Row, deftly clipped the mini GPS device underneath his hood. He knew it wasn't a perfect solution. The unit could fall off, be discovered, or the battery might run down. There was a solar charger which he doubted would work at all given its location, but it had a motion charger too. The two deadbeats moved around constantly so that would hopefully be good enough. The thing really didn't use much power anyway and a single charge could last over three weeks. He wouldn't need it to last anywhere near that long.

What was really amazing was how Carl had found the device in the first place. He wasn't into gadgets and definitely not up on the latest trends in electronics. He'd simply gotten lucky--the combination of a random web search and the fact that he couldn't spell for shit. He seemed to have good timing, though. He'd stumbled upon the Retrievor website at the tail end of their community funding campaign. He was able to secure the device for a couple hundred bucks plus a $5.95 per month service contract. He'd had the unit for weeks and twice attached it to Ricky's Lexus just so he could make sure the thing really worked. It performed as advertised, and he'd gotten a bonus too. Not that it came as much of a surprise, but Carl now knew his boss couldn't be trusted.

According to the company literature, the Retrievor mini GPS unit was intended to track household pets or maybe put on a child's car so parents could more easily keep tabs on their kids. Carl knew better. The thing wasn't much bigger than a quarter and weighed next to nothing. You don't design something that small and discrete just so you can find Fido when he wanders off. It was a people tracker plain and simple, and this was the first time he had the chance to really put his new toy to the test. So far, it was passing with flying colors.

What he still wasn't sure about was how to use his exciting new power. He knew what Ricky wanted. He was just as sure that, in the end, it would prove to be completely pointless. He could grab Skid Row and Bullfrog right then, scare the piss out of them once again and tell them they had to pay. For what? He could give them an hour, a month or a year. It would work out just the same because there was no way a couple guys like that could ever come up with that much money. They'd inevitably miss whatever deadline they were given and then Carl would be called upon to take it to the next level. He knew what that meant and knew he didn't like it. He was trying to figure out what he could do and that's when his phone gave a chirp.

Carl looked and saw that Skid Row had turned a corner and was now headed east. He wondered where he was going, why he cared, and why this one job was suddenly making him so uncomfortable. It hadn't bothered him any when he was tossing Geno around that germ factory of a restaurant. He was one of the *scumbags.* Skid Row and Bullfrog were too. They were living in the woods for Christ's sake. So shouldn't he treat them all the same? No, Carl decided, because they were in way over their heads. He'd known that the first time he laid eyes on them.

Standing outside the trailer, they'd looked as helpless and hopeless as anything he'd ever seen. He'd also known at a glance that his world was not the same as theirs. They might be outcasts. They might be down on their luck. They weren't druggies, hoods or criminals and the best thing they could do was stay away from Ricky Fixx. Carl had come on strong thinking that would scare them off and that would be the end of it. Instead, Skid Row proposed his ridiculous plan to sell drugs. Ricky should have kicked them out then but the cheapskate had evidently seen what he thought was an opportunity.

"Bastard!" Carl muttered, gripping the steering wheel and feeling trapped. He wanted to tell Ricky either that he couldn't find Skid Row and Bullfrog at all, or that he'd found proof they'd left town. They'd be off the hook then but he'd end up in shit so deep he'd need a snorkel. He wished he could tell his boss to fuck off. Unfortunately, Ricky was pissed at him already and Carl hated to think what might happen if he pushed him any further.

That got him thinking about what he'd discovered when he secured the Retrievor unit to Ricky's car. The GPS didn't just track current whereabouts. It could tell you everywhere the target had been. As it turned out, while Carl was busy rearranging Geno's testicles and showing him the error of his ways, Ricky had been parked nearby, in fact, practically right across the street. Carl was pretty observant and hadn't seen anything, and that meant Ricky had deliberately stayed out of sight. Why? That one was easy. He was gathering dirt. There was no other explanation.

Carl wasn't a killer... except for Marco of course, and that was an accident. It wasn't like the guy was a pillar of society anyway but that made no difference. He was dead and Carl was directly responsible. He'd done other things too, plenty of other things, and always on Ricky's orders. Of course, Carl had no proof of that, or almost none. But what did Ricky have? That was the big question. If he'd been following him around, watching him do all the dirty work, it was a good bet Ricky had some sort of a record. Was he merely covering his ass or did he have something more devious in mind? Carl had known Ricky a long time and thought he had a pretty good idea.

"Bastard," he said again, wishing he'd done more to protect himself. From now on, he'd start being a lot more careful.

Carl started his truck, deciding it was high time he blew off some steam. According to his new best friend, Skid Row and Bullfrog were just four tenths of a mile away. So what if they didn't deserve it. He was going to hit them like a freight train. But then he froze.

"Don't tell me," he groaned, grabbing his phone and squinting at the screen intently. The ganja icon wasn't moving. "Shit!" he yelled, shaking the phone like that might do some good. Either the GPS unit had fallen off or just stopped working.

Okay, he thought, keenly aware of his suddenly racing heart. *I know where they were a few minutes ago. If I can get there fast enough, I'll still be able to pick up their trail.* And if not? Carl had toyed with idea of telling Ricky he'd lost them but, now that he might actually have to do it....

"I'll find 'em," he said, dropping the transmission into gear and spitting up gravel as he careened out of the lot. He was immediately stopped at a red light.

"Dammit!" he swore, tempted to drive right through. Then he looked down and saw that the icon was no longer stationary. It hadn't moved much but enough to make him breathe a huge sigh of relief. It was obvious what had happened. They'd been walking all morning and stopped to rest. Now they were off again.

"I'm an idiot," he said, waiting for the light to turn green and then pulling slowly through the intersection. He was still going to see Skid Row and Bullfrog but he wanted to do it on his terms. If he just swooped down on them, they might realize he had some way to track them. Better to let them come to him, and he thought he knew just how to do it.

-39-

"Chicken and biscuit. CHICKEN AND BISCUIT. CHICKEN AND BISCUIT!"

"What's his problem?" Bullfrog whispered, staring at a middle-aged black man who for the past thirty seconds had been running up and down the loading ramp behind a small diner, each few steps punctuated with those same three words. The diner was closed, and if the darkened interior and graffiti-covered doors and windows were any indication, wouldn't be opening again anytime soon. That didn't seem to dampen his spirits, nor did the fact that the few people within earshot had all stopped to watch the spectacle. The man had a long, lanky frame, and his large grin revealed teeth that were surprisingly straight and white. He wore Army fatigues, a dark green pea coat, a cowboy hat, tall boots, and a long silver chain that hung from his waist and jingled with every step.

"That's Delmont," Skid Row said. "He's always hangin' somewhere downtown. You've never seen him before?"

Bullfrog shook his head. "I don't think I want to see him again either. What the heck is he yelling about?"

"Chicken and biscuit. Can't you hear him?"

Bullfrog gave him a look. "Everyone can hear him, but why chicken and biscuit? What does that even mean?"

"How should I know? He likes it I guess. It's about all he ever says."

"Shut up sucka!" Delmont shouted as a jackhammer started up a few blocks over.

"I forgot," Skid Row said. "He doesn't like power equipment."

"Is he dangerous?" Bullfrog asked, still staring and giving the man as much room as possible as he and Skid Row moved past.

"No, man. He's cool. Keeps to himself, you know?"

"CHICKEN AND BISCUIT!"

"Comes into McDonald's all the time, morning or night, and always orders the same thing."

"I'm sure I can guess."

"Chicken and biscuit," Skid Row confirmed. "Here's the thing. The mighty McD's does not have that particular menu item. They sell chicken; they sell biscuits. They just don't sell them together."

"And how's he handle that?" Bullfrog asked as Delmont did another lap up and down the ramp.

Skid Row shrugged. "We wasted beaucoup time telling him we didn't have it. Dude wasn't gettin' it at all. 'Chicken and biscuit, chicken and biscuit,' every fucking day. Then we tried substitutions: burgers, chicken sandwiches, shit like that."

"Did it work?"

"Depends on what you mean. He took whatever we gave him, but he knew it weren't no chicken and biscuit. He'd sit there eating and shaking his head at us the whole time. Fucking downer, man."

"You weren't afraid he'd go crazy on you? He might have PTSD or something."

"I don't know if he ever served. It's not like you can have a real conversation with the guy, and plenty of dudes just dress the part. I do know one thing. If he's an example of America's finest, we're doomed. Delmont's harmless, though. He just wanted his grub."

"But you weren't giving it to him."

Skid Row smiled at that and put a hand on Bullfrog's shoulder. "Only one dude I know who'll go all bat shit just because he doesn't get what he wants from the Golden Arches. "

"Very funny," Bullfrog said, pushing his hand away but he was smiling too.

"We came up with a strategy," Skid Row said. "Instead of ditching all the breakfast goodies when we switched over to lunch, we started putting one biscuit aside. If Delmont came in, we'd throw a chicken patty on there and give him that. Still wasn't no chicken and biscuit but it did the trick. He never complained anyway." Skid Row paused. "Actually, I think he was there the day you came in."

"SHUT UP SUCKA!" Delmont yelled as the jackhammer started up again.

"I didn't notice," Bullfrog said; "but speaking of food, how much is left in the till?"

"Huh?" Skid Row asked, shaking hair out of his eyes and looking baffled.

"Money," Bullfrog explained. "How much do w…, do you have left?"

"Oh. Right." Skid Row dug into his pocket and came out with some crumbled bills and a few coins. "Definitely no pot of gold," he said, frowning as he counted. "Looks like eight dollars and twenty-nine cents. Should we go for steak or lobster?"

"Why not both? You are talking about ramen flavors, right?"

"Dude, you kiddin' me? We can't afford flavors. These are desperate times Kimosabe."

They walked along in silence until they passed some low rent apartments and Skid Row spotted a rusted toilet bowl sitting on the stoop outside one of the ground floor units. Someone had attempted to turn it into a planter and a few very dead flowers hung over one side. "Three points," he said automatically.

"What?"

Skid Row glanced Bullfrog's way. "Oh. Nothin'," he muttered. He hadn't realized he'd spoken out loud. "Forget it."

"But I heard you say something about three points. What was that?"

"It's not important. Trust me."

"Come on," Bullfrog coaxed.

Skid Row was embarrassed but thought he may as well fess up. "It's just a game. I call it Ghetto Bingo."

"So how do you play?"

"It's not a real game," Skid Row explained. "I mean, you can't win or anything. I made it up. I look for weird shit and award points based on how ghetto it is."

"Like what?"

Skid Row gestured with his chin. "A toilet in the Yard isn't that uncommon; not around here. I'd normally give it two points. But turn your shitter into a garden and it's worth more."

"I get it. So what about something like that?" Bullfrog pointed at a second story window where someone was using a bed sheet in place of curtains.

"You see that everywhere. That's only worth a point. Same goes for homeless people, drug deals, graffiti, shopping carts, abandoned vehicles and crap like that."

"What about a homeless guy dealing drugs out of an abandoned vehicle?"

"Definitely worth more," Skid Row said. "You're getting the idea. Actually, there used to be this dude that hid his drug stash in his artificial leg."

"And how much was that worth?"

Skid Row laughed. "Five years in the state pen. Don't think we'll see him again for a while."

They turned a corner and had to walk past a Chinese takeout. Skid Row did his best to ignore the wave of mouthwatering aromas while wondering how in hell he could feed both of them with the little bit of cash he had left.

"When can you pick up your next paycheck?" Bullfrog asked as if he'd been reading Skid Row's mind.

He thought for a moment. "Day after tomorrow. Afternoon, though. The big wampum drop is usually around two."

"Okay. And between now and then, do we need to buy anything other than food?"

"I fucking hope not." But then Skid Row held up a finger. "Unless we find a BOGO on weed."

"A What?"

"Buy one get one, dude. I don't think I could pass up that sort of opportunity."

Bullfrog looked at him and shook his head. "Then it's probably a good thing we won't find one."

"That's your problem right there my friend," Skid Row said. "You don't properly appreciate the inestimable qualities of high grade hash."

"You may be right about that, but the only hash we can afford comes in a can."

"A sad state of affairs for sure. Poverty sucks ass."

"Agreed. Let's hope it's only a temporary condition."

"Amen to that. And when can we get out of here?"

"Gotta be around noon now," Bullfrog said, staring up at a completely overcast sky. "That means you can get your check in a little over forty-eight hours. If you're leaving this up to me, I say you pick it up as soon as possible, cash it, and then we head straight to the bus station."

"But I'll get another check next week," Skid Row pointed out, his feet suddenly feeling heavy. "Don't we want that too?"

"I guess that depends. You said it wasn't gonna be much."

"No thanks to you."

"And how long do I need to keep apologizing for that?"

Skid Row didn't answer so Bullfrog continued.

"You need to decide if it's worth waiting around the extra nine days. It is getting colder out, and--"

"And the longer we're here the better the chance we encounter Tweedle Dum and Tweedle Dick."

"It's something to consider," Bullfrog said. "Although I still don't think we'll see them, especially if we stay close to home."

Home? Skid Row started gnawing a fingernail but stopped when he tasted blood. He looked and saw that every one of his nails was chewed down to about nothing. When had that happened? He brushed at his hair and, realizing he'd been doing too much of that too, jammed both hands into his pockets and tried not to think about how totally weird and awkward that felt.

"Something wrong?" Bullfrog asked, giving him an odd look.

Skid Row actually laughed at that one. "Congratulations," he said. "You just asked the stupidest question in the history of stupid. We got no home, no job and no food. The only thing we do got is a couple maniacs chasing us around claiming we owe them a bunch of money we don't have. And you want to know if something is wrong. Fucking brilliant. And you're supposed to be the smart one."

"I don't know about that."

"Yeah, well I'm starting to have my doubts too."

Skid Row's hands had somehow found their way out of his pockets again and his right index finger was back in his mouth before he even noticed what he was doing. The twinge of pain was a quick reminder. "Shit," he swore, and this time clasped both hands together inside the big front pocket of his sweatshirt. He wished he had a piece of gum or even a toothpick, something to at least keep his mouth busy for a while; but mostly, he wished his situation--their situation were different. Maybe it would be someday but he'd have bet his last dollar it was going to get worse before it got better.

One thing that was making him nervous was the whole idea of packing up, such as it was, and leaving Binghamton for good. He didn't understand why that was giving him such problems. It wasn't like the city had ever done him any favors. Why stay? There was really only one reason that came to mind and Skid Row didn't think he was ready to deal with it.

He looked at Bullfrog and considered trying to explain what he was thinking. Skid Row didn't know if he could do it because he'd never had that sort of conversation with anyone. Until a couple days ago, his entire social network consisted of his McDonald's co-workers, most of whom didn't even know where he lived, and those he shared a roof with at the Y. They mostly fell into one of two categories. There were the Zatts types, the guys who believed or at least acted like they believed they were the kings of the roost. They got into fights, got into more serious trouble and usually got kicked out before too long. The majority of the other residents were more like him. They kept their heads down and mainly kept to themselves for reasons they never discussed. Skid Row knew a lot of people. He had a lot of acquaintances. There wasn't a true friend among them. Bullfrog was becoming that and the realization made him strangely self-conscious.

He knew he was acting dumb. Bullfrog had opened up to him right away. Of course, his situation was totally different. Unlike Skid Row, he had nothing to be ashamed of. He was doing just fine before losing his parents and his inheritance. Under those circumstances, it was a miracle he hadn't ended up just like Delmont, running around and screaming at power equipment.

Bullfrog definitely made his share of mistakes but his actions were justifiable. What was Skid Row's excuse? True, he hadn't seen his mother in so long he couldn't remember the sound of her voice. It cut him to the bone when she left, even though she'd really never been much of a mother in the first place. He understood that now. But at the time, he'd taken his hurt, anger, confusion and hostility and transferred it all onto William, who'd done his best to provide for a son he probably never wanted. Even so, it had been Skid Row's decision to leave and he really couldn't blame his father for not doing much to try to stop him. He'd chosen his own path. He could, however, still turn back the clock. So far as Skid Row knew, both his parents were still out there somewhere. That meant he could find them if he really wanted to. With William, he doubted it would even be that hard.

Damn, he said to himself, clasping his hands together more tightly. He didn't understand what was happening. Until recently, he hadn't had any desire to reconnect with or even think about his past. Entire weeks and even months had gone by when he hadn't thought of his father at all. He was fine with that and had always assumed they were both better off. So why, all of a sudden, had that changed? Why was he so confused? What would happen if--?

“Okay if I do the shopping?" Bullfrog asked as they rounded a corner and a Weis grocery store came into view.

"Sure," Skid Row said, relieved to have something else to think about. "You think we got enough money?"

"Leave it to me. We'll be eating like kings."

"Should I distract them while you stuff a prime rib up your shirt?"

They entered the store, and neither of them noticed the familiar dark blue pickup truck, empty, and positioned in a distant corner of the lot.

-40-

"Hi, this is Sara. So sorry I missed you. Leave a message and I'll call you back as soon as I can. Have a great day!"

Cullen sighed and glared at his phone like it had somehow betrayed him. He pressed the end button and tossed the thing onto his desk. No point leaving another message. He'd done that at eight o'clock and again at nine-thirty. It was now almost noon and she still hadn't returned his call. The woman was mad no doubt. Better make that livid. Of course he'd known that already. After her blow up in the kitchen the night before, they'd hardly exchanged another word. Cullen had assumed a generous donation to her charity would help break the ice between them. Instead, it seemed to have made it that much thicker.

What really ticked him off was that she hadn't even given him a chance to explain what he wanted to do. She didn't know or seem to care where the money was coming from or how much could potentially be involved. He didn't get that. If his wife was as concerned about those kids as she let on, always harping about how tough they had it, shouldn't she at least try to be a little more open-minded when he was going out of his way to help them? So he'd have to put more time into his training. What was the big deal? It was only for a couple of weeks and it was for a good fucking cause. Why couldn't the woman see that?

He gave his phone another withering look. If it rang right then, he was fully prepared to rip into her about how insensitive and selfish she was being. He waited a beat and, when nothing happened, stood and stalked to the window. He was getting himself worked up and Cullen knew that wouldn't do. He still had a lot of things to take care of and needed to keep a level head. A more understanding spouse would have made that a whole lot easier but he supposed he could deal with that later. In the meantime, that weasel Ricky Fixx was still breathing down his neck.

Cullen's promise of a hundred large had bought him a two week reprieve. He understood that to mean Ricky would leave him alone but the slimy little jerk obviously had other ideas. Cullen spotted his car twice during his predawn run and again when he was exiting the YMCA after his swim. He thought he saw Ricky's goon once too but couldn't swear to that. Regardless, the message was clear. He would get the extra time he requested but he'd better not try anything cute. That was just great. How was he supposed to concentrate on his training if he was looking over his shoulder the whole time? He could ask Ricky to back off a bit but Cullen already knew how much good that would do.

He'd knew he'd have a better chance of getting everything sorted out if people would just leave him alone for a while. That, evidently, wasn't going to happen. He'd have Sara hounding him whenever he was at home and Ricky on his tail anytime he wasn't. His office was his only real sanctuary but he couldn't stay there for the duration.

Cullen extended a finger to part Venetian blinds. He preferred keeping them open but, lately that made him feel far too exposed. He was on the fourth floor, higher up than most other buildings on the street; yet, at his desk with his back to the window, he couldn't shake the unsettling feeling that the whole world was looking in at him.

He moved to the edge of the window frame and peered down on the street. He took his time studying faces but didn't see Ricky, Carl, or anyone else he recognized. No one looked back at him and nothing looked even remotely out of the ordinary. If anything, Court Street seemed a little quiet for a weekday afternoon. He paused long enough to watch a striking brunette stroll past and then let the blinds fall back into place.

Oddly, failing to detect anything suspicious didn't make him feel any better. So Ricky wasn't parked in front of the building. What did that prove? He could still be lurking somewhere nearby, in a parking garage or just around the corner. Cullen tried telling himself it didn't matter. *Let him sit out there all day. What do I care?* He knew Ricky wasn't about to lay a hand on him anyway, not as long as he held the promise of all that money. That was his insurance policy. So why did he still feel like the walls were closing in around him?

He returned to his desk but didn't sit down, instead drumming his fingers on the back of his chair and surveying his twenty by twenty foot space. Would his plan really work? He thought so, assuming he played it just right. And if not? His office was full of high-end furniture, some original artwork and a few other knick-knacks and collectibles. He could sell it all and still not have anywhere near enough to pay what he owed.

Even with the money he'd given Mrs. Banyard, his personal and corporate finances were still a mess. He thought he could handle that once he dealt with the most immediate threat. There was only one way to do that. He needed to win the triathlon and line up enough sponsors so he could pay Ricky in full. If he failed--Cullen used a thumb and forefinger to massage his temples--he'd have no choice but to come clean with Sara. That would lead to some major lifestyle changes. He thought about moving into a smaller home or even, God forbid, an apartment. It would suck but they'd cope. What he couldn't imagine, didn't want to imagine was how Ricky and that monster he hung out with would respond if they didn't get their money.

Cullen slumped into his chair and again glanced at his phone. Then his eyes, seemingly of their own accord, drifted to the louvered wooden doors that concealed a small but well stocked wet bar. How nice it would be to while away the afternoon hours getting totally shit-faced. That, he knew from long experience, wouldn't solve his problems but it could effectively put them on hold for a few hours. He swallowed and licked his lips, imagining the delicious, smoky burn of a fifteen-year-old Glenfiddich single malt Scotch. He had a brand new bottle not six steps away.

Cullen began to rise but then shook his head and sank back into his chair. If he went down that road now, he may as well give up on everything. For at least the next couple weeks he had to stay focused, and that meant staying away from the booze. With a reluctant sigh, he reached over and mashed the button for the intercom.

"Yes?"

"Hi, Carrie. Would you mind stepping in here when you have a chance? It can wait if you're in the middle of something."

She didn't respond but was standing in his doorway five seconds later.

"That was quick," he said, doing a fair job keeping his gaze above shoulder level while not focusing on how perfectly her form-fitting green dress caressed every one of her incredible curves.

"I'm running a little behind today. I was about to go to lunch. Do you need something first?"

"Uh, yes," he said. "That press release. Did you get a chance to work on it?"

"All done. I'll get if for you."

She spun to leave and Cullen's breath caught in his throat. *Unbelievable.* "Hold on," he said, his tongue suddenly feeling two sizes too big.

"K. What's up?"

She leaned back into the room and he wondered if she was torturing him on purpose. He would have given a hundred dollars to slide his hands over that dress just one time.

"Sit down for a second," Cullen said. He was hoping that, seated, she might look a little less goddess-like and he could have a real conversation without being distracted by wild sex fantasies.

"Did you have a lunch date?" he asked as she floated into a chair. "I don't want to hold you up."

"Nope. I thought I'd go to Di Rienzo's for a sub. I can bring one back for you."

"That would be great. Thanks."

Cullen was surprised. Carrie didn't look like she'd been within half a mile of a sub in her entire life. He'd always assumed she was one of those health food nuts. Nice to know that wasn't the case. And with her bringing lunch in, he wouldn't have to leave his office until the end of the day. He thought of Ricky then and hoped he was sitting in his car out there somewhere, hungry, cramped, uncomfortable and needing badly to pee.

"That release needs to go out today," he said, "but I'd like to add something first."

"Sure. Do I need to take notes on this?"

"No. It's just one thing." He paused because it was important he explain himself properly. "I'd like to set up a separate fund--a separate account I guess is a better way to put it. Sponsors can pay into that and that's where the check will be drawn from when Cyber Force makes the donation to the children's center."

Cullen watched Carrie's reaction closely to see if anything in her body language suggested she knew he was feeding her a line of crap. What he wanted, what he needed really, was a legitimate-sounding account his various contributors would confidently pay into so they didn't make their checks directly payable to the charity. He would of course have complete control of the new account and could, when necessary, divert funds accordingly.

"Here's my thought," Cullen said. "We set this thing up now, and if we want to do more stuff like this in the future, it will make it that much easier. Cyber Force is in a position to do a lot of good in the community and I'd like to take more advantage of that."

"That's wonderful," Carrie said with a dazzling smile. "So you want the information about this new fund included in the press release?"

"Exactly!"

Cullen was relieved. She was so openly enthusiastic he knew his plan must have sounded good. And why not? It sounded pretty damn good to him when he'd come up with it. He wasn't sure how it would fly but the first test appeared to be a success.

"Have you set this account up already?"

"No, and I don't have a name for it either. I was thinking about the Cyber Force Benevolent Children's Fund but that sounds too stuffy. Besides, not knowing what we might do with this later on, I don't want to tie the name to a specific cause."

"That makes sense."

"Yeah, so maybe you could think about it while you're out. See what you can come up with. I'd like a name that's heartfelt but also somewhat generic."

"Of course. I'll have something by the time I get back." Carrie rose to leave. "Should I get Janet Banyard's number so you can talk to her about setting this up?"

"I don't think so." *That ornery old bitch is too interested in my finances already. The last thing I'll do is give her anything else to sink her nasty claws into.* "First Niagara gets enough of our business now," Cullen explained. "I'll use someone else for this."

-41-

Carl pulled up outside the trailer feeling rather proud of himself. He checked his phone and grinned. If the information the Retrievor app provided was accurate, and he knew now that it was, it appeared Skid Row and Bullfrog had barely moved since he left them, slack-jawed and completely dumbfounded clinging to their small bag of groceries and staring after him as he turned out of the Weis market lot and drove away. He almost laughed when he thought about how they'd looked when he strolled up behind them in the checkout line. He couldn't wait to share the details with Ricky. Of course, there were some aspects of the story he wouldn't tell, not yet anyway. He needed to be sure he knew which way the wind was blowing first. Even then, Carl thought he might have to withhold some things. He was the sole possessor of vital information. That was new territory for him and he had to admit he found it liberating. It would be a shame to give that up, so unless it became necessary, why should he?

Carl was whistling a Katy Perry tune when he mounted the steps and entered the office. Blinking against the dim light, he shrugged out of his coat and tossed it onto the couch. Then he looked at Ricky and the song died on his lips, his good feelings all but forgotten.

"What the hell happened to you?" he asked, dropping into a chair. "You look like hell."

"Thanks. That's sweet of you to say." Ricky rubbed at the dark circles under his eyes like he could somehow wipe them away.

"You have a rough night or what?"

"No, Mom,"" Ricky scowled. "I was in bed by eleven. You writing a fucking book?"

“Okay,” Carl said. "Forget I mentioned it."

Ricky stared at him for a second and then yawned and ran a hand over the stubble on his chin. "Sorry," he said sullenly. "I didn't have a rough night just a damn short one. I've been up since three-thirty and it feels like I've been run over."

"That's about how you look too."

"Yeah. You sort of said that already."

"So what's the deal? Nobody gets up that early on purpose"

"Andrew Cullen does, or thereabouts, and I wanted to make sure I was ready."

Carl gave him an odd look. "For what?"

"To follow him, dumb ass. What do you think?"

"I think you've lost me," Carl said, leaning forward, his palms on his knees. "He's supposed to be running that triathlon, right? And that's where he's getting' the money to pay you?"

Ricky yawned again and nodded. He picked up a foam coffee cup, drained it, made a face and threw the cup toward the trash can. "That's his plan anyway."

"But he has to win," Carl stated. "You think he can do it?"

Ricky shrugged. "What do I know from triathlons? Dragging my sorry ass out of bed is about all the workout I can handle. He seems to thrive on it, though. Running, biking, swimming--it never stops. He probably uses two hands to jerk off just for the extra muscle toning."

"So this Southern Tier Triathlon or whatever, you said it's not for a couple weeks yet. He doesn't have the money now so why bother following him? What do you get out of it?"

"It's called intimidation," Ricky said. "I shouldn't have to explain that to you. He bought himself a two week reprieve but that only goes so far. I need to make sure he remains properly motivated."

"And you really think that's necessary?"

"You better believe it. Cullen's a schmuck and he's already proven he can't make good decisions. There's no telling what he might try if we drop completely out of sight until the race is over. He needs to know he'd better stick to the program or there's gonna be trouble."

"You're gonna keep following him around then?"

"No," Ricky said, looking at Carl pointedly. "We are. It will be more effective if he sees both of us. Besides," he stretched and tilted his head from one side to the other. "I can't do this crap every day. That's not how I'm wired."

"Hold on," Carl said, straightening. "I can't be chasing him all over town. I've got enough going on already."

"Relax. I'll handle most of it. And I'm not even talking about a constant tail. I just want to pop up often enough that he knows we're around. Know what I mean?"

"I guess that depends on how much you want from me."

"The occasional drive-by. That's it. You won't have to go looking for him either. His routine is predictable."

Carl suspected it wouldn't be as easy or as casual as Ricky was making it sound. But, it wasn't worth arguing about. With Skid Row and Bullfrog effectively under his thumb, he could devote as much or as little time to Andrew Cullen as he saw fit.

"Guess I can do that," he said.

Ricky looked at him sharply. "Hey, don't do me any fucking favors. And just so we understand each other, you'll do what I tell you. Got it?"

Carl bristled but Ricky didn't give him the chance to speak.

"Don't sweat it," he said, with a smile that didn't quite reach his eyes. "Those two losers are still your priority. Concentrate on them and help me out when you can. Is that fair?"

Carl nodded but he was still annoyed. Nothing he did was good enough. He'd busted his butt for Ricky for years, busted a lot of other butts along the way, and all he ever got for his efforts was insufficient pay, a disgusting work environment and all the criticism he could eat. At least Ricky was planning on carrying most of the load on this one. Carl wondered about that but wasn't about to start asking questions. It all sounded pretty pointless to him. Cullen had already seen the pictures Ricky took of his wife and kids. If that didn't motivate the man nothing would. Tailing him might scare him more but where was the benefit in that? Maybe Ricky thought it would make him run faster. It wasn't Carl's problem either way, and he decided to keep his distance as much as possible.

"So let's say he does win that thing," Carl said. "The prize money is fifty grand. Explain to me again how he thinks he can pay you twice that."

"It's pretty clever, actually. He's got sponsors. It's like March of Dimes or something but on a larger scale. He'll make a donation to charity but says he can skim enough off the top to pay us."

"How honorable." *Talk about scumbags. Andrew Cullen could be their king.*

"I'm not here to make moral judgments. Here's how I see it." Ricky suddenly looked energized and alert. "No matter what happens, I can't lose. He pays what he owes or we keep after him. We'll get our money in the end."

"But what if he gets caught?"

"What if he does?" Ricky had his palms up as if he couldn't possibly be less concerned. "He's the one taking the risk. It's got nothing to do with me."

Carl bit his lower lip, thinking the whole scheme had disaster written all over it. He considered expressing those concerns but could tell from Ricky's expression it wouldn't do any good. He decided to save it for another time.

"You gonna go home and get some sleep?" he asked, figuring a change of subject was best.

"I don't know about that but I at least want to shower, shave and change. I didn't do any of that this morning."

No kidding. Ricky was in the same clothes he'd been wearing the day before and it looked like he hadn't even bothered running a comb through his hair before leaving the house.

"So go crash for a while," Carl said. "I can swing by Cullen's office if you want. I assume that's where he is now."

"Oh, he's there," Ricky said, staring up at the ceiling and then checking his watch. "You don't need to bother with him, though. Even if I take a little siesta, I'll be back long before he leaves for the day."

"You sure?" Carl asked, again wondering why Ricky was being so agreeable but also glad he'd have the afternoon to himself.

"Positive. I'd like you focusing on the other task for now. Any progress on that front?"

Carl studied his fingernails for a moment and then looked up, his face completely blank. "I found them if that's what you mean."

Ricky blinked and sat back. "YOU WHAT?"

"I found them," Carl repeated simply. "I told you I would."

"I know but...." Ricky stared at him. "I didn't think you could do it so fast."

"Well, I did." Carl was enjoying Ricky's reaction but did his best not to show it.

"And why didn't you mention that sooner?"

"You didn't ask."

Ricky looked at him and shook his head. "So talk to me. What happened and where are they now?"

"Actually," Carl said, deciding to field the easier question first. "I sort of got lucky."

"Explain."

"Well," Carl began, but then he felt his phone vibrate in his back pocket. He assumed that meant the boys were finally on the move again. He wanted to check but couldn't do it with Ricky sitting right there. There was no need anyway. They could run but they couldn't hide. He knew it and by now he figured they must have reached that same conclusion. Carl felt bad about that but still wasn't sure what he should do. He couldn't keep letting them slip through his fingers. He couldn't keep making excuses, not if he wanted to keep his job. He was beginning to have his doubts about that but knew damn well Ricky wouldn't let him just walk away. He was trapped, at least for now, and that meant he'd have to keep his boss happy.

"I wasn't sure where to start looking," he continued, trying to cover the soft buzzing sound by flipping pages in his notebook. "I've seen those two all over town. That makes it tough to zero in on any one area."

"That shouldn't be a problem for someone with your skills."

Ricky's tone was flat and Carl couldn't tell if that was a real compliment or if he was just being an ass. It was probably a little of both.

"I spent a while just driving around and hoping I'd spot them. I checked out all the places I'd seen them before and came up with nothing."

"So?"

"So I had this old city map in my truck," Carl said, speaking slowly because he was making his story up on the fly. "I thought I'd mark out all their previous locations and that might indicate where to look next."

"That's good," Ricky said. "And I guess it must have worked."

"Actually, no. I never even got started because my pen was out of ink."

Ricky froze, his expression hovering somewhere between bewilderment and irritation. "I assume there's a reason you're telling me this. If you don't mind, could we cut to the fucking chase? I've got things to do"

"Sure," Carl said, biting the inside of his cheek. "As I was about to say, I stopped at the grocery store to get a new pen and that's where I found them."

"In the fucking grocery store?"

"I told you it was lucky." Carl crossed his legs, feeling more comfortable because the next part of the tale at least bore a resemblance to what had actually taken place.

"What were they doing there?" Ricky asked, looking like he thought the whole thing might be a put on.

"Just buying groceries."

Carl explained how he'd first seen Skid Row and Bullfrog in the produce section and then tailed them all over the store. Thanks to his new Retrievor app, he'd already had a pretty good idea of where they'd been headed. It was no trouble to get there ahead of time and take up a good position to intercept. The main thing was to make it appear random. That was true for Skid Row and Bullfrog as well as for Ricky.

"I don't know how they're gonna pay you," Carl said, still wishing he could drop the whole thing. "They definitely don't have the money."

"And you know this because…."

"You've seen them. They look like they live on the street. They also spent twenty minutes shopping and all they bought was a head of cabbage, some ramen noodles and a bag of dried beans."

"Who eats that shit?"

"I guess it makes sense if it's all you can afford."

"Great," Ricky said. "So they're smart shoppers. You better be able to tell me more than that. You did talk to them, right?"

"Of course," Carl said. "I didn't want to make a scene so I had to wait for the right time to move in. When they were finally ready to check out, they got in line behind this old woman with a whole bunch of crap in her cart. I stepped right up behind them. There was nowhere they could go."

"They must have been shittin' bricks."

"That's about how I would put it. They didn't even see me at first. I just reached over and tapped that little one on the shoulder. They were so surprised I thought they were going to drop everything and take off."

Carl smiled for Ricky's benefit but remembered the desperate, haunted look on Bullfrog's face. He didn't say anything but his left eye started to twitch and, for a second, Carl was afraid that might lead to a repeat of what had happened outside the laundromat the day before.

"They couldn't go anywhere," he explained. "Not with the woman's cart blocking the aisle. That gave us a chance to chat."

"With the woman and the cashier right there? Are you crazy?"

"It was cool," Carl said. "They were arguing about the price of paper towels and paying no attention to us. I did all the talking anyway and I kept it nice and quiet."

"What'd you say?"

"Not much. I just re-enforced the idea that I could find them anywhere, anytime. I also told them that, the next time I did find them, they'd better have some money for you."

"That's good," Ricky said, rubbing his hands together. "So where are they now?"

Carl paused and looked down.

"Don't fucking tell me," Ricky growled. "You lost them again?"

"I didn't lose them," Carl said; "because I didn't have the chance to follow."

"What?" Ricky asked, veins popping out along his neck. "You were right fucking there!"

"Yeah. And you know who else was there? Girl Scouts! Right outside the store selling cookies. A lot of them had their parents with them, and a couple city cops were kind enough to stop by to support their effort. Skid Row and Bullfrog walked away and there wasn't a thing I could do."

"You've got a truck!" Ricky almost screamed. "You couldn't watch to see which way they were going and then catch up?"

"We were at a Weis," Carl said, getting angry but keeping his voice under control. "That store has entrances off two different streets. They went out one side and I was parked on the other. They were out of sight by the time I drove around the block."

"I don't believe this," Ricky said, jumping to his feet, shoving his desk chair and sending it crashing against the wall. "Can't you do one damn thing right?"

"I did find them," Carl pointed out, surprised at how little Ricky's outburst bothered him. "I can do it again."

"Yeah. Master fucking tracker. You got lucky! You told me that."

"I would have found them anyway."

"Prove it!" Ricky said. "I want to know where they are and what they're doing to get my money. You think you can handle that?"

Carl nodded, afraid of what he might say if he opened his mouth.

"Good," Ricky snapped. "So go!"

Carl left the office and was whistling Katy Perry again by the time he reached his truck.

-42-

As soon as Carl was gone, Ricky grabbed his keys and headed for his own car. He had to get some rest; but mostly, he needed to get out of the trailer, clear his head and try to figure out why the brief conversation with his partner bugged him so much. Something was nagging at him but he couldn't quite put a finger on it.

Ricky drove home, making one small detour so he could reassure himself that Cullen's vehicle was still where it was supposed to be. Of course, with his insane exercise regiment, he was often miles away from wherever he'd parked. Ricky couldn't do anything about that. Also, with the office blinds closed tight, he had no way to verify if the man was really in there or not. That ticked him off, but he knew he couldn't do anything about that either.

Slowing as he cruised past the Cyber Force building for a second time, Ricky touched his phone and considered dialing Cullen's office number. He finally decided it wasn't worth the trouble because, if Cullen wasn't there, Ricky was too tired to go chasing after him anyway. He knew he could find him later on, and that made it a lot easier to leave him alone now.

Ricky had to drive an extra lap around his own block before he found a parking spot that wasn't blocking either a fire hydrant or somebody's driveway. He wished he had his own garage but also wished the east side of Binghamton wasn't such a slum. Feeling tired and angry, he locked the Lexus and kicked a few broken kids' toys out of his way as he cut across the postage stamp-sized, sorry excuse for a lawn. The neighbor's dog snarled at him, as always, and Ricky spit at the mutt before climbing the creaking back stairs and entering his cramped second story apartment.

He shrugged out of his suit coat, groped for the wall switch, dropped keys on the table just inside the door, scooped up a small stack of mail and headed for his kitchen, all the while wondering why he felt so out of sorts. Okay, he wasn't exactly living in the lap of luxury but he thought there was a good chance that could change soon. He thought he should be happy but what he mostly felt was irritation. If Cullen won the triathlon, if he came through on his promise of a hundred large, that would be the biggest payday Ricky had ever received by far. He could finally get out of that trailer, move to nicer digs and maybe start focusing on clientele a little higher up the food chain.

Cullen had been one very large pain in the ass, but Ricky believed he could prove to be well worth the effort. If nothing else, it was a step up from smacking a guy like Geno around for what would probably amount to a few hundred bucks a week. Ricky had been doing that sort of work for what felt like decades and he was tired of it. He wanted to get to a point where he no longer needed to chase dirt bags around for chump change. He was too good for that and he'd damn sure paid his dues. He was owed something in return and felt it was high time he start collecting.

First things first--Cullen had to come through on his promise. Ricky wasn't too worried about that. Even if he didn't win the stupid race, he should be able to pay the fifty grand he planned on skimming from his donors, and that would exactly double Ricky's original investment. That was a far better return than he could get on the stock market, a shrewd real estate deal or pretty much anything else he could think of, legal or otherwise. He could stop there and be way ahead of the game. Or, because he'd still have Andrew Cullen very firmly by the balls, he could continue to squeeze until he had every penny. Ricky would get his money one way or another, and, he thought, possibly a whole lot more. He had an idea he believed could pay dividends beyond his wildest dreams.

Ricky opened the fridge, reached for a can of beer, but changed his mind and grabbed the carton of milk instead. He already had a twinge of heartburn and figured alcohol would only make it worse. He saw that the milk was a few days past the sell by date but it passed the sniff test so he figured it was still okay. That was good since his only other options were water and coffee.

He took a quick swig from the carton and then poured the rest of the milk into a plastic Tioga Downs Raceway cup. He found a half loaf of white bread, checked for mold spots and, finding none, began assembling a sandwich of salami, yellow mustard and Kraft Singles. As he peeled off the plastic, he noticed that the Kraft package didn't seem to include the word cheese anywhere. He did see the words *food product* and decided the less he knew about that the better.

Ricky leaned against his stained and cracked, pea green and piss yellow, 1970's era kitchen counter, chewing absently as he considered what his future might hold. He thought he could be on the verge of something big, perhaps even momentous. Then again, if history were any indication, something or someone--he couldn't help thinking of Carl--would come along and fuck the whole thing up. He was determined not to let that happen. That meant keeping Carl in the dark, at least in the short term.

He stared unseeing at his grease-stained kitchen window. How many more Andrew Cullens were out there? How many other white collar assholes were running around, spending far beyond their means and getting into trouble? How many of those very same assholes could use some friendly assistance in the form of a short-term, high-interest, off-the-books loan? Most important, how many of them would jump at the chance, risky as it might be, to get their lives back on track? Ricky intended to find out.

He finished the sandwich, drained his cup and set it next to the sink, thinking all the while. Those people were out there. They had to be. Cullen was a perfect example. He might even know others in similar situations. And with his assistance, perhaps in exchange for some debt forgiveness, he could help make the necessary connections.

Ricky doubted he'd have much trouble persuading Cullen to help out. What choice would he have? If he still had a loan hanging over his head and someone like Carl waiting to collect, giving up a few names and making some simple introductions would seem a lot more appealing than the alternative. There was no reason it shouldn't work. So why did Ricky still feel like things were beginning to unravel?

As he made his way to the bathroom, peeling off clothes as he went, he tried telling himself his only real problem was lack of sleep. After all, he'd gotten up WAY earlier than he was used to and hadn't slept all that well beforehand. He kept dreaming that he'd slept through his alarm, missed Cullen, and then spent hours driving futilely all over town, catching occasional glimpses of his quarry but never getting close enough to be sure. After a few rounds of that same sequence, Ricky had a hard time determining if he was asleep or awake. It almost came as a relief when his alarm finally did go off. He was still in a foul mood when he got up, and trailing Andrew Cullen all over everywhere only made it worse.

He turned on the tap in the shower. Pipes hissed and squealed and eventually produced a thin stream of water about five degrees cooler than he would have liked. He washed and shaved quickly, toweled off, and then pulled on a pair of ratty gray sweatpants and a long sleeve black t-shirt. He wouldn't be caught dead dressed like that outside his own apartment but he didn't plan on going anywhere for awhile. He'd earned some down time and Carl, that big son of a bitch, should again be out looking for the two deadbeats. How in hell did they keep getting away? It was almost like Carl was letting them do it, but that made no sense at all so Ricky rejected the idea.

He stretched out on the bed, pulled an old afghan up to his chest, grabbed the remote and pointed it at a 60-inch HD television. He watched local news long enough to catch the weather, which sucked, and then began thumbing through channels until he found a soap opera showing a couple lesbians getting it on in the back of a private jet. He'd never thought of dykes joining the mile high club but supposed it must happen. That would probably be a good premise for a porn flick. *Fly the friendly skies?* You better fuckin' believe it.

Once he'd built up some capital, Ricky thought he might go into the movie business. He didn't know the first thing about it but assumed being a porn producer must come with some pretty sweet benefits. Besides, how hard could it be to aim a video camera at some wannabe *actors* while they went at it? Drop in some Barry White music, come up with a suitably raunchy title and you were good to go.

Ricky adjusted his pillows and tried to get comfortable. The soap opera scene shifted to a board room and a bunch of high-strung people yelling at each other. One especially bitchy looking woman, who'd apparently come back from the dead, was warning everyone about a hostile takeover and some schmuck named Pierre. He went back to channel surfing and, finding nothing, turned the set off.

Ricky wanted to get some shuteye, but after a full ninety minutes of tossing and turning, he finally groaned and sat up. If anything, he felt even worse than before. His eyes were gritty and all his muscles seemed to ache at once. He decided it was all Carl's fault for putting him in such a negative frame of mind.

Maybe, Ricky thought, he'd made a mistake with Andrew Cullen and following him around served no real purpose. That still didn't give Carl the right to question his judgment. Ricky had no patience for that, especially when it came to his shit-for-brains partner. The sensible approach would have been to admit his error. Instead, he'd gotten his back up and dug his heels in. He'd basically talked himself into a corner, and there was no longer any graceful way to back down. He would have to continue to follow Cullen and hope it did some good.

"That's fine," Ricky said, standing and crossing the room to the closet. "At least I'll have some help. He don't know it yet but the big man's gonna be putting in some serious overtime."

Ricky spent a few seconds wrestling with the closet door. One of the hinges was broken, and getting the damn thing open was always an adventure. He eventually succeeded and reached in to pull the string for the single overhead light. There was a flash and a pop followed by darkness.

He blinked, wondering if his day could get much worse, and then headed for the kitchen where he rummaged under the sink for new light bulbs. He found one cardboard sleeve which, of course, was empty.

Ricky returned to the closet and, one by one, brought each suit over to the window so he could see which looked the least soiled. He'd already trashed one suit climbing Cullen's fucking tree and only had three others. They were all overdue for dry cleaning and he was running out of shirts, socks and underwear too. Maybe he'd send Carl out to do his laundry. That would totally tick him off *and*, Ricky thought, *serve him right.*

As he dressed, he realized his difference of opinion with Carl regarding the handling of Andrew Cullen was only part of the problem. The guy had been acting differently for a while now. It started, as best Ricky could recall, after Marco was killed. Carl was scared at first, as well he should have been, but once it looked like he was in the clear, something seemed to have changed. It was about the time Skid Row and Bullfrog showed up on their doorstep, although Ricky couldn't imagine how they could have anything to do with it. Still, all of a sudden, Carl seemed less submissive and more... confrontational wasn't the right word but certainly more assertive. Ricky didn't like that. He just wasn't sure what he could or should do about it.

-43-

"This is totally freaking me out, dude."

"You mean Carl?'

Skid Row stared at Bullfrog from across their camp fire. "Well what do you think? He's fucking everywhere."

"I wouldn't say that." Bullfrog stirred a pot containing some beans, cabbage and water.

"I don't know why not. We see him every time we go out."

"So what are you saying? He knew we'd be at the grocery store? You think he's psychic?"

"Shit. I don't know." Skid Row brushed hair out of his eyes and began picking at a piece of loose rubber on the bottom of his right sneaker. "You said they couldn't follow us. You said we were safe. I gotta tell you, dude. I ain't feelin' safe right now."

"Would this be a bad time to remind you that you're the one who wanted to stick around?"

"Would this be a bad time for me to kick your ass?"

"Hey, I'm just sayin'…."

"Well don't. I know this is all my fault."

"I didn't say that."

Skid Row continued to tug at his sneaker. "You didn't have to. And how the hell can you be so calm? I know you were freaked out too."

"I was, and I'm sure I'll be again later. Right now my focus is lunch. Aren't you hungry?"

"I was but," Skid Row stared into the pot with distaste. "That shit looks like something I ate last week and now it's come back for revenge."

"It's good food," Bullfrog said. "And it will stick to your ribs"

"That slop would stick to anything. Who taught you how to cook?"

"I'm making do with what we've got. You don't have to eat it, but it will be good when it's done."

"I'm sure."

Bullfrog gave the pot another stir. "At least this didn't cost us anything."

"Who'd want to pay for it?" Skid Row grumbled, directing his comment at his shoe.

"The point is we can buy different stuff tomorrow. We've still got some money."

"And that's another thing." The bit of rubber Skid row had been working at finally tore free and he flicked it into the fire where it began to hiss and bubble. "Where does he get off buying our food? I mean, what the hell was that about?'

"Maybe he was just being nice."

"Fat fucking chance. If he wanted to be nice he should try leaving us alone for a change."

"Agreed," Bullfrog said. "But do you want to know what I think?"

"That depends. You gonna say something stupid?"

Bullfrog gave him a look and then went back to his cooking. "I think he was afraid we'd make a scene."

"Meaning?"

"He might have thought we'd start yelling or something."

Skid Row probably would have done just that, had he been able to find his voice. When Carl showed up, out of fucking nowhere again, he'd wanted to curl into a ball and cry like a baby--Carl standing right there grinning down at him. In the end, he'd been too shocked and scared to do a damn thing. He'd frozen up solid as Frosty's icicled asshole.

"I know he wasn't going to start thumping us right there in the store," Bullfrog said. "He couldn't draw attention to us either. I think he was trying to make our meeting look natural. Remember the way he started talking to us, like we were buds or something?"

"As if." Skid Row took a quick look around their small clearing. "All last night, I kept thinking about what you said, about how they couldn't really have spies all over the place. I mean, they couldn't, right?"

"Right."

Skid Row watched while Bullfrog opened ramen noodles, crumbled the pasta into the pot and stirred in the seasoning packet.

"Yeah, well, you almost had me believing it. I figured we'd be okay as long as we kept a... low profile? Isn't that what you called it?"

Bullfrog nodded and began dishing up the food.

"Okay," Skid Row went on, a pained expression on his face. "Then how are they doing this? That Carl bastard finds us everywhere we go."

"He hasn't found us here."

"Not yet," Skid Row said, taking in the waterfall, their campfire and the trees surrounding them on all sides.

"You serious?"

"Fuckin'-A," but then he shook his head. "I don't know. I don't know anything. The dude's in my head now. Don't you feel the same way?"

Bullfrog shrugged and handed over a bean can full of food.

"And you want to hear something really messed up?" Skid Row asked, realizing suddenly that Bullfrog's disgusting little concoction didn't smell half bad.

"What's that?"

"When we were at the store, right before we got into the checkout line, I'd sorta been thinkin' about him, you know? I was surprised we'd walked all that way there and hadn't seen him yet. I'd just been thinking that and then--"

"And then he was there."

"Fuckin' strange, dude. I mean cosmic. It was like I summoned him or something. That crazy or what?"

Bullfrog studied him for a while. "Do you even believe in stuff like that?"

"Shit no. I mean, I never have. But like I said, he's in my head now. I'm thinking all sorts of weird stuff."

"Such as?"

"I don't know," Skid Row said, taking a tentative bite then glancing up at the tree tops. "It ain't important."

They ate in silence until the food was gone and then Skid Row stood, grabbed a couple large chunks of wood and tossed them onto the fire.

"Can I tell you what I can't figure out?" Bullfrog asked, taking their cans and pot to the stream and beginning to rinse them out.

"Does it have anything to do with Carl?'

"Of course."

"That dude is so big. Even his fucking smile scares me."

"Yeah," Bullfrog said, his mind clearly somewhere else. "But here's what I don't get. He seems to find us with ease, whether it's coincidence or not I don't know, but then he doesn't really do anything."

"He dumped you on your ass yesterday."

"Okay," Bullfrog said, nodding as if to concede the point. "And he's got you so scared you think he's supernatural. But what has he really done other than pick up our grocery tab?

"Well," Skid Row said. "You still think he stole that bag."

Bullfrog stared at him. "And you don't? After everything we--"

"Relax, bro. I know it was him. But he's not the reason we're in this perpetual pity party. That one's on me."

"I think I had a part in it too. You were fired because of me. Why don't we call it a group effort?'

Skid Row was silent for a moment. He understood what Bullfrog was trying to do but it wouldn't fly. Even if he still had his lousy job, even if

Bullfrog had never set foot in McDonald's and the two had never met, Skid Row would still be homeless now and--full disclosure--he'd been stupid his whole life.

His history of poor decision making went back literally as far as he could remember, starting in kindergarten when he'd swiped a kid's bike so he could get home a few minutes faster. When his mom bolted, he'd never made any attempt to work things out with William. Instead, he'd simply walked out. Why? It was easier, or seemed so at the time. He was always doing what was easier, saying he wanted a better life but coasting along for years because that required less effort. His half-baked, half-assed plan to take over for Marco was yet another chapter from that same old book. And as usual, his big brainstorm was really nothing more than a brain fart, another failed attempt at a quick fix and that's why accepting full responsibility felt perfectly natural.

"I should have listened to you," Skid Row said, feeling miserable and, for some reason, hoping Bullfrog would come down on him as hard as he was trying to come down on himself. "You didn't want to do it. You told me it was a bad idea. I wouldn't let it go." He shook his head and couldn't meet Bullfrog's eye. "I'm sorry."

"You sure are," Bullfrog said, looking at him curiously.

"Huh?"

"Well just listen to yourself," he said, hands on his hips. "That's about the sorriest crap I've ever heard. How are you ever gonna get anywhere with an attitude like that? Here's a thought. Instead of beating yourself up, how 'bout we put our heads together and see what we can figure out."

"About what," Skid Row asked, frowning up at him but then sighing and getting to his feet.

"For starters, Carl. What's his game? What does he want?"

"To make us feel like idiots?"

"Be serious," Bullfrog said. "What is he really after?"

"Money, I guess. That's what he says."

"Right! So why hasn't he tried to get it?"

"Maybe 'cause he knows it would be a waste of time. Anyone could see that."

"Okay, then why does he keep coming around, making vague threats but not following through?"

Skid Row thought about that. After inexplicably paying for their groceries, Carl had all but frog marched them out of the store. His intent had seemed plain enough and Skid Row thought they were doomed.

Yet, once they reached the entrance, he seemed to hesitate. He'd pushed them to the right, only to pull them back the other way after a step or two. They'd ended up exiting right next to a group of Girl Scouts enthusiastically selling their cookies. Two cops were close by.

"You're lucky," Carl had growled, gripping them both by the shoulders but looking, Skid Row thought now, amused. He supposed that hadn't registered at the time because he'd been so focused on what else Carl was saying.

"You boys run back to your camp now. I'll find you when I want you. It will be soon, and you'd better have Ricky's money or else." He'd given them a shake and a quick shove and that was it.

For quite a while they'd been too dumb-founded to do much more than stand and stare at each other. Then, they'd done what he said, getting away from there as fast as they could.

"He let us go," Skid Row said, that realization finally dawning. "He led us out that way on purpose."

Bullfrog nodded slowly. "I think so too. I just don't know why."

-44-

Ricky had been at his office for the past hour, thinking about Carl and getting progressively more irritated. He checked his watch, again, and saw that it was going on six. He'd sent a text to Carl at 5:17 which gave explicit instructions that he was to call. As yet, he hadn't done it. If that didn't change in the very near future, Ricky would either have to drive back over to Cullen's office so he could be there when he left for the day, a responsibility he'd planned on delegating, or let that go until morning. That wouldn't be a big deal, but Carl's prolonged silence was.

He looked at his phone and re-read his message. *Call me ASAP!* There's no way that could have been misinterpreted, not even by Carl. He was a dunce, sure, but he spoke English and knew how to read. Of course, there was no way to verify that he'd actually seen the text. He could have lost his phone, had it turned off, or left it in his truck while he was off stalking Skid Row and Bullfrog or whatever else he might be doing. Those were all perfectly plausible scenarios and Ricky guessed Carl would use one of them as an excuse.

Normally, he would have given his partner the benefit of the doubt, because in the past Carl had always been reliable. Ricky could text him at two in the morning and still receive a response within seconds. The--he glanced at his watch again--more than half hour time lapse was unheard of and Ricky didn't like it one fucking bit. Carl was ignoring him. He felt it in his gut and it confirmed what he'd already been suspecting. Something had changed and definitely not in a good way.

Ricky stood behind his desk, hands in his pockets to try to get them warm. This was the first time in months he hadn't needed to turn on the old window air conditioner. The office seemed too quiet without the incessant hissing, rattling and wheezing. He had the heat on instead and it didn't feel like it was doing a thing. To make matters worse, the insufficient trickle of warm air stirred up whatever pathogens had been long dormant in the vents and under the floorboards. The entire trailer smelled like a combination of Geno's food poisoning palace and Ricky's mountain of dirty laundry. He considered opening the door but decided the cold was worse than the smell. What he really needed were some candles or a big honking can of Lysol.

Ricky knew he had a decision to make. Whatever was going on with Carl, he had to nip it in the bud before it became a much bigger problem. Their business model was simple: Ricky led, Carl followed. That's how it had always been and how it needed to stay if they were to remain successful. But if Carl was having other ideas, if he was beginning to question Ricky's judgment and decision-making, what would be the best way to rein him in?

That's easy, Ricky thought, looking down at the mess on his desktop. *Crush him like a fucking bug.*

He had options, and the first was to come down hard and heavy. Carl was the muscle in the outfit. He bullied, threatened and, when necessary, cracked heads. But when it came to their personal dealings, Ricky had always worn the boots. He used them to kick Carl in the ass. It was a perfect arrangement and, Ricky thought, mutually beneficial. He also thought Carl needed him a lot more than the other way around. They were like George and Lenny. Ricky never read *Of Mice and Men* but he knew what it was about. George was smart and tough. Lenny was big, stupid, and always getting into trouble. Ricky knew how it ended too and he wondered if he should borrow a page from that story and put a bullet in Carl's ugly head. It might be satisfying but could cause more problems than it solved.

Silently cursing his partner, he opened his top desk drawer where he kept an old .38 revolver. It wasn't loaded nor had it been the entire time the weapon had been in Ricky's possession. Like his laptop computer, it had been given to him by T. J. Tyson one of the many times the bookie didn't have the cash to cover his debts. Ricky didn't like guns and had never actually fired one. He also assumed the revolver was hot and may have been used in the commission of serious crimes. He only kept the piece for show, and never carried it unless Carl was unavailable and he felt the need to intimidate.

After much practice in front of his bedroom mirror, he'd learned how to stand just so. With the subtlest shift of his body, his suit coat would fall open slightly, just enough to reveal the dark wooden grip protruding from his waistband. He'd practiced drawing the weapon too, and did so in a way that made him look like he knew what he was doing. He'd be screwed if he ever had to take his act any further than that.

Ricky started to slide the drawer closed but then paused, reached in and lifted the gun out. It felt heavy, solid and deadly. To Ricky's untrained eye, it also looked like it had seen better days. He noticed a bit of rust along the barrel and on one side and rubbed at it with his thumb. When he spun the small cylinder, there was more resistance than he thought there should be. How could you tell when a gun needed to be cleaned? Would the thing even fire if it was loaded? Maybe he should get some ammunition and find out. With his luck, though, it would probably blow up in his face. There were ways to deal with that.

Carl, buddy, take this out back and see if she'll still shoot straight.

But that was no good either. He did enough damage with his bare hands. The last thing Carl needed was a firearm. He'd owned one briefly and it hadn't ended well. That was a couple years ago now. Ricky never quite got the story straight but, so far as he could tell, Carl was waving the gun around and threatening to shoot a guy in the knee cap.

As was normally the case, the dispute was over a payment that was past due. Tempers flared, one thing led to another, and the gun, which Carl always swore was neither loaded nor cocked, somehow discharged. The man's knee caps thankfully remained intact but the bullet struck him in the nuts and the poor bastard nearly bled out before emergency personnel arrived at the scene. Carl was long gone by that point and the victim, who already had a police record as long as an eighteen-wheeler, never fingered him as the shooter. All gunshot wounds have to be reported to law enforcement but he claimed he shot himself and, even though he couldn't produce the weapon, there wasn't much of anything the police could do.

Oddly, the mishap helped solidify Carl's reputation as a bad ass. The stories that emerged after the fact were totally ridiculous and most included words like castration and dismemberment. It bothered Carl quite a bit but Ricky never made the slightest attempt to dispel the rumors. It boiled down to one simple fact. The fear factor was good for business and everyone was afraid of Carl. By association, that meant they were afraid of Ricky too. He'd done his best to capitalize on that and thought it had all worked out pretty well.

But what, Ricky wondered now, stalking from one end of the trailer to the other, would happen to his business if he could no longer rely on Carl's services? Carl was his partner and Ricky had always thought of him as such. Be that as it may, it was still his business and definitely not a joint venture. He called the shots. He made the plans. It was Ricky Fixx the clients wanted to talk to. They might be scared of Carl but that wasn't the same as respecting him. Even Carl respected Ricky; at least, he had. For some reason, though, it felt like the sand had begun to shift.

Spinning suddenly, he took up what he believed was a good shooter's stance: legs wide, knees bent, and elbows locked. He tilted his head and sighted down his arm, taking careful aim at the door, the window and then the chair Carl usually occupied. Ricky could see him sitting there and the big fucker was actually laughing at him. He shook his head and tried to blink the image away. What the hell had gotten into him? So Carl hadn't called him back yet. And yes, maybe he had been a little insolent of late. That didn't necessarily mean anything was happening. Or, did it?

"Fuck," he swore, returning to his desk, dropping the gun into the drawer and slamming it closed. He sank into his chair and noticed that, if nothing else, he was no longer cold. Ricky ran a hand across the back of his neck and it came away damp with sweat. He got up, went into the bathroom and checked his reflection in the cracked mirror. His face was flushed, and he could feel the heat radiating from his skin. That wouldn't do. Carl was going to call at some point, if not show up here. And when he did, Ricky had to be in control.

Taking a few deep breaths, he washed his hands and splashed cold water onto his face. Back at his desk, he sifted through the items scattered in front of him. They were a fair but not quite comprehensive representation of Carl's work history, and the pictures of him manhandling Geno were right on top of the pile. Unfortunately, he didn't have any real evidence of Carl's nastier exploits. There were no photos of him burning that car dealership to the ground, skewering Marco with an axe handle or shooting a meth head in the crotch. He didn't even have any shots of Carl with a weapon. In short, Ricky could make trouble for him but probably not enough to get him out of the way for good.

"I need more," he said, picking up a thumb drive and bouncing it in the palm of his hand. But then he had a thought. Carl was gullible as all hell. If it came right down to it, Ricky might be able to scare him off by showing him a picture or two and implying he had a lot more than he did. Did Carl have the balls to call his bluff? Ricky doubted it, but also knew there was too much at stake to take the chance. He needed solid proof of Carl doing something truly malicious. Skid Row and Bullfrog came to mind, and Ricky realized they might be more expendable than he'd thought.

His phone still sat dark and silent, and he knew his top priority was determining how best to handle the immediate situation. Whatever Carl was up to, he needed to understand that Ricky was still the boss and wasn't about to put up with his shit.

In the past, verbal abuse had always been enough to keep him in line. This time, though, Ricky believed a different approach would prove a lot more effective. Although it seriously rubbed against the grain, he'd paste a smile on his face and blow a ration of sunshine up Carl's fat ass. Massage his ego until his attitude improved. By the time that happened, and Ricky doubted it would take long, he planned on having enough dirt on Carl to bury him for good.

Ricky scooped up his cell phone and began typing a new text. It was a little kinder and gentler than the first. The only thing missing was that little smiley-faced emoticon. He pressed the send button and laughed, tilting back and spinning around in his chair. He kept the phone in his hand because he knew he'd be receiving a return text soon.

-45-

Carl ran his tongue over his teeth in search of any bits of chili dog he might have missed. He felt a twinge of heartburn and decided that in future, two foot-longs and one large order of fries were probably enough. Also, it might be better to let his food settle a while before digging into his hot fudge sundae. He rubbed his stomach and wriggled in his seat until he managed to loosen his belt a notch.

Stake-outs were dull work. That was his problem. And when Carl was bored, he ate. Why he was even on this stake-out was a question he hadn't quite figured out. He knew Skid Row and Bullfrog were hunkered down just over five hundred yards due east of his current position. He knew that if he needed to, he could go in there, locate them and flush them out even without the help of his new best friend. Mentally, Carl had started referring to the Retrievor unit as Fido because it seemed as reliable as the family dog. When he could track their whereabouts simply by looking at his phone, why in the world was he wasting his time sitting in the cab of his truck and getting progressively colder by the minute?

He pushed that thought aside and considered cranking the engine to let the heat run for a few minutes. He finally decided against it. There was always the chance his boys would hear the rumble from his big diesel. Carl knew that wasn't likely at—he did some quick math--almost a quarter mile away. Really, the evening was so still and calm he just didn't want to break the silence. Instead, he zipped his coat up a little higher and dug his hands into his pockets. At least his truck provided a little warmth. That was more than Skid Row and Bullfrog had. Sleeping outdoors and living on cabbage and beans--was that really all they could afford? Where did they go when it rained? Why were they homeless in the first place? Carl shook his head and wondered why he even cared.

He had his own problems and being overly concerned about a couple down-on-their-luck drifters would do him no good at all. He'd already helped them by way of his small handout at the grocery store. He'd done his part. Whatever happened next was out of his control. He didn't agree with whatever Ricky thought he could get out of all this. He'd made that clear but, in the end, it really wasn't his decision. He needed to accept it and move on. Still....

And on the subject of moving on, Carl decided it was time to go for a stroll. He could think, stretch his legs and, if his trek just happened to take him a few hundred yards east, maybe see what sort of camp they'd set up and exactly what they were up to. He wasn't planning on doing anything other than satisfying his own curiosity. Carl had his window cracked a couple inches and thought he smelled smoke. Maybe they were roasting marshmallows... *or fucking cabbage leaves. Who knew?*

Carl had his left hand on the door handle when his cell phone gave a soft chirp. "Hello, what's this?" he asked in what he thought was a passable British accent.

At first, he figured Skid Row and Bullfrog were moving again but then he realized the tone was wrong. Someone had sent him a text and he was sure he knew who it was. He sighed and checked the screen. He then had to check again because he thought his eyes must be playing tricks on him.

"Are you free? I thought we could meet for dinner. My treat."

Carl sat back and scratched his head. He took a look at Ricky's previous message which he'd read for the first time almost forty-five minutes earlier. *"Call me ASAP!"* He couldn't miss the difference in tone.

"5 minutes," he typed and hit Send. He set his phone aside and wondered what Mr. Fixx had up his sleeve.

Are you free?

That was his first clue something strange was taking place. Ricky never asked a question like that because he really didn't give a shit. When he said jump, he expected Carl to drop everything and find the nearest trampoline. And then that last part. They'd met for dinner plenty of times but Ricky had never once offered to pay. He was more the type to order a twenty dollar meal but only put ten on the table when the check arrived.

"Not good," Carl said, seeing right through Ricky's evident kindness and generosity. He was trying to play him. Carl felt sure of that, but didn't know how he should react.

He still had two minutes left of the five he'd requested but went ahead and sent Ricky another text. *"Just ate,"* he typed. *"What's up?"*

"So I'll buy you a drink. How about Uncle Tony's?"

"What the hell?" Carl had never known Ricky to be reasonable or accommodating and it was totally throwing him off. He bit his lower lip and began typing again.

"Tracking S & B now. Could we do it later?' He took a breath, pressed Send and imagined Ricky reading his message, swearing and then hurling something, probably that hideous pole dancer paperweight, against the wall of the trailer. Carl knew full well that Ricky didn't like

being put off and it didn't make the slightest difference if it was work-related or not.

He remembered the time he'd shown up a few minutes late for a pickup. When he pulled up at the street corner Ricky was there, red-faced and fuming. Carl was red-faced too because it was a hot, sunny day and he'd spent the past ten minutes frantically changing a flat tire. He was sweaty, out of breath and his hands were covered with grime. Ricky still blew up at him, like it was somehow his fault, and then gave him the cold shoulder for the rest of the day.

Carl knew it would be worse this time around. He hadn't responded to Ricky's first text and, although he had an excuse at the ready, he knew it wouldn't be accepted. Ricky hadn't said anything about that yet but he would. Carl assumed he was waiting until they were face to face.

An interminable seventy-six seconds passed before the next text came in. Carl stared at his wrist watch, its tiny second hand seemingly in perfect time with his thudding heartbeat. After the first forty-five seconds, he decided Ricky wasn't going to text again. He'd call. Carl would have to answer and Ricky's yelling would be so loud that Skid Row and Bullfrog would hear it even if they were clear across town.

With considerable effort, he tore his eyes away from his watch and used his coat sleeve to wipe a sheen of sweat from his forehead. He felt like a scared kid waiting for Dad to come home to lay down the law. Why? Why was he so afraid of the little twerp? Why did he let him push him around? Why, Carl wondered, didn't he just stand up for himself for once?

He had tried, sort of. At times, most recently with the two drifters, he'd let Ricky know he was unhappy. The problem was he could never stick to his guns. Ricky would get pissed, Carl would back down, and in the end allow himself to be manipulated just like always. It was stupid and weak and Carl knew it needed to stop.

No more, he thought, deciding that this time if Ricky gave him shit, he was prepared to give it right back, but his boss surprised him once more.

"No problem," Ricky's new text said. *"Call when you're done and we'll meet then. It's open bar. Good luck."*

Carl stared, blinked, and stared some more. "What is your game?" he asked, and then he started his engine and drove away.

-46-

"I really appreciate your support," Andrew Cullen said, cradling the phone against his shoulder and doodling in the margin of the list of talking points he'd prepared.

"Oh, there's no need to thank me. Your generous donation is what's making this possible. Cyber Force is honored to be involved and I'm just happy I can do my part to benefit such a worthy cause."

Cullen wrote $7,500 next to Prestige Home Furnishings. Then he added a little smiley face because that brought his pledges for the day up to almost a hundred and twenty thousand bucks.

"What's that, Sir?"

He gave his smiley a Mr. Monopoly style mustache and top hat.

"Well let me see." Cradling the phone between his ear and shoulder, Cullen noisily riffled through the papers on his desk. He made sounds like he was adding up figures in his head. "I don't have an exact total," he said. "It looks like we're up to about sixty thousand so far."

Mr. Monopoly got an eye patch and the body of a snake.

"I'm encouraged but we certainly hope to do more. I know everyone wants to help. This economy makes it difficult."

Cullen never thought he'd have much trouble finding donors. What had surprised him was the size of some of the donations. The seventy-five hundred from the furniture store was a big one but he'd received a few of ten grand and more. And of course, the more he took in the more he could safely skim without being caught.

"That would be perfect," he said. "Just make your check out to the Tri-Cities Tomorrow Fund. I'll send my assistant around to pick it up in a day or two."

Cullen thought involving Carrie would make his endeavor appear even more on the up and up. He also decided it was best not to have Cyber Force in the name of his bogus charity. Yes, people wanted to help but they wanted their recognition too. No one would make a substantial contribution under another business's name. That's what Cullen believed anyway and it seemed to be proving true.

"Oh, absolutely," he said. "I'll do what I can to acknowledge all of our supporters. The information will be in the press releases and all our promotional materials. Of course, there will be significant media coverage too. I'll have to prioritize and, well, you know how it is. The larger donors will get top billing."

Cullen listened and smiled to himself. They were all the same.

"I'm sure that could be arranged. And the additional thousand dollars really isn't necessary."

He gave Mr. Monopoly pointy ears with large diamond studs.

"Well, if you insist. That's incredibly generous. Thank you."

Cullen checked the special calendar he kept under his desk blotter. A substantial part of his Cyber Force business came from antivirus software. But, he didn't just eliminate viruses; he planted them too—little, custom-made time bombs designed to go off at his discretion. It was devious but kept his customers coming back, and it appeared Prestige Home Furnishings was due for detonation within the month. Under the circumstances, he decided to put that off a bit.

See that, he thought, making a note. *I can be a nice guy too.*

After a few more minutes of polite chit-chat and a vague promise to get together for lunch--*Aint happenin,' pal*--he hung up the phone and sat back with a self-satisfied smile. The way things were going, he thought he might be able to pocket enough to pay off Ricky even if he failed to win the race. He just needed to make sure he didn't get too greedy.

Cullen knew he was a gambler and a risk-taker by nature. His brazenness had served him well over the Years. That was true in matters of business and pleasure. They often went hand in hand. Make a big bet. Win a big pot. Have some bimbo sucking you off in your hotel suite fifteen minutes later. If he had a dollar for every time something like that happened, maybe he wouldn't have had to go to Ricky for help.

Of course, the dollars had been there. That only changed when, all of a sudden, every hand was a bust and every roll of the dice seemed to come up snake eyes. He'd hit a rough patch but he believed—hell, he knew--his luck had to improve. That was the gambler mentality. No matter how bad things got, every bet he placed had the potential to right the ship. That was why, when he found himself in a hole, he got a bigger shovel and kept on digging.

To Cullen, working the phone, making his pitch and convincing people to contribute to his charity felt a lot like bluffing an opponent out of a pot. It made him think he was back in the saddle, like things had finally started to turn around. He could, Cullen supposed, pay Ricky off right then or at least as soon as he collected all the money that had been promised. He owed Ricky a hundred grand. Fine. That would still leave twenty grand that, if wagered wisely, he could turn into a lot more. It probably wouldn't take more than a few hours at the blackjack table. A little guts, a little luck and he'd be riding high again.

Cullen remembered the redneck asshole he'd met last time he was at the casino. What was his name? Jimmy or John Boy or maybe Billy Fucking Ray? What was the difference? He was a shit and Cullen could imagine how nice it would be to sit down next to him and blow his backwoods ass right out of the water. A couple things stopped him. Although Carrie had no idea how much he'd be bringing in, she was enough in the loop that he couldn't simply take the money and run, even if he planned to refill the coffers a short time later. She might start asking questions. She could, Cullen supposed, even say something to her big-shot lawyer daddy. He closed his eyes and shuddered at the thought. Leo Flynn typically didn't practice that kind of law but he had the clout and the connections to rock Cullen's world in a big way. He vowed not to do anything to cause Leo's baby girl the slightest suspicion.

And then there was Sara. Cullen wasn't sure what had happened there but she seemed suspicious of him already. Why? He'd managed to keep his financial problems secret. As for his other missteps, he'd been careful--extremely careful. All of his liaisons were out of town and in places he wasn't likely to be recognized. He'd never come home smelling of perfume or with lipstick smears on his collar. He had that one bite mark but he was quite sure Sara had never seen that. He couldn't remember the last time she'd given that particular region of his body a close inspection. Maybe if she had, if she'd been more attentive to his needs, he might not have been so tempted to seek his pleasures elsewhere. In his heart, though, he knew that was crap. He was a red-blooded, horny almost fifty-year-old and had never had much luck controlling his urges. He couldn't blame that on Sara. He still loved her, more than anything in the world, and that's why he'd been so cautious, always covering his tracks. He did it out of respect for her and their marriage. But what about the recent cold front that had blown in? She acted like a woman scorned. Was it possible that, despite his best efforts, she'd suspected all along?

Cullen's gaze wandered around his office and finally settled on the framed picture of Sara and the girls. He focused just on her, noticing how fresh, young and happy she looked. But was there something else in her eyes? They seemed penetrating, like she was looking right into his soul. He wondered if, even then, she knew who he really was.

"No way," Cullen said. They'd been happily married for years and it was only recently that some cracks had started to appear. Besides, it wasn't like he was a bad husband or father. So he had a few vices. Everyone did. He compensated by providing for his family very, very well. She didn't know about the other women anyway. She couldn't. All she knew was that he hadn't been around as much as she would have liked. He could make up for that, and he would just as soon as the triathlon was over and he was on firmer financial footing.

But then Cullen thought about his last real conversation with his wife and couldn't help wondering if, somehow, he wasn't quite seeing the full picture. What had she said? *When's the last time you passed a bar without stopping for a drink*? It was something like that, and the subtext was clear.

So she'd known he'd been hitting the bottle some. That was no biggie. He was under a lot of stress and had already made the decision to cut back on the booze. What made him nervous was this new realization that she wasn't as much in the dark as he'd assumed. And if she knew about his drinking, wasn't it at least possible she knew about the gambling too? How much further did it go? He thought it was his little secret, but what if no one was buying his act? When he stepped away from the poker table to call Carrie with his well-rehearsed story about high-level business dealings, did she take him at his word or roll her eyes and then go home and tell her boyfriend all about the total loser she worked for?

"This is nuts," he said, standing and moving automatically towards his wet bar. He took a few steps, realized what he was doing and then stopped short. He wanted a drink badly but that was the last thing in the world he needed right then.

"Dammit!" he swore, his voice echoing off dark wooden paneling. His eyes shifted to the door but he knew there was no one around to hear him. His small staff had all left for the day and the cleaners weren't due for a while. There was an insurance office right below his own but they were all gone as well and who the fuck cared anyway? Pissing off his neighbors was the least of his problems.

"I got 99 problems and a bitch ain't one," Cullen said, thinking about the Jay Z song even though it didn't exactly fit the situation.

He spun in a slow half circle, unsure what to do with himself. He knew he was over-thinking the whole thing, assuming the worst when there was no sensible reason to jump to that conclusion. Sara was plainly furious with him and it had to be based on something more than missed family dinners and a few too many vodka and tonics. However, she'd never been one to hold her tongue. If she knew about the gambling, the women, or any of the rest, she would have come right out and said it. The fact that she hadn't should indicate that he was still in the clear, at least for the time being. Somehow, though, he didn't feel reassured. Maybe that was because when he'd told her about his charitable endeavor, she'd immediately accused him of having an ulterior motive. That stung, even though her assessment had been spot on.

Cullen looked at his desk phone. He still had his list of perspective donors he could call, but given that they were mostly nine-to-fivers, he'd probably be wasting his time. His heart was no longer in it anyway. He could call his wife and try to make nice, or better yet, head home right then, maybe even hit the florist along the way. Should he grab some take-out too? But really, what was the point? Carnations and fortune cookies wouldn't be enough to get him out of the dog house. He needed to fix their finances and everything else would fall in line. He capped his pen and then headed into his bathroom to change into workout clothes.

-47-

Ricky picked up his glass and was surprised to see that all it contained was a few ice cubes. *When did that happen? And where had everyone gone?*

When he'd first entered the pub, most of the bar stools were occupied. That was fine. He hadn't been in the mood to socialize anyway. Ricky chose a table against the back wall, and it gave him a good view of his surroundings. He just hadn't been paying much attention. While he was busy with his drink, or maybe it was drinks, he'd somehow missed a mass exodus. The place hadn't entirely emptied out but he now had plenty of options should he feel the need to relocate. He knew what he should really do was order something to eat. Instead, he caught Gus's eye and raised one finger.

Ricky stood and had to hold onto the edge of the table briefly to steady himself. That surprised him too. He didn't think he'd had that much, but he realized he couldn't be TOO sure one way or the other. That ought to tell him something. *Oh well,* he thought. *It takes a drunk to catch a drunk,* and then he smiled.

"So how's life treating you Gus old boy," Ricky asked, stepping up to the bar and helping himself to a handful of pretzels.

The bartender eyed him over the tops of the beer pulls. "I'm perfectly fine, Mr….."

"The name's Ricky. Ricky Fixx." He spit a few pretzel crumbs onto the bar.

"And you're a friend of Mr. Cullen. Is that correct?" Gus picked up a towel and deftly wiped the crumbs away.

Ricky hesitated, trying to remember the story he'd told the last time he'd been in there. Hadn't he claimed they were college buddies or something? He finally just nodded, deciding it was best not to elaborate. "Has he been in tonight?"

"I haven't seen him," Gus said, getting a new glass and adding ice, a generous amount of Jim Beam and a thin red cocktail straw. "I expect he's busy training. You know he's got that triathlon coming up."

"Oh sure," Ricky said. "We talked about that."

"It's a wonderful thing that he's doing, and I'm sure it will help take his mind off his recent loss."

His loss? What was the old buzzard prattling on about now? But then Ricky remembered his tale about the dead professor. He'd have to pay closer attention to what he said because Gus didn't seem to forget anything.

"We're contributing," Gus added, looking at Ricky as if he was expecting some sort of response.

Ricky picked up his drink and took a sip, as much to stall as anything else. *Contributing? What the hell had he missed?*

"He's making a big donation to a center for underprivileged children. You must know about that, being a close friend and everything. It's been all over the news too."

"Of course," Ricky said, feeling stupid. "It just slipped my mind. One of those days, you know?"

"I understand perfectly," Gus said, looking sincere but placing just enough emphasis on the last word to make Ricky wonder if the man knew he was full of shit.

"Uncle Tony's is contributing a thousand dollars to the cause," Gus went on. "Mr. Cullen has been a good customer for years and we're proud to support him in such a worthy endeavor."

Ricky took another large sip from his drink, figuring that was better than putting his foot in his mouth again. He stood awkwardly for a moment then raised his glass, turned, and headed back to his table. He looked over his shoulder once, which proved to be a mistake because he veered off course and bumped into a chair. And as he righted himself, he saw that Gus had been watching him the whole time.

Well fuck him, Ricky thought, because something in Gus's snooty expression suggested that he didn't approve: of Ricky, his suit, his haircut, his choice of whiskey or anything else associated with him.

"Fuck him," Ricky thought again, except he must have said it out loud that time because a stiff looking man and his obviously frigid wife both turned to frown at him. *And fuck you two too,* Ricky thought, giggling slightly as he dropped into his chair. His good humor didn't even last as long as his drink.

So Andrew Cullen had been busy. He was big news all of a sudden and Gus seemed to think he was some sort of hero. Ricky was tempted to go burst that bubble right then. What would Gus say if he knew the real story? What if he saw candid photos of Mr. Socially Consciousness gambling, womanizing and doing all the rest? Ricky had some of those photos. They were his ace up his sleeve just in case the ones he'd taken of Cullen's wife and kids hadn't done the trick. Even if the jackass won his stupid triathlon and paid every cent he owed, Ricky could keep on pulling his strings just as long and hard as he wanted. What would good old Gus say if he knew that? Would it change the self-righteous sneer that Ricky knew was lurking right behind his smile?

Unfortunately, he couldn't act just yet, not without blowing the whole thing to pieces. He had the power to send Andrew Cullen's reputation right down the toilet. He could rock his world, but doing so would also mean he'd never see one penny of his money. That was a tall price to pay for a little satisfaction and Ricky wasn't so drunk that he lost sight of the need to bide his time. Cullen would get his in the end, and wasn't that what really mattered?

He is clever, Ricky thought, reaching for his glass but then thinking better of it. Carl was on his way there, presumably, and it wouldn't do for him to be totally bombed when he finally showed up. Ricky squinted at his watch but couldn't tell the difference between the minute hand and the hour hand. It was either seven forty or about twenty-five minutes to nine. Ridiculous that he couldn't pinpoint how long he'd been there even to within the nearest hour. He finally gave up and pulled out his phone. Seven forty-two. At least it wasn't as bad as he'd feared. He'd still had too much to drink in too short a time. That was dangerous, especially because the game he was playing required a certain amount of delicacy.

Ricky looked around for the waitress but she was nowhere in sight. He debated, and then stood and worked his way carefully back to the bar. Trying to keep his conversation with Gus to a minimum, he ordered coffee and a hot corned beef sandwich with fries. He returned to his table, but not before Gus made a few more comments about the awesome Andrew Cullen.

A lot you know, Ricky thought, but he held his tongue.

Cullen had been smart, a lot more so than Ricky first realized. It seemed he'd suddenly become the talk of the town. That was good for his donor campaign, and whether by design or not, it also put him that much more in the public eye. That meant Ricky couldn't or at least probably shouldn't keep as close tabs on him as he might want. He wasn't about to back off completely. No way. He'd just have to be a lot more careful. And wouldn't Carl love hearing that, since he already said following Cullen so closely wasn't necessary to begin with.

"I ain't doin' it 'cause of you," Ricky muttered, swirling the ice in his glass. "So don't get any ideas."

As if he'd been waiting for the proper time, Carl pushed through the door farthest away from where Ricky was sitting. He spotted him immediately but walked straight to the bar and ordered a bottle of Bud.

"Put it on his tab," he said, nodding and pointing a thumb in Ricky's direction.

"I see you're alone," Ricky said, once Carl had pulled out a chair and sat down. "Should I assume you struck out, or did you find them and let them go again?"

Ricky hadn't meant to start the conversation with such hostility. As usual, though, something about Carl rubbed him wrong. It may have been the stupid expression on his face or the fact that it had taken him so damn long to respond to the text. He didn't think he was being unreasonable. He'd bought him a drink and offered to buy dinner and Ricky thought that was at least worth a little punctuality.

"Was I supposed to bring them with me? I'm not sure this is their kind of place."

"So what? They're out in your truck then?"

They would be if I wanted them to. "It's a big city," Carl said, draining half of his beer in one long gulp and setting the bottle aside. "I was on their trail but then..." he gestured at the room in general. "You made it sound pretty important that we get together."

"So it's my fault?" Ricky asked, raising his voice a little too much. He glanced around and was relieved to see that no one but Gus was paying them any attention. He looked away and concentrated on not letting his temper get the best of him.

"I did want to see you," Ricky said just as his food arrived. He fell silent as the tired-looking waitress placed his plate, a bottle of ketchup, and a napkin-wrapped bundle of silverware in front of him.

"Anything for you?" she asked, directing her question at Carl but not really meeting his eye.

That, Ricky knew, was a common reaction. In his experience, most people went out of their way not to look at him because he was so freaking massive. Carl knew that too and tended to use it to its fullest advantage.

"I'm good," he said, the words coming out like distant thunder.

"Okay then." She held her tray up as if it were a shield. "My name is Angela. Just let me know if you change your mind." With that, she backed away, turned and pushed through the swinging door into the kitchen.

"Was that necessary?" Ricky asked.

"What?"

"You probably scared her. You think she'll want to come back?'

"What do you care? You've got your food and it looks like you've already had enough to drink."

Damn. Was it that obvious? Ricky cleared his throat and sat up a little straighter. "I'm drinking coffee," he said, even though his half full whiskey glass was still right next to him.

Carl looked but didn't comment and Ricky made a show of stirring cream and sugar into his cup.

"So what's this about?" Carl finally asked, leaning back, crossing his arms and tilting his head to one side.

Ricky took his time arranging his napkin on his lap and spreading extra Thousand Island dressing on his sandwich. It smelled good. He just wasn't that hungry. He'd only ordered the food to help counteract the alcohol he'd already consumed. With some reluctance, he took a large bite, pretending to savor it like it was the best thing he'd ever tasted. Really, he was just buying time because Carl wanted answers and, all of a sudden, Ricky had none to give.

"I think," he began, trying to remember why seeing Carl had seemed so all-fired important, "we need to get on the same page."

"Meaning?"

Ricky paused to wipe his mouth. He'd gotten fed up with Carl's attitude. He remembered that much. He just couldn't remember what he'd planned on doing about it. It had something to do with Cullen; at least he thought so, but the pieces no longer fit together in his head. Ricky cursed himself for ordering however the hell many drinks he'd ordered. After a second, though, he decided it didn't matter. Carl was a dim-wit and Ricky had always managed to put him in his place. No reason he couldn't do it again now. Getting some help from Jim Beam might even make it easier. And with that, a new plan started to form.

He had, Ricky now recalled, decided to take the kid glove approach and catch Carl off guard by blowing sunshine up his butthole. Why that ever seemed necessary was beyond him. The free beer was all the sunshine the big bastard was going to get. If Ricky wanted results, if he wanted the respect he'd earned and damn well deserved, it was time to play some hard ball. He poured a slug of Jim Beam into his coffee, took a sip and fixed Carl with his most serious stare.

-48-

"It's time to stop fucking around!" Ricky said, setting his cup down and placing both palms firmly on the table top.

Carl recoiled inwardly but willed himself not to shrink away or show any of the fear that caused his heart to race or the skin to crawl along the back of his neck.

Already, this wasn't going as he'd expected. He'd read Ricky's text, at first with suspicion but then bewilderment. Maybe it was wishful thinking but he'd convinced himself that whatever Ricky wanted to talk to him about, it had to be something good. Instead, it took him all of about two seconds to see that his boss was pissed, in the drunk sense as well as the just plain pissed sense. The only thing Carl could figure was that Ricky's good mood had come out of a bottle, and disappeared at least a drink or two before he arrived. *Should've stayed away,* he thought, knowing it was too late for that now.

"I don't understand," Carl said, fiddling with the button on his left shirt cuff. "Did I do something wrong?"

Ricky actually laughed at that but without a hint of humor. "Wrong?" He spat the word out like it had a bad taste. "When's the last time you did one fucking thing right?"

That didn't seem fair, especially since Andrew Cullen owed far more money than Marco, Skid Row and Bullfrog put together. Carl briefly considered pointing that out but then thought better of it. Ricky didn't give him the chance anyway.

"Hell," he continued. "You can't even talk to a waitress without scaring the shit out of her. You're a God-damn menace. That ever bother you?" he asked. "Do you scare yourself when you get up each morning and have to look at that ugly mug in the mirror? Is that why you haven't shaved in like ten years? Too fucking frightening?"

He kept going like that but Carl tuned him out, placing his hands in his lap rather than reaching across the table and crushing Ricky's head like a giant, slime-filled pimple. Let him rant. He'd heard it all a hundred times before. It bothered him a little less these days and he was able to take it for what it was--typical short man syndrome. Ricky was no midget but, next to Carl, he must have felt like one. He needed to talk tough to feel tough. Even so, Carl's nerves were as brittle as dry leaves. He wanted to get out of there and wondered how Ricky would react if he simply got up and left.

Without being obvious about it, he scoped out the pub while waiting for Ricky to run out of steam. It seemed like a decent enough place. The old guy behind the bar had looked their way a few times but didn't seem terribly interested in their conversation. Carl caught his eye and nodded to indicate another round. About the last thing Ricky needed was more alcohol, but he might be easier to handle if kept well lubricated.

Of course, it would be nice if the little turd would lower his voice some. He was not only too loud but spitting out four letter words like they were going out of style: a five-and-a-half- foot-tall vulgarity Pez dispenser. Carl was pretty sure that's why their waitress had departed so abruptly. He'd at least made the effort to smile at her. Ricky had just stared at her tits the whole time. She totally knew what he was doing but he didn't stop, not even when she shot him a nasty look and held her serving tray up in front of her chest.

Carl saw her exit the kitchen and, taking a circuitous route to avoid walking by their table, make her way to the bar. The old guy had the drinks ready and was saying something to her. She shook her head emphatically, hands on hips to punctuate whatever she'd said in response. She shook her head again and then retreated to the far end of the bar where she began wiping off tables. She never so much as glanced toward Ricky and Carl but her body language was plain as day. The bartender watched her for a moment then sighed visibly and carried the drinks over himself.

"Thanks," Carl said, cutting Ricky off mid-impropriety. He'd been in the middle of a tirade about *those stupid fucking deadbeats* and hadn't seen the bartender approach. He also hadn't liked being interrupted. His eyes blazed and he looked like he was gearing up to unleash a fresh stream of venom.

"Put 'em on his tab," Carl said before Ricky could get started. "We'll go ahead and settle up now."

"Of course," the bartender said. "It's my pleasure." He started to move away but then stopped, looking concerned. "Shall I call him a cab?" he half whispered, glancing warily at Ricky.

"That's not necessary," Carl reassured him. "I'll make sure he gets home safe."

"Fuckin' old buzzard," Ricky muttered as the bartender moved off.

Carl sipped his beer and wondered what was coming next. He also wondered what he was doing there in the first place. When they had business to discuss, they normally did it either at the office or in the front seat of Ricky's car. Why the change of scenery? Why the pretense of kindness when Ricky was obviously as irritable and angry as ever? Did he even have anything on his mind or was his urgent summons nothing but bullshit? At the very least, Carl supposed he'd have to wait until the following morning to find out because, in his current state, Ricky didn't look ready or able to carry on a coherent conversation.

"I gotta hit the head," he announced, taking a quick swig of his drink and pushing back from the table. "Do me a favor and try not to hurt anyone while I'm gone."

Ricky returned a few minutes later and Carl was surprised to see him looking more alert. His eyes were more focused, his cheeks less flushed, and the front of his hair was slightly damp from where he'd apparently been splashing water on his face.

"Hey, Gus," Ricky called, grabbing his empty coffee cup and walking to the bar, the extra little sway in his step barely even noticeable. "Could I trouble you for a refill?"

"It's my pleasure, sir."

Ricky was smiling when he sat back down and that made Carl uneasy. He realized he had to at least consider the possibility that even Ricky's drunkenness was part of his act, to what end Carl couldn't even guess. What he knew was that Ricky Fixx was a snake and could not and should not be trusted.

"As I said before," Ricky began, seeming to enjoy Carl's discomfort. "It's time to stop fucking around."

Carl said nothing because he had no idea what Ricky was talking about.

"I don't know if you've noticed but things haven't been going so hot lately. We've been losing a lot more money than we're taking in. That's what's called an unsustainable business model. You with me so far?"

Carl nodded because he was expected to but he didn't say what he was thinking, which was that it really ticked him off when Ricky talked down to him as if he were some sort of simpleton.

"I pay you to do a job," he went on, tipping back and draping an arm casually over the back of his chair.

All his movements were deliberate, well-rehearsed, and Carl wasn't in the slightest bit impressed, except he realized he was grinding his teeth and gripping his beer bottle so tightly he thought it might shatter. He took a breath and tried to relax, which would have been a lot easier if Ricky would just shut up.

"Let's face it," he said. "You're a walking disaster. You overdo everything. I'm surprised you can wipe your ass without accidentally giving yourself a toilet paper enema. I can see you're getting upset but I'm just telling it the way it is."

Carl looked down at the table. He figured Ricky probably saw that as submissive, a tacit admission of his guilt, but what he was really doing was counting to ten and hoping he could get there before his rising fury got the better of him and he gave Ricky an enema compliments of the King of Beers.

"You go to collect a little money and a guy ends up dead. How does that even happen? How do you impale somebody by mistake? Can you explain that to me?"

Keep talking and I'll be happy to show you.

"And that's what I don't understand about this deal with Skid Row and what's-his-name. You've been chasing them all over town and they aren't any the worse for wear. I'd actually like you to rough them up a little bit. Smack 'em around. If one of them ends up dead, what's the difference? It's not like anyone's gonna miss 'em, and maybe that would motivate whoever's still around to pay what's owed."

"They don't owe you anything," Carl said softly, his gaze only coming up as high as Ricky's chin.

"What's that?" he asked, cupping a hand around one ear. "Did you say something?"

"I said they don't owe anything." Carl sat up a little straighter. "You gave them product and then you took it back."

"Correction," Ricky said. "You took it back.'

"Whatever. It was on your orders. They didn't do anything wrong either way so why are you trying to hold them responsible?"

"Let's go back to that dead guy," Ricky snapped. "He did owe, and thanks to you, that's money we'll never see."

"You're never gonna see it anyway. Skid Row and Bullfrog can't pay. I keep telling you that."

"And I keep wondering why in fuck you care. Do you even understand what we do for a living? We're not winning any good conduct medals. You get that, right?"

"That doesn't mean—"

"I'll tell you exactly what it means," Ricky said, leaning in close. "I call the shots and that's the end of the story. If I decide I want your opinion on something, I'll go down to Kinko's and print you up some nice flashy business cards that say consultant. But until that happens, I suggest you do what the fuck I say or things are going to get nasty. And believe me, I can make it real nasty for you if I want so don't push it!"

Carl licked his lips, gathered himself and nodded. There were about a hundred things he wanted to say—make that a thousand—and he couldn't bring himself to say any of them.

Why? He wondered. *Why do I continue to let him push me around and talk to me like a dog?* It was infuriating and demeaning, yet every time he thought he might finally man up, he proved once again that he had about as much backbone as a garden slug. Carl hated himself for that but still felt unable to do anything about it.

"That's good," Ricky said with a smirk. "I'm glad we're on the same page. As I see it, we're dealing with two different situations. We have Andrew Cullen and the promise of a nice big payoff. Meanwhile, there's the two jackasses wandering around and making you look even stupider than usual. I wouldn't have thought that was possible but there you go.

"You got a point?" Carl asked, his tone sullen.

"My point," Ricky beamed, "is that I'm a genius." He held his coffee cup aloft as if making a proclamation.

"Do tell," Carl tried to sound snide but Ricky didn't seem to notice.

"I think you'll like this," he said, "because it lets you off the hook, sort of, and it begins with two words you probably never thought you'd hear me say."

Ricky paused and Carl knew he was waiting for him to ask the obvious question. He was determined not to take the bait, instead picking at the label on his Budweiser bottle. He hoped to look unconcerned, even indifferent, but could feel a thin trickle of sweat sliding down his back.

"You're right," Ricky said, looking Carl squarely in the eye.

He didn't reply because he figured there had to be a catch. As far as he could remember, Ricky had never told him he was right about anything. It seemed damn unlikely he meant it now.

"I'm serious," Ricky said, almost like he'd been reading Carl's mind. "You said there was no reason to follow Cullen. Isn't that right?

He nodded cautiously.

"I agree with you and we're not gonna do it anymore. What do you think of that?"

What Carl thought, what he knew from long experience, was that Ricky wasn't capable of a simple change of heart. He wouldn't admit a mistake either, unless he could somehow benefit from doing so.

Ricky wanted a response. Carl could see that but he wasn't ready to give one so he sat, waited, and didn't miss the flash of anger in Ricky's eyes.

"As for our other problem," he said, scowling and staring at Carl intently. "I think you were right about that too."

"What?" Carl asked, unable to help himself.

"Those two jerkoffs. You keep saying they can't pay what they owe."

"They don't--"

"Forget it," Ricky said with a wave, "because it don't matter. Just to prove that I can be kind and generous, I am prepared to forgive one hundred percent of their debt."

You what? Ricky was neither kind nor generous and had never backed down when it came to matters of money. *Conclusion? There had to be an angle.*

"So what do they have to do?" Carl asked, feeling like he was stepping into the lion's den.

"What makes you think they have to do anything?" Ricky was all innocence and charm, and that put Carl on instant high-alert.

"So I can stop following them?" he asked, already knowing the answer.

"Well no," Ricky replied. "Not exactly."

"Then what?'

"Before we get to that, I want to make sure I understand the situation. Is it safe to say that, up to this point, you haven't gone after those two as aggressively as you could have?'

Carl swallowed. There was no way he was answering that one and Ricky seemed to know it.

"Well," he said, smiling and running a hand over his chin. "It's either that or you're not as good at your job as I thought. I have my own theory. Suffice it to say that if you were properly motivated, I do believe this hunt would have been over already."

"It's not like I haven't been trying to find them," Carl objected. "I have found them, more than once."

"So you say, but we're still sitting here talking about it and I have yet to see any proof."

"Then what do you want?"

"Oh, it's very simple," Ricky said. "I'll even give you choices."

Here it comes.

"You will find them. You have until noon tomorrow. That gives you," Ricky made a show of checking his watch, "a little over fourteen hours. That should be more than enough."

"And then?"

He shrugged. "Up to you."

I'll just bet.

"You can persuade them to pay. If they still can't or won't, you have my permission to break one of Bullfrog's legs. Check that. I order you to break one of his legs."

Carl shivered at the pure callousness. He sounded as calm and casual as if he were at the drive-thru ordering lunch. *Yeah, give me a cheeseburger, large fries and, uh, go break that fucker's legs.*

"But you said..." Carl stammered, his mouth suddenly dry.

"That I would forget about the money? Indeed I will. And I can tell by the idiotic look on your face that you don't like that first choice I gave you so here's one more. Bring them to me. Now!"

Ricky pointed at his watch and Carl knew the clock was ticking.

-49-

Skid Row awoke and could see thin slivers of moonlight filtering through the tree tops. That made no sense to him, because for the past couple nights he'd slept behind the waterfall which made it impossible to see much of anything. What was he doing out in the open? He remembered eating dinner and then sitting and talking with Bullfrog next to the camp fire. He supposed he must have fallen asleep right there.

The fire had gone out, nothing remaining but some glowing embers and occasional wisps of smoke. There was just enough ambient light to see by. So far as he could tell, everything looked the same as always. Bullfrog was nowhere in sight, but Skid Row figured he was tucked away in the natural hiding spot he'd found. He considered joining him but then decided he was plenty comfortable right where he was. And that got Skid Row thinking about what had woken him in the first place.

He took another look around, this time paying closer attention. He had his sleeping bag, which Bullfrog had evidently draped over him before going off to bed. Skid Row propped himself on an elbow and squinted into the darkness. He saw their wood pile, their bag of supplies tied to a tree branch, and Bullfrog's small stash of cook pots and other odds and ends. His own box of junk was behind the waterfall, as were Bullfrog's clothes and other personal belongings. There wasn't a whole lot else to see other than rocks, tree trunks, shrubs and dried up scrub grass, and the light mist that seemed to always hang in the air. It was all perfectly ordinary. Then why, Skid Row wondered, did he have the unmistakable feeling he was being watched?

The waterfall, no more than thirty feet away, wasn't loud but its soft, steady, unchanging thrum made it tough to distinguish any other sounds. Skid Row thought he heard an owl or some other nocturnal bird a ways off but he couldn't be sure. In his current state, the night seemed oddly, even unnaturally still and that made him uneasy. He could tell something was wrong. He turned his head slowly from side to side, holding his breath and trying not to make a sound as he strained to listen. He heard water, the increasing rush of blood in his ears and then....

The crack of a branch was startlingly close and, to Skid Row, as loud as a gunshot. He saw their stash of food and his first thought was BEAR! His instinct was to flatten himself on the ground and cover his head. It wasn't the manliest response to the situation but there was plenty to be said for self-preservation. Skid Row guessed the beast had smelled the remains of their dinner and come on the run.

Although he'd never seen one before, spending most of his time in the downtown area, he'd heard there were bears all over Broome County. Almost against his will, he turned toward the sound. He had no desire to face a big ass black bear up close and personal but also didn't want to mistakenly be in between one and its food. He imagined sharp teeth, powerful limbs and long, deadly claws. What he saw instead was even more terrifying.

The fast moving shadow emerged from the trees, making a low, guttural sound and lumbering toward him like something out of a horror movie. He was still thinking bear but something about the creature, its size, movements and up-right posture, didn't add up. Skid Row stared, temporarily incapable of doing anything else. He wasn't about to try to fight and, although flight seemed like a great option right then, he couldn't convince his muscles to respond to the panicked signals coming from his brain.

As he looked on, the figure drew closer and began taking on more of a human form. He was big, burly and, Skid Row noted distractedly, wore boots. Another couple steps and he could make out wild hair and then the untamed beard.

Carl, he thought, realizing at the same time that he wasn't too surprised. He wasn't paranoid either. As Skid Row had suspected, they'd been followed the whole time. He knew he was about to die and his only regret right then was that he wouldn't be around long enough to tell Bullfrog *I told you so.*

"Quiet!" Carl hissed, not exactly shouting but also not making much effort to keep his own voice low.

Skid Row was confused until he realized he'd started keening like a scared little girl, his breath coming out in a series of high-pitched and totally pathetic moans. No wonder Carl wanted him to shut up. He tried to get himself under control but, for the time being, subsiding to puppy-like whimpers was the best he could manage.

Carl stared at him and shook his big head in obvious disgust. "Where's your friend?" he asked, stooping as he looked all around.

"Who?" Skid Row asked, opting to play dumb rather than give away Bullfrog's location.

One of Carl's big hands came down on his shoulder. "You don't want to go there," he said, squeezing hard enough to show he was serious.

Skid Row was fairly sure nothing was broken but thought he might be wiping his ass left-handed for the next couple days. He tried to move away but Carl only squeezed tighter.

"You better talk to me."

He'd be happy to do that, if it was only talk Carl was after, but Skid Row had a feeling he had come there to do some real damage. He was probably waiting until he had the two of them together, in which case Bullfrog's absence was the only thing keeping Skid Row in one piece. He had to distract, stall, and hope Bullfrog would remain hidden until Carl got bored and went away. That seemed like a tall order but what else could he do?

"I really don't..." he began, deciding to continue the ruse that he didn't know who Carl was looking for.

"Don't!" Carl stuck a finger in Skid Row's face. "Don't lie to me. I know you and Bullfrog are still together and I need to talk to both of you."

Talk? That sounded a lot better than dismemberment, but it also sounded like a big pile of horse shit. Talking was something people did during the daytime, not at whatever the hell time at night. Skid Row had no reason to believe anything Carl said and was determined not to volunteer any information.

"I was sleeping," he protested, rubbing his eyes for effect. "How should I know where he went?'

"No ideas?" Carl asked, for some reason checking his phone.

Skid Row shrugged and tried to look indifferent. "We weren't getting along too good. I guess he split. Good riddance. That's what I say to that."

"Uh huh," Carl said, tapping his foot as he surveyed their campsite. "And when was the last time you saw him?"

"It's been hours," Skid Row said. "I don't know."

"You sure about that?"

"Yeah, well, seeing you before scared him pretty bad. He's been talking about leaving. I guess he did it." Skid Row raised his hands like the whole thing was out of his control.

Carl studied his face. "Then you two weren't here together earlier tonight?"

"Mm... no. Just me."

Even in the dark, Skid Row could see Carl wasn't buying it and that his stall tactic had failed. That meant it was time for action. He tried to slink away, but still sitting on the ground, couldn't manage much more than a clumsy backwards crab walk. Carl watched him for a second and then his right arm rocketed forward. Skid Row thought he was going for the throat, just like he'd done outside the laundromat. Instead, Carl reached behind him, tugged briefly at the back of his sweatshirt and came away with something small and circular. Skid Row caught a glimpse of it pinched between two fingers before Carl tucked it into a shirt pocket.

"What the fuck was that?" he asked, indignation taking the place of fear.

"You were here," Carl said, ignoring Skid Row's question. "Both of you. So I want to know where Bullfrog is now."

"Yeah? And I want to know what the hell that was!"

"Ricky says you owe him two thousand dollars. Unless you've got some money for me, you're in no position to make demands."

Skid Row got to his feet so he could at least come close to facing Carl eye to eye. "I really don't give a crap. I want to know what that was."

"It doesn't concern you."

"You just took it off my shirt!" Skid Row rubbed at the back of his neck like he was afraid the spot might be infected. "How can you say it doesn't concern me?"

He felt his ears getting red, a sure sign he was either overtired or majorly pissed off. He still didn't know what Carl was doing there or how in the world he'd ever found them, but something in his gut told him the answer was in Carl's left breast pocket and almost within arm's reach. Skid Row thought about making a mad lunge. Carl wouldn't expect it and what did he have to lose anyway?

He was gathering his strength and courage when a softball-sized rock whizzed past his ear so close he both heard and felt it. He ducked reflexively and then gaped when he saw Carl's hand shoot up and catch the stone just before it hit him in the head. Had it found its mark, he probably would have been knocked out cold, which had to be what Bullfrog was counting on. How Carl had managed to not only see the danger in the dark but react so quickly Skid Row had no idea. He was thankful he hadn't flung himself at the man because it surely would have ended in disaster.

"Nice toss," Carl said, dropping the stone on the ground as he turned casually toward the waterfall. Bullfrog was there, his arm still half-cocked.

"Thanks," he said. "I played a little ball in school."

"My sport was hockey," Carl replied. "Goalie and defenseman. I think I still hold the state collegiate single season records for saves and penalty minutes."

That made sense, Skid Row thought. "The dude had freakish speed, smooth and deceptive. It wasn't hard to imagine him out on the ice, busting heads and creating all sorts of chaos. Carl didn't have the typical hockey player build. He was tall but a good 200 pounds north of lanky. Maybe he was slimmer in his late teens or early twenties, maybe not. Either way, he must have looked like a locomotive bearing down, a high-speed wrecking ball on skates.

To Skid Row, the only real surprise was learning that Carl had gone to college. He didn't look the type and it was impossible to picture him crammed behind a tiny desk in some lecture hall somewhere.

"Went in on a sports scholarship," Carl explained, continuing Skid Row's train of thought. "Some scout saw me play and recruited me. It wasn't a good fit. I couldn't meet the academic standards and only lasted a year." He paused then, like he hadn't expected to share so much personal information.

"So now you harass people for a living?" Bullfrog asked, plainly unimpressed by the story. "Nice career move."

Skid Row could see that Bullfrog still held a rock in his other hand. Carl must have seen it too but he looked unconcerned.

"You should put that down," he said. "I don't want you guys getting hurt."

"You think we're scared of you?" Bullfrog asked, actually coming a step closer as he shifted the rock from his left hand to his right.

Skid Row knew first-hand what could happen when his friend was pushed too far and he thought they were getting dangerously close to that point. When Bullfrog was still hidden, Skid Row thought there might be a chance of getting out of this because Carl said he'd wanted to see them together. Maybe Bullfrog overheard that conversation and that's why he made his grand appearance. Too bad his aim hadn't been a little better. If they'd had any leverage before, it was gone now and, in Skid Row's opinion, their position would get a lot worse if Bullfrog threw that second stone. The best thing would be for him to shut up and calm down but he didn't seem inclined to do either one.

"You've been following us all over," he said, taking another couple steps. The ten yards that had separated them was now down to about eight. "Why don't you fuck off and leave us alone?"

Skid Row cringed and Carl's eyes narrowed. They'd had it. That was going to be the end of their story. Even bad hockey players knew how to fight and Skid Row wondered how much weirder Bullfrog would look with no teeth and one of those small, knobby ears torn half off his bald head. It occurred to him then that their secret get-away was not only a good place to hide out but an ideal location for disposing of bodies. And that gave him another disturbing thought. Who would ever even notice they were gone? At least that Marco dude got his name and picture in the paper. He and Bullfrog would vanish with all the fanfare of a couple fallen leaves.

Damn depressing, Skid Row thought, for some reason thinking of his father.

"I guess you haven't noticed," Carl said, staring at Bullfrog but obviously speaking to both of them. "I've mostly left you alone."

"What?" Bullfrog asked, thrusting his chin forward but looking a little less sure of himself. "We see you everywhere we go."

"I bought your groceries."

"Yeah," Skid Row said. "And what the hell was that about?"

"You really don't get it?" Carl looked at each of them in turn. "I've been protecting you."

Bullfrog scoffed but he dropped his stone and came over to stand next to Skid Row.

"Why should we believe that?"

"Simple," Carl said. "I was told to break your leg and I haven't done it yet."

-50-

"That's freakin' wild," Skid Row said, shaking hair out of his eyes as he turned the miniature tracking device over and over in his hand. "And it works anywhere?"

"That's what they say." Carl signaled to a waitress and she came over to refill his coffee cup. "You boys want anything else?"

They shook their heads. They'd both ordered the Denny's Grand Slam breakfast with pancakes and put away every scrap. Between hurried bites, Bullfrog told him they hadn't been eating much the past few days and Carl had no trouble believing it. Skid Row in particular looked scrawny enough to drift away in a strong breeze. His baggy sweatshirt somehow made him look even skinnier. Bullfrog had a stockier frame but he wasn't carrying too many extra pounds either. Carl was tempted to buy some food to send with them but decided to hold off on that for now. He believed such an act would represent more of a commitment than he was prepared to make. Then again, he'd already come this far.

"So why are you doing all this?" Bullfrog asked. He set down his fork, wiped his mouth with a napkin and then dropped it on the plate in front of him. "The grocery store, this food, finding us and letting us walk away…?" He shrugged. "The first time we met you, you threatened to dump us in the river. Why stick your neck out for us now?"

Carl stared down at his own plate. He'd only ordered a cinnamon Danish and that was long gone. He dragged a finger through a smear of icing and stuck it in his mouth. The truth was he didn't know how to answer Bullfrog's question. He didn't know why he cared what happened to him or Skid Row, or why he was willing to defy Ricky for their sake.

The sudden surge of conscience, if that's even what it was, didn't sit well with him but he knew he had to stand up for what he believed. What that was exactly remained something of a mystery and Carl assumed that was why he lacked the courage to confront Ricky face to face. He'd made his displeasure known. That was as far as he'd dared push it.

Part of the issue, Carl had to admit, was the inexplicable fear he had of his boss. It wasn't physical. No one had ever scared him that way. The hold Ricky Fixx held over him was something entirely different.

Carl had known for years that Ricky had no scruples. That made him dangerous, as did the knack he seemed to possess for always knowing just which buttons to push. But even more than any of that, Carl always had the sense that Ricky would turn on him almost without provocation. There were never any overt threats. It was more the way Ricky carried himself, like he always had a couple aces tucked up his sleeve. He was better connected and absolutely more ruthless. Basically, he had the power, and Carl's defense was to follow the path of least resistance. That meant a role of subservience. It worked for a while, but he felt he'd reached the end of that particular road.

"You two are in trouble," he said, side-stepping Bullfrog's question.

He glanced at them, but then his eyes automatically moved to the window. It was bright inside, full dark outside, so he couldn't make out much more than a smudged reflection of the few late-night diners and the pale-skinned, big-haired waitress, the only employee they'd seen since sitting down. She was busy filling napkin dispensers, bent over and giving Carl a view he could have done without.

He thought she'd probably been attractive once upon a time. He put her in her mid to late forties, although she looked like she'd spent every one of those years serving coffee, lugging heavy food trays, getting her ass pinched—which he doubted happened much anymore–and working long hours for crap pay and even crappier tips. He noticed her chipped fingernails, prominent varicose veins, too-heavy eye makeup and bleached-blonde hair with serious gray roots. He couldn't see any tattoos or unusual piercings but would have bet she had some hidden somewhere beneath her unflattering uniform. *Rode hard and put away wet,* he thought, turning his attention back to the table.

"What I said before about the broken leg," he paused and took a sip of his water. "That was no joke."

Carl's Retrievor device fell from Skid Row's hands and clattered onto the table.

"You fucking serious?" he asked.

"Would we be here if I wasn't?"

Bullfrog snorted. "How would we know? You've been messing with us for days. You and that Ricky guy. How do we know this isn't just part of your game?"

"I'm not playing a game. I'm trying to help you."

"Like you did when you stole that bag?"

Carl shook his head. "That wasn't my idea."

"You did take it then?" Skid Row asked, and Carl couldn't tell if he looked more annoyed or hurt.

He wished he could deny it but he knew he'd have to be totally up front if he wanted to gain their trust. And somehow, that had become important to him.

"The day you two showed up at the trailer...," Carl hesitated as he searched for the right words. "I'd screwed up in a big way and it cost us a lot of money. Ricky was--well, let's just say he wasn't happy. I felt like I had to do something to make good."

"What'd you do wrong?" Skid Row asked.

"It doesn't matter. You two came along with the stupidest scheme I've ever heard of."

Bullfrog shot Skid Row a look and Carl guessed they hadn't both been in favor of the plan.

"Wait a minute," Bullfrog said, sitting back and crossing his arms. "This screw up you mentioned. Any chance it had something to do with that Marco guy?"

Carl flushed and turned away but not quickly enough. Bullfrog had obviously noticed his reaction and his body stiffen as realization dawned.

"You killed him," he said, and Carl heard Skid Row's sharp intake of breath.

The lights inside the restaurant suddenly seemed a lot brighter and Carl thought he could actually feel the heat from the overhead fluorescents. With Skid Row and Bullfrog both staring at him now, he picked up his water and drained the cup in one long gulp. He wanted to use a napkin to mop his forehead but dropped his hands in his lap instead.

Bullfrog's revelation had rocked him for sure, and Carl could tell Skid Row was just as stunned. His face had gone a few shades paler than normal and he kept gasping and gulping like a fish that had just been pulled from the water. Carl knew the feeling.

His heart was racing a mile a minute, but he told himself he had nothing to worry about. Bullfrog didn't really know anything. He'd made a lucky guess; that was it. Carl knew exactly how Ricky would handle something like that. He'd deny everything, looking Skid Row and Bullfrog square in the eye as he lied through his teeth. He could do the same thing, and thought he'd get away with it too, but even as he started to form the words, something told him it was time to put his cards on the table. He took a breath and nodded.

"Holy shit," Skid Row said, starting to chew a fingernail but then clasping both hands in front of him.

"Why?" Bullfrog asked, his expression unreadable.

"He owed money," Carl explained. "He didn't have it and things just got out of hand."

"So Ricky told you to…" Bullfrog began but then trailed off, apparently unable to finish the thought.

Carl knew where he was going. "No!" he said, immediately jumping to Ricky's defense without really knowing why. If the tables were turned, he was sure Ricky wouldn't do him that same favor.

"It's my job to collect. I went to see Marco a few days ago and he told me he couldn't pay, that he needed more time. I told him that wasn't an option. He tried to punch me and then started to run away." Carl shrugged his massive shoulders. "All I wanted to do was stop him."

"You succeeded," Skid Row mumbled.

"If you don't mind me asking," Bullfrog said. "How much did he owe?"

"A few thousand,"

"A few thousand," Bullfrog repeated, gazing up at the ceiling.

"I didn't mean to do it," Carl said, feeling like he needed to explain himself. "I didn't want to hurt him. I was just doing my job."

Bullfrog looked at him. "Right. And your job is to do what Ricky tells you, yet now you're saying Marco's death was 'accidental,' that Ricky had nothing to do with it."

Carl had nothing to say to that. He knew how it sounded. He also knew he'd told them the truth. If they chose to read more into that and if by doing so they transferred more of the blame onto Ricky, well, there wasn't much he could do about that and he thought it might actually work to his favor.

"I don't know much about the drug culture," Bullfrog said. "From what I've read and heard, I guess it's a big problem in Binghamton."

"That's for sure."

"So I'm thinking Marco brought in a ton of money for you two. It is just the two of you, right?"

Carl nodded and Bullfrog glanced Skid Row's way.

"He did okay," Carl said. "I mean, I know how much I collected. I just don't know how much was profit. To hear Ricky talk, it wasn't that much."

"I wouldn't know about that," Bullfrog said, but he looked at Carl like he thought he'd been played the fool.

He's probably right about that.

"Do you have other people selling for you?" Skid Row wanted to know.

"Just him," Carl said. "Ricky didn't like the drug trade a whole lot. Too much gang activity."

"Still," Bullfrog said. "He wouldn't have eliminated Marco if he didn't already have another plan."

"I told you that was—"

"An accident. Yeah, I know. I'm just wondering what you guys would have done if we hadn't come along when we did."

Interesting, Carl thought. Despite everything he'd said, Bullfrog at least still seemed convinced that Marco had been a hit. Stranger still, even though Carl had basically made a murder confession, Ricky was the one getting most of the blame. Maybe that was because he'd showed them some mercy and bought them a couple meals but Carl thought there had to be something more to it.

"You can believe what you want," he said, "but I'm telling you there was no other plan. We would have gotten out of it altogether. That's pretty much what's happened anyway."

"Then why involve us if Ricky never intended to have us take Marco's place?"

Carl studied them both. "He seemed to think that if I told you you owed us money and scared you enough, you would find a way to pay."

"That's fucked up, dude," Skid Row said. "I've got like four bucks to my name and I'm the one holding all the money. Do you think Ricky would take a deposit? Maybe just break one of Bullfrog's toes for now?"

"I know it sounds crazy but Ricky was serious. He's always serious."

They sat a while, and Carl tried to figure out what the other two were thinking. Skid Row mostly looked confused and nervous. He kept brushing his hair back, even when it wasn't hanging in his face. But Bullfrog? He was a lot tougher to read. He had to be nervous too, just because of what Carl had just told them, but he stayed practically motionless and his face gave away nothing. His eyes did occasionally move toward the door and Carl guessed he was ready to get out of there, or maybe just away from him.

"So tell me about Miracle Max here," Skid Row finally said, again picking up the Retrievor unit. "You stuck it on me a couple days ago. Is my life so fascinating that you wanted to follow me all the time? I mean, seriously, dude. What was the point?"

"I needed to keep tabs on your whereabouts."

"But why? You said we should have just left town and that you didn't really want to find us." Skid Row shrugged. "So why didn't you just leave us alone? Would Ricky have found us without your help?"

Carl laughed at that. “Ricky would have a hard time tracking Dorothy down the Yellow Brick Road.”

“Then what’s the deal?”

He sighed and signaled to the waitress for their check. “I didn’t have a choice. Ricky makes my life miserable if I don’t do what he wants.”

“Nice work environment,” Bullfrog said.

“It’s not that bad, usually. But like I told you before, I was already in the dog house. I needed to show results but I was also trying to protect you. You may not believe that but it’s true. This,” he took the Retrievor from Skid Row and slipped it back into his pocket, “allowed me to watch you from a distance. I wasn’t sure what Ricky had in mind and thought that was the best way to go.”

The waitress brought their check, dropped it on the table and told them to have a good night. Carl thanked her and reached for his wallet and they all stood to leave.

“Before,” Bullfrog said; “you told us we had to pay or Ricky would....”

“Bust one of his legs,” Skid Row chimed in.

“Thanks,” Bullfrog muttered. “Our other choice was to go to Ricky. If we do that, what do you think will happen?”

“I don’t know,” Carl said, heading for his truck; “but I doubt we want to find out.”

-51-

Andrew Cullen unlocked his front door, feeling rather good about himself. After leaving the office, he'd run a hard twenty miles. That was the furthest he'd gone in months. He had never enjoyed running and that was always the weakest part of his triathlon competitions. Thankfully, he was blessed with natural speed and endurance and he was usually able to do well enough to get by. Of course, the stakes were much higher now and he didn't have anywhere near enough time to train properly. Even in his wildest dreams, he knew he couldn't win the running segment. It just wasn't his thing. But, he planned on kicking serious ass in the pool and on the bike and he hoped that would be enough to put him over the top.

Even with the long run and the stop back at his office to shower and change, he got home quite a bit earlier than he'd expected. It wasn't even eleven o'clock yet. And, for the first time in, he wasn't even sure, he was stone sober. Although he'd been tempted, he hadn't had a single drink with lunch or dinner. His entire evening meal consisted of a couple protein bars. That was an improvement over the numerous other bars he'd been overindulging in recently. He had good news too, plus a big bouquet of pink roses. They'd always been Sara's favorite and he was looking forward to seeing her smile again.

"Hello," he called, quietly because most of the house was dark. The girls were definitely in bed by now. All the better because he had plans and they required privacy. Cullen saw that there was a light on in the living room so he headed that way.

"Delivery for Mrs. Cullen," he said, pausing just shy of the doorway but holding the flowers out in front of him. "There's postage too but I'm sure we can work something out."

No answer.

From his position, he couldn't see far into the room but sensed Sara was there. He sighed and stepped forward, and saw her sitting in front of the fireplace. She had her back to him and hadn't even bothered turning around to see what he was holding. She'd heard him, though. He could tell that from the stiffness of her posture. He could also tell she was still angry. He still thought he could thaw the ice once he told her about his day.

"That's a nicer place to sit when there's actually a fire going. Would you like me to start one for you? It is a little chilly in here."

He thought his lousy pun might elicit some sort of response. It didn't. She maybe stiffened a little more but otherwise just sat and stared into the cold ashes.

"Listen," he said. "I'm sorry about last night. I'm sorry about everything. I know I haven't been around much. I'll make it up to you. I promise. I'll make it up to the girls too. We'll go on vacation. I'll take some time off once this triathlon is out of the way."

"The girls are in school," Sara said, with all the warmth of a January blizzard. "They have sports too. We can't just leave."

"Okay," Cullen said. He set the flowers on an end table, grabbed a piece of newspaper from the hearth and began crumpling it into a ball. "So we'll do something else. How about a weekend trip to one of those indoor water parks? It would be a blast."

Sara didn't reply, which he took as a sign of acquiescence or at least indecision. That was good and he decided to press his advantage.

"I need to tell you about my day," he said, crumpling more paper. "This charity thing is going to be huge. I've collected over a hundred thousand dollars in donations," *give or take*, he thought, knowing it was actually nearly twice that.

"Almost everyone I've talked to wants to contribute. I didn't see that coming. I think it's the connection to the children that's really carrying this thing. It's amazing."

He paused but she still didn't reply. Cullen tossed his bits of paper into the fireplace and began arranging kindling on top.

"Anyway," he said, thinking now that he may have misinterpreted her silence. "I set up a new account called the Tri-Cities Tomorrow Fund. The donation will be made in that name. If everything goes well, I think I may do this every year."

He wasn't sure why he'd added that last part, but once he said it, he realized there was no reason he couldn't go back to the well at some point if he needed to.

"Speaking of accounts," Sara said, as Cullen stood and began searching the hearth and then the mantel for matches. "You had a phone call."

"Yeah? Who from?'

Sara's tone was matter of fact and Cullen had no inkling that she was about to destroy any illusions he might have about saving his marriage.

"Janet," she said, her tone almost conversational. "She'd like you to call her back."

"Sure," he replied. "I'll do it in the morning." He found a pack of matches behind one of Sara's cherished Alaska figurines and had actually started to remove one before it clicked.

Janet? Janet Banyard? Had she really just said that? But he knew he hadn't misheard. Maybe, he thought desperately, it was a different Janet. The name wasn't that uncommon, although he couldn't think of any others that he knew personally. It had to be her.

He was screwed. That's all there was to it. Sara and the Banyard bitch had never met before. As far as he knew, they'd never even spoken. Yet now they were on a first name basis? *Must have been a nice little chat.*

"Did she say what she wanted?" he asked, making the effort to sound unconcerned even though he could feel his nuts shriveling up like a couple old apples.

"Oh, she said lots of things."

Until that moment, Cullen had been hoping and even praying that Ms. Banyard had kept their business dealings confidential. Just because she'd called him at home for the first time ever didn't necessarily mean she'd divulged important information. Except it did. He'd known that in his heart and would have even without the note of betrayal in Sara's voice.

"She told me you made a payment on some accounts that were in arrears."

That fucking word again. Maybe that was how she liked it. Or maybe that was the only way her husband would give it to her so he wouldn't have to look at her face. *That's the only way I'd do it*, Cullen thought, and his nuts shriveled a little more.

"I assume," Sara said, "you went to the bank right after selling your Jag. Was there even anything wrong with the engine or did you just need to unload the car?"

This time it was Cullen with nothing to say. He had several explanations at the ready, but he didn't want to start laying down his cards until he had some idea of the hand she was holding. If her stricken expression was any indication, she had a straight flush, probably ace high. She might not know everything yet but she definitely knew enough and he could see that it was tearing her apart.

"I'll make this right," he said. "I will." He started to reach for her but she wasn't even looking at him anymore and he let his arm fall to his side.

"How?" she asked, so quietly that he had to read her lips.

"I'll pay it back. You've got to believe me. I'll straighten out our personal finances first and then I'll concentrate on the business."

She was looking at him now and her eyes were daggers. "You drained the business accounts too?"

Oops.

"How far does this go, Andrew? Have you been dipping into the girls' trust funds?"

"No!" he said, indignant. "I would never."

"Good to know you've got such high standards."

In truth, he had wanted to borrow at least a little bit from the trust funds but the accounts were in Sara's name too and he was afraid it might come back to her.

"It's not as bad as you think," he said, all reassurance and sincerity. "Really."

Sara wasn't buying it. "Is that supposed to make me feel better? Until a few hours ago, I didn't think anything. I didn't know anything because you did all of this," she waved a hand vaguely, "and didn't even tell me."

"I know," he said. "I'm sorry."

"You're sorry?" She stared at him. "That's the best you can do? Janet told me we could lose the house. Do you understand what that means?"

"Of course," he said; "but it won't come to that. I promise."

"Don't even say that, Andrew. You've been breaking promises as long as I've known you. I can't trust you anymore."

"Then take a look around," he snapped, his temper getting the better of him. "I think you've had it pretty easy."

Sara drew back and, for a second, he thought she was going to spit at him.

"Even if that were true," she said through clenched teeth. "Even if raising two daughters, running a household and doing all the other things you never found the time for was as easy as you seem to think, does that somehow give you the right to take it all away?"

"No," he said, "of course not." He realized he'd gone too far and tried to back pedal. "I just meant that you've had it pretty good."

She glared at him and he knew he'd stepped in it again.

"What I'm saying is that I provided for you very well. You've got to see that," he added, hating the pleading tone in his voice. "We're not going to lose our house. We're not going to lose anything."

That got an eye roll. "So you sold your precious Jag because you're suddenly in love with Toyotas? Let me also direct your attention to our bank balance because it's a whole lot smaller than it used to be. Any idea how that might have happened?"

"I can handle it, Sara. You just need to give me time. None of this has affected you. If it wasn't for that nosey bitch at the bank, you wouldn't even know."

She pounded a fist on the arm of the chair. "That's my whole point! You put this entire family in jeopardy but decided to keep that as your little secret. If you'd told me what was going on, if you'd been upfront and honest, I could have helped you and we might have avoided all of this."

"I don't need your help," Cullen answered, with more hostility than he'd intended. "I can take care of this on my own."

She looked at him, her face devoid of emotion. "I hope you can," she said, "because you're on your own from now on. I'm leaving and I'm taking Kristin and Kayla with me."

Cullen felt like he'd been sucker-punched. "You can't do that," he said, getting weak in the knees. He groped for the wall, missed and nearly fell. Sara made no move to help him.

"It's already done," she replied. "The girls are at my parents'. I've got a bag packed. I'll get the rest of our stuff later."

"But you can't." Cullen stared at her in disbelief.

He wasn't surprised Banyard had called the house. That had long been a possibility. But even when he'd considered the various scenarios and repercussions, he never once thought Sara would walk out on him. It was crazy. And then Cullen realized what she was doing and it almost made him smile. She was a stay-at-home mom. She had no means of support and had no way to care for herself and the girls. Bottom line, she needed him and couldn't leave even if she'd wanted to. This whole thing was a scare tactic. He had to give her credit too because it had almost worked.

"Let's talk about this in the morning," he said. I'll sleep in the guest room tonight. That will give you a chance to cool off."

"Sleep wherever you want," she said, standing. "I won't be here when you wake up."

"You're serious?"

Without a word, she turned and left the room.

"Where are you going?" he called after her. He heard the jingle of keys and, a few seconds later, she slammed the door that led to the garage.

She'd already engaged the automatic garage door opener and the door was half way up and Sara had the car engine running before Cullen slid to a stop next to her window.

"Hold on!" he said, banging his palm against the glass. "Can we at least talk about this?"

She lowered her window about an inch. "There's nothing to talk about, Andrew. It's over."

"You can't mean that. We've been through so much together."

She set her jaw and put the car in gear.

"This isn't right," he said. "You can't just leave. You can't take my girls from me."

Sara turned to look at him. He saw sadness in her eyes but resolution too.

"Try and stop me," she said. "I doubt you can afford a lawyer. No decent one would represent you anyway. You're an alcoholic with a gambling addiction. I know you cheated on me too. For the girls' sake, I've kept that to myself; but don't push me, Andrew. If you do, I'll fucking destroy you."

She stepped on the gas, tires squealed and he had to jump back to avoid getting his feet run over. Without so much as a backward glance, she swung out of the driveway and sped off down the road.

"She'll be back," he announced to the empty garage, and he believed it too. He just had to show her what she was missing out on. There was only one way to do that. He had to win the triathlon, pay off Ricky, make his sizeable and very public donation, and all would be good. He knew it was only temporary but losing Sara was still a setback. However, maybe it had a positive side too. No one would be pressuring him to come home on time. That meant he could be all-in on his training. He was determined to make that pay off in the most literal sense of the word. Cullen thought about going for another run right then. Instead, he turned and walked toward his bicycle. What he needed was speed.

-52-

Skid Row stared out the passenger window as Carl slowed and turned onto a side road. He'd been so distracted he'd completely lost track of where they were other than knowing it was somewhere on the west side. How, he kept wondering, had Bullfrog figured out what Carl had done? More to the point, how had he missed it? He knew Marco had been selling for Ricky. He knew Carl did all Ricky's dirty work and that Marco was dead. It seemed so obvious now, yet he'd failed to put those pieces together and it made him feel stupid. Skid Row also didn't understand why, knowing what they did, he and Bullfrog had willingly gotten into a car with a confessed killer. *What were we thinking?* Whatever was coming next, he supposed they deserved it.

"How much further?" Bullfrog asked, bumping against Skid Row's shoulder as Carl rounded another turn.

The truck had no back seat which made for a tight squeeze up front, and Skid Row knew that Bullfrog, occupying the middle, didn't want to sit any closer to Carl than he had to. No wonder. With his wild hair, bushy beard and massive body, he really did look like a murderer. If Skid Row had any sense, he thought he should push the door open and go running off into the night. Oddly, though, he wasn't as scared as he thought he probably should be and that too made him uncomfortable.

"Another few blocks." Carl said as they passed what probably had once been a gorgeous home.

It was large: three stories tall with covered porches on every level. Of course, like so much of Binghamton, it had seen better days. The house had long since been converted into apartments, six from the look of it, and although Skid Row couldn't make out many details in the dark, he would have bet his remaining funds that it was decades overdue for a paint job and other basic maintenance. No longer stately, it now just looked sad. There were signs of life, though.

A guy who looked to be about Skid Row's age was sprawled on the front steps, partially illuminated by a nearby street light. Skid Row could clearly see his Mohawk and matching sneer. He held a bottle in one hand and, while Skid Row watched, he tipped it up and drank. He then passed it to someone sitting in the darkness behind him. He sensed that there might have been several people there but he couldn't really tell. Carl's dashboard clock read 1:17. That seemed like an odd time for a whiskey social but who was he to judge? At least they had a porch to drink on, which was more than he'd ever been able to say for himself.

"You sure it's okay for us to crash with you?" Bullfrog asked, sounding like he had serious reservations about the idea. Skid Row did too, although he was looking forward to having a roof over his head again.

"Safest place for you," Carl replied. "I don't think Ricky even knows where I live. Besides, it gets you out of the weather. I only have one bed but even a carpeted floor has got to be better than sleeping on the ground. Why have you guys been doing that anyway? Don't you have family or anything?"

Skid Row saw Bullfrog's jaw tighten so he thought he should field that one. "We both lost our jobs recently. I had a place I was staying but I lost that too." He shrugged. "Shit happens." He tipped his head toward Bullfrog. "We only just met. We seemed to be on similar downward trajectories so we joined forces. We're all sorts of bad ass now."

"And that's why you went to Ricky?"

"We needed dough. That seemed like the quickest way to get it."

"Sorry it didn't work out."

"No thanks to you," Skid Row said. "We never had a chance."

"I was doing my job," Carl answered, and Skid Row thought his comment had struck a nerve. *Well, too bad.*

There was definitely some sort of weird dynamic going on between Carl and Ricky. Skid Row wasn't sure what that meant but sensed that Carl was dealing with his own misgivings. That could explain why he was being so nice to them. Regardless of his motivations, he'd offered them shelter of sorts and Skid Row was more than happy to take advantage of it if only for one night.

"If you don't mind me asking," Carl said, "why didn't you guys just leave? It doesn't sound like there's anything keeping you here."

"Lack of dinero," Skid Row said. "But I got a paycheck coming in a couple days. Once I have that, me and Bullfrog here will be in the wind."

"And go where?"

"Wherever it blows, dude. I don't really care."

Carl looked at him. "So stay with me until you get your check. No one will even know."

"You will," Bullfrog retorted, his tone making it clear they could only trust Carl so far.

He seemed to think about that. "Then what could I do to make you feel more secure?"

"For starters," Skid Row said. "You could tell us more about that bug, or whatever that thing was you stuck on me."

Carl smiled. "It's not a bug. I couldn't hear any of your conversations. I wouldn't have wanted to. It just told me where you were."

"That's the part I don't get." Skid Row thought about trekking all over town and all the while feeling like he was being watched. Bullfrog told him that couldn't be, but it appeared Skid Row had been more right than either of them could have imagined.

"You said a couple times that you were just doing your job. You also said you were supposed to scare us or whatever. I can't speak for my man here but you freaked me out plenty. I don't mind telling you that."

Skid Row studied Carl from the opposite end of the bench seat. "You still never did anything that made me think we had to come up with that money right away. You never really threatened us, you know? So if you were under orders, and if you knew where we were every second, why didn't Ricky just make you come get us and finish it?"

"He didn't know," Carl said. "I thought I'd explained that. I bought the Retrievor and Ricky doesn't know anything about it."

"Come on."

"Cross my heart," Carl said, actually going through the motion, and then he chuckled. "And Ricky was the first person I tested it on."

"No way, dude," Skid Row said.

"It's true." Carl's face clouded. "I found out something about him and...well I guess it's one of the reasons we're all here now."

Skid Row wanted to ask but thought that should maybe wait until later. "So he has no idea you've seen us?"

"Oh, he knows that much. I told him you keep giving me the slip."

"As if."

"Yeah, well I don't know how much he was buying the story. I think that's why he turned up the heat. I also think he has a job for you."

"WHAT?" Bullfrog asked, turning to stare at him. "What kind of job?"

"I don't know. And trust me, you don't want to know either."

"Why not? Maybe we could do something to pay off that money."

Carl frowned. "He said that if I brought you two to him, your debt would be forgiven."

Bullfrog gaped open-mouthed and then slapped the dashboard. "Why didn't you say that before? We could get this whole thing over with. Take us to him now."

"You really don't want me to do that."

"Don't tell me what I want! If he's got something in mind, I'd at least like to talk to him about it. We both would."

Skid Row nodded reluctantly but he wished Bullfrog hadn't been so quick to speak for him. He felt sure there was more going on than either of them realized.

"I shouldn't have said anything," Carl muttered, braking and pulling his truck to the curb in front of a small house.

He killed the engine, but before the cab was plunged into darkness, Skid Row saw his pinched expression and knew he didn't care for the direction the conversation had gone.

"We're here," he said. "Let's get inside."

"I don't think so," Bullfrog said. "I'm not going anywhere until you tell us more about Ricky's offer."

Carl sighed. "You can't think of it that way. Whatever he wants you to do, you'll come out on the losing end. Trust me."

Bullfrog snorted. "Little late for you to say that."

"I'm trying to help you." Carl shifted in his seat and the springs groaned. "Haven't I proved that yet?"

Bullfrog started to say something else but Skid Row didn't give him the chance.

"We appreciate it," he said. "Really. But you can buy us all the eggs and pancakes you want. If Ricky still says we owe him, where does that get us? If we have a chance to get out of this, we want to at least find out what it is."

"Damn right," Bullfrog echoed.

"Fine," Carl said. "I'll tell you everything I know or can guess. It's not much but maybe it will help you make up your mind. Can we do it in the morning, though? It's late and we're all tired."

Skid Row looked at Bullfrog and then shook his head. "I think that's a negative," he said.

Carl sighed again. "Okay, so I'll take you back to your camp." He started to reach for the key as Skid Row and Bullfrog exchanged another look.

"That's not necessary," Bullfrog said with reluctance; "at least not now. Let's take a walk. Tell us what you can and we'll see where it goes from there."

Carl hesitated but then pushed his door open with a creak. "You're the boss," he said. "Lead the way," and they all piled out of the truck.

Skid Row totally understood Bullfrog's reservations. He had plenty of his own. Of course, whether they were in Carl's house, in his truck, or walking down a darkened street in the early hours of the morning, they were completely at his mercy. Whatever he might have in mind, they'd be powerless to stop him. Skid Row knew it and Bullfrog had to know it too. Carl was letting them call the shots, though, and that simple gesture made Skid Row feel a little more secure.

"One question," Bullfrog said as they headed off down the block. "You said before that you learned some stuff about Ricky when you had that tracker thing on him. What did you mean by that?"

Carl didn't answer immediately, and that gave Skid Row a chance to notice the shadows they cast in the pool of light from a nearby street lamp. Carl took one step for every two of Bullfrog's. He looked even more like a giant, his silhouette stretched out a good twenty feet. And Bullfrog, even elongated as he was, somehow looked even more like a frog, his odd gait more pronounced than usual. Skid Row thought his own shadow looked ghostly. That wasn't an image he wanted right then so he turned away.

"What I found out," Carl began, "was that Ricky was following me. Actually, that's the wrong word because he always knew where I was going. He'd give me a job and then arrange to show up at the location ahead of me."

"For what?" Skid Row asked.

It was Bullfrog who answered. "He was spying on you."

"Worse than that," Carl said. "I think he was making a record of my activities."

"By record," Bullfrog said, "you're talking about pictures?"

"Maybe audio or video too. I don't really know."

"You sure that's what he was doing?"

"It's the only explanation I can come up with."

"Then he's blackmailing you," Bullfrog said.

"He hasn't, yet. That doesn't mean he won't."

"And these… jobs," Skid Row said. "I guess it wouldn't look good for you if they were made public?"

"I'm more concerned with the police than the public." Carl looked at them. "I know I'm no saint. I'm also not ashamed of what I do, not usually anyway. Ricky works with a lot of scumbags. It doesn't bother me to knock one of them around if it's warranted. When it's not, I guess that's when I've got a problem with it."

"And that's why you're willing to help us out?"

Carl nodded. "But I don't blame you for not trusting me. Why would you?"

"So let's talk about Ricky's offer," Bullfrog said.

They rounded a corner and Skid Row accidentally kicked an empty soda can. It clattered down the sidewalk and a dog started to bark.

"I told you I don't know much. I think it has something to do with Andrew Cullen."

"Who?" Bullfrog asked, looking at Skid Row like he might know.

"The name wouldn't mean anything to you unless you've been following the local news lately."

"We saw the thing on Marco," Skid Row said. "Nothing since then."

"Cullen's a local businessman. I guess he's pretty successful but that's not why you would have heard of him. Anyway, he's into gambling and stuff. He got into some trouble and had to borrow a bunch of money from Ricky. Long story short, he dicked us around for a while and now owes a hundred large."

Skid Row whistled.

"So what does that have to do with us?" Bullfrog asked.

"I think Ricky feels like this Cullen guy might be playing him a little bit. He doesn't like that."

"He doesn't want us to--" Bullfrog began and his eyes got big.

Carl laughed. "I highly doubt it. Cullen is the cash cow. Ricky wouldn't want anyone to hurt him unless there were no other alternatives."

Then what's he want?"

"It's kind of weird," Carl said. "Cullen isn't a celebrity or anything but he's pretty well known. He signed up to compete in this big triathlon and that's where he plans to get the money to pay Ricky off. It's a total scam but we don't need to get into that. Cullen has this connection to a local charity and that's getting him a lot of extra attention."

Skid Row brushed a strand of hair out of his eyes. "Dude, I got no idea what you're talking about."

"Yeah, you've kind of lost me too," Bullfrog said.

"I told you it was weird."

"It sounds like it's fucked six ways from Sunday," Skid Row said. "What's it got to do with us?'

"The race isn't for a couple weeks." Carl said. "Because of all the media hype, Ricky can't get as close to Cullen as he wants to. He can't keep tabs on him and messing with people is a big part of his game."

"So he wants us to do it?" Bullfrog asked.

"That's what I'm guessing.

"That ain't gonna work," Skid Row said. "We don't got wheels. How are we supposed to get around?"

"Cullen has a downtown office," Carl explained. "That's where a lot of his workouts begin and end. From what I gather, Ricky wants you to just sort of be around and make sure Cullen knows you're there."

"That's fucked up," Skid Row said. "It ain't like we're scary looking. Why would he give a shit if we were there or not?"

"It seems like there's got to be more to it," Bullfrog added.

Carl studied them. "I'm sure there is. I just don't know what and that's what concerns me. I know Ricky well enough to know he won't let you off that easy."

"So what do we do?"

Carl didn't reply and it was plain to Skid Row that he wasn't sure what to say. They all stood and looked at each other and the night seemed eerily quiet. They hadn't seen any other pedestrians, which wasn't a surprise given the hour, but no cars had gone by either. It was like the entire neighborhood was asleep. Then Skid Row heard a strange noise, soft at first but growing louder. It was a sort of whirring with frequent metallic-sounding clicks. He turned his head from side to side and tried to pinpoint the source. Nothing was moving but they were approaching a cross street and Skid Row thought the noise must be coming from there.

It continued to increase in volume, and second's later, a bicycle shot past in front of them. The rider wore dark shorts, a royal blue top with reflective orange stripes and his royal blue helmet was similarly adorned. Skid Row was shocked because he'd never seen a bicycle moving that fast. He had nothing to compare it to but thought the guy had to be going fifty miles an hour. He was in a sort of standing crouch, hunched over the handle bars and pumping his legs furiously. The sheen of sweat on his cheeks glistened under the streetlights. Before disappearing from sight, he glanced to the side and Skid Row got a good look at his face.

"THAT'S HIM!" Carl shouted, loud enough that Skid Row and Bullfrog both jumped. Skid Row somehow knew what would happen next. He watched in horrified silence as the rider turned to look over his shoulder. He saw the three of them standing there and Skid Row couldn't miss the flash of realization and then fear when he recognized Carl. He slumped, and for a brief moment, seemed to lose control of his arms and legs. A moment was all it took. The bicycle swerved and then the front wheel started to slide in the loose sand and grit between the edge of the street and the curb.

Just lay it down, Skid Row thought. At that speed, the road burn would hurt like hell and probably result in a trip to the emergency room but that was obviously still the best option. Andrew Cullen must have seen it differently. He fought for control, presumably believing he still had time to save the bike. He was wrong. The front wheel struck the curb dead on and immediately folded like a taco shell. The metallic whirring was replaced by a series of sounds Skid Row hoped he'd never hear again. The front half of the bike frame caved in on itself and the rider was catapulted over the handle bars. He was only a few feet off the ground but traveling at high velocity and an awkward angle.

"No," Carl said softly, right before Andrew Cullen flew head first into a fire hydrant. Skid Row heard the sickening crunch and he knew it was all over.

-53-

"No. No. No. No. No!"

Carl kept repeating that same word while shifting from one foot to the other, wringing his hands in front of him and looking frantically this way and that. It was totally whacked, and Skid Row suddenly flashed back to his last day at McDonalds and that weird frog dance thing Bullfrog had done right after being told he wasn't going to get a free cheeseburger and right before he lost his mind and flung himself over the countertop. Carl's movements were strikingly and disturbingly similar. However, to Skid Row's tremendous relief, where Bullfrog had been angry, Carl just looked scared. His eyes were huge, his skin as white as paste, and all Skid Row could think of was a kid who'd been caught not only with his hand in the cookie jar but with that jar shattered all over the kitchen floor.

"No. No. No!" he moaned, staring at Andrew Cullen's motionless body while Bullfrog and Skid Row gaped at him.

"Settle down, dude," Skid Row said, taking a step backwards.

He was getting more than a little freaked out by Carl's reaction. Okay, so the guy was dead. They'd all known that the second his head bonked off the fire hydrant with the sound of an egg being dropped onto concrete. He figured he'd be hearing that sound for months. It was like biting into a stale potato chip but about a thousand times louder. There was no blood, thank God, and Skid row was a little surprised his noggin hadn't split open like a melon. Dude was still a goner, though. No doubt about that.

The scene was grim for sure but Skid Row wasn't about to piss himself or anything. Carl, on the other hand--huge, strong, scary Carl--looked like he was ready to burst into tears.

"Yeah, take it easy," Bullfrog said, looking at Skid Row with concern.

"But he's d.... He's dead," Carl whimpered.

Well no shit. Even if the sound hadn't clued them in, the interesting new angle of Cullen's neck, lying practically flat against his right shoulder, was a definite sign his bike-riding days were over.

"Yes," Bullfrog said, placing a hand on Carl's back. "He is dead. It happened fast and I'm sure he never felt a thing."

"But he's dead!" Carl repeated and seemed unable to tear his eyes away. He started to shake and Skid Row was afraid the big man would collapse right there on the sidewalk. What the hell would they do then?

"It's okay," Bullfrog was saying, patting Carl's back now. "It's not your fault." He walked around to position himself between Carl and the crumpled figure on the ground. “He lost control of his bicycle. That's all.”

“But I...” Carl began and then his voice trailed off.

“You yelled out and startled him. That doesn't make you responsible. Skid Row and I will back you up on that. ”

“Yeah, man. It's cool.”

After a few beats, Carl blinked and seemed to focus on Bullfrog for the first time. He was still about as white as Cullen's athletic socks but maybe starting to lose the glazed look in his eyes.

“I've done it this time,” he said, biting his lower lip and glancing nervously up and down the street.

No cars had gone by. No one had shouted and come running. As far as Skid Row could tell, it was just them, Andrew Cullen, and one seriously fucked up bicycle. He didn't think it mattered anyway. Like Bullfrog said, none of them were to blame for what happened.

“What should I do?” Carl asked, his gaze flitting from Skid Row to Bullfrog and back again.

“It's no big deal,” Bullfrog said. “You call the police and tell them everything. There's nothing to worry about because we'll all be telling the same story.”

“I ain't afraid of no cops,” Carl retorted, his baffled expression saying plainly that he was surprised anyone would even make the suggestion. “I just don't know what I'm gonna tell Ricky.”

“That one's easy,” Skid Row said. “Don't tell him shit. Why would you? No one but us even knows you're here.”

Carl bit his lip some more.

“I'm serious,” Skid Row said. “Just chill. We go back to your place and that will be the end of it.” He might have said more but Bullfrog shot him the hairy eyeball and it was clear going back to Carl's was not what he had in mind.

“Well what do you want to do?” Skid Row asked with a shrug. “We can't hang here all night and I don't feel like walking all the way back to camp.”

Carl started to say something but Bullfrog cut him off.

“We need to call the police!” he said, hands on his hips. “This guy is dead and they need to know about it. I'm going to find a phone.”

Carl cleared his throat. “I don't think so,” he said, his voice low and dangerous.

Bullfrog stared at him but didn't seem to know how to respond.

"I'm sorry," Carl said, looking troubled but also completely serious. "I can't let you leave until we figure this out."

"What's to figure out?" Skid Row asked. "We phone the fuzz or we bolt. Ricky don't need to know either way."

"He'll find out," Carl said, his eyes downcast. "He always finds out. It will be worse if we try to hide it, and he'll make us pay even if we weren't responsible."

"Wait," Skid Row said. "No comprendo. What's with the *us* and the *we*? This is your problem. Me and Bullfrog got nothin' to do with it."

"That's not how Ricky operates," Carl said. "Cullen owed a lot of money. I told you that. Ricky's not going to just take the loss. He can't afford to. He'll make someone else pay."

Bullfrog staggered like he'd been punched. "Well it ain't gonna be me," he said, his hands out in front of him. "I've wanted to get out of here for days. I think it's time."

"But we got no money," Skid Row protested. "I thought we were waiting 'til I got my check."

"Not if that lunatic is after us. I'm outta here tonight. Are you coming or not?"

Skid Row knew he should leave but the thought of hitting the road virtually penniless scared him to death. He'd also never been great at making decisions, and didn't want to make the most important one of his life with some dead guy ten feet away. He wanted to go to Carl's house, or any house, where he could get a good night's sleep and then take some time to process all the new information. Unfortunately, it was pretty clear he wouldn't have that luxury.

"Listen," Carl said. "I can't let you guys contact the police, but if you want to walk away from here I won't get in your way."

"We can just leave?" Bullfrog asked, suddenly looking less sure of himself.

"You can do what you want. I have to warn you, though. Ricky won't let this one go. He'll send me to find you and bring you back."

"Would you do it?"

Carl seemed to stare at something far off in the distance. "I've known Ricky a long time. He has a way of making me do what he wants. He might also have pictures and stuff. I already told you about that. I guess what I'm saying is that I might not have much choice."

"You can't use that tracker," Skid Row said. "We know about it now and we'd find it."

Carl looked at them and sighed. "I don't need a tracker. I bought it because it made my life easier and I like toys. I would have found you anyway. Leave right now and I can promise I'll have you back here within a week."

Somehow, Skid Row knew he wasn't bluffing. "Then we're fucked," he said, wishing that he'd never known Marco, never asked Zatts for information, never saw Ricky, Carl or that old trailer. Come to think of it, he sort of wished he'd never met Bullfrog either. He had a real friend now but at what cost? "It doesn't have to be that way," Carl said thoughtfully, his eyes drifting over to where Cullen was still sprawled on the ground."

"What are you talking about?" Bullfrog asked, in a tone that said he might not want to know.

"I'm not sure yet." Carl stroked his beard. "I just know we've got to get this guy out of sight while we still can." Then, to Skid Row's amazement, he smiled.

-54-

"I don't like this," Bullfrog said, grimacing as he grabbed one of Cullen's legs and began to lift.

All things considered, Carl didn't care for it either. Every fiber of his body was telling him to get out of there. However, if Ricky learned what had happened, and Carl had no doubt he somehow would, he knew he'd never hear the end of it. Ricky wouldn't simply fire him. Carl would be okay with that, but that wasn't how Ricky did things. He'd want to make Carl pay and, if at all possible, suffer.

In the past, the punishments he'd doled out rarely amounted to much more than verbal abuse. Carl resented that but he could deal with it. This time, he knew it would be different. Andrew Cullen's untimely demise meant a net loss of a hundred thousand dollars. He didn't blame himself. Ricky wouldn't be as understanding or forgiving. How he would react Carl could only imagine. The only thing he was sure about was that it wouldn't be pretty.

"I'm with him," Skid Row said, tilting his head toward Bullfrog while struggling with Cullen's other leg. "This definitely ain't cool."

"No," Bullfrog said; "but it probably is a felony offense."

Carl gave him a look. "What are you talking about? He's already dead and we had nothing to do with it." He stared into Cullen's lifeless eyes. *Almost nothing anyway.*

"You still can't move the body. You're interfering with a crime scene or something."

"There was no crime," Carl insisted. "You said that before."

"Okay, but you still can't move him. It's wrong. And you know what will happen if we get caught?"

Carl had no idea, and he bet Bullfrog didn't either. However, they all knew what they were doing was both stupid and dangerous. It was also, at least in Carl's opinion, necessary.

"Let's just get this over with," he said.

He had Cullen under the arms and could feel the heat and moisture from his sweat. He could smell him too and he thought the guy's bladder might have let go. That was gross but Carl forgot all about it when Cullen's head suddenly flopped backwards with the sound of snow crunching under foot.

"Whoa," Skid Row said, staring as if he thought Cullen's head might fall right off. "Nasty."

"He broke his neck," Carl said. "That's what happens." He tried to make it sound like the grim scene was no big deal but had to swallow against the bile rising in his throat.

"Let's just get him into the truck." Carl shifted his grip so he could cradle Cullen's head in the crook of his arm. "The longer this takes, the more chance someone will see us."

In truth, he could have moved Cullen easily without any help from Skid Row or Bullfrog. They were actually slowing him down. They were also implicating themselves, and that's what he wanted. He wasn't about to screw them over. He just figured they'd be more likely to go along with his program if they thought they had a stake in it. Unfortunately, in terms of the program itself, he hadn't exactly come up with anything yet. He still believed Cullen's accident presented them with an opportunity, and that opportunity would become clearer in time. For now, his only focus was getting the guy off the street and out of sight.

"What makes you think we haven't been seen already?" Bullfrog asked. "We've been here at least ten minutes."

Carl didn't think it had been that long but he couldn't be sure. At least Cullen had done them the favor of wiping out on a poorly lit side street and right in front of a secondhand book store. The place looked like it probably didn't see many customers in broad daylight let alone the middle of the night. There were houses on either side and a few across the street. None of them had shown anymore signs of life than Cullen himself. Either the occupants were asleep or, just as likely, the homes were empty.

Carl's main concern was that Skid Row and Bullfrog would take off while he was jogging back to get his truck. He wanted them to stay, but hadn't really given them any reasons why they should. Had he been in their place, he would have vanished faster than a fart in a windstorm. They hadn't done that, possibly because they were afraid of Ricky or, like him, too scared to think straight. Whatever the case, they'd stuck around and were in for the long haul now because their fingerprints were all over Cullen's legs and ankles.

"What are we gonna do with this dude?" Skid Row asked once they'd managed to get him into the bed of the truck.

Carl didn't answer, instead grabbing Cullen's bike and tossing that into the truck too. He then spread out an old tarp so both body and bicycle were hidden.

"You do have a plan, don't you?" Bullfrog asked as Carl eased the tailgate closed.

"I've got some ideas," he said.

"Care to share them?"

"Do you want to have a discussion or do you want to get out of here?"

Without waiting for a reply, he walked to the driver's door, pulled it open and slid onto the seat. He again thought Skid Row and Bullfrog might bolt. They had a perfect opportunity. It wasn't like he could aggressively give chase, not with a fresh corpse bouncing around behind him.

Carl wondered what they were thinking, and what he'd do if he were in their shoes. That got him thinking about Ricky, and what he would do once he learned his precious cash cow was dead.

A hundred large lost forever. It didn't seem possible. Carl let out a low moan and considered slamming his head through the windshield. He couldn't believe that, once again, he was smack in the middle of such a royal fuck up. It wasn't fair. He could plead his innocence but it wouldn't do any good. Ricky was going to hit the roof. He'd go absolutely ballistic, and that would be the case whether he thought Carl had a hand in Cullen's death or not. It was, as far as Carl was concerned, a no win situation, or it would be unless he could somehow change the rules of the game. Otherwise, Ricky would have his way and Carl, Skid Row and Bullfrog could all be destitute together, and that might be the least of their problems.

The big question now was whether or not he could convince them to help out. They hadn't joined him in the cab, but they hadn't run away either. They were still behind the truck, and Carl adjusted his rearview mirror so he could see them more clearly. Skid Row looked lost. He had his hands jammed into his jeans pockets and he kept shaking his head like he didn't want to hear whatever it was Bullfrog was saying. Carl did want to hear and he was tempted to lower his window. He placed his finger on the button, hesitated, and then moved his hand away, deciding they deserved their privacy.

He tilted his mirror to one side, but not before getting a good look at Bullfrog, stomping one foot while flapping his arms as if trying to hail a cab. Carl figured he'd lost them for sure. He still couldn't tell which of the two had the stronger personality, but Bullfrog had definitely been more vocal. If he was arguing to vacate the premises, and Carl already knew that's what he wanted to do, it didn't seem like Skid Row was likely to put up much of a fight.

Carl could hear the murmur of voices, one voice really, low and earnest. That would be Bullfrog, laying everything out and explaining that there wasn't a single good reason for them to hang around any longer. Carl was almost glad he wasn't part of their discussion because there wasn't much he could say. He knew what would happen next. That voice would fade and they'd be gone. He wished them luck and wondered how he should proceed. He still had Andrew Cullen, his one big bargaining chip. Somehow, though, without Skid Row and Bullfrog's assistance, he felt like any bet he made would come up a loser. He thought he might better go to Ricky, be as honest and open as he could and hope for the best. In other words, he could kiss his ass goodbye. It was the coward's way out but what choice did he have?

Carl noticed then that he could no longer hear Bullfrog talking. He couldn't hear anything. So he'd been right. They made their decision and obviously believed they'd be better off on their own.

"That's it," he said, and his hand wandered to his shirt pocket where he'd tucked the Retrievor unit away. Maybe he shouldn't have told them about it. If he'd kept his big yap shut, Skid Row would still be wearing the device and Carl could find him, find them in a matter of seconds. He could then talk to them and persuade them to.....

He slumped in his seat and shook his head. What was wrong with him? They were history. He needed to forget about them and move on. He'd spent the past few days trying to protect them. What sense did it make now to involve them in whatever sort of doomed scheme he might cook up?

Carl sighed and reached for the ignition, wishing they'd at least said something before they left. He'd bought them a couple meals and thought he deserved that much.

"Oh well," he said and sighed again, and then Skid Row yanked open the passenger door.

"This bus going downtown?" he asked, climbing into the cab with Bullfrog following.

"Thought you two split," Carl said.

They exchanged a look.

"We discussed it," Skid Row said. "But with no money or nothin'...." He shrugged. "We figured it couldn't hurt to hear what you had to say."

-55-

Not ten minutes later, Carl pulled up in front of what looked like an old auto salvage yard. Skid Row breathed a sigh of relief. The short ride had been torture. The roads were full of potholes and each time the truck bounced he heard the rattle of bicycle parts along with dull, muffled thumps he didn't even want to think about. He'd never seen a dead body, let alone touched one, and the close proximity to the former Andrew Cullen was really starting to freak him out.

"This where we're gonna dump him?" Bullfrog asked, sounding scared but also curious.

Skid Row was too busy biting his nails to say anything.

Carl looked at them both. "We're not dumping anyone," he said. "We just needed someplace safe to talk and work out a plan."

"I thought you already had one," Bullfrog said, his tone quickly changing from curious to accusatory.

Skid Row wondered about that too, but he was focused more on the other thing Carl had said, his reference to their current location as safe. That wasn't the word that immediately sprang to mind.

In the pale moonlight, he could just make out the rows of vehicles, one piled haphazardly on top of another. He saw cars, vans, pickup trucks, and sitting by itself off to the right, something that might have been a golf cart. It was hard to say for sure because it was partially in shadow and had been compacted to the size of an amusement park bumper car.

"What is this place?" Skid Row asked, staring at a drooping fence constructed of red wire mesh supported by thin metal posts placed at insufficient intervals. There was a gate too, made of wooden slats so rotted he thought he could punch right through them--not that he would want to. The place had all the charm of a quarantined haunted house. Skid Row looked but couldn't find any signs indicating the name of the business. He did see any number of placards warning of security systems, surveillance cameras and trained attack dogs. Why any of those things would be necessary for such an obvious dump he couldn't even guess.

"You don't need to know," Carl said. "It's safe, and that's all that matters right now."

Bullfrog gestured through the windshield. "But what about all the cameras and stuff?"

"There are no cameras here," Carl replied. "Trust me on that one."

Skid Row already knew Bullfrog didn't trust Carl any further than he could throw him. He had his own doubts too. A lot of those stemmed from that little tracker thing. Monitoring their movements seemed so shifty. On the other hand, Carl had apparently done what he could to provide a buffer between them and Ricky. For that, Skid Row thought they should hear him out. Bullfrog didn't, insisting they'd heard plenty already. Eventually, though, he'd given in and agreed to hang around a little longer. Skid Row felt bad about that because he was starting to think he'd steered them wrong yet again.

"But all those signs," Bullfrog said, his eyes jumping from one to the next. "They can't all--"

"This facility is owned by one of Ricky's associates," Carl said with some impatience. "He's in the salvage business but has several other interests too." He looked at them flatly. "You don't want to know what they are."

Skid Row had no trouble believing that one.

Carl continued. "Let's just say he doesn't want to attract attention. That's why this place looks like it does. He's trying to keep people away."

"I get that," Bullfrog said. "But if he's cooking meth or whatever...."

Carl's eye twitched and Skid Row guessed that hit the mark. Bullfrog didn't seem to notice.

"Wouldn't he want all the dogs and stuff?"

Carl actually chuckled at that. "I'm sure he would, but those signs in front of you are about all the security he can afford. He's got some vices and that's where most of his money goes."

"You're sure?" Bullfrog asked.

"Positive. I also know that, even if he had cameras, he wouldn't dare say a word about anything he saw us do here."

That sounded ominous as all hell and Skid Row decided he didn't want to know. "And what are you planning on doing?" he asked instead, swallowing and glancing nervously over his shoulder. He couldn't help wondering if Cullen and bicycle were about to suffer the same fate as that miniaturized golf cart. He hadn't seen a car crusher but knew there had to be one in the vicinity. The pulverized evidence was all around him.

Carl must have sensed what he was thinking and blinked in surprise. "We're here to talk," he said. "That's all. I didn't want to stay out on the street and this is private and out of the way. There's no way we'll be observed."

That seemed true enough but didn't make Skid Row feel any more at ease. "So why didn't we just go to your trailer or whatever you call it?" That place gave him the creeps too but at least it was a little closer to civilization. Not only was the salvage yard far removed from any other home or business, Skid Row could only see one working street light and that was at least a hundred yards away. If it weren't for the moon and Carl's headlights, they'd be completely in the dark.

"I thought of that," Carl said, reaching under his seat and beginning to feel around. "Ricky keeps some pretty strange hours. I didn't want to risk running into him. Besides, I know there are no cameras here, but when it comes to Ricky Fixx, I can't be sure. Now where in hell," he muttered, and then grunted with satisfaction.

Skid Row heard something jingle as Carl retrieved a small ring of keys.

"You guys wait here," he instructed, pushing his door open, getting out of the truck and walking away without so much as a backward look.

Skid Row's eyes immediately dropped to the ignition where Carl's other keys still dangled.

"You know how to drive a stick?" Bullfrog asked.

Skid Row looked at him. "It's been a while since I drove anything, but yeah, I can do it."

"Then what are we waiting for? This is our ticket out of here. We can get so far away that Ricky will never be able to touch us."

"You think?"

"When are we ever gonna get another chance like this?"

"You think he's doing it on purpose?" Skid Row asked, peering out at Carl, standing in front of the gate and fiddling with a rusted padlock. Opening it seemed to be taking a lot longer than it should.

"What?" Bullfrog asked, clearly mystified.

"Well," Skid Row said, again looking at the keys. "He has tried to help us, I mean, with Ricky and stuff."

"And you think he's intentionally giving us his truck?" Bullfrog's tone suggesting he found that idea preposterous.

"I don't know," Skid Row said. "It's possible. This whole thing is so fucked up."

"Yeah, and that's why we should get out while we can."

Skid Row thought about that, and decided it really didn't matter if Carl's actions were deliberate or not. He'd presented them with a get out of jail free card and they'd have to be nuts not to use it.

"Okay!" he said, sliding into the driver's seat. "Let's do this!" He had his foot poised over the clutch when he froze.

"What are you waiting for? Bullfrog asked. "Start it up and let's get out of here!"

Skid Row didn't move.

"Come on!" Bullfrog pleaded, grabbing his right hand and trying to force it onto the gear shift.

Carl turned around then but had the headlights enough in his face that he didn't appear to notice that Skid Row had taken his place behind the wheel. He gave them a short wave and then, proving he'd managed to get the lock open, swung the gate wide. When he let go, it began to close again on its own and Carl started searching the ground for something he could use to prop it open.

"Please!" Bullfrog begged. "We're running out of time."

"I don't have a license," Skid Row said, as if that had just occurred to him. He'd had one once but it had expired and, given his situation, there wasn't much point having it renewed.

Bullfrog stared at him. "Who cares about that? Don't speed and there's nothing to worry about."

"We've got a dead body in the back."

"So we'll get a ways down the road and ditch it. No one would be able to connect it to us."

"Almost no one," Skid Row said, half to himself.

"What?"

Skid Row pointed out at Carl, who'd found a couple large stones and was positioning them in front of the gate.

"I was just thinking. What if he wants us to take the truck so he can call and report it stolen?"

Bullfrog slapped his forehead. "I thought you trusted him."

"I do," Skid Row said. "Sort of. It's just..... I've seen how scared he is of Ricky. He already told us he thinks Ricky will blame him for that dude being killed."

"What does that have to do with anything?"

Skid Row shrugged. "Maybe nothing. Or, maybe Carl sees us as a way out. He calls the cops and they nail us before we've gone five miles."

"There's no way they'd catch us that fast."

"No? So where's that little tracker thing right now?"

Bullfrog's eyes got wide and Skid Row could see he was starting to catch on.

"It could be stuck under the seat, and that's why it took him so long to find those keys. We'd go down for that guy's death and Carl would be off the hook with Ricky."

"Is that why he's keeping us around? Just so he can screw us over?"

"Don't know," Skid Row said. "I just want you to know the score. Say the word and I'll drive out of here right now."

Bullfrog looked at Skid Row, at Carl, and then he sighed and shook his head.

-56-

"I appreciate you two stickin' with me," Carl said, driving around to park behind the rundown two-bay garage that also passed for office space on those rare occasions when the salvage yard was used for its designated purpose.

"We'll listen to what you've got to say," Bullfrog said. "But we're out of here if we don't like what we hear."

Carl had to give him credit. The guy might look like a frog but he had some serious spunk. Still, he had the impression Skid Row was the main reason they hadn't already left.

"That's fair," he replied, "and I'll do you one better. If you decide you want to leave, I'll take you to the train station, the bus depot or anywhere you want to go. Cool?"

They exchanged a look Carl couldn't interpret but he thought it had something to do with whatever happened while he was out of the truck. They'd had some sort of disagreement. That much he could tell. And they both seemed more nervous now. Skid Row in particular kept looking around the interior of the cab and trying to surreptitiously reach under the seat. He couldn't imagine what the kid was up to. If Carl didn't know better, he'd think he was jonesing. Bullfrog had already made the comment about the place being a meth lab, which it was on a part time basis. Maybe that had sparked Skid Row's craving. Carl doubted that, though. He'd been around plenty of tweakers and could usually recognize the signs. Skid Row was thin, sure, even gaunt, but he had clear skin, good teeth and didn't seem overly paranoid or delusional.

"No money for trains and busses," Bullfrog said with a scowl. "That's what got us in this mess in the first place."

"So I'll give you a ride out of town. I can throw a few bucks your way too. That's about the best I can do. I warned you, though," Carl said, raising one finger. "Depending on what happens with Ricky, I may have to come after you again. It's nothing personal. I just want you to know that it may be out of my hands."

"What's up with that anyway?" Skid Row asked, his right hand exploring the crevice around the seat belt.

Carl watched him out of the corner of one eye. *Okay, so maybe he was a little paranoid.*

"Seriously," Skid Row said. "Why don't you just tell him to fuck off? You're way bigger than him. Kick his ass and be done with it."

Carl couldn't count the number of times he'd fantasized about doing just that. "If only it was that simple," he said, reaching under his own seat and grabbing a flashlight.

"So why can't it be? I mean, what does he have on you anyway?"

Carl stared out at the darkness. "It's getting a little cramped in here," he said. "Can we continue this inside?"

They piled out of the truck, and using the flashlight so they didn't trip over any of the random auto parts scattered all over the ground, Carl led them to the back of the building where he stopped in front of a locked door. He pulled out his ring of keys again.

"Why do you have those?" Bullfrog asked. "Is this place really yours?"

"I promise it's not," Carl said. "Like I told you, the owner is one of Ricky's associates."

"Right. And we're supposed to just believe that?"

Carl suddenly found that he wasn't appreciating Bullfrog's spunkiness quite so much.

"Believe what you want but I'm telling it like it is. Ricky has a lot of different business interests. He's got some unusual arrangements with some of the people he works with. Sometimes, they feel like they need to do him favors. That's all I'm gonna say about it."

"This guy owe Ricky money then?" Skid Row asked.

Carl shot him a look. "It isn't always about that." Even though that's what it came down to about ninety-nine percent of the time.

The dirt bag owner of the salvage yard didn't owe now but that wasn't the case a few months back. Carl had occasion to pay him a visit. Subsequently, the guy now supplied Ricky with some product and had turned over a set of keys. They'd never been used but Ricky said they might someday come in handy.

Well, he was right about that one, Carl thought, unlocking the door and stepping inside.

"Yuck," Bullfrog said and then sneezed.

Carl had to pinch his nose to stop from doing the same thing. With his free hand, he groped for the wall switch. He found it and a couple overhead lights sputtered to life.

The place looked the same as ever, which wasn't saying a hell of a lot. Metal utility shelves reached from floor to ceiling and covered one side plus the entire back wall. They were mostly bare or held automotive parts so old and rusty they'd never be of any use. The rest of the "inventory" was in cardboard boxes, plastic or wooden milk crates or just dumped on the floor. Carl noticed stacks of old tires, the crumpled rear half of a Chevy Nova, a Honda motorcycle with no handlebars or wheels, an air compressor that didn't seem to have a hose, a portable engine lift, the very one he'd threatened to use to remove the owner's testicles, and all sorts of junk he couldn't identify. That was all as expected. What he hadn't counted on was the cloying chemical stench that hung in the air. It had always been there but now seemed a lot more pervasive.

"Freaking foul, dude." Skid Row said, his face buried in his sweatshirt. "Can we open a window?"

Carl shook his head. "Not without a crow bar. They're all painted over. We'll leave the door open. It faces the back of the lot so no one will see the light."

"And why are we here?" Bullfrog asked, moving into the doorway and taking several deep breaths.

"I told you. It's isolated and I thought it would be a good place to talk."

"Then do it," Skid Row said, "because I'm gonna hurl if I have to stay in here much longer."

Carl started to lean against a large slop sink but reconsidered when he saw the layer of brownish sludge crusted all over the outside. He straightened and folded his arms. "We need to figure out what to do with Andrew Cullen."

Bullfrog stared at him. "We should have called 911 but it's a little late for that now."

"It is," Carl agreed. "And I don't think that would have been in our best interests."

"Maybe not yours, but now you've managed to wrap us up in your mess. Thanks a bunch!"

"I'm trying to help you," Carl said. "Can't you see that?"

"How?" Bullfrog asked. "How is any of this helping us? Until about a half hour ago, we'd never heard of Andrew Cullen. Now he's dead and you somehow convinced us to help move the body. Pardon me if I don't see the benefit."

"I'm protecting you from Ricky."

"So you say." Bullfrog retorted. "But I haven't seen one thing that makes me think it's true. He glanced at Skid Row but kept talking to Carl. "You keep telling us Ricky is going to do this or Ricky is going to do that. How do we know it isn't a big bunch of crap? You're the one that keeps following us around. You even stole the bag with the drugs. You told us yourself"

"I was..." Carl stammered

"Following orders," Bullfrog finished. "Yeah, we know. How about you show us some proof because I'm starting to think you're full of shit."

Carl stepped forward, his fists clenched. He wanted to grab Bullfrog by his stubby little neck and send him into the slop sink head first, and might have done it too had it not been for Skid Row standing there, pulling at his hair and looking miserable. Bullfrog looked pretty miserable too and Carl could see where they were coming from. He walked over to stand in front of the window, even though the thick layer of black paint prevented him from seeing anything more than a heavily smudged version of his own reflection.

"I'm sorry," he said, turning to face them. "I really was trying to help. You asked me to prove it and," he shrugged,"I'm not sure I can do that. I guess I made things worse by bringing you here. I want to bring Cullen inside, just to get him out of my truck. When I'm done, I'll take you wherever you want to go. The Retrievor's in my pocket." He pulled it out to show them. "So you don't have to worry about that. And," he fished out his wallet and inspected the contents. "I've got about forty bucks here. You can have that too."

"We don't want your money," Bullfrog said, his expression suggesting otherwise. "We'll take that ride, though. You can drop us downtown somewhere. We'll figure it out from there."

Bullfrog started to move toward the door but Skid Row held out a hand to stop him. "What does he have on you?" he asked, staring directly into Carl's eyes.

"You mean Ricky?"

Skid Row nodded and brushed hair away from his face.

"I wish I knew. Until I found out he was following me, I didn't think he had a thing. I mean, I just never thought about it."

"Ironic, huh?" Bullfrog said as he gazed out into the darkness.

"How's that?'

Bullfrog turned to look at him. "You follow us. He follows you. Doesn't that strike you as kind of funny?"

"Our intentions were different. I promise you that."

"Hold on," Skid Row said, glancing around. "If Ricky was keeping tabs on you, following you or whatever, doesn't that mean he might know where we are too?" He looked at the door as if he thought Ricky might stroll in at any second.

"He doesn't know shit," Carl scoffed. "If you're gonna believe one thing I say, you can hang your hat on that one."

"How do you know? You said he's got photos of you and stuff."

"I think he does," Carl answered. "But he only got them when he knew exactly where I was going to be. Getting someplace ahead of me isn't the same as tracking me down."

"You're sure?" Bullfrog asked.

"I can't be a hundred percent sure but I've known Ricky a long time. I know how he operates. He's gonna take the path of least resistance and do what he can to hedge his bets."

"What the fuck does that mean?" Skid Row asked.

Carl smiled wryly. "It means he's lazy but dangerous. That's what we have to keep in mind. And one other thing: he's into self preservation."

"So he'll send you up the river to save his own ass."

"In a heartbeat," Carl said.

Bullfrog ran a hand over his mouth. "So you said you don't know what he has on you. What could he have? What's the worst case scenario?"

Carl had already given that a lot of thought. Unfortunately, there was a whole lot he didn't know and had no way to find out. How long had Ricky been gathering evidence against him, assuming that's what he'd been doing, and how often did he do it? Based on what the Retrievor had indicated, Ricky had been near Geno's the day Carl had tossed the grease ball around his pizzeria and presumably had pictures of that encounter. That was the only one he knew about for sure. Everything else was conjecture.

Worst case scenario? Carl couldn't count the people he'd knocked around on Ricky's instructions. He'd twisted arms, blackened eyes, and engaged in various forms of vandalism and arson. Just based on sheer volume, he supposed Ricky could have compiled quite a portfolio. There was, however, one thing he absolutely did not have. Despite all the times Carl had said he was going to kill someone, he'd only actually done it once. It was Marco. It was an accident, and Ricky had no physical proof. Carl was sure about that because of how surprised and pissed off Ricky had been when he found out.

"I guess it could be worse," he said, kicking an axle and a section of exhaust pipe out of his way to give him room to pace. "I've done a lot of bad stuff. Depending on what Ricky's got, he could cause me a lot of trouble."

Bullfrog studied him. "But you think you could use that Cullen guy to what? Turn the tables on him?

"I think so. I mean, I did. I'm not sure now. You don't have to worry about it, though. You guys are out of it. Give me a second to get him out of the truck and then I'll be ready to roll."

"What will you do?" Skid Row asked.

Carl had been wondering that very thing. Unless he came up with something, Ricky was going to have his nuts for lunch. His best bet was probably to make Cullen disappear and then pretend he didn't know anything about it. That should work at least for a while.

"I got some ideas," he said, realizing how pathetic that sounded.

"Like what?" Bullfrog asked, and Carl couldn't miss the note of challenge in his voice.

"My first thought was to call Cullen's wife and demand a ransom."

"You want to ransom off a dead guy?"

"She wouldn't know he was dead, dipshit," Skid Row said, giving Bullfrog a shove.

"That's right," Carl replied. "I'd have her drop off the money somewhere. I just wouldn't come through on my end of the deal."

"That's stupid," Bullfrog said. "She'd call the cops."

"I know. All sorts of people would get involved and it would turn into one giant mess. On top of that, even if Ricky got his money, he'd wonder what happened to his golden goose and he'd never let that go."

"And that's your master plan?" Bullfrog asked, looking dumbfounded. "That's why you dragged us out here?"

"No," Carl said. "That's just one idea. I've got others."

"Uh, huh. Well I can't wait to hear them."

"We need to set him up," Carl said, looking to Skid Row, to Bullfrog and then back again. "We need to get Cullen and Ricky in the same place."

"What for?" Skid Row asked.

"To force Ricky to do something that makes him look guilty."

"You're talking about framing him," Bullfrog said.

Carl hesitated and then nodded. "I guess I am. I just haven't figured out how to make it work. I can set up the scene easy enough. I could even do it here."

"But how you gonna get Ricky down here?" Bullfrog asked. "It's like two o'clock in the morning."

“I don’t know,” Carl admitted, hanging his head. “I can’t just call him. I can’t do anything to make him suspect I might be involved. He’d see right through that.”

“Then you’ve got nothing,” Bullfrog said. “You should have left him on the street like I said.” He turned to Skid Row. “You ready to rock?”

“Chill for a sec,” Skid Row said. Then to Carl, “Are you hoping to make money on this?”

“I don’t care. I just want him off my back, and yours too.”

“Then we’ll call him,” Skid Row said. “Sort of anyway, but we’ve got some work to do first. Follow me.” Without another word, he turned and went outside.

-57-

Ricky opened his eyes and blinked. He was facing his bedroom window and a shaft of light sliced through the small tear in the shade. He could see it was still full dark out and wondered what had wakened him. When he'd fallen into bed, his good-for-nothing, girlfriend-beating, welfare-collecting, crack head downstairs neighbor had been blasting god-awful gangster rap music. That apartment was blessedly quiet now. The entire street was quiet. Maybe that was the problem. He was so used to thumping music, shouting matches and police sirens that the uncommon stillness had interrupted his dreams.

Ricky figured he must have been dreaming about sex. He had no memory of it, unfortunately, but he was rock hard and had his left hand buried in his shorts. He groaned, rolled over, and knocked his elbow against the edge of the nightstand.

"Shit!" he said, squinting at the clock.

Twenty-seven minutes past three. He groaned again and sat up, struggling to free his legs from the tangle of sheets and blankets. He was a little nauseous and had the beginnings of what he thought would be a world class hangover. Ricky used the heel of his hand to rub one eye and then the other. He still didn't know what in hell he was doing up but decided he may as well tend to his bladder and pop a Tylenol or three while he was at it.

Pinching his temples between thumb and fingers, he stood, took one step and tripped over a pile of dirty clothes he'd left in the middle of the floor. Ricky swayed and nearly fell on his face. With a curse, he started to kick the clothing aside when he heard a soft buzzing.

"Mother fucker," he hissed, instantly recognizing the buzz as his cell phone and an incoming text message. Ricky knew that's what had roused him. He also knew the text had to be from Carl and, given the time, it had to be bad news.

"What has the moron done now?" he asked, dropping to his knees and blindly fumbling through coat pockets while he tried to remember if he'd given Carl any jobs for the night. They'd been at the pub, he recalled, and they'd talked about those two deadbeat losers Carl couldn't seem to get his hands on. *And after that?* They'd discussed other things too but the details of that conversation were a tad fuzzy. No wonder. Ricky's head was banging like a cheap whore and his tongue felt like it needed a shave.

He finally got his hands on the phone, picking it up but then dropping it again while attempting to enter his four digit pass code.

Settle down, he told himself, realizing he was probably getting worked up over nothing. Other than finding and collaring Skid Row and Bullfrog, Carl had no pressing responsibilities that Ricky could think of. So even if he'd screwed up royally and somehow managed to kill them both, definitely not out of the realm of possibility, what difference would it really make? It wasn't like anyone would miss them. He supposed Carl might have implicated himself. Instead of an axe handle and a semi-private construction lot, maybe he beat them to death in full view of a dozen people. Really, though, Ricky couldn't imagine anything like that happening. Carl was capable of it, sure, but for some unfathomable reason, he actually seemed to like the little creeps. Ricky was fairly sure that's why they were still on the run.

He pushed that thought aside because it still ticked him off. He'd given Carl one simple task and, as usual, the guy had not only botched it but made it more complicated. The two jerk-offs just weren't worth all that trouble. Still, something had gone wrong. Ricky felt that in his gut. Silently cursing his partner, he took a breath and entered his code, correctly this time. Moments later, he was bent over the toilet and puking violently into the bowl.

The text, it turned out, had not been from Carl at all. Ricky sat back on his haunches and wiped his mouth on the back of his arm. He stared at the screen in a state of complete shock. The sender was Andrew Cullen and the first four words of his text were what had Ricky scrambling for the bathroom.

OUR DEAL IS OFF!

Things went downhill from there. Ricky read it through three times just to make sure he hadn't somehow misinterpreted Cullen's meaning. Unfortunately, it was as plain and clear as the sharp stench of vomit that now filled the tiny room. Ricky leaned back and rested his head against the tiled wall.

COME TO MY OFFICE NOW, Cullen's note said. *WE NEED TO MEET AND RENEGOTIATE. BE HERE WITHIN THE HOUR OR I WILL CONTACT THE POLICE AND MY ATTORNEY.*

The tight-assed fuck had put every letter in caps like Ricky might not have taken him seriously otherwise. No worries there. His heart was pounding and he could actually hear the blood rushing in his ears. Something that sounded disturbingly like a whimper escaped his throat. *What in hell had happened?*

He stood on shaky legs and had to clutch the sink to avoid collapsing back to the floor.

OUR DEAL IS OFF.

Fuck you, Ricky thought. *It was all your idea!*

He spat, turned on the cold water tap, and cupped several handfuls into his mouth. He then splashed water onto his face and used a dirty hand towel to dry off. When Ricky was done, he supposed he felt a little more human but definitely not any better.

He didn't understand. Who did Cullen think he was anyway? Ricky hadn't gone looking for him. Cullen came to him, borrowed money and then wasn't able to pay. True, Ricky had done everything he could to turn up the heat. Cullen should have expected that. He'd agreed to the terms and understood the risks. But bottom line, it was Cullen himself who proposed the hundred thousand dollar payoff. Ricky had nothing to do with that. He'd simply accepted the offer and agreed to give the deadbeat more time. He didn't have to do that and now his generosity was biting him in the ass.

"That's what you get for being nice," he said, picking up his phone and considering either smashing it against the wall or grinding it under a heel. That, he knew, would only compound his problems but he felt like he needed to strike out in some way.

"FUCK HIM!" he suddenly shouted, spinning and slamming his bare right foot into the side of the shower stall. Ricky heard a satisfying thwack, and then he was back on the floor, cradling his foot in his hands and hoping none of the bones were broken.

Still wondering what exactly had gone wrong, he showered and dressed as quickly as he could, while simultaneously trying to keep all his weight on his left side. His right foot was throbbing and had swollen to nearly twice its normal size. He had no luck getting that foot into his customary black wingtip so had to go with an unlaced running shoe instead. That struck him as ironic since he doubted he could so much as jog if his life depended on it.

It was close to four when Ricky limped down his apartment stairs. Based on the time the text had come in, he still had a half hour for the short drive to Cullen's office. What would happen once he got there he couldn't even guess. He would have appreciated some back up and had sent a couple texts to Carl, but as yet had not received a response. Ricky was too nervous to be pissed.

Cullen had said he wanted to renegotiate. Ricky wasn't sure how to take that but told himself it wasn't all bad. He believed there was still a chance to work something out. There had to be or Cullen wouldn't have bothered contacting him at all.

Other parts of his message were encouraging too. That bit about going to the cops was total bullshit. The guy had too much to lose. For one thing, Ricky had followed him closely enough to be fairly sure Cullen's pretty little wife had no clue what he'd been up to. He couldn't bring in the cops without bringing her in too, and Ricky would bet his left nut Cullen wasn't ready to go there. As for consulting his attorney, that was even more laughable. Cullen had not only borrowed money from a loan shark but was planning on ripping off business owners all over town. He definitely wouldn't want the legal spotlight pointed at his activities.

That all made sense, and by Ricky's estimation, he was still the one holding most of the cards. Only one thing troubled him. Cullen's text had been insistent not to mention downright rude. That was odd. From the time he and Ricky first met, Andrew Cullen had been sneaky and conniving but also submissive. He was clearly afraid of Ricky and even more afraid of Carl. Why then would he suddenly start acting so aggressive? Ricky had no answer to that, which was very disconcerting. He didn't like walking into a situation without knowing exactly what to expect. He'd been to Cullen's office probably a dozen times but had never ventured beyond the sidewalk out front. Now he was being asked, make that ordered, to meet the guy on his own turf and at a time of night when nothing good ever takes place.

His head still hurting, either from hangover, stress or both, Ricky stopped his car at an empty intersection, took a quick look around and then made a left turn through a red light. The streets were all deserted, and if he wanted to he could have made it to Cullen's office in less than five minutes. Instead, he made another left turn, taking him in the opposite direction from where he needed to go. It was all about controlling the situation. Ricky really had no choice but to do what Cullen said. That didn't mean he had to rush right over and crawl in on his hands and knees. He wanted to make Cullen sweat and maybe even think he wasn't gonna show.

He slowed as he neared the Red Oak Diner, thinking he might stop in for a head-clearing cup of coffee, but soon saw that wouldn't be an option. Back in the day, the Red Oak was open twenty-four hours. He thought so anyway. Regardless, it obviously wasn't now. The interior of the restaurant was dim and it didn't look like any of the employees had even arrived yet. Ricky knew he could get his coffee at the gas station a couple blocks ahead but decided not to bother. He debated, drumming his fingers on the top of the steering wheel as he made his way downtown. Then, already knowing it wouldn't do any good, he picked up his cell phone, went into the call history and selected the top number. There was a pause, a click, and then he was listening to the same voicemail message he'd heard three times already.

"You've reached Andrew Cullen at Cyber Force Technology. I'm sorry but I'm not available to take your call. If you need immediate assistance...."

"Damn it!" Ricky said, ending the call and tossing the phone aside. He felt like Cullen was playing him and he didn't like it one tiny fucking bit. The guy was in his office. He had to be or he wouldn't have requested the meeting. So why wasn't he answering his office phone or his cell? Ricky even sent him a text and got no response to that either. It was bullshit and no way to handle a negotiation. If he'd had any choice in the matter, Ricky would have said the hell with it and gone home right then. He had no choice, though, not if he ever wanted to see any of the money Cullen owed.

As he approached, uncharacteristically keeping well below the posted speed limit, the first thing Ricky noticed was the row of empty parking spots outside the Cyber Force building. That struck him as odd too. At the very least, he assumed he would find Andrew Cullen's new Avalon there, but it was nowhere in sight. As Ricky drove past, he glanced up and could make out faint illumination filtering through Cullen's window blinds. He figured that had to be from a desk lamp. It cast strange shadows, one of which might have been Cullen's silhouette but Ricky couldn't be sure.

"I see you," he said, driving to the end of the block and turning the corner. He wanted to park close by but not so close that Cullen would see him coming. And if the jackass had gone completely off his rocker and called the cops after all, Ricky definitely didn't want to leave his car right out front. He was all about being inconspicuous.

He considered another lap around the block to reconnoiter but decided he'd only be putting off the inevitable, not to mention making his presence more obvious. Ricky checked his mirrors and then pulled to the curb, gliding to a stop without ever touching the brake pedal. He killed the engine and, feeling slightly foolish, reached up and flipped the switch so the dome light wouldn't turn on when he opened the door. He exited the car as quietly as he could, standing and looking up and down the street before nodding to himself and easing his door closed. He then pressed the button on the key fob to lock up. The dome light remained dark but the head and taillights flashed accompanied by a bleep from his horn. The sudden noise broke the stillness of the early morning, caused Ricky to jump halfway out of his shoes and made him feel like an incompetent asshole.

"Fucking idiot," he muttered, suddenly glad Carl wasn't there to back him up. He didn't want witnesses to his stupidity.

His right foot a little better but still aching, Ricky gimped his way to the end of the block where he took up a position behind a utility pole. He was mostly hidden but had an unobstructed view of Cullen's window. Nothing had changed. There was definitely a light on in there and Ricky noticed the same shadow he'd seen before. He squinted but couldn't make out any more detail. It might have been Cullen but could have just as easily been a filing cabinet or potted plant. Whatever the case, it didn't appear to be moving.

Ricky watched a moment longer then glanced around and, seeing no one, started across the road. He felt exposed but concentrated on moving as casually as he could, no easy task given his awkward gait. He whistled softly, just a guy out for a predawn stroll. Then Ricky put his hands in his pockets because he figured that's what innocent people did, and that's when he realized just how empty his pockets were.

"Son of a bitch," he said, stopping in the middle of the street and feeling incompetent all over again.

What was I thinking?

Anytime Ricky expected trouble, he made a point of having Carl nearby. That had always worked well. Tonight, however, his oversized partner was MIA. Ricky should have planned accordingly. He had that handgun at the office. It would have been easy enough to bring it along. Instead, he had nothing. He couldn't threaten or even defend himself. He was younger than Cullen, sure. But if things got physical, Ricky knew he wouldn't stand a chance.

He looked back in the direction of his car, which he could no longer see from where he stood. He knew he had a pocket knife in the glove box. The blade was dull and maybe two inches long. In other words, it was useless. *And in the trunk?* He tried to think. His snow brush was probably still there, along with jumper cables, a half a jug of wiper fluid and a bag of cans and bottles he hadn't gotten around to returning. That was about it, *except for the spare tire.* He'd never used it before but it was there, and that meant the jack and tire iron were somewhere there too. It would set an interesting tone for their meeting if he strolled in swinging something like that.

Several minutes later, Ricky was climbing the fourth and final flight of stairs to Cullen's office. He could have taken the elevator and that would have been much easier on his bum foot but he didn't want to announce his arrival with the chime of elevator doors. He'd entered the lobby and, after poking around long enough to satisfy himself that he was alone, found the fire stairs and began working his way slowly up, pausing at each landing to rest and listen. His hands and pockets were as empty as they had been before. Ricky still wasn't sure he'd made the right decision on that one. Andrew Cullen was a businessman though, and it was best to try to deal with him on businessman terms. That meant talking, which Ricky figured he could do with the best of them. And if things started to go south? He'd found a short but surprisingly weighty statuette on the reception desk in the lobby. It was up Ricky's shirt now and he could feel it digging into the small of his back. It was no tire iron but might still do the job in a pinch.

Ricky mounted the last step, waited for his breathing to return to normal, and then pushed the door open and poked his head through. Cyber Force was maybe forty feet down the hall on the left. The hallway itself was dark with only some low level security lighting to show the way. Even in the relative gloom, Ricky could tell Cullen had done pretty well for himself. He could make out paneled walls in a dark finish and the carpet was so thick and well padded that even his labored steps were practically silent. Everything smelled new and rich. But as Ricky well knew, looks could be deceiving and desperate people sometimes did desperate things. *So what had Cullen done?*

OUR DEAL IS OFF!

Ricky kept going back to the same question he'd been asking himself since before he left his apartment. What was this all about? Andrew Cullen wanted to see him, presumably, but he hadn't exactly laid out the welcome mat. The unlocked front door had been the only real sign anyone even knew he was coming.

"You could have at least turned some fucking lights on," Ricky said, a little freaked out by the darkness and quiet.

He made it to the Cyber Force door where he again stopped to listen. It would have been helpful if the door had a window or even a peephole but it was a solid hunk of wood and Ricky could tell by the look that it was thick and heavy. He still pressed an ear to one of the panels and strained to hear. There was nothing, but as he started to pull away, he thought he heard a muffled thump. Ricky pressed his ear to the door again and held his breath. The sound wasn't repeated and he guessed he must have imagined it.

He was reluctant to stroll right into whatever Cullen had planned for him but really had no choice. He raised a fist to knock, thought better of it, and then twisted the knob and pushed the door open. It swung silently and revealed a small but well-appointed reception area. No lights were on, but Ricky could see a desk, a few plush chairs against one wall, a coffee station, and a large piece of abstract art that, to him, looked like a sea horse getting sucked off by a dwarf. Ricky also saw three closed doors and one that was partially open. That was obviously the source of the light he'd seen from outdoors and he knew he'd found his man.

-58-

Ricky didn't immediately realize anything was wrong, probably because he was too busy being pissed. He stood in Cullen's doorway, glaring across the room while trying to decide what to say to the self-serving son of a bitch, posed smugly behind his big, fancy desk. Plenty of things sprang to mind, but Ricky had enough business acumen to know he shouldn't call the guy a dirty cocksucker right off the bat. His temper and impulsiveness were getting the best of him though, and he was on the verge of doing just that when something made him stop.

He took a half step forward, cocking his head to listen. Then, feeling like he was being watched by someone other than Andrew Cullen, he glanced around to make sure they were alone. The reception area was empty. He knew that because he'd just walked through there. The outer door was still closed and there was no way anyone had snuck in behind him. There were no obvious hiding places either, except for maybe under the desk. And the way the chair was pushed in tight, he could tell there wasn't enough room there for anything much larger than a dog. So why was the hair beginning to stand up on the back of his neck?

Ricky turned to face his host again, taking in the leather furniture, the floor-to-ceiling bookshelf, the wet bar, the wall-mounted television and the two other doors. One was in the corner immediately to his right and the other on the opposite wall. Ricky assumed closet and bathroom but either door might have opened into a conference room or another office. He noticed that the door on his right was cracked open an inch or two. The interior was completely dark but he was still tempted to walk over to investigate. Ricky didn't know what Cullen would think about that but decided he really didn't give a shit. Maybe he'd make himself a nice cocktail and then tour the whole place. He was sure Cullen's booze would all be top shelf; and although he didn't especially want a drink right then, he did want to send a clear message that Ricky Fixx was not to be pushed around.

"Pretty nice digs," he said, winking at Cullen while moving toward the bar. "Don't mind if I do."

He received no objections and, making a concerted effort to hide his limp, got as far as the center of the room before stopping short, sensing that something wasn't kosher. He looked at Andrew Cullen more closely and realized that, not only had the guy not spoken, he hadn't so much as blinked from the moment Ricky walked in. He simply sat there, his stillness exuding arrogance and superiority. That's how Ricky saw it anyway, recognizing the behavior because he'd used that same shtick countless times, perched at his raised desk platform so he could stare down at Carl. But something about Cullen's body language was different and definitely not right.

Ricky was a jumble of nerves, and he guessed that was why he hadn't picked up on it sooner. He also still hadn't gotten a good look at Cullen's face. He blamed that on the gooseneck desk lamp, angled sharply downward so it pointed directly at what looked like a single sheet of paper. Cullen's torso was brightly illuminated by the lamp's small, circular beam, but everything from the shoulders and above was in relative shadow. Taking another hesitant step, Ricky saw now that Cullen's head was tipped back a bit too far to be comfortable and his neck seemed to have a curious, almost unnatural tilt. His mouth was open slightly too and the overall effect reminded him of someone who'd fallen asleep on an airplane or bus. He'd wake up in a few hours so sore he could barely move. Except Cullen wasn't sleeping. His eyes were wide open and his facial features were frozen in an expression of mild surprise.

"Oh, fuck," Ricky breathed, the pieces finally falling into place.

His first frantic thought was heart attack. It seemed to make sense. Even though Cullen was in good shape from all the biking, swimming and other crap, he drank like a fish and was under a tremendous amount of stress. Much of that was self-inflicted but so what? He was probably lucky his ticker hadn't timed out years before.

"Stupid bastard!" Ricky said, wondering why things couldn't go his way even one fucking time. Whenever he thought his ship was finally coming in, someone would set off a depth charge and the whole thing would blow up in his face. The S. S. Andrew Cullen was only the latest.

Ricky started to reach for the desk phone, thinking he should call 911 on the off chance it wasn't already too late. If Cullen could be saved, he'd surely be so grateful that he'd—

Ricky let his outstretched arm fall to his side. He wasn't calling anyone. It didn't take a coroner to see that Cullen had run his last marathon. Besides, what could he say anyway? Once he explained the nature of the emergency, the 911 operator would ask for pesky little details like his name and location. Ricky couldn't give either one. He could give Cullen's location, but how was he supposed to explain his own presence there?

I just happened to be in the neighborhood.

Yes, I know it's four o'clock in the morning. I was walking my dog.

I saw the light from outside and just knew something was wrong. The front door was open so I let myself in, made my way all the way to the fourth floor and that's when I found him.

Yeah, right. He'd be in custody before he even finished his story. But even as he began mentally shredding the hundred large he knew he'd never see, Ricky had deduced that his initial diagnosis was wrong. Dead wrong. Whatever killed Andrew Cullen, it was no heart attack.

The guy was in his office. If his heart was going to give out, wouldn't it have happened during one of his crazy workouts and not well after the fact? Ricky was no doctor but that seemed to make sense to him. But, Cullen was in workout clothes and that sort of confused the issue. He had been exercising, not preparing for a meeting. Ricky wasn't exactly a client but he'd still assumed Cullen would be dressed more appropriately.

Ricky focused again on Cullen's head and neck. If he didn't know better it really looked like.... Without knowing exactly why, he touched Cullen's shoulder and gave it a gentle shake. He didn't exert much force but Cullen's head wobbled and fell forward so far that, for a horrifying second, Ricky was afraid it was going to tumble onto the desk.

"Jesus!" he said, leaping back, putting too much weight on his bad foot and almost landing on his ass. He had to grab the edge of the desk to steady himself. In doing so, a sheet of paper fluttered to the floor. Ricky ignored it, his eyes instead fixed on Cullen. He swallowed hard and was afraid he might puke. He'd never seen a broken neck before but had no doubt that's what he was looking at. It was like all the muscles had been replaced by so much overcooked pasta. It sounded that way too, everything all soft and mushy. It was fucking creepy and Ricky sank into one of Cullen's visitor's chairs while he tried to collect his thoughts.

What in hell? he wondered, thinking he might just need that drink after all. With some effort, he tore his gaze away from Cullen's body and looked around the room. He tried to come up with a scenario where what he was seeing made sense. A guy might conceivably suffer a heart attack while sitting behind his desk. Hell, some people had heart attacks in their sleep, but a broken neck? That didn't happen spontaneously or without an obvious cause.

His throat suddenly very dry, Ricky was on his feet before he even realized what he was doing. "I gotta get out of here," he said, looking at Cullen's motionless form one more time. It didn't seem possible but he knew what had happened. There was no other explanation. Andrew

Cullen had been murdered. Ricky didn't know why or how. At the moment, he didn't' even care. He just knew he needed to get away from that office and the Cyber Force building as fast as he could. He was almost to the door when he spied the paper on the floor.

"Damn," he muttered, stopping in his tracks. If he didn't want anyone to know he was there, he thought he should leave things just as he found them. He hadn't made a drink, thankfully, and Ricky didn't think he'd touched anything other than the doorknob and Cullen's shoulder. *Could you leave fingerprints on fabric?* He didn't know, and decided he'd have to take his chances with that one. He wasn't laying another finger on the guy and most definitely wasn't' about to try to readjust his head. He got queasy just thinking about it.

Using his coat sleeve, Ricky plucked the piece of paper from the floor and slid it onto Cullen's desk, positioning it under the lamp right where it had been before. Ricky started to turn away but then remembered he'd grabbed the desk when he almost fell. He thought he'd only touched one corner but started wiping one whole side just to be safe. As he ran his sleeve back and forth, he actually looked at the paper for the first time. It was on Cyber Force letterhead and Andrew Cullen's signature was scrawled at the bottom. Ricky figured it was a contract or some other type of business form but it was all hand written. That seemed strange. He didn't think much of it but looked a little closer and then froze when he saw his own name. Forgetting all about his prints, Ricky snatched up the paper and began to read.

"Looks like it worked," Skid Row said, peering out between the blinds. As he looked on, Ricky hurried across the street, glancing over his shoulder every few steps.

"You see him? Bullfrog asked. "What's he doing?"

"Tough to tell from here," Skid Row replied. "But if I had to venture a guess, I'd say the man is currently shitting his pants. No question we got his attention." Then he turned to Carl. "Any idea why he's limping?"

Carl shrugged. "I noticed that when he came in here. He was fine when I saw him a few hours ago. He was also pretty drunk. Maybe he fell down the stairs."

Skid Row looked out the window again. "Dude ain't drunk anymore. Might wish he was, though."

"I bet," Carl said, pulling out Cullen's cell phone. "If I didn't say it before, I sure am glad you found this."

Skid Row pushed hair out of his eyes. "It was luck. I felt it in his pocket when me and Bullfrog were helping you get him into the truck."

"And it's a good thing you did or this wouldn't have worked."

"Do you think he still believes Cullen really sent that text?" asked Bullfrog.

"No telling," Carl said. "But knowing Ricky, he probably thinks he has the situation under control. Let's prove him wrong. I almost feel bad doing this," he added, showing no remorse whatsoever.

-59-

Still clutching the paper, Ricky exited the Cyber Force building and made a beeline for his car. He didn't think he really had anything to worry about but wanted to get away from there as quickly as he could. He still couldn't believe Andrew Cullen was dead. He also didn't understand or even want to consider how it might have happened. Ricky knew Cullen was a gambler, a womanizer and a drunk so the fact that he'd met a bad end came as no big shock. Had he romanced the wrong lady or gotten into serious debt with someone other than him? No way to know. One thing was clear, though. He'd pissed off somebody enough to get his neck broken. But as troubling as that was, Ricky had something far more pressing and personal on his mind. Whoever was responsible for Cullen's death had also gone to great lengths to try to pin the murder on him.

Before rounding the corner, Ricky looked back, and for the briefest moment, thought he saw movement in Cullen's office window. The louvered blind shifted slightly, and wasn't the strange shadow from the desk lamp a little different now? Did it somehow look…larger?

No way, he thought, patting his front pockets until he found his car keys. He'd just been inside the office and knew full well there was no one else there. Why then could he still not shake the feeling he was being watched?

Ricky drove down Court Street, not sure if he should go to his office or turn around and head home. He finally decided he was too wired to even consider going back to bed. He continued a ways further and then, on a whim, made a sharp left turn into the TA truck stop. He needed his coffee now, and thought some breakfast might be good too.

Ricky chose one of the booths against the wall and sat where he could keep his eye on the door. He wasn't sure why he bothered, given that he had no idea who, if anyone, he should be on the lookout for. He had Cullen's note tucked into his shirt but didn't pull it out until he'd perused the menu and the waitress, looking surprisingly fresh and perky given the hour, took his order and moved off. Ricky still waited, anxiously rolling a bottle of hot sauce back and forth in his hands until she returned with a carafe of steaming coffee, filled his mug, offered cream and sugar, both of which he refused, and then retreated behind the counter.

He took a sip and sat back, surreptitiously inspecting the other diners. The clientele was primarily male, and if they weren't all truckers, they still looked the part. He saw lots of flannel, blue jeans, ball caps and work boots. A gray-haired man with a thick mustache chewed the end of a pencil as he worked a crossword puzzle. Another guy, quite a bit younger, seemed to be in the middle of a heated conversation via text. It appeared things weren't going his way. He kept squinting at his phone and frowning, lips moving slightly as he typed out a response. The table closest to the door was occupied by two large men arguing over a card game. As far as any of them were concerned, Ricky wasn't even there. Even the waitress seemed to have forgotten his existence. She leaned a hip against the counter, her attention divided between a television and a fingernail and emery board.

Ricky relaxed somewhat, and started paying a little more attention to the restaurant itself. He'd driven past a thousand times but had never stopped in. It was larger, brighter and cleaner than he would have expected. The decor surprised him too, the walls lined with large framed pictures. They were striking in their overall weirdness. One showed a cat wearing cat-shaped sunglasses. Another featured a man with a bird cage on his head. Still another showed a boy about to eat a banana while other children peered through the bars of a fence in envy.

Along with the bizarre artwork, the back of each booth displayed famous quotations from the sorts of people Ricky definitely would not have associated with a truck stop. They included the likes of TS Elliott, Oscar Wilde, Mark Twain, Abraham Lincoln and Ralph Waldo Emerson. The one that especially struck him was by someone named Miguel De Cervantes. It said, "He who loses wealth loses much; he who loses a friend loses more; but he that loses his courage loses all." Ricky had already lost some wealth. His courage had been dealt a blow too. And although he hadn't lost Carl, he couldn't help wondering how much his partner could still be counted on.

Figuring he still had a few minutes before his food arrived, Ricky pushed his coffee cup aside, pulled out the piece of paper, and with shaking hands, smoothed it out on the table in front of him. Someone, a murderer presumably, knew far too much about his business and his dealings with Andrew Cullen. The evidence was all there. The first few lines read like a run-of-the-mill suicide note. Cullen apologized to his wife, his kids and his friends for being such an asshole. He expressed deep regrets, but just like the first time he'd read it, Ricky noticed that he didn't go into detail about any of the things he'd done. It was all very general, like someone had googled suicide note template and then filled in the blanks. But then the tone changed, and it was the final paragraph that made his blood run cold.

I didn't know where to turn, he read. *I made mistakes and put my family at risk. I was desperate to make things right. Seeing no alternative, I went to Ricky Fixx, a man I've known for many years.*

Fucking liar! Ricky thought, even though he already knew Andrew Cullen was not really the note's author.

Ricky calls himself a businessman but he's really just scum. He loan sharks, runs some hookers, sells drugs and is involved in numerous other illegal activities. I know this because we were once friends.

Ricky balled his hands into fists but continued to read.

Our lives went in different directions but I'm ashamed to say that we did keep in touch. When I hit rock bottom, I knew Ricky could and would help. He loaned me money which I paid back in due course. He was not satisfied, demanding that I pay more. I refused and he became angry. He made threats, but I was afraid to go to the police because I knew they'd discover the things I'd done. I couldn't live with that and I knew there was only one way out. I'm sorry.

Ricky read and reread the final few sentences, pinching the bridge of his nose while the words swam before his eyes. The note was signed, and even though Ricky didn't think he'd ever seen Cullen's signature, he knew damn well it wasn't his. How could it be? Even if the guy was that scared, which Ricky thought was bullshit, Cullen hadn't gone out for a late night run, returned to his office, sent that totally fucked up text about their deal being off, and then somehow broken his own neck. The text proved Cullen had something on his mind, unless....

Ricky closed his eyes, his head spinning. The note was obviously bogus. So what if the text was too? Could it be?

"Here we go."

Ricky was so startled that he snapped to attention, in the process banging a knee against the bottom of the table and causing the flatware to jump.

"Are you okay?" the waitress asked, looking toward the counter as if she wasn't sure she was safe.

"I'm uh... I'm fine," Ricky said, straightening his tie and giving his best effort at a smile. "Sorry about that." He picked up a napkin and wiped at a puddle of coffee that had sloshed out of his cup. "I was doing some paperwork and I guess I sort of forgot where I was."

"Must be important stuff." She came forward and her gaze dropped to the tabletop. Ricky noticed and swept the paper out of sight.

She looked at him strangely. "I've got your breakfast." She placed a couple plates in front of him. "Can I get you anything else?"

"Not just now," Ricky said. "And I don't mean to seem rude. I'm a lawyer." He gestured at his suit coat like that might give validity to his claim. "I've got a big case today and I need to keep everything confidential. You understand."

"Sure," her clouded expression making it plain she was ready to end their conversation. "I'll just get your check then."

Once she was gone, Ricky began nibbling at a piece of rye toast. He realized he didn't have much of an appetite. He again thought about Cullen's text. It had seemed weird at the time. In fact, it made no sense at all. Both the content and the timing were odd. That was assuming the message had actually come from Cullen. Initially, Ricky had no reason to doubt that, but now?

He took a bite of hash browns and pushed his plate away. Just like the would-be suicide note, the text came from Cullen's killer. That was the most obvious explanation. The big question was why? For whatever reason, someone was targeting Ricky. They had wanted him to go to Cullen's office, which he had done. But once he got there, he not only discovered Cullen's body but found the note too. He actually should have seen it much sooner the way it had been left out in plain sight. Again, why? He'd removed the note, which would have been anticipated. In doing so, he'd eliminated the threat and anything that might implicate him. So what in hell was the point?

Ricky was still mulling that one when his cell phone chimed. "It's about damn time," he growled, ready to lay into Carl in a big way. But just like before, the text wasn't from him. The sender was again listed as Andrew Cullen.

Neat trick, Ricky thought, remembering how Cullen looked the last time he'd seen him.

With trepidation, he glanced at the screen. The first thing he saw was a bubble with a thumbnail image too small to make out. The second bubble contained a three-word message: *YOU FORGOT SOMETHING.*

Ricky clicked to enlarge the picture. He blinked, his throat tightening. Then, he tossed some bills on the table and ran for the door.

-60-

"How do you know he'll come back?" Bullfrog asked, hugging his knees as he sat on the tailgate of Carl's truck.

"No choice," Skid Row said, thumbs hooked into the front pockets of his jeans. "Dude's gotta be totally flipping out right now."

"But he didn't do anything."

Skid Row made a face. "We didn't do anything either and look where it got us. Perception is reality. Know what I'm sayin'?"

"Yeah, and I'm saying we got lucky. What if he'd found me in there? I would have been screwed," Bullfrog said. "Did anyone stop to think about that?"

"Chill, man. It's over."

Bullfrog shot him a look. "Easy for you to say. You didn't--"

"We were right down the hall the whole time," Carl interrupted, one foot propped up on a rear tire. "All you had to do was shout and we would have come running."

"Skid Row to the rescue? Is that supposed to make me feel safe?" Bullfrog studied the tops of his boots. "I was a sitting duck in there. We should have come up with a different plan."

"You volunteered," Skid Row said. "I think you're just pissed because I came up with such a totally epic idea."

"By my count, that brings your total up to one. And who says it was a good idea anyway?"

"Eat me," Skid Row said, freeing his right hand from his pocket so he could give Bullfrog the finger. "You think you could have come up with something better?"

"I think a house plant--"

"Enough!" Carl said, straightening up and glaring at each of them. "This isn't helping. Bullfrog, you did a nice job in there and, like Skid Row said, you did volunteer."

"What choice did I have?" He jabbed a thump at Skid Row. "He's never used an iPhone. He probably would have set off the flash or done some other dumb ass thing."

"I could have gone in," Carl said. "I told you I would."

Bullfrog stared at him. "I'm picturing a gorilla trying to hide behind a stop sign."

Carl wanted to be angry but really couldn't. He saw the point. As adept as he was at remaining still and quiet, his size would have made it difficult if not impossible to stay in Cullen's cramped bathroom for any length of time without giving away his position. Bullfrog hadn't wanted to do it, but he'd agreed because there was really no other way.

In truth, Carl still hadn't been crazy about sending the kid in there. If given the choice, he would have preferred to set Cullen's iPhone up somewhere out of sight, start recording video and then just sit back and wait for Ricky to walk in and incriminate himself. Video requires a lot of memory, though, and there was a good chance it would run out before Ricky arrived. They couldn't risk it. They'd talked about setting up their little sting elsewhere, but once Skid Row found the phone, wallet, and then Cullen's keys, doing it at his office made the most sense.

"He's got like two hundred bucks here," Bullfrog had argued, flipping through Cullen's billfold. "That would get us quite a ways down the road."

They'd discussed it, and Carl did his best to keep his comments to himself. In the end, and much to his relief, Skid Row and Bullfrog decided to hang around for the same reason they hadn't left already. Without some real resolution, they thought they might never get Ricky off their backs.

As uncomfortable as Carl was letting Bullfrog do the dirty work, no matter what happened, he didn't think he'd be in serious danger. Ricky was, by nature, a pussy. His sharp tongue was his deadliest weapon. However, he'd never been threatened before, not like this, and Carl couldn't be sure how he'd react if he happened to find Bullfrog lying in wait. It was best to not even think about it. He knew that but of course couldn't help it.

And so he'd waited, just down the hall and around the corner, straining to listen and flinching at the slightest sound. Skid Row was there too, asking whispered questions, constantly brushing at his hair or biting his nails and making a nuisance of himself. Carl wanted to tell him to shut up and be still but was afraid that would lead to a noisy confrontation. He shushed Skid Row a few times and the guy finally got the point. He was just nervous. Carl understood that because he felt the same. He just handled the stress differently, repeatedly flexing his muscles as he worked through various scenarios in his mind. What would they do if the ruse was discovered? What if they couldn't get any good evidence? What if Ricky was wise to them already and didn't take the bait? That last possibility was the one that concerned Carl the most because, for all his faults, he knew Ricky was no idiot and wouldn't be tricked easily.

But in the end, he had appeared, making his way to the fourth floor by stair, as anticipated, and moving slowly and with great caution. Carl heard him open the stairwell door, creep down the hall and let himself into the Cyber Force offices.

The next few minutes were excruciating. Carl made a point of not consulting his watch but he could feel the seconds tick past, each one as agonizing as a quarter hour in the dentist's chair. He kept expecting to hear cries for help or some other signs of struggle. He longed to find out what in hell was taking so long and might have gone to look if not for Skid Row's surprisingly determined grip on his arm.

"Relax," he'd whispered. "It'll be all right."

Carl wanted to believe him but he'd picked up on the note of tension in Skid Row's voice. He was scared too, and why not? It seemed like Ricky had been in there far too long. What could he possibly be doing? Unfortunately, it was only too easy to imagine him seeing through their scheme, finding Bullfrog's hiding spot and then....

Carl didn't have the chance to finish that thought because the door flew open again and Ricky was out and making his way back down the hall, his quick, labored steps expressing his eagerness to get away. Carl risked a peek and was thrilled to see Ricky limping toward the elevator, a familiar-looking sheet of Cyber Force letterhead clutched in one hand. Carl held his breath, afraid Bullfrog would reveal himself too soon but he remained hidden and the only sounds were Ricky's low curses punctuated by repeated mashings of the elevator button. After only a few seconds the elevator arrived with a soft ding. The doors slid open, closed again and Ricky was gone.

"Can I make an observation?" Skid Row asked, hopping onto the tailgate and squatting down next to Bullfrog. "We got what we wanted, right? So there's no need to get our undies in a bunch. It's all good."

Bullfrog frowned at him but Carl could see his heart wasn't in it. Skid Row must have sensed that too. He put a hand on Bullfrog's shoulder and after a few seconds they were both smiling. Carl was feeling pretty good about things too, because for the first time he could remember, he'd actually put one over on his boss.

"Let's see it again," Bullfrog said, reaching a hand out for Cullen's phone.

Carl gave it to him and Bullfrog used an index finger to scroll through the images. The first two weren't great. They showed Ricky in Cullen's doorway and then in the middle of the office. In the first one, Cullen couldn't be seen at all, and in the second, he was just visible in the corner of the frame but his face was in shadow.

"I never thought of that," Carl said, watching over Bullfrog's shoulder. "The way we positioned that lamp made it tough for you to get anything good."

""For a while, I didn't think I'd get anything at all. The angle sucked and I couldn't open the bathroom door any further. He would have noticed. I just waited, snapping pictures and hoping for the best."

"Fucking epic," Skid Row said.

Bullfrog continued to scroll. "I figured Ricky would walk over to the desk right away. Instead, he just stood there in the middle of the room, carrying on a conversation like he actually thought Cullen would answer him."

"He didn't know he was dead?" Skid Row asked.

"Not at first. I guess the lighting made it hard to tell."

"That was the point," Carl said.

"I know but," Bullfrog shrugged. "It looked pretty damn obvious even from where I was."

"You see what you want to see," Skid Row said, his tone surprisingly serious.

Carl looked over, not sure if Skid Row was a flake, as he often appeared, or if the kid had a little more going on upstairs then he let on.

"So what was Ricky saying?" he asked, turning to Bullfrog.

"Not much." He ran a hand over his mouth. "He said, 'Nice place,' or something like that, and then I think he said, 'Don't mind if I do.'"

"What's that mean?"

"I'm not sure. He was kind of facing the bar. Maybe he was going to make a drink."

"That sounds like Ricky," Carl said. "Anything else?"

"Yeah. He called Cullen a dumb bastard, or something along those lines. But by that point, I'm pretty sure he knew he was dead."

"Why do you say that?"

Bullfrog rocked back on his heels. "Body language I guess. He sort of stiffened, and that's when he went over to Cullen and I got that other picture. Here it is. He held the phone out.

Carl peered at the small image even though he'd seen it several times already. Ricky's face was in profile but as clear as it could be given the lighting. He had an arm extended and may have actually been touching Cullen's shoulder. It was Cullen's head that made this particular picture worth a thousand words, or a possible life sentence. It was tilted at a sickening angle and obviously falling forward. Carl shuddered involuntarily.

"I didn't think we'd get anything like that," he said, mostly to himself. "I was hoping for one clear shot that showed them both in Cullen's office."

"So we got the bonus plan," Skid Row said. "And thanks to my man Bullfrog here, I'd say Ricky is thoroughly fucked."

"You got that right," and Carl wondered if Bullfrog's picture was a little too good. He definitely wanted Ricky scared, but not so totally panicked he'd become irrational.

"You know," he said, biting his lower lip. "We might have enough right here."

"Come again, Holmes." Skid Row leaned in so he could look at the picture again. "Are you saying we should just back off?"

"No," Carl said, although he wasn't sure. "I guess I mean that we might not need to do anything more."

"We've gotta do something," Bullfrog said. "We sent the picture, and by now, I'm sure Ricky has seen it."

"Right," Carl said. "And he might be ready to make a deal. It does look pretty bad for him."

"Bad enough that he won't try to use whatever he's got on you?" Bullfrog jumped down from the tailgate and began walking back and forth behind Carl's truck. "Remember," he said. "Ricky still doesn't know where that picture came from. As far as he knows, Andrew Cullen sent it."

Carl opened his mouth but Bullfrog kept talking.

"I know," he said, waving a hand. "Unless Ricky is an idiot, he's figured out Cullen didn't send the text, the picture, or write that suicide note. He also knows someone is trying to set him up. He probably assumes Cullen was murdered. That's definitely how it looked."

"And that's what I mean," Carl argued. "We may not need to do anything more."

Bullfrog stared at him. "You're missing the point," he said. The one thing Ricky doesn't know is that we're behind it all. As soon as we tip our hand, we're going to lose a lot of leverage unless we play it just right."

"Why do you say that?"

"Simple," Bullfrog said. "You're scared of him and he knows it. If he can, he'll use that against you."

"The little dude's correct," Skid Row said. "We can't take any chances with him."

"But he wouldn't..." Carl began but then clamped his mouth shut because he knew better. The sad truth was that Ricky Fixx would stop at nothing to save his own ass. At times, he'd gone to ridiculous extremes out of spite or for no other reason than to prove that he could. It was a power trip or something and Skid Row and Bullfrog were a perfect example of his pure yet often senseless vindictiveness. He had nothing to gain from hounding them but he'd done it just the same.

Carl was parked under a bridge, and he realized they were only a block or two from Skid Row and Bullfrog's original camp. It seemed like so long ago since he'd snuck in and made off with that gym bag. Had it really only been a few days? So much had changed, and it was all because of the accidental death of one lowlife pusher. Carl hadn't meant to kill Marco. He hadn't really wanted to hurt him at all. Yet that one act was what brought Skid Row and Bullfrog to Ricky's doorstep and everything else followed.

It's my fault, Carl thought, and he knew he'd have to see it through until he was sure they'd be safe.

He gazed off in the general direction of Cullen's office and wondered what Ricky was doing right then. As Bullfrog suggested, it was a good bet he'd already seen the photo. What was his next move most likely to be?

Carl's phone vibrated in his back pocket. He scowled but left his hands on his hips. Ricky's calls and texts were something he should have considered but, in the stress of moving Cullen, helping Bullfrog compose the note and all the rest, that one little detail had sort of slipped through the cracks.

He didn't have to read the latest text to know what Ricky wanted. He was looking for help and probably wondering why he hadn't heard from his partner. Unfortunately, there was no good way Carl could respond. What was he supposed to say at—he checked his watch—four thirty-six a.m.? That he was busy? Ricky wouldn't buy it, which meant Carl had to ignore him. That, he knew, would piss Ricky off to no end and may well be making him suspicious.

Nothing to be done about that, he thought, reaching into his pocket and powering the phone down so he wouldn't be bothered anymore. They'd forced Ricky's hand. He hoped so anyway. And soon enough, Ricky would find out his anger and suspicions were the least of his problems.

"Let's roll," he said, climbing into his truck and starting the engine.

Skid Row and Bullfrog slid onto the seat next to him. "Back to Cyber Force?" Skid Row asked.

Carl shook his head as he pulled a tight U-turn. "Like you said, we can't take chances. That means we shouldn't show ourselves too soon."

"So what are we doing?"

Carl looked at them. "We're going to let him walk into a trap there's no way out of."

-61-

"Bitch! BITCH! BITCH!"

Ricky threw his cell phone and watched it bounce off of the dashboard, strike the window and then land on the floor on the passenger side of the car. He hoped it was broken. What good was the damn thing anyway? He'd already been delivered a double dose of bad news that morning, and it wasn't like his fat ass, good-for-nothing, dickhead of a partner was going to take any of his calls. Where was that son of a fuckstick anyway? Ricky had bent over backwards to get Carl's sorry hide out of one jam after another. He rarely saw any gratitude and now that he needed help, the big jerk was nowhere to be found.

"Thanks for nothing," Ricky said, dropping the Lexus into gear and peeling away from the truck stop. He'd only eaten a few bites of his breakfast, which he thought was probably for the best because the sight of that photo made him sick to his stomach. The image was a little off center and the lighting wasn't good but Ricky was able to make out his own face plain as day. Of course the star attraction was Andrew Cullen, and if the person viewing the picture didn't know any better, they would probably assume Ricky had just killed him.

I didn't do it! he screamed silently, knowing that line would sound even more ridiculous to the cops than it did inside his own head.

He checked the speedometer and saw that he'd accelerated to nearly sixty, in a thirty-five mile an hour zone no less. Ricky looked for flashing lights as he eased off the gas. The last thing he needed was to get pulled over, especially with Cullen's damn note sitting right there on the seat next to him. He may as well hand the police a signed confession. Ricky didn't know why he still had the note with him but knew he'd better tear it up, burn it up, or flush it down as soon as he could.

For a little while, he'd almost convinced himself that disposing of that one piece of evidence was all he needed to do. A simple click of his lighter and he'd eradicate the only shred of physical proof connecting him to Andrew Cullen. Ricky mentally congratulated himself on handling that situation so well. How many other people would have been that cool and collected under pressure? Oh, sure, he'd about jumped out of his skin when Cullen did his impression of a fucking bobble-head but Ricky thought he got himself under control pretty damn quick given the circumstances.

He knew what was supposed to happen. He'd figured it out before he'd even made it out of the building. It was real cute too. He was supposed to stroll in, see Cullen sitting there with his broken neck, totally freak out and run away with his tail between his legs. Then, when the body was later discovered by some unfortunate member of his staff, probably that smoking hot secretary with the world class caboose, the cops would be called in and Ricky would be toast. They'd find the suicide note, if that's even what it was intended to be, along with his fingerprints every-damn-where. He'd never be able to talk his way out. Hell, his only alibis for the night were Carl, wherever he was, the ancient bar tender at Uncle Tony's and the large quantity of alcohol he consumed while he was there. He would have been framed like Roger fucking Rabbit. Again, that's what was supposed to happen. But Ricky was smarter than whoever was trying to set him up. He'd found the note, taken it away with him and that put him in the clear, or so he'd thought until his phone chimed, he'd gotten a look at that picture, and realized how totally screwed he was.

Gripping the steering wheel as he headed back downtown, he thought again about the placement of the note: on top of the desk, right out in the open and practically under a fucking spot light. Ricky was meant to see it. He understood that now. He also understood that he'd been an idiot. The whole thing had so obviously been staged. How had he not picked up on that? And there was something else too. The note itself was crap and even an imbecile could tell Cullen hadn't written it. So why was it there at all? That was the question he should have asked himself, but in his haste to get away, he'd failed to do so.

Ricky knew the score now, well after the fact and far too late to do anything about it. That initial text summoning him to the Cyber Force office had not actually come from Andrew Cullen. Someone had gotten hold of his phone. Now that he was starting to connect the dots, Ricky knew he should have realized that sooner. In a way, he supposed he had. He'd at least recognized that the message was out of character. And regardless of the circumstances, why would Cullen ever want to meet in the middle of the night? Quite simply, he wouldn't. But Ricky hadn't thought it through because he'd been too focused on getting his money.

He groaned, knowing he'd been played like a damn drum. So the text was to get him to the office. He'd followed instructions, but what choice did he have with a hundred large on the line? Ricky didn't think he should beat himself up too much for that one. But Cullen's note?

That part was slick and Ricky grimaced because he had to give credit where credit was due. That seemingly incriminating sheet of paper was nothing more than a well-worded distraction. As intended, he'd seen it, read it, and then reacted exactly the way he was supposed to, fleeing the scene rather than taking the time to poke around.

Things could have worked out very differently. Hell, they almost had. Before he realized Andrew Cullen was no more, Ricky had considered making a drink and then doing a little reconnoiter, just because he could. He thought about the layout of the office, and in particular, the door on his right as he walked in. He remembered how it was cracked open just so, and that odd feeling that he was being watched. He'd clearly been right, and Ricky wondered how things might have turned out if he'd acted on impulse and gone to see who was hiding back there.

He glanced at his phone, still face down on the floor of the car. He could delete the image and the texts, but deleting something doesn't make it go away. Just ask Hilary Clinton about that. The only way Ricky could really ensure his safety was to somehow track down Cullen's phone and whoever had it and put them both out of commission. That would take some time, which meant he had a little cleanup work to do first.

Ricky knew Cullen's staff would show up around eight or so. Call it seven just to be safe. Technically, that still gave him over two hours to do what had to be done. He couldn't take anywhere near that long, though, because he knew the downtown area would start to wake up even before sunrise. The one thing he couldn't chance was witnesses so he planned to be well on his way by the time the clock struck five. That only gave him thirteen minutes but he thought that would be plenty. His task was simple enough. When Cullen's people arrived, Ricky needed to be sure they didn't find anything out of the ordinary or have any immediate cause to raise the alarm.

It's got to be the money, he thought, grinding his teeth so hard his jaw was starting to ache. Why else would anyone go to such lengths to mess with him? Get a little dirt, apply the pressure and demand a payoff. *Nothing like some good old-fashioned extortion.* As a businessman, Ricky actually admired the ploy and had done similar things once or twice himself, although never to such an elaborate extent. He preferred to rely less on subtlety and more on fear and Carl's brute strength. Whoever was pushing his buttons would find that out soon enough.

"Carl, old buddy," Ricky muttered, slowing to make a turn. "That's how you're gonna repay your debt." *And this time*, he decided. *You don't have to hold back. You can kill the son of a bitch with my blessing.*

Unfortunately, that couldn't happen until he identified the son of a bitch in question. For whatever reason, Ricky felt sure he was dealing with just one guy and didn't think it would be difficult to track him down. After all, how many people knew anything about his arrangement with Cullen? The only person Ricky told was Carl and he'd already ruled him out. It wasn't because of the broken neck. That was just the sort of thing Carl would do, although probably by accident. However, he'd made it clear he thought they should be leaving Andrew Cullen alone. Carl always wore his heart on his sleeve so Ricky knew he was serious. But even if Cullen and Carl had some sort of coincidental run-in with a tragic outcome, it would never occur to Carl to try to pin it on him. He'd have no reason to think like that and wouldn't be smart enough to pull it off anyway.

Ricky thought about it and decided there was only one other possibility. Cullen, the pompous asshole, had confided in someone. That had to be it. And then that person, seeing an opportunity, either turned on him or shared his secret with somebody else. It didn't matter which way it happened. The only thing that did matter was who.

One of the employees? Ricky shook his head, immediately dismissing the idea. Any rumors of financial troubles could put the whole business on shaky ground. Cullen wouldn't risk that. So who did that leave?

A friend? An exercise partner? Someone like... him? That gave Ricky pause. Would Cullen really go to one loan shark to try to deal with another? It didn't seem likely, but how likely was it that someone in Andrew Cullen's position would consort with criminals in the first place? He'd found Ricky, and plenty of other people were in the same line of work. You couldn't find them in the Yellow pages. That type of business was all word of mouth. You had to know a guy who knew a guy. Cullen apparently knew a guy, or so it seemed. Ricky wasn't holding out much hope he'd find a name, address or phone number, but since he had to return to the office anyway, it couldn't hurt to open a drawer or two to see what turned up.

He checked his rear view mirror, then checked it again until he was satisfied he wasn't being followed. A Pepsi delivery truck chugged past and turned the corner a block ahead. Otherwise, the street was pretty well vacant. Ricky wanted to park somewhere out of sight but he knew that would make his job tougher and more dangerous. There was no time for stealth. He had to get in and get out, and the quicker the better.

His palms sweaty, he stopped his car right in front of Cyber Force Technology. Ricky looked up at Cullen's window and saw that his light was still on and still casting that strange shadow. Everything else appeared just as it had the first time he'd been there. The watcher was presumably gone, but Ricky would verify that as soon as he got inside. He'd made too many mistakes already and swore he wouldn't make any more. He waited a beat, took a breath and pushed open his car door.

Ricky didn't want to run so he moved with what he hoped looked like determination and purpose. If anyone asked, he had a lot to do and wanted to get an early start on the day. He was a very busy man. He was also a man with a bum foot and that made it hard to walk with anything resembling authority. He hoped he wouldn't have much trouble when it came to the heavy lifting. Then Ricky had a sobering thought and it almost stopped him in his tracks. The front door of Cyber Force had been left open for him before. What if it was locked now? What if Cullen was still up there and Ricky had no way to get to him?

"I'll fucking break in," he said, legs trembling as he mounted the steps. He looked around and saw that there were ground floor windows circling the building. He knew he could gain access that way if he had to, but was it worth doing something that desperate? Maybe he'd get lucky and Cullen's time of death, once determined, would prove he had nothing to do with it. On the other hand, the lousy prick might have got his neck broken sometime after Ricky left the bar, when there was no longer anyone around who could vouch for his whereabouts. One thing he knew for sure. With his history with the cops, no one was about to give him the benefit of the doubt. Unless he came up with some way to establish his innocence, there was a good chance he was going down.

Thinking a rear-facing window would give him the best shot at breaking in unseen, Ricky tried the door, already knowing it would be locked tight. Instead, the knob turned easily in his hand. He breathed a shocked sigh of relief, glanced up and down the street and let himself into the lobby. Ricky rode the elevator to the fourth floor and less than two minutes later pushed open the door to Cullen's office.

He knew what to expect but was still surprised when he saw Cullen slumped in his desk chair, his head lolled forward so far it seemed to defy the laws of physics that his whole body hadn't toppled to the ground. Ricky couldn't see his eyes, thankfully, but thought Cullen's posture looked more rigid than he remembered. He supposed that might have been his imagination. It was also possible that rigor mortis stuff was already setting in. How long did that take anyway? How long did it last? Ricky didn't know but it was going to be a lot harder to do what had to be done if Cullen was stiff as a board. One way or another, he'd have to make it happen.

There was, he realized, one benefit to coming back there. He could cover his tracks a little better. He'd left in a hurry before and might have left a stray fingerprint or some other bit of evidence behind. He could take care of that now and—Ricky snapped his fingers as an idea dawned—maybe stage his own murder scene. Someone was trying hard to set him up. What if he could find a way to turn the tables?

For some reason, he was still staring at Andrew Cullen, specifically a small patch of pale flesh at the top of his forehead and right on the edge of his receding hairline. He hadn't noticed it before but the skin appeared to be slightly discolored and, Ricky thought, a little swollen. *What the heck?* Had someone popped him, and done it hard enough to snap his neck? Ricky again thought of Carl and again decided that was stupid. But what had happened? How had Cullen managed to get himself killed and why had it suddenly become Ricky's problem? He felt like the answer was right there in front of him but knew he couldn't stand around trying to figure it out. With effort, he tore his eyes away so he could concentrate on the job at hand.

Ricky surveyed the room. This time, he was going to make sure it really was empty. The door that had been slightly ajar before was open wider now, as if he needed more proof someone had been there. Ricky peered into the darkness but couldn't make out much more than the edge of the white tile floor.

Bathroom, he thought, moving a step closer. He took another step and then froze when he saw the outline of a man. He was dressed in a suit and tie and, based on the height of the tie knot, had to be at least six and a half feet tall.

Holy fuck! Ricky thought, shrinking away and looking frantically around for a weapon. *What was the guy still doing there?* He had to be the picture taker. Had he been waiting around in hopes Ricky would return? If so, why?

Ricky didn't know what to do. He glanced toward the outer door and then at his gimpy foot. Not much chance for a quick escape, but maybe that wouldn't be necessary. It occurred to him that the guy hadn't made a move yet. That was strange. Even if he somehow hadn't seen him, he must have at least heard Ricky come in. So why was he still standing there? *Simple*, Ricky thought. *He didn't know I was coming back and he wants no part of me now. Bright boy.*

Feeling slightly emboldened, he leaned forward to try to get a better look at who he was dealing with. The build was unfamiliar, long and lean as best Ricky could tell, but the position of the bathroom door along with the interior darkness made it impossible for him to see anything above the neck or below the waist, unless he wanted to get a whole lot closer.

Ricky thought he had the upper hand but the obvious size difference still made him nervous. He needed something to help level the playing field. *A bottle of booze?* Cullen's bar was well stocked and some of the bottles looked pretty hefty. One solid thunk to the side of the head and the fight would be over. The only problem was that the bar was a little too far away and Ricky couldn't get there without turning his back. *Plan B?*

He looked for other options and, after a few seconds of seeing nothing usable, his eyes fell on the statuette he'd brought up from the lobby the first time he'd been there. Ricky remembered concealing it inside his shirt. It must have fallen out and, in his panicked exodus, he hadn't even noticed.

Fucking beautiful, he thought, figuring the thing had his DNA all over it. That would have been one more nail in his coffin.

It was halfway under one of Cullen's visitor chairs and several feet from where Ricky stood. To retrieve it, he'd pretty much have to walk right in front of the bathroom door. He debated, and finally decided that was his best option. He just needed to play it cool and casual. Whoever was in the bathroom obviously planned on staying there. That was fine. Ricky would go about his business as if he'd never seen him. The guy wouldn't know any better until it was too late.

The plan worked in theory but Ricky soon realized how damn near impossible it was to act casual when you're in a room with a corpse. There was nothing he could do that would appear natural or normal to anyone watching. Ricky still did his best, taking a couple steps and then dropping to one knee while muttering something about his shoe lace. He retrieved the statue, stood, paused as if deep in thought, and then turned and lunged for the bathroom.

He had it all choreographed in his head: two long strides, then yank the door open with his right hand while swinging the statue with his left. He would have preferred to attack right-handed but the positioning would have been wrong, and it turned out not to matter anyway. In the excitement of the moment, he again forgot about his bad foot. He put weight on it, lost his balance, and crashed into the door with his shoulder. It slammed shut with Ricky on one side and the mystery man on the other. So much for the element of surprise.

Ricky thought about just leaving but he was in deep and knew he had to see it through. He gathered himself and flung the door open, his arm already cocked to strike. There just wasn't anybody there, unless you counted the finely tailored navy blue suit hanging on a hook on the bathroom wall. Ricky had seen the reflection in the mirror over the sink and naturally assumed it was a person.

"FUCK!" he screamed, hurling the statue at the mirror and watching both shatter into a million pieces. Then he collapsed against the door frame when he realized what he'd done. So much for searching the office to try to figure out who was targeting him. So much for covering his tracks. He had no choice now but to get the hell out of there.

-62-

Ricky stood in the bathroom doorway, his heart pounding at what felt like five times its normal rate. He was such a schmuck. A harmless reflection of Cullen's freaking dry cleaning and he'd totally flipped out. The lighting was poor and that, Ricky supposed, was at least partially responsible for his momentary lapse in judgment. It still didn't come close to justifying how royally he'd just screwed up.

He took a step back so he could get a better look at the damage. To his surprise, he saw that the mirror's decorative frame was not only still in place but looked perfectly straight, not that it would do anyone any good anymore. All the glass was in shards. Some had fallen into the sink or onto the countertop but most were scattered in a large, glittering arc on the floor. Ricky noticed bits of the broken statue too. He stooped and gingerly picked up a few of the larger pieces and slipped them into his coat pocket. He didn't think any of the others were big enough to hold a fingerprint but he ground them under his heel just the same. There wasn't much he could do about the rest of the mess. He definitely wasn't about to start touching everything. Ricky considered, and then used a foot to slide all the glass into the corner behind the door. He then pulled the door closed with the hope no one would open it again for a while.

He checked his watch and saw that it was five minutes to five. *Damn!* When he'd entered the office, Ricky only had three objectives. They weren't complicated and he hadn't anticipated problems. First, he wanted to give the place a good wipe down. Second, time permitting, he'd open a few desk drawers and see if he could figure out who Cullen had been spouting off to. Third, and most important, he needed to get the body out of there. Ricky knew that last part would involve some risk, especially when it came to transferring Cullen from building to car. Like it or not, that was a risk he had to take and he was fully prepared. What Ricky hadn't prepared for was being freaked out by an empty fucking suit. And now, two thirds of his brilliant plan was down the drain.

Of course, five o'clock wasn't a hard deadline. He figured he could safely take ten or even fifteen minutes to search the office and obliterate any trace evidence. He knew he should do those things, but couldn't shake the disquieting feeling that every extra tick of the second hand increased the chance he'd be caught.

"It's your fault!" he said, grabbing the back of Cullen's big leather desk chair and pushing it toward the door. "You could have paid me when you were supposed to and saved us both some trouble."

Cullen's head bobbed sickeningly as his chair bounced over the threshold but he otherwise gave no response.

"Lot of help you are."

Ricky shoved him into the reception area and then returned to the office. He didn't have time to do what he'd wanted to, but knew he should at least make things look as normal as possible. The secretary would obviously notice her boss wasn't there, but Ricky wanted her to assume he was just late for work. Between his drinking, gambling and exercise schedule, he doubted a late arrival was a rare occurrence.

Feeling the stress of every passing moment, he used his sleeve and hurriedly wiped at the bathroom doorknob, the edge of Cullen's desk and both arms of the visitor's chairs even though he couldn't remember touching either one. *Better safe than behind bars.* He then adjusted Cullen's desk lamp, although he had no idea how it was normally positioned.

Once that was done, Ricky searched the floor to make sure there were no more telltale pieces of paper with his name written all over them. He saw nothing so he stood in the middle of the room, turning a complete circle to see if anything else looked out of place. As far as he could tell, Cullen's office appeared no different than any other. Whoever went into the bathroom would realize something had happened there. Maybe they'd think Cullen was drunk and broke the mirror himself. Ricky couldn't worry about that now. He just needed to cover his ass, which he thought he'd done. After one last glance around, he returned to the desk, used his sleeve to turn off the light, and then crossed to the door, pulled it closed and wiped the knob free of prints.

Satisfied, he breathed a small sigh of relief, feeling like he was a little closer to extricating himself from the pile of shit he'd somehow stepped into. Of course, he knew he still had an avalanche of crap hanging just over his head. That would be the case until he figured out who'd sent him that picture. If only he'd had more time to search the office....

Ricky shook his head, as if doing so could make all his problems disappear. He told himself it was all about keeping things in perspective. He could do what needed to be done as long as he stayed a step ahead of whoever had put the crosshairs on him. And once Cullen was permanently out of the picture, *pun intended,* the real picture wouldn't pose as much of a threat. Sure, it might look bad—Ricky's hands on a very dead-looking guy--but that didn't prove a thing.

He paused, blinking in the dimness of the windowless reception area. The only sources of light were a series of small yellow and green indicators on some sort of electronic device on the desk. He assumed computer modem, router or docking station. They gave off a soft glow which, once his eyes adjusted, was enough to see his way to the door without falling on his face. He could also make out the amorphous shape of Cullen in his desk chair. Ricky was a little disappointed, thinking how convenient it would have been if someone had come along and ferried him away. He didn't have that kind of luck and knew he'd have to deal with the S.O.B. on his own.

Already feeling ridiculously exposed, Ricky grasped the big chair once more, maneuvered it to the door and, after looking right and left, pushed it out into the hallway. He again did his bit with the sleeve and the doorknob and then hurried toward the elevator. This was the part he'd been dreading most because he was so out in the open. If anyone should come along, there wasn't a single thing he could do. It wasn't "Weekend at Bernie's." He couldn't pretend Andrew Cullen was still alive, not with his head flopping around like a rag doll. Anyone with one good eye would immediately realize he was dead.

Ricky kept both of his eyes trained on the elevator doors. The whole building was empty. He knew that, or at least thought he did. The only sounds he could hear were his own footsteps, the occasional creak of leather from his hands against the chair back, and the slight whir and hiss of the chair wheels as they rolled over the carpet. The elevator itself was stone silent, and as Ricky drew near, he could both see and hear that it was not in use. He still couldn't help thinking the doors were about to slide open and a dozen cops would spill out. And if that happened, he would have no choice but to abandon Cullen right there and make a mad dash for the stairwell.

Ricky pushed the button, flinched when he heard the elevator start moving and actually jumped backwards when the doors finally did open in front of him. He took a breath and shoved Cullen inside.

The ride to the lobby seemed to take an eternity. All the while Ricky questioned the sanity of what he was doing. Up to that point, he'd committed no crimes, at least not when it came to Andrew Cullen and his premature passing. Ricky still had no idea what happened to him but something told him it hadn't taken place in the office. Everything was too clean and orderly. So he wasn't even guilty of interfering with a crime scene, unless whoever deposited Cullen there left some fingerprints behind that Ricky had later wiped away. Destroying evidence might be a felony but it didn't hold a candle to murder. What, he wondered, would happen if he left Cullen in the elevator and just walked away? He'd eventually hear from the picture sender and he or she or they would make some sort of demand, probably for money. If Ricky refused to pay, the picture would presumably be sent to the police. Would it be enough to put him away? Ricky didn't know, and that was why he had no choice but to see his plan through to the end.

He hadn't yet decided where he'd take Cullen, mainly because it didn't matter unless and until he could get him out of the building, into his car and away without anyone spotting him. That, Ricky knew, would be far easier said than done. He didn't have to cover much distance. He could see his car through the lobby window and it was no more than twenty feet away. However, he'd somehow have to get Cullen out of his chair, down the few steps to street level and then into his back seat. Ricky was no wimp. He did work out on rare occasions and considered himself pretty fit. He was also less than a hundred percent because of his foot and Andrew Cullen outweighed him by a good fifty or sixty pounds. It was all dead weight too. Moving him would be like moving a refrigerator. Ricky thought about how much he could use Carl's help. He also knew no help was coming. The idiot must have turned off his phone or left it in his truck when he'd gone home and gone to bed. Whatever lame ass excuse he came up with, Ricky wouldn't accept it but instead do everything he could to make Carl sorry. That, unfortunately, wouldn't help him at the moment. He had to try to focus only on those things he could control.

Ricky dug into his pants pocket and pressed the button on the key fob to unlock his car doors. He then moved to the window and peered outside, wanting to make sure there was no one in the vicinity. Passing traffic was always a possibility and one he couldn't do a damn thing about. He'd just have to be cautious, time it right and hope to get lucky for a change. In all likelihood, any cars going by would be traveling quickly enough and the occupant or occupants wouldn't give him a second look. Pedestrians were a different story. If someone was walking by when he exited the Cyber Force building, Andrew Cullen slung over his shoulder, there was no way that would go unnoticed.

At first, Ricky didn't see anything more intimidating than a few bags of garbage stacked on the curb awaiting pickup. Then, as he was about to turn away, his gaze fell upon a blanketed figure crumpled in a doorway on the opposite side of the road and at the far end of the block.

"Shit," he said, cupping a hand over his eyes and leaning against the glass to try to get a better look. It was too dark and too far away to make out much. He saw a boot, part of one leg, and everything else was hidden under a brownish blanket or tarp.

"Loser," Ricky whispered, knowing the guy had to be a hobo, a wino, or some other total waste of humanity.

He watched a minute longer, looking for movement or any signs of life. He saw none, which supported his wino theory. The shit bag was probably either dead or passed out drunk. Ricky was relieved, but still not crazy about walking out there when someone was close enough to observe. He really had no choice, so studied the short stretch of sidewalk from door to car as he worked out what he'd do next.

As it turned out, Cullen was even heavier than he'd expected. He tried to lift him out of the chair and got nowhere. Swallowing his revulsion, Ricky leaned down and worked his hands under Cullen's arms and around his back until he had him in what amounted to a sitting bear hug. He braced himself, all the while trying to ignore Cullen's odor of dried sweat, stale cologne and what smelled like urine. He'd have to shampoo his car once this was all over with. Better yet, he'd make Carl do it, preferably with his fucking tongue.

Ricky heaved, lifting up and back simultaneously and managing to get Cullen about half way out of his seat. Then, the laws of physics kicked in and the chair started rolling across the marble floor. Ricky started to back pedal, but couldn't go far because his hands and arms were pinned. He tugged in a futile attempt to free himself but that only made the chair gain speed. He had just enough time to think, *oh shit,* when he, Cullen and the big desk chair all crashed into the wall. Ricky fell forward and was sprawled in Cullen's lap. He took a second to catch his breath then, realizing where he was, extricated himself as fast as he could. He stared at Cullen in disgust while brushing at his suit coat like he could wipe away all the dead guy germs.

"That bastard will be going to the dry cleaner too," Ricky said, thinking of Carl and his growing list of chores.

If Carl was there, they could load Andrew Cullen into the bed of his truck, chair and all. With neither of those things at his disposal, Ricky knew he had to come up with another plan. He also knew he was running out of time. As if he needed a reminder, he looked outside just as a Willow Run Foods truck rattled down Court Street. For some, the new business day had already begun.

Ricky again considered running away but decided he'd give it one more shot before giving into his growing sense of desperation. He knew or at least believed he could get Cullen to his car once he was out of the chair. The easiest way would be to dump his ass onto the ground and then just drag him. Of course, once he was out on the sidewalk, he'd instantly attract the attention of anyone and everyone who happened to see him. Ricky wasn't sure it would make a difference, but thought he should try to make what he was doing appear as innocent and normal as possible. That meant Cullen had to be on his feet.

"Get up , bitch," Ricky said, not relishing the idea of putting his arms around Cullen again. He sighed and looked around the lobby, hoping to find something he could use to brace the chair while he lifted Cullen out. He saw nothing so dropped to his knees to see if the chair's casters could be locked. No luck there either. Ricky heard another vehicle roll past and that was followed by a horn blast a few seconds later. He looked towards the door and knew it was now or never.

Fast and hard, he thought, moving over to stand in front of Cullen once again. He placed his right foot, the bad one, against the base of the chair with his right knee wedged against the cushion between Cullen's legs. It felt awkward but he thought it should work as long as his foot didn't give out again. He positioned his other foot a little further back and imagined what it would be like when he got Cullen up and was supporting a hundred percent of his weight. Ricky thought he'd have the proper leverage, but there was only one way to find out.

Trying not to breathe in any of Cullen's stench, he grasped him around the mid section, gathered himself and gave a mighty yank. He heard a crack, but couldn't tell if it was the chair, one of Cullen's ribs or his own muscles and tendons. Like the first time, he got Cullen half way up and was afraid he was going to lose him again.

"No!" Ricky groaned, tightening his grip and leaning backward as far as he could. It didn't seem to do much good, but he must have gotten that extra inch or two he needed because the center of gravity suddenly shifted and Cullen popped up like he was on springs.

"Fuck!" Ricky said, stumbling backwards. He managed to keep his balance but knew he wouldn't be able to keep it for long. He also knew he'd miscalculated again. He'd had this ridiculous fantasy of somehow walking Cullen out to the car. He realized now how stupid that was because Cullen's legs were no more supportive than his broken neck.

There'd be no way to keep him in a standing position for any length of time. Ricky also knew that, if he let Cullen fall, he wouldn't have the strength to pick him up again. He was already starting to lose the battle so Ricky grasped one of Cullen's wrists, did a sort of half turn, and ended up with him draped over his shoulder in something resembling a fireman's carry. That was about the best he was going to do so Ricky staggered toward the door.

No cars were going by. That was the good news, but getting Cullen into the back seat of the Lexus proved even more difficult than it had been to get him out of his chair. Ricky was carrying him over the wrong shoulder. Either that or his car doors were hinged on the wrong side. It amounted to the same problem. He got the door open, but couldn't figure out how to deposit Cullen inside unless he transferred him to the opposite shoulder, which definitely wasn't happening, or twisted his own body around so he'd basically be dumping Cullen in backwards. Neither scenario seemed to offer much of a chance at success.

Ricky was still working it through when he heard the sudden wail of a police siren. It was several blocks away but sounded like it could be headed in his direction. His legs immediately turned to Jello and he nearly dropped Cullen right there.

This is bullshit, he thought, hooking an arm behind Cullen's knees, bending forward and practically rolling him over his head and into the car. It wasn't a perfect fit. Cullen's head—or maybe it was his ass—thumped against the roof and Ricky had to do some pushing and shoving to get all his limbs inside. He did it, and even managed to shut the door without anyone seeming to notice what he was up to. All that was left was to get Cullen's desk chair and return it to his office.

Ricky took one step in that direction and heard the siren again. It was definitely closer, definitely coming his way and that was all it took for him to completely lose his nerve. Let them find the chair. Let them dust it for fingerprints. He had to go!

-63-

"There he is!" Skid Row said, pointing through the windshield with one hand while grabbing at Carl's arm with the other. "Right there—Dude, slow down!"

"What do you think I'm doing?" Carl asked, pulling his arm away. He'd been angling toward the curb even before Skid Row started going nuts and didn't need all his theatrics. "We might have a problem," he added, his eyes narrowing as he noticed something Skid Row evidently had not.

"What do you?—Oh shit!" Skid Row exclaimed, reaching for the door handle.

"Sit still," Carl ordered.

"But he's hurt!"

"No reason for you to hurl yourself out of a moving vehicle. Let me get parked."

He slid to a stop, wondering what had gone wrong. Bullfrog had been given instructions to do nothing more than observe from a safe distance. He'd seemed willing enough, and showed no desire to put himself in harm's way. Yet, it appeared that's what he'd done. As Carl looked on, Bullfrog staggered toward them, clutching his stomach and bent nearly double, tears streaming from his eyes.

Carl thought he'd been shot. He couldn't see any blood but that didn't necessarily mean anything. And it looked like Skid Row was thinking something similar. He'd gone pale, his fingers scrabbling at the door handle ineffectually. He seemed to lack the coordination required to both pull the handle and push the door open at the same time.

"I'll get him," Carl said, pushing his own door open. "You stay put."

Skid Row said something, but Carl couldn't tell if it was an actual protest or a moan of fear and anxiety. It didn't matter because Bullfrog had reached the truck. He headed for the passenger door first but then veered to one side, slumping against the bed momentarily and then peeling off the old tarp he'd used to hide under and dumping it inside. Carl watched him through the side window. Bullfrog still had a hand over his gut but he'd straightened up somewhat and seemed to be moving okay. He also wore an expression Carl couldn't interpret. His eyes were still wet but it didn't look like he was in any pain. To the contrary, it almost looked like…

"Oh my God!" Bullfrog said, yanking Skid Row's door open and practically falling into his lap. He started to say something more but then began convulsing. At least that's how it looked to Carl. His entire body shook, his breath coming out in odd little hiccups. It was scary as hell until Carl realized Bullfrog was laughing and couldn't seem to control himself.

Skid Row stared down at him, obviously not knowing what he should do.

"Are you hyperventilating?" Carl asked. "Do we need to slap you or get you a paper bag?"

Bullfrog shook his head as he pulled himself into the cab.

"Then what's your deal?" Skid Row asked, sliding over to make room on the seat. "We thought you were…I don't know, dude, but you looked pretty fucked up."

Bullfrog shook his head again, using the heel of one hand to wipe at his eyes. "You guys missed it," he said. "It was…" But then he started giggling, wheezing and choking.

Skid Row and Carl looked at him, looked at each other, shrugged, and then waited in silence for Bullfrog to pull himself together.

"First," he finally said, brushing at his eyes again and then reaching for the seatbelt. "You gotta do something about that tarp. It smells like an old chicken coop. I was afraid I'd start sneezing and give away my position."

"Sorry," Carl said. "I keep it in the back of the truck for when I'm out and I need it for camouflage or to keep warm."

"Like when you hide out in the woods so you can steal stuff from guys that never did nothin' to you?' Skid Row asked.

Carl looked at him but didn't comment.

"Listen," Bullfrog said. "I don't care what you do with it. Just wash the thing once in a while. I'm surprised Ricky couldn't smell it from all the way down the block."

"He didn't see you, did he?"

"Nah. Well, he looked my way one time but I think he had other things on his mind."

"You know I would have done it if I could," Carl said. "But with my size…" he gestured vaguely.

"I know," Bullfrog replied. "You're too well-fed to be convincing as homeless. I, on the other hand, have had a lot of practice."

"And did you get anything good?"

"You could say that. I just hope the pictures came out."

"It was dark," Carl said. "Even with all the street lights."

"I'm not talking about that." Bullfrog plucked Cullen's phone out of a front pocket and handed it over. "I know I got a good shot of Ricky coming out of the building. He had Cullen across his back. I'm just not sure what I got after that because my hand was shaking so bad."

"Why?" Skid Row asked.

"I started laughing. I've got to tell you. That was the funniest damn thing I've ever seen."

Carl stared at him. "He was moving a dead body. You find that amusing?"

"No," Bullfrog said, shaking his head, "of course not. It was just…." He paused, his eyes unfocused as if he was picturing the scene, and then the giggles started again.

"Dude," Skid Row said. "This is all sorts of fucked up. You gonna be okay?"

"Yeah." Bullfrog swallowed and sat up straighter in his seat. He kept a hand over his belly like that might help keep the laughter inside. "What happened to that guys sucks and there was nothing funny about it. I know that. It was Ricky."

"What about him?" Carl asked, beginning to scroll through the images on the phone.

"He came out just like I said. He had Cullen on his back and it looked like he was really straining."

"I'm sure of that," Carl said. "Ricky ain't built for heavy lifting."

"He was moving fast too. I don't know if that's because he was scared or because he just couldn't help it. He almost fell when they came down the steps."

"I gotta tell ya," Skid Row said. "None of this is tickling my funny bone."

"I'm getting to that. So Ricky almost makes it to his car when this police siren starts up. It had to be a good half a mile away. Anyway, he flipped out. He lost it. I guess he thought the FBI was closing in or something."

"So what'd he do?"

"He started running. For a second, I thought he was going to dump Cullen right there on the sidewalk. But then he got to his car, and I could tell he didn't know how to get him inside. Square peg and a round hole, except the peg probably weighs two hundred pounds."

Bullfrog paused and then went on. "Ricky managed to get the rear door open. I'm still not sure how. He had Cullen over one shoulder and practically upside-down. He stood there for a minute, spinning in a circle and looking totally panicked. Then they kind of tumbled into the car together. I know it wasn't funny but…" he shrugged, his eyes starting to tear up again. "It didn't even look real. You know what I mean?"

"I guess so," Carl said, squinting at one of the pictures. It showed part of a car door along with Ricky's ass and Cullen's head in uncomfortably close proximity.

"What about those sirens? Maybe someone saw Ricky and called the cops."

"If so, they never showed up, at least not while I was there. If anything, it sounded like they were moving further away."

"He must have heard it differently," Carl said, a slight smile playing at the corner of his mouth.

"Oh, I'm sure he thought they were ready to drive straight up his butt. He was definitely running scared. He got Cullen into the car and then took off like a shot."

"I wonder where he was headed," Carl said, sitting back and stroking his beard. "What do you say we find out?'

-64-

Ricky slid around a corner, punched the accelerator and sped to the end of the block. He ran a stop sign and would have run a second had it not been for the rusted Chevy van that backed out of a driveway in front of him. He swore and slammed on the brakes. Tires squealed and he heard a thud from the backseat. That would have been Andrew Cullen rolling onto the floor.

"Shit!" Ricky said, glancing at the rearview mirror. He'd been doing that every few seconds, each time expecting to see red and blue strobe lights. He saw nothing and no longer heard anything either. That should have put him at ease, but Ricky couldn't completely escape the thought that the police would all converge on him as soon as he rounded the next turn. But if the jerk-off blocking the road in front of him didn't get his ass in gear he'd never make it that far anyway.

"Come on!" Ricky said, his fingers nervously tapping the steering wheel as he waited for the van to get out of his way. He hadn't yet figured out where he was going but knew he had to get as much distance as possible between himself and Cullen's office.

The van finally started rolling, unfortunately in the same direction Ricky had been going. That meant he had to follow along at a snail's pace. He considered honking the horn or pulling a fast U-turn. Instead, fighting feelings of helplessness and frustration, he blew out a breath and thumped his head against the back of his seat. He tried to convince himself that the asshole crawling along at twelve fucking miles per hour was actually a blessing in disguise. He'd been speeding through one residential neighborhood after another, ignoring every traffic law and practically daring the cops to pull him over. That was immensely stupid, and if they did stop him, what in hell could he say? Even if he could somehow explain away the reckless driving, his story would probably fall apart once he got to the dead guy in the backseat.

Ricky reflexively checked his mirror once more. There was still nothing back there and he wondered if when he'd torn away from the Cyber Force building, the police hadn't been as close as he'd thought. So maybe he'd panicked a little. He could admit that much but who could really blame him? When he'd gone to bed, his biggest worry was the hangover he knew he'd have in the morning. All signs of that were gone, replaced by a still-throbbing right foot, a corpse he now had to deal with, and the assurance that he'd probably spend the rest of his life in jail if he made a single mistake. And that was the trouble. He'd lost his cool, and as a result, messed up on multiple levels.

Cullen's broken mirror wasn't a huge deal because there was really nothing to connect it to him. Still, the staff would realize something was up as soon as someone opened the bathroom door, which they'd do almost immediately because they'd already know something was up when they found their boss's desk chair in the fucking lobby.

Careless! Ricky thought, flipping the Lexus's air conditioner on, turning the dial to high and adjusting the vent so it blew directly onto his face. According to the thermometer, the outside temperature was only forty-two degrees but he was sweating like a pig. He undid the top button of his shirt and pulled the damp fabric away from his skin. He couldn't wait to take a cold shower and prayed it wouldn't be in a place where he was afraid to drop the soap.

The van stopped at a four-way intersection, signaled and made a right-hand turn. Ricky had planned on going straight but after a brief hesitation, he signaled and followed the Chevy. He wasn't sure why. Making such sluggish progress was maddening. However, it was giving him a chance to collect his thoughts. Ricky rationalized that the mistakes he'd made up to that point were from reacting too quickly. Maybe he'd do better if he was forced to slow down.

After having so much trouble getting Cullen into his car, not to mention the added anxiety from the wail of nearby sirens, Ricky knew he lacked the nerve to take that desk chair all the way back to the fourth floor. That didn't mean he should have left it behind. He could have tried to hide the thing, or better yet, tossed it into his trunk to dispose of later. A missing chair might be suspicious but still preferable to one that was conspicuously out of place.

He supposed it wasn't too late to go back. He thought about that and decided the risk would far outweigh any possible reward. Sure, someone would soon know Cullen was missing. They might even suspect foul play. There was still nothing to indicate the man was dead and Ricky figured it would stay that way for at least a day or two, unless his body was discovered. He needed to make sure that didn't happen and Ricky was convinced returning to Cyber Force would be playing with fire. So he knew where not to go. That was helpful but didn't address the more immediate problem of how and where to make a body disappear.

The Chevy's brake lights flashed and the van made an abrupt right-hand turn. Ricky almost followed until he realized it was the driveway to what looked like some sort of clinic. He slowed but then continued on his way, suddenly at a loss as to what to do next. He couldn't keep driving around. It would be light soon and his opportunity to ditch Cullen would be gone. He racked his brain and tried to come up with somewhere he could safely go and not have to worry about being spotted.

Ricky's first thought was the Broome County landfill. He didn't know when they opened but doubted it was before six. That should give him enough time as long as he hurried. It was plenty remote too, way the hell up Airport Road and actually not that far from Cullen's house. That had potential, and Ricky appreciated the irony of taking a piece of trash like Andrew Cullen to the dump. The more he thought about it though, the less the idea appealed to him.

For starters, he was pretty sure the place was fenced in, probably to prevent people from doing exactly the sort of thing he had in mind. There might be security cameras too. He couldn't chance that. But the main issue was logistics. Landfills were no longer big, open holes in the ground. Everything went into a dumpster which meant Cullen would have to go into a dumpster and Ricky doubted he had the strength. There was also the possibility, even the likelihood, his body would be discovered in short order. So what did that leave?

Ricky's criteria were simple. He needed someplace out of the way enough so Cullen wouldn't be found, but also where Ricky wouldn't have to lift or carry him any real distance. It had nothing to do with his foot. Cullen was just too heavy and that narrowed his options tremendously. He considered the train yard or a park or some other wooded area but ruled all of that out for lack of access. He needed to be able to just dump and run and couldn't do that at any of the places he'd considered.

Ricky drove past a sign for the Binghamton Zoo and fantasized about feeding Cullen to one of the lions. "Here kitty, kitty," he said, wishing it could be that easy. *Or*, he thought. *Maybe it could.*

His biggest problem was time. It was after five-thirty and he had less than an hour before sunrise. There was already more traffic on the road and plenty of indications the city was waking up. Ricky reminded himself that he didn't need Cullen to disappear for good but just for awhile. If he could manage to keep him out of sight at least until that night, he figured that would give him all the time he needed to arrange a proper burial. He also knew he'd have Carl by the short and curlies by then and could count on his help. That put his mind at ease and it wasn't long before Ricky came up with what he thought was a perfect solution.

He actually smiled as he made one left turn and then another, and was soon headed back downtown. To his chagrin, Ricky realized he'd been over-thinking the whole thing because he had the perfect hiding spot all along and barely had to go anywhere. In fact, if he'd thought to stuff Cullen into the trunk instead of the backseat, he could park his car wherever he wanted, lock up and walk away and have nothing to fear, at least in the short term,. As it was, he knew he'd still be okay. He just needed to take appropriate measures. The Water Street parking garage should serve his purposes quite well. He'd find a spot in a dim corner and back in so no one had a clear view into his car. Cullen was already on the floor and there was a decent chance he wouldn't be seen even if someone happened to look in. But just to be safe, Ricky decided he'd get the carpet out of the bottom of the trunk and cover him with that. It might look a little strange but not enough to cause concern.

Less than five minutes later, he was on the third floor of the garage and had already picked out his spot, against the far wall and partially blocked by a support pillar. Ricky figured he could leave his Lexus there for a month and no one would notice. Feeling extremely satisfied with himself, he parked and was about to get out of the car when his cell phone buzzed. He frowned because he'd long since given up on Carl and couldn't think of anyone else who might try to reach him at that time of the morning.

Wrong number, Ricky thought, pulling his phone out and checking the screen, which sported a new hairline crack that snaked from one corner to the other. He could still see it clearly enough, although, at the moment, he wished that wasn't the case. The text message was only three words long and all in caps just like before.

I SEE YOU.

"Mother fuck!" he said, craning in his seat and looking all around. He had a full view of the garage from one end to the other. It was completely empty. *Unless,* Ricky thought, someone was hiding in the far stairwell or ducked down behind the green Camry or old black Aerostar. No other vehicles were in sight.

Ricky stared at his phone again. It didn't seem possible! No one could have been there waiting for him because he hadn't even known where he was going until a few minutes before. Had he been followed? Ricky thought about all the times he'd checked his mirrors to see if the cops were tailing him. He'd never seen a thing. Of course, he'd been on the lookout for flashing lights and nothing else. He was still fairly certain there'd been nothing else to see. And for anyone to follow him, they'd have to know he was at Cyber Force and he hadn't seen anyone there either.

"He's just fucking with me," Ricky said. "He knows that one picture isn't enough to take me down so now he's pushing my buttons to get me to do something stupid. Well it ain't gonna work!"

Ricky believed that, but his fingers trembled as he reached for the ignition. He knew he shouldn't overreact. He was perfectly safe and his best bet was to stick to his plan, leave the Lexus there and catch a cab or bus either home or to his office. The car and Andrew Cullen would still be there when he came back to get them later that night. He would have bet his reputation on that.

Ricky paused, car key in hand. No one in the world could possibly know where he was right then. There was just no way. He stared out at the deserted parking garage, trying to decide what he should do. And then his phone buzzed a second time. He groaned and squeezed his eyes closed. He had no idea what this new message would say but could already feel his stomach twist into a knot. With serious apprehension, he braced himself, steeled his nerves and opened his eyes again.

Ricky careened around a corner and the Lexus's tires slid on the smooth concrete. He slowed but not in time to prevent the left front bumper from brushing the wall. The impact wasn't much but he heard the shriek, saw the sparks and knew he'd be headed to a body shop soon. At the moment, that was the least of his worries. Someone had seen him at Cyber Force, and they'd gotten close enough to take a fucking picture.

I'm dead, he thought, turning onto Henry Street, not because he wanted to but because the light was green so he didn't have to stop at the intersection. The road was open in front of him and Ricky wanted to push the accelerator to the floor. Instead, and with tremendous effort, he forced himself to obey traffic laws, even fastening his seatbelt, something he almost never bothered with.

He made one random turn after another, all the while checking his mirrors and looking all around. If anyone had been watching him in the parking garage, they were out of luck now. He was good to go. He just needed to find another suitable place to leave the Lexus. There were other parking garages nearby and they definitely had appeal, but Ricky was spooked and decided he should come up with something else.

Besides, if his would-be watcher was in the area, nearby was the last thing he wanted.

Sometimes, Ricky thought. *The best place to hide is right out in the open.* After some indecision and a few wrong turns, he took Highway 17 to 201 and headed for the mall.

-65-

"Why don't we just call him?" Bullfrog asked. "I'll talk. I can disguise my voice so he won't know it's me."

"Dude," Skid Row said. "We only talked to Ricky that one time. You were scared to death and barely said a word. You really think the vocal subterfuge is necessary?"

"Vocal what?" Bullfrog asked, scowling at him.

"Subterfuge. It means--"

"I know what it means," Bullfrog said. "Who told you?"

Carl was staring at the Retrievor app but, out of the corner of his eye, he saw Skid Row give Bullfrog the finger.

"So can we call him?" Bullfrog asked. "We have a picture of him in Cullen's office and one of him moving the body. That should be enough, right?'

Carl thought so, but he was afraid of leaving even the slightest bit of wiggle room because he knew how slippery Ricky could be. It came from being a snake. His indecision must have shown.

"Great," Bullfrog said, crossing his arms and slumping down in the seat. "So we're just gonna keep chasing him all over the county, letting him know we're onto him but never doing anything about it?"

"We will do something," Carl insisted. "You'll see."

"And when's that gonna happen?"

"Where is he now?" Skid Row asked, saving Carl from answering Bullfrog's question.

"Based on these coordinates," Carl said with a frown, "it looks like he just turned into the Oakdale Mall."

"What's he gonna do there?"

Damned if I know, but then Carl had a thought. "Probably nothing," he muttered, only half to himself.

"So you think he's just taking Cullen on a tour of our fair city? Sounds kinda weird, dude."

"When he went into the parking garage," Carl said, turning to look at them. "I figured he was gonna try to hide Cullen's body in there somewhere."

"But where?" Skid Row asked.

"I don't know," Carl said with a shrug. "It seemed strange to me, and it wasn't like we could drive in there to see what he was up to, not without him seeing us too. That's why I sent that last text. I needed to spook him to get him back out into the open."

"Done deal," Skid Row said. "It don't get much more open than a mall parking lot."

"Right." Carl tugged at the end of his beard. "That's kind of what I was thinking, and I may have figured out what he's doing."

Bullfrog nodded slowly. "He's just gonna leave his car there. There's no reason it would attract any attention."

Carl looked at him. "That's what I think, and I bet that's what he was doing at the parking garage too."

"Are you two crazy?" Skid Row asked, staring at them wide-eyed. "He's got a fucking corpse in the back seat. You don't think anyone would notice that?"

"Not if he covers him up. Then it looks like every other car there."

Skid Row glared at Bullfrog, looking like he wanted to retort but obviously having nothing to say. He started biting a fingernail instead.

Carl had to give Ricky credit. It was not only a sensible plan but damn gutsy too. He'd counted on a less rational response, one that would make him more vulnerable. Thankfully, he could still track Ricky's every move and that made it easy to tighten the screws.

"We need to flush him out again," Bullfrog said, finishing Carl's thought.

"I think so too. We have everything we need against him. We just have to make sure he knows that, and I think we need to do it face to face."

"Are you ready for that?" Bullfrog asked.

Carl swallowed and nodded. "Yeah," he said. "He'll keep getting worse unless I do something about it. This is long overdue."

"Where?" Bullfrog asked.

"That's up to him," Carl said, shrugging. "We'll make him run until he stops somewhere secluded enough that we can close in."

"And what if he never does?"

"He will," Carl said. "He's got no choice."

"Then let's start wearing him down," Bullfrog said. "What do we say to him this time?"

Skid Row stuck his hand out. "Give me the phone. I've got this one."

-66-

When Ricky's phone buzzed, it surprised him so much he'd jumped in his seat like he'd been stabbed. He'd pulled into a parking spot seconds before, and that was only after driving two full laps around the lot. No one had followed him. No one! He hadn't seen a single person or another moving vehicle. He had the place to himself. Still, he'd chosen an isolated spot on the back side of the mall, in the rear corner behind Sears.

Feeling relatively safe for the moment, Ricky was thinking ahead and decided he didn't want to draw undue attention to himself by having a taxi pick him up there at that time of the morning. He'd walk across the street to the Dunkin Donuts, order the largest coffee they sold, and grab a cab from there. He could go to the office and spend as much time as it took to figure out who was messing with him. He had no doubt he would. There couldn't be that many options. And once he had his answer, he'd take great pleasure in dealing with the punk. He could simply turn him over to Carl but Ricky thought it might be more satisfying to handle this one personally. It had been a long time since he'd really gotten his hands dirty and he wondered if he still had his old set of brass knuckles.

As far as he could tell, there was no reason his plan wouldn't work. He'd been careful, decisive and, he thought, smart. The pictures of him were troubling but that threat would go away as soon as the sender was identified and made to see the error of his ways. Ricky was looking forward to that. And once it was done, he could return to the mall, retrieve his car and dispose of Mr. Andrew Cullen permanently.

He was actually whistling when he killed the engine and started to open his door. He'd had a rough few hours but was back in control again. It still sucked he'd lose out on the hundred large Cullen promised him but that wasn't the end of the world. There were plenty of other rich assholes out there. He just needed to find them. His experience with Cullen proved it could be done. He'd just need to be more cautious next time. He'd been too nice, too patient and accommodating, and that's what got him into trouble. Ricky would not let that happen again. At least he could learn from his mistakes, unlike the stiff in the back seat. It would all work out. That's what he thought anyway, and that's when his phone blew up again.

CHRISTMAS SHOPPING ALREADY?

Ricky gaped at the screen in absolute horror. It just wasn't possible. He was too stunned even to swear. He opened his mouth but all that came out was a whimper. He read and reread the message, his new feeling of confidence smashed as quickly and completely as Cullen's bathroom mirror. What was happening was beyond his comprehension. It was like there were eyes on him when he could see full well there wasn't anyone around.

The first picture was easy enough to explain away. Someone was concealed in that bathroom. It he'd only gone ahead and opened that door, but there was no point beating himself up about that now.

That second picture was the one Ricky found so disconcerting. The angle was horrible, the backend of his car blocking most of the shot, but the photographer had to be right there on the street. That made no sense. He'd looked and seen nothing, except for that boozer in the doorway. Not to be judgmental but people who slept on sidewalks didn't generally carry cameras or cell phones. And like the first picture, it had come from Cullen's phone. That suggested that the picture taker and Cullen's killer were one and the same. Did that mean he was capped by a fucking wino? Random murders happened all the time, but how would Cullen have ended up back in his office, and what did any of it have to do with him? Ricky was at a complete loss and it was terrifying.

Not bothering to look around this time, he cranked the engine, threw the Lexus in gear and stomped on the gas. The car shot forward and then almost came to a dead stop, Ricky nearly slamming his chin against the steering wheel as he bounced over the cement parking barrier that, in his haste, he'd failed to see. The sound seemed deafening in the early morning stillness and he was afraid the commotion would wake up everyone within a ten mile radius. He then compounded his problem by hitting the brakes. The Lexus shuddered to a stop but the car wasn't sitting right and Ricky could tell the front end wasn't completely on the ground.

"SHIT!" he said, opening his door to see what was going on. The impact had knocked the barrier askew and one end of it was now wedged between the wheel well and the back of the left front tire. Ricky shifted into reverse and tried to back up. He got nowhere at first, and revving the engine only made the right tire spin and smoke. The left didn't seem to want to do anything.

"This is not happening," he said, fearing he might actually be stuck there. He put the car in drive, and tried moving forward. He only got a few inches before the right tire started spinning again. "Shit, SHIT, SHIT!"

Ricky wondered if he could use his jack to crank the left side of the car up enough that he'd be able to pull the barrier out of the way. He doubted it, and knew he didn't have the time even to try. He could already see a hint of daylight on the eastern horizon. The sun would be up soon and Ricky needed to get the hell out of there and he needed to do it before some well-meaning jerk saw him and came over to offer help.

Fighting back tears of panic, he shifted into reverse, then drive, then reverse again, goosing the accelerator each time, rocking back and forth and getting a little further with each repetition. Ricky closed his ears against the racket emanating from his undercarriage, even if it did sound like someone was attacking the frame with a chainsaw. He still didn't stop. The front of the car rose, fell, rose again and Ricky knew he was getting close. He went through the cycle one more time and when he knew he was at the top of the arc, he shifted and punched the gas hard. The Lexus lurched bounced and something cracked loud enough to make him flinch. A football-sized piece of silver molding shot into the air, hit the ground and cart-wheeled into the shrubs a few feet away. Ricky didn't care because he was free. He sped out of the lot without a backward glance.

Back on 17, he noticed how the Lexus started pulling to the left once he got up to about sixty miles per hour. So he'd be due for body work as well as an alignment. That was just beautiful. As he drove, he found himself checking his cell phone every few seconds. He hadn't received any more texts yet but knew he would soon enough.

How are you doing this? Ricky wondered, trying to decide where to go next and if it would even matter. He didn't waste time with his mirrors or looking out the back window. What was the point? He hadn't been followed before. He was absolutely sure of that. Yet someone, somehow, had still known he was at the mall the moment he got there.

"How?" Ricky whispered, shrinking down in his seat and feeling like he was being watched from above. The idea was ludicrous . He knew that much. Even if the cops were onto him, which they were not, it wasn't like the under-funded Binghamton Police Department owned a state-of-the-art, super stealthy, completely silent helicopter that could fly around in the dark and track his every move. Whoever was after him, Ricky knew it wasn't the cops. He almost wished it was because he figured they'd be a lot easier to ditch.

How do you get away from somebody you can't even fucking see? That was the question he kept asking and Ricky had no answers.

Not knowing what else he could do, he settled on randomness and unpredictability. He was on 17 East but got off at the first exit and looped around so he was headed west once more. He exited again, made a left and then a right, and then started turning down one unfamiliar side street after another. It didn't take long before he'd totally lost his bearings. It was almost comforting. If he was unsure of his own whereabouts, how could anyone else zero in on his location?

There were a few houses just ahead and Ricky slowed so he could get a better look. He had a hard time making out much detail in the predawn gloom but took in the dingy, cracked windows, flaking paint, and unkempt lawns. He also saw how, alongside one of the houses, a thick tangle of weeds had overrun what had once been a concrete driveway. The place had to be abandoned and Ricky considered driving around and leaving his car in the back yard. He'd be out of sight from the street and probably the neighbors too. His only reservation was knowing he'd have to hoof it quite a ways to get back to a main road.

Ricky started to turn in but he was still a little jumpy and decided he should drive around the block one time to be sure he really was alone. He hadn't seen any people or other cars but knew from his experience at the mall that that didn't mean a thing. He crept along at a walking pace, peering this way and that and even lowering his driver's side window so he could stick his head out to listen. Nothing sounded out of place, and what he mostly heard was dry leaves crunching under his tires. There may have also been the low rumble of a truck's engine but it was at least a block away and faded out before Ricky could be sure he'd heard it. He was no longer focused on that anyway because he'd spotted something more promising than the abandoned house.

South Side Pack and Mail had been closed for the past two years. That was because Drew Pierce, former owner, had been in federal prison for about that long. In addition to his above-board packing business, Drew supplemented his income by shipping contraband pharmaceuticals. They mostly came from Canada and he was paid by a third or fourth party to re-package and re-route. Ricky knew that because for a little while he'd helped move some of Drew's product. Carl, of all people, had gotten wind of a possible sting and Ricky broke off his association just in time. He'd been lucky. Pierce had not. It would be another five years before he was even up for parole.

The packing store itself was about as welcoming as the nearby homes. The front windows were covered with plywood and someone had used that space to write FUCK OBAMA in red spray paint and letters about two feet high. Ricky also noticed the heavy chain and padlock dangling from the front door. That was fine. He had no desire to go inside. What he wanted was out back.

The store had a small rear lot and Ricky remembered how it was only a few feet from a deep culvert. It was behind a chain link fence, but last time he'd been there, an entire section of the fence was missing. It seemed unlikely anyone had been by to make repairs. Drew used to joke that, if the narcs showed up, he'd have a perfect place to dump the drugs. He hadn't been quick enough, but Ricky was sure Drew wouldn't mind if his dump spot was used for another purpose. He could back in, open the rear door and give Cullen one big shove. All Ricky would need to do then was drive away. The body might never be found and he would have all the time he needed to deal with his tormenter.

The first indication his plan might not work out so well was the tire pressure warning light that had just started flashing on the dashboard. Obviously, that hunk of cement had done more damage than he thought.

"Fuck me," Ricky said, smacking the heel of his hand against his forehead. *What else could go wrong?*

He checked and, to him, the tire looked normal. It wasn't visibly flat anyway. He figured he had a slow leak and decided he could do what he had to do, get a safe distance away and then assess the situation. If it became necessary to ditch the Lexus somewhere, he'd much rather do it once his passenger was gone. Ricky started to turn the car around, but then heard the one sound he'd come to dread. He looked at his phone and the new text message.

I HOPE YOU HAVE A LOT OF STAMPS.

"NO!" he screamed, twisting around in his seat and looking in all directions. He then stared at Cullen as if he might somehow be responsible. His body was face down on the floor but Ricky sensed the bastard was laughing at him.

"Fuck you," he whispered, his voice quavering. Ricky's vision blurred and his head felt like it was ready to split wide open. He didn't even know what the hell street he was on and he'd gotten there completely by accident. No one had seen him. No one was around to see him, yet....

He looked at his phone again and that smug fucking text. *STAMPS.* He wasn't just being pursued. He was being taunted. That would have pissed him off royally if he wasn't so scared.

"What do you want?' he asked, balling his right hand into a fist and pounding it against his thigh. If he only knew who he was up against and why in hell they'd decided to pick on him. He was tired, frustrated, and had never felt so powerless in his life. He was also sick of being jerked around.

"Let's get to the bottom of this, he said, grabbing his phone. His first instinct was to fire off a vulgarity-laden reply but knew that would accomplish nothing. He took a breath, swallowed his pride and typed the first two words of *who are you and what do you want?* when realization struck.

His iPhone, pretty much every smart phone in the world, had a built-in GPS. Ricky didn't know how the thing worked but remembered hearing stories about people being tracked down electronically. All they had to do was—he struggled to come up with the word—triangulate the signal. So maybe someone had triangulated his sorry ass and that's how they were able to find him so easily. He figured that had to be it, and he could break the connection just by turning the thing off or, better yet, removing the battery. That's what he assumed anyway, but how did you get the battery out of an iPhone? They weren't made to be opened. Ricky considered the problem, turning the device over and over in his hands. Battery or not, he finally decided there was only one way to be sure the GPS really was disabled. He hesitated and then dropped the phone out the window, driving over it on his way out of the lot.

"Find me now," he said, praying he was right because there was only one place left he could go.

-67-

Ricky turned onto Conklin Road, grateful his office was less than a mile ahead. The steering wheel felt heavy in his hands and he could tell his left front tire was seriously fucked up. The sound it made was low and hollow and, a few times, he thought he smelled smoke. He knew it would get him the rest of the way and, after that he didn't much care what happened. For some reason, destroying his phone made him feel even more helpless than before. He also had the unsettling notion it had done no good.

Driving back from the Pack and Mail, he hadn't tried any evasive maneuvers. He stayed below the speed limit, and took the shortest route from point A to point B. That still gave him plenty of time to think. He went through it all in his head, from the moment he'd received that very first text. Ricky eventually came to one sobering conclusion. He realized he should have put it together a lot sooner because all the information was right there the whole time. He'd been so focused on how it was all done—and that part was still a mystery—he hadn't given near enough thought to the only question that ever really mattered. Who?

Ricky pulled into the lot, parking his Lexus behind the trailer. He tried to convince himself he was wrong, that there had to be another explanation, but he couldn't even feign surprise when a second vehicle drove in and stopped right behind him. There was no need to look. The sound of the engine was familiar, and would have been even if he hadn't heard that same one from a distance not fifteen minutes before. Ricky still glanced in the rearview mirror and then hung his head. Moments later, Carl opened the passenger door and lowered himself into the car.

"How'd you do it?" Ricky asked, wanting to be angry but lacking the energy it required.

Carl didn't answer but instead turned and reached into the back seat. Ricky heard the rustle of clothing and couldn't imagine what he was up to. Then, Carl grunted and tossed something into his lap. It bounced off his leg and fell to the floor. The item was black, round, and not much larger than a piece of hard candy. Ricky bent to pick it up, noticing that it weighed next to nothing.

"What the hell is this?" he asked, poking it with a finger.

"It's called the Retrievor," Carl said without inflection. "It's a mini tracking device."

"Fucking GPS," Ricky murmured. "I knew it. You stick that on Cullen somewhere?"

"In his shoe. We didn't think you'd find it there."

"Never thought to look. Probably wouldn't have known what it was anyway."

Ricky paused, his mind reeling. *Where had a lunkhead like Carl gotten his hands on miniature electronics? How long had he been using them? What else had he used them for?*

Ricky had plenty of other questions too, but only one seemed important right then. His eyes flitted to the mirror even though Andrew Cullen was completely out of sight on the floor of the car. "So why'd you kill him?" he asked.

"I didn't," Carl said, taking the tiny GPS and slipping it into a pocket.

"Get real!" Ricky snapped, turning to look at the man he now considered his ex-partner. "That's the same crap you said about Marco."

"I didn't do it," Carl insisted. "He wrecked his bike, went over the handlebars and landed on his head."

"And you know that because…."

"I saw it happen. I was there but I never laid a finger on him."

"Fine," Ricky said, tempted to tell him he was full of shit. However, he suddenly realized Carl wasn't exhibiting any of his normal nervousness. There was no foot tapping or rolling and unrolling of the sleeves. He wasn't even writing in his damned note book. He just sat there, plainly not caring if Ricky believed his story or not. Carl maybe looked a bit uneasy but also resolved and that caught Ricky off guard.

"Fine," he said again. "You didn't kill him. You didn't have anything to do with it. So why didn't you come to me?"

"Why do you think? You would have blamed me just like always. And then, you would have tried to make me pay. Thanks, but I'm done going down that road!"

"We could have talked about it," Ricky said.

Carl stared at him. "Oh, you're good at talking. You just never listen."

Ricky waved his hands in a way that took in Cullen, the trashed Lexus and all the rest. "And that's why you did this?" he asked, shock and bewilderment starting to give way to anger.

"It wasn't just that," Carl said. "We got tired of you pushing us around."

"Okay," Ricky said. "I get that. I guess I may have been a little heavy-handed at times. I'm sorry if I came on too hard." *And you're gonna be sorry when....*

He never finished the thought because something Carl had said just clicked. It was his use of the plural pronoun. *WE got tired of you pushing us around.* And before, when they'd been discussing that GPS thing, he'd said *WE didn't think you'd find it there.* Ricky was almost sure of it.

"Wait," he said, craning around to look out the rear window. "Who the fuck is we?" He saw Carl's truck, and noticed something he hadn't before. There were two passengers in the front seat. Squinting into the early morning sun, he couldn't make out much detail, but one figure had long hair and the other didn't appear to have any. "That's not..." he said, the betrayal finally hitting him full force.

"Skid Row and Bullfrog," Carl finished. "We've sort of been working together."

"I..." Ricky began but had no idea how to continue. He'd known Carl was soft on those two, and suspected he'd let them evade him at least once or twice. But Ricky never imagined the three of them had fucking joined forces. How had that even happened? Did they hatch their plan that first night when Carl stole the bag? Was it possible they'd been plotting against him ever since? More perplexing still, how had Andrew Cullen gotten involved? Carl said he didn't kill him, but there was no use of the plural pronoun that time. As improbable as it seemed, could Skid Row and Bullfrog somehow have been responsible for his death. If so, what else were they capable of?

"There's two ways we can play this," Carl said, seemingly oblivious to Ricky's inner turmoil. "Agree to our terms and all this goes away."

"And if I don't?"

He held up a cell phone. "We'll take you down. We've got everything we need right here.

"But you can't!" Ricky protested, trying to think of a way out. "I didn't fucking do anything!"

"Neither did they," Carl said, jabbing a thumb toward the back window. "I kept telling you that but you wouldn't let up. We're giving you an out. What you do with it is up to you."

"So if I don't go along...what? Those pictures go to the cops or something?"

"That's the idea."

"What if I don't think you'll do it?"

"You could test me," Carl said, his jaw set, "but I wouldn't recommend it."

"And the terms?" Ricky asked, hating the new note of uncertainty in his voice.

"They'll keep you out of jail. What more do you need to know?"

"Nothing I guess."

Ricky stared, looking for any sign Carl might be bluffing or at least willing to negotiate. The return gaze was dark and unyielding. He then thought of the evidence he'd spent years compiling. It was all in the trailer, not fifty feet away. Of course, next to the pictures of him with Andrew Cullen, none of what Ricky had against Carl was worth a puddle of spit. He knew that but couldn't accept that everything he'd worked for was over, or that he'd somehow underestimated Carl so badly.

The *choice* he'd been given was no choice at all. He was being asked to forfeit his dignity, and to do it in front of the two scum bags that started the whole mess. Even with everything at stake, he would never stoop so low; not when there was a third option available.

"Why don't we talk about this inside?" he suggested, his left hand drifting toward the door handle. "I'm sure we can reach an agreement."

"Maybe I didn't make myself clear," Carl said, "but there's nothing to talk about. I need your answer now."

"Okay then," Ricky replied, glancing over for a moment and then dropping his eyes, hoping he appeared appropriately submissive. "I guess you wi--"

He lunged for the door, getting it open and rolling out in one fluid motion. Carl made a grab for him but only got a fist full of coat sleeve. Ricky tugged and the sleeve tore free. He fell but was up again in an instant, sprinting towards the trailer for all he was worth. Carl was already in pursuit, shouting at Skid Row and Bullfrog to stay where they were. Based on all the commotion, it didn't sound like they'd listened.

Good, Ricky thought. *You can all come inside and we'll end this right now.*

He rounded the corner, bounded up the steps and hit the door on the run, thankful he'd left it unlocked. Ricky risked a glance behind him and saw Carl bearing down. He knew he didn't have time to maneuver around his desk so he vaulted over, landing hard on his right foot. Something snapped but he was way too jacked up to feel any pain. He stumbled and crashed to the floor.

Carl yelled something but Ricky was so focused on his task that he paid no attention. He groped for the desk drawer and, seconds later, was clutching the old hand gun. He didn't aim or even take time to think. He just pointed up at where he knew Carl had to be and squeezed the trigger.

Nothing happened.

Ricky was confused, but then he knew what he'd done. In his panic, he'd forgotten to release the safety. He fumbled with the weapon but it was already too late. Carl's fist came down like a wrecking ball, striking his arm with enough force and follow through to also clock him a good one in the side of the head. The gun skittered away and Ricky was left seeing stars.

"That was foolish," Carl said, looming over him and clearly willing to hit him again. "My offer is still on the table but this is your last chance. What do you say?"

Ricky sat, staring up at Carl and realizing how small and pathetic he must look. He wondered how it had come to this, and for some reason, the Miguel De Cervantes quote popped back into his head. *He that loses his courage loses all.* I accept," Ricky said, so softly he could barely be heard.

-Epilogue-

"You really think we're in the clear?" Bullfrog asked, staring at Carl as if he couldn't quite believe it.

"Looks that way. According to the report, Andrew Cullen's body was discovered at the bottom of an embankment just off Airport Road with his damaged bicycle nearby. It's believed he crashed while training for a triathlon. Cause of death was a broken neck. The accident occurred late last Thursday night and there were no witnesses."

"And that's it?" Bullfrog asked.

"Officially, yes."

"But there had to be suspicions of foul play. What about his office?"

"Ricky did leave a mess. We're partly to blame for that. Our scare tactics worked a little too well."

Skid Row shifted in his seat but remained quiet, as he'd done most of the morning. He brushed at is hair, even though it now stopped well short of his collar.

Carl checked an address, slowed and made a turn.

"That's what I mean," Bullfrog said. "You look at that stuff and it's pretty obvious something more than a bike wreck took place. Why aren't the cops investigating?"

"You want them to?'

"No but...."

Carl raised a hand. "I told you Ricky knows a guy at the police department. He usually gives us pretty good information. Based on what he said, Cullen's wife sort of helped us out."

"Why?"

Carl chuckled. "I don't think she meant to. I doubt she has any idea what really took place."

"But wouldn't she want to find out?"

"Not necessarily. It seems Mr. Andrew Cullen held a two million dollar life insurance policy."

"Don't rock the boat baby," Skid Row said, finally speaking up.

"You got it," Carl cruised through an intersection, peering at the road signs as they drove past. "She had to know some of the stuff he was into and probably didn't want anyone digging too deep."

"But the cops must have realized there was something going on," Bullfrog argued, his expression dubious. "They wouldn't drop it just because she said so."

"True," Carl agreed, but you're talking about a respected local businessman. He sat on committees, owned his own company and employed a dozen people. Guys like that are treated differently than you and me."

"It still doesn't make sense."

Carl sighed. "The system isn't always fair. What do you want me to say? It's working out well for us, so don't look a gift horse in the mouth."

"I never got that one," Skid Row said. "Who would want a fucking horse anyway?"

Carl looked at him and then turned his attention back to Bullfrog. "From what I heard, the wife told police her husband was stressed because of the triathlon. A lot of people were backing him and he wanted to do well. According to her, he sometimes dealt with anxiety by drinking too much."

"So he got tanked and trashed his own office?"

"Trashed is a bit strong, but alcohol consumption could explain what probably looked like erratic behavior."

Bullfrog plucked at the sleeve of his new Carhartt jacket. "I'm sorry but I can't help feeling guilty. We know that's not what happened."

"We don't know he wasn't drunk," Skid Row said. "That might have been why he wrecked in the first place. Besides, it's not like we were responsible."

"Right," Carl said. "And the place we ended up leaving him was a lot nicer than where he died. I think it turned out about as well as it could have, for almost everyone involved."

"I guess," Bullfrog said, still not sounding convinced. "I just hope I never have to touch another dead body as long as I live."

"Amen to that," Skid Row agreed. "Total skeeves."

Carl made another turn and then pulled to the curb and stopped at the end of a long driveway, alongside a sign for Bartolo Construction Company. "I almost forgot," he said. "I read this morning that most of the people sponsoring Cullen in that triathlon are going to honor their pledges. He obviously won't be competing, but a sixty-five thousand dollar donation will be made in his name to some children's center."

Bullfrog shook his head. "So he'll get a hero's burial. I don't know what to think about that."

"I do," Skid Row said, lowering the window visor to check his reflection in the mirror. He frowned and straightened his shirt collar. "I think it's great. Cullen might have been a shit but his family's taken care of and a bunch of kids will benefit too. It's all good."

"I suppose," Bullfrog said, turning to look at Carl. "And what about you? I'm assuming you won't be working for Ricky anymore."

"For him? No. We may still work together in some capacity. We've had discussions but nothing has been decided. If anything, it will be a much more equal partnership."

"You're not afraid he'll try to screw you over?"

"I'm sure he's thought about it. That's his nature. He's always scheming. But there's nothing he can do. That reminds me." Carl reached into his shirt pocket and pulled out a small, red thumb drive. "Keep this in a safe place. That's our insurance policy. Ricky knows you guys have it and that I've got a copy too. He wouldn't dare make a move against any of us."

"I don't know," Bullfrog said. "He did try to shoot you."

Carl smiled wryly. "Like I said, I haven't made any decisions. I probably won't for a while. I'm gonna take a little time off. I need to think and I've got a few other things I want to do."

He and Skid Row exchanged a look. The back of the truck was full of camping gear, and unbeknownst to Bullfrog, Carl was on his way to Maine where he hoped to track down a certain amoral attorney and persuade him to return the inheritance he'd stolen.

Glad I'm not in his shoes, Skid Row thought, glancing up the drive at the new ranch-style home that looked to be in the final stages of construction. "Well," he said, reaching for the door. "I guess this is our stop."

"You sure this is what you want?" Carl asked. "You guys talked about leaving town. I'll take you to the bus station and I'm sure Ricky would be happy to buy you a ticket anywhere you want to go."

"We were gonna split, but a lot has changed since then. Besides," Skid Row indicated his new boots and jacket identical to Bullfrog's. "I think he's been generous enough."

"And you've got a place to stay?"

"We'll figure it out. Thanks for giving us somewhere to crash the past few nights."

"You can stay longer. It's no trouble."

"We appreciate it," Skid Row said, "but I got something else in mind. I think it will work out."

"Yeah, you told me, and I think you're doing the right thing. Key's under the mat if you change your mind."

"Here goes nothing," Skid Row said, mostly to himself. He watched Carl's truck disappear around the corner, and then turned to study the mini excavator, the sections of drainage pipe, the large pile of gravel, the shovels and the big red wheelbarrow. It was all foreign to him. It wasn't that he was afraid of hard work. He just didn't know if he could do it there and under such circumstances. His haircut felt weird. His new clothes felt weird. And even though he'd gone through various scenarios in his head, he really had no idea how he and Bullfrog would be received.

Skid Row fingered his front pocket and the money tucked away there. Carl had given them each a hundred dollars, compliments of the Ricky Fixx rehabilitation fund. If things didn't go well, at least they'd have something to tide them over for a while, and that made him feel a little better.

His legs still trembled and he had to grip the handrail as he mounted the front steps. With Bullfrog in tow, he crossed the narrow porch and stopped when he got to the doorway.

"Where do we go?" Bullfrog asked, his voice just above a whisper. "Are we supposed to just walk in?"

"How the hell should I know?" Skid Row hissed. "Just give me a minute."

He peered into what he assumed would end up being a spacious living room. A few pieces of dry wall were in place but it was mostly framework. Sawdust covered the floor and there were building materials piled everywhere. A thick yellow extension cord snaked through an open window and Skid Row could hear a gas-powered generator at work somewhere out back. He heard voices too and moved cautiously in that direction.

"You two need something?"

Skid Row froze and looked up. He'd seen the ladder propped against the wall but hadn't realized there was actually someone using it. The man wore a hard hat, a large tool belt and was doing something with a thick spool of wire.

"Uh, yeah," Skid Row said, wishing his voice didn't sound so thin and weak. "We're looking for the foreman. Is he around?"

The man squinted down at them and didn't seem to like what he saw. He muttered something Skid Row couldn't hear and then spit a stream of tobacco juice into a small paper cup.

"Excuse me?" Skid Row said, meeting his gaze and standing as straight as he could.

The man muttered something else, but then shrugged to indicate that whatever they wanted, it wasn't his problem. "He's out there," he said, cocking his head. "And watch your step," he added, just as Bullfrog kicked a metal can and sent it tumbling across the floor.

"Smooth," Skid Row said and Bullfrog gave him a shove.

They worked their way toward the back of the house, following the sound of voices. They eventually ended up in the kitchen, where three men and a woman were having a heated discussion involving three-way switches and a ceiling fan. Skid Row had no idea what they were talking about but he'd stopped paying attention because he was so fixated on one of the men. He was a few inches taller than the others and wore a different colored hard hat.

"We can't do it that way," he was saying. "Look here." He flattened out a diagram on top of a makeshift plywood counter. "We need three-way switches at each entrance, and the customer wants overhead lighting on a dimmer. That means we..." He tailed off when he noticed Skid Row and Bullfrog in the doorway. "I'm sorry," he said. "Can I--" and then his jaw dropped open.

"Sebastian?" He blinked like he couldn't quite believe his eyes. "Is that you?"

Skid Row cleared his throat as he took in gray hair--actually longer than his own--the familiar wiry frame, heavily callused hands, and ruddy skin that showed all the Years of hard work and exposure to the elements.

"Yeah," he said, stuffing his own hands into his pockets to keep them from shaking. "It's been a while. Good to see you... Dad."

Acknowledgements:

For starters, I'd like to thank Alan Colosi for not dying when, in the spring of 2014, he went over the handle bars of his bicycle and broke his neck. His accident occurred not long after the release of *A Shot at Redemption,* my debut novel. I'd been kicking around some ideas for my next literary project but hadn't yet come up with anything I liked. For whatever reason, Alan's wheels slipping out from under him somehow got my mental wheels turning. I recall the very moment inspiration struck. At the time, our sons were both members of the Windsor High School varsity tennis team. We were watching a match and Alan, wearing a horribly uncomfortable looking silver neck brace, told my wife and me what happened to him. He talked about the wreck itself, the incredible care he received from the EMTs, his treatment plan, and just how lucky he was not only to be alive but to still have all four limbs in perfect working order. I knew immediately that I would be fictionalizing his mishap and that, in my telling, it wouldn't turn out so well.

As unlikely as it may sound, the entire plot structure of *Parlor City Paradise* was crafted around that one unfortunate incident. I also had Alan very much in mind when I created Andrew Cullen. They share the same initials. They are also both successful business owners with a passion for physical fitness. That's really where the similarities end. To the best of my knowledge, Alan is not, nor has he ever been, a womanizer, a compulsive gambler or a drunk. He's got a good sense of humor, though, and didn't mind at all when I told him he'd be portrayed as a total slime. In fact, I don't think he'd have it any other way. So thank you, Alan, for inspiring me, for being such a good sport and for not being dead.

As I alluded to in the novel, Binghamton was once extremely affluent. I won't bore you with the details but the entire area fell on hard times. The bottom really dropped out in the early 1990's, and just a few years back, businessinsider.com still listed Binghamton among the top five most depressing cities in America. There's no question the situation has started to improve and plenty of indications that trend will continue. That's why, although most of the characters in this book occupy the lower rungs on the social ladder, the overall tone of the story is more uplifting, at least that was my goal.

Perhaps you picked up on the note of irony in the title. I really wanted a cover image that embraced that same spirit. Specifically, I was looking for one picture that captured the best and worst Binghamton had to offer. I wanted to show the desperation along with the promise of something better. I had no idea how to achieve such a thing so I sponsored a photo contest and I am extremely grateful to all those who participated. I was afraid I wouldn't get anything good. Instead, I was presented with the challenge of narrowing down all the potentials to the one I liked best. I'd especially like to thank Kaitlyn Hession. She sent me several excellent pictures, one of which is now on the cover of the book. Two more are displayed on the back. I apologize to the e-book readers who don't get a back cover. I suppose that's the price you pay for digital. Thank you also to Olivia Kristek and Kaylee Stone. One of their photos is displayed on the back as well.

And once again, I need to thank Robin Gilbertson for the cover design. Prior to the release of "A Shot at Redemption," I had never required the services of a cover designer and Robin, despite more than two decades of experience, had never designed the cover for a thriller novel. I think it's safe to say she knocked it out of the park. When I was ready for my next cover design, I didn't even consider other options. With little input from me, she worked her magic and gave me exactly what I wanted.

Finally, I must thank Janine Holbrook, Michaele Stoughton, and all those who read early drafts of this novel. That goes double when it comes to Michael Sova II. He's my son, the aforementioned tennis player. As a rule, it is a bad idea to have close friends or family members serve as beta readers because they can have a hard time distancing themselves enough from the author to be duly critical. Michael didn't have that problem. He read the story and then told me every single thing he didn't like about it. And, without exception, his feedback was spot on. I'd like to thank him and every other reader that gave me a well deserved dose of humility. This novel is vastly better because of your efforts and your honesty.

Made in the USA
Middletown, DE
24 May 2016